HEATHER GRAHAM

HAUNTED

MIRA®

ISBN 1-55166-750-9

HAUNTED

Copyright © 2003 by Heather Graham Pozzessere.

Visit us at www.mirabooks.com

Printed in U.S.A.

To the one and only Miss Barden...Liz
With lots of love and best wishes

the street was about to die of cancer. He had known when Brad Taylor was going to break his leg during a football game. A lot of the kids called him a freak. But despite her little spat with Hunter, she had always held her own in school. She could bring Josh to the prom, and he'd be accepted, because he'd be with her. Oh, they'd talk about her—and him—behind their backs, but what did she care? Hunter had already hurt her just about as badly as she could be hurt; she was cut right to her eighteen-year-old heart.

And besides, the whole high school thing was over. A new life was about to begin.

Josh hemmed and hawed at first, skeptical. "Darcy, I'll just look like the geek you dressed up and brought along."

But she'd laughed and assured him, "Josh, honestly, you're a good-looking guy. Tall, lean, great eyes, and if you don't mind, we'll shop together. But if you'd feel uncomfortable, we won't go. We'll just see a movie or something that night. I mean, if you're willing to keep me company."

He'd smiled at that. "I'd rather be in your company than anyone else's, that's for sure. But you don't have to take me. Half the school would go with you."

"That's doubtful and it doesn't matter. If you don't want to go, I don't want to go."

At that, Josh had given her a strange smile. "If you want to go to the prom with the class nerd, lady, I wouldn't dream of stopping you."

To her amazement, the planning was fun. Although he usually dressed like a couch potato himself, Josh had a good eye for clothes. Hand in hand they went shopping together. They ran into a number of her friends at the mall, and she was delighted to see their eyes widen at first, and then seem to focus more deeply on Josh. He was able to help Cissy Miller with a math problem she'd been dragging around for days, and over tacos at the food court, he found a new friend in Brenda Greeley, a really beautiful girl, and the head cheerleader.

When they got back to shopping, he made Darcy try on a dress she hated on the rack, and loved once she slipped into it. It turned out that one of Josh's computer buddies worked in the store, and he was able to give her his employee discount, so she could afford the gown. The young man's name was Riley O'Hare, and he told Darcy he was actually in her auditorium class. She apologized sincerely for never having met him, and when they left the shop, she thoughtfully told Josh that she had never known that she could be so rude or careless herself.

"Darcy, you? Never," he told her devoutly. "Rude and careless is when you don't acknowledge someone when they talk to you, when you can't even lift your hand for a wave. Or when you push over a thin guy just 'cause he's not on the football team, or can't really join in on a jam with a guitar. Darcy, you know that I love you, and it's one hell of an overused term, but you're a special kind of girl, you know?" He looked embarrassed suddenly. "Hey, come on, we've got to find something for me. I can't take out a girl like you looking the way I usually do."

So next came Josh's turn, and when she advised him on a shirt and suit, somewhat funky and retro, he, too was delighted, thinking that he looked something like a New Age Mozart.

There was only one fly in the ointment that day.

Mike Van Dam.

He was friends with Hunter, and dating Brenda. Darcy realized later that he must have seen them in the food court, and seen Brenda talking to Josh. When they were leaving the mall, the door suddenly swung back on Josh, who was carrying the bags filled with their purchases. Mike, broad shoulders thrusting forward, was suddenly there, standing over Josh, who had wound up on the floor. "Hey, there, geek-boy, having a problem standing?" He reached a hand down, which was accepted by Josh, except that as soon as Josh was halfway up, Mike released him. Josh fell again, hard, on his tailbone.

"Mike, what the hell is the matter with you?" Darcy

demanded, infuriated, reaching down to give Josh a hand herself. Mike caught her by the shoulders, spinning her around.

"What the hell is the matter with you, Darcy? Trying to make fools of us all by taking up with the riffraff, the scum of the school?"

She jerked free from him. "Mike, you idiot. What? Are you going to live in your little high school tough-guy haven for the rest of your life? Scared for your future, because football star and all, you just might not get into college, and a decade from now, you'll still be on the couch, an armchair quarterback, while Josh is making his way up the ladder in a top law firm?"

That got him, and she knew it did. Josh was on his feet by then. Mike stared at him furiously.

"I carry mace," Darcy warned softly.

Mike cocked his square-jawed head, blue eyes burning, cropped blond hair seeming to stand on edge. He made a clicking sound and pointed a finger at Josh. "You're a dead man," he told him.

Josh stared back at him, a strange smile of amusement and irony curling his lips. "Maybe. But so are you," he said very softly.

Mike was about to go into another fit of rage. Darcy grabbed the bags and pushed Josh out the door. For a moment, they could hear Mike raging behind them. "What's that supposed to mean, geek-boy? You'd better be careful, I'll—"

They never heard the rest of the threat. The door had swung shut once again.

Darcy looked at Josh uneasily as she quickly led him to the car. "What was that all about? You didn't have one of your little premonitions there, did you?"

Josh laughed and shook his head. "No, kid, no. But he doesn't know that."

Darcy laughed as well, delighted. Josh had probably managed to scare Mike through the next many nights.

The night of the prom came. As long as Darcy had

known Josh, she barely knew his father. His mom had died when he was an infant, and his dad had almost never been around. All Josh had ever said about him was that he was the head of a company with offices in D.C., which was why he had to spend so much time away from their small town in southern Pennsylvania. He was a nice enough man when Darcy saw him, though he had seemed ancient from the first day they had met. She hadn't realized, though, until Josh picked her up for the prom just how much money his dad must make. Josh's graduation present had been a brand-new Volvo, a sporty one at that.

Josh brought her the most beautiful corsage she had ever seen. Her mother fussed around the two of them, taking picture after picture while her father beamed.

Josh, she discovered that night, was also an amazing dancer. Flushing, he informed her that he'd had some experience because his father had brought him to cotillion classes when he'd been in junior high.

Her friends were good that night, especially Brenda, and even the guys had to toe the line somewhat, since their dates seemed to accept Josh. Hunter, however, never approached her once. She saw that he and Mike were watching them from a distance, however, and that Mike looked as if he were about to explode when she and Josh won the "Wild and Wacky" dance contest.

Hunter just looked sad.

Darcy smiled at Josh, and he looked at her, curiously arching a brow. "Thank you," she told him.

"Me? Thank you! I'm like a male Cinderella tonight. Prince-not-so-charming, feeling like the beau of the ball."

She shook her head. "No. You made me realize that my life wasn't over without Hunter, and that there is a world ahead."

He caught both her hands, squeezing them tightly. "Don't you ever forget that, Darcy, you hear? The world is out there, and it's yours. It's a beautiful world." He spoke urgently, staring into Darcy's eyes. "Even when things don't seem quite right. Some people, just with a smile here and there, a kind word, make it all a better place for everyone around them. You're one of those people. Remember that. There are times in life to be sad, to feel pain, but you're a giver. Don't ever let yourself be downed by fear, hardship, or even sorrow that's so deep, you may not feel like going on.''

A chill swept into her. ''Josh, you're scaring me.''

''Sorry, Darcy.'' He seemed to return to himself again. ''Hey, I don't believe it. They're playing a Charleston! Want to try it?''

''Why the hell not?''

In a while, she forgot his words, because they did just have so much fun.

She was vaguely aware of the amount of drinking going on, the punch being spiked, and even the drugs. Brenda was upset because she was sure Mike was getting smashed. She was uneasy about the guys driving, but she had no control over any of it and decided that she was just going to enjoy the miracle that occurred; Hunter had thrown her over just before their senior prom, and she was still there, and having the best time of her life.

At last, it was time to go. Darcy had booked a room at the hotel where most of the kids were going after the prom, but she didn't want to go. Josh agreed that a perfect end to the evening might be watching a few movies, then seeing the sun come up. They were in his brand-new Volvo and heading out of the parking lot when the first warning that they were never going to make it occurred.

There was a tap against Josh's bumper. Just a tap. It barely jerked them forward.

Josh turned around, swearing softly. ''Too much alcohol in there, or kids who just can't drive.''

With lights blaring around them, they really couldn't see who was behind them.

Josh pulled out on the road.

''Care if I rifle through the CDs?'' Darcy asked him.

''Be my guest.''

She was oohing over his Beatles collection when the

next tap against the bumper came. This one was harder, slamming against the car.

"Dammit!" Josh swore.

"What the hell...?" Darcy said, looking back.

She didn't really need to look back. A car pulled alongside them. Mike was at the wheel, in his souped-up old Chevy. The car was a battle-ax with an engine that might have made the grade at the Daytona 500. His window was down. He had a beer in his hand while driving.

"Ass!" Darcy said.

Josh was quiet, staring ahead. He didn't seem frightened. Only...strangely resigned.

Mike was making signs for her to roll the window down.

"Might as well do it," Josh said.

"He's an idiot. Just drive," Darcy told him.

She looked straight ahead as well. To her amazement, Mike slammed his Chevy's tank side right against the Volvo.

She was wearing her seat belt; still, she slammed against Josh. Amazed, she straightened as Josh deftly maneuvered to keep the car on the road.

"Josh, I'm so sorry!" she gasped, real fear starting to trickle down her spine. She'd known that Mike could be a real jerk. She hadn't known that he could be this insane. She stared furiously over at the Chevy, still driving neck-and-neck with them.

The problem with small-town Pennsylvania, of course, could be the roads. Miles and miles of them in almost total darkness, with no one around for help.

Mike knew that. She could tell the minute she saw the grin on his face.

Then, to her great dismay, she saw that Hunter was sitting next to him, in the passenger's seat.

She rolled her window down. Surely, Josh's father was going to have a fit about the car. And someone was going to wind up really hurt.

"Stop it! You idiots!" she shouted.

"Ah, come on, you want to play with the geeks?" Mike called back.

Wind was racing by them. Darcy was afraid her voice wouldn't carry. "Hunter! Make him stop this, now!"

Hunter leaned forward and she saw his face. He was as white as a ghost. "Darcy, I'm trying!"

Mike laughed and slammed the car again. Darcy heard the terrible screech of metal against metal.

"Stop! We'll just stop, Josh," she said. "Hunter won't let Mike hurt you. He's still sober, I can see."

Just as she finished speaking, the Chevy began to veer insanely. She grabbed hold of her seat with a death grip as the Volvo veered accordingly. There was a split second in which she saw Hunter trying to seize the Chevy's steering wheel.

Then it all went out of control. The Chevy jackknifed with a roaring vengeance against the nose of the Volvo. Then it flipped, and rolled over and over in front of them. Josh pumped the brakes, but simple physics sent them flying into the body of the Chevy.

For a moment, Darcy felt the weightlessness of flight herself. An air bag suddenly exploded in her face. She felt a thud unlike anything she had ever known before, and the world suddenly turned to an absurd cartoon vision as stars in a field of black velvet swam before her eyes. Then, one by one, the stars twinkled out, and there was nothing but an ebony darkness.

Ashes to ashes.

Dust to dust.

Darcy attended Josh's funeral with blackened eyes and heavy bruises. They told her that it was only thanks to the integrity of Josh's Volvo that she was still alive.

Mike wouldn't be buried for another two days. Somehow, again miraculously, Hunter had survived as well. Darcy thought that she must still be in shock, unable to really absorb what had happened because, as she stood by Josh's grave site, supported on either side by her parents, she was able to look at Hunter. She could even think that, to his credit, he'd had the balls to come here, and that he was weeping like an infant.

The accident had been a wake-up call for the entire school, she thought, for those who had shunned Josh for years had come. He might well have been amused, she thought. But again, every face showed shock and sorrow. Those who had thought themselves young and immortal had discovered that life was fragile and death could come at any time. Who, in their realm of experience, had ever imagined that taunting a nerd could come to such a tragic end?

Josh's father, grave, tall, ancient, and bowed, tenderly kissed the coffin, and laid a flower upon it. His grief seemed beyond tears, and still, when the last words of the priest had faded into the bizarre and beautiful blue beauty of the day, he came toward her. He managed a gentle smile, as if her pain could be as deep as his own, and reached for her hand. She took it, let him lead her to the coffin, where he offered her a flower to cast upon it.

It was a strange moment, for those who had attended seemed to want to come to him, to offer their condolences. Yet, he and Darcy stood in their own little world, and people hesitated, then let them be. Even Darcy's parents, loving, kind people, allowed them that moment.

They stood in silence for the longest time. Oddly, Darcy became aware of a bird chirping. At last, she found her voice. It was broken and trembling, but she managed the words she wanted. "I'm so sorry. So, so, sorry. I—I'm responsible. That can't help you any, I know," she babbled. "But he was my friend, truly, my best friend, always there, and oh, God, I didn't know…I…."

"Please," Josh's father said softly. "Darcy, you did nothing wrong. It's never wrong to be a real friend. He loved you. Not romantically, of course. You didn't love him that way, either. But he knew you really, truly cared about him. You were a special person to him. Incredibly so."

She looked up at the old man who seemed bowed with sorrow, and yet so accepting. She offered him a teary, rueful smile. "Please, you're trying to comfort me. You've lost your only child."

He looked back at her a long time. "I always knew that I would," he said quietly. "And still, what a fine, bright boy! The love we shared will remain in this old heart as long as it ticks. I was privileged to have him as long as I did. Remember this, those we love do live forever in our hearts. You'll remember his voice. The things he said that made you laugh. I can't explain this, but...Josh wasn't really for this world."

"He has gone to a far better place," she whispered, wincing at the way the words, sincerely meant, could sound so trite.

"He was different, Darcy. You must have known that."

"Smart, sweet, wonderful," she whispered.

Josh's father was still smiling. He reached into his wallet suddenly, producing a card. "I doubt if I'll be around the old homestead here much anymore. Please, take this. If you ever need help, if you ever need to just talk, call me. Come see me. You have great folks of your own, Darcy. I know they'll help you through. But if you're ever confused, lost...call me. Remember that I am—was—his dad. I'll always be there for you. You were always there for my boy." He hesitated. "And you may find that you need me. Remember this, please, I'll always be there."

He touched her head gently, then walked away, leaving her at the coffin. She stood there for several seconds, feeling the breeze touch her face, noting again the unbelievable blue of the sky. Down by the road, her parents were waiting. They would give her all the time she needed.

She saw that Hunter, leaning on his crutches, was waiting as well.

She didn't think that she could bear to talk to him.

She knelt down in the earth at the head of the coffin, suddenly overwhelmed with bitterness. "Oh, Josh, I will never speak to him again,'' she whispered softly, then shook her head. "God help me!"

She closed her eyes. It seemed that Josh's voice entered her head. "Darcy, hey, don't be so hard on Hunter. You know, he realized that Mike was being a homicidal jerk. He tried.''

The voice was so real that her eyes flew open.

The day hadn't changed. The sky was still blue, the breeze still soft. The coffin still lay in the mechanism that would shortly bring it deep into the ground.

Tears welled in her eyes again. She closed them tightly, and prayed. Then she rose, kissed the coffin, and murmured. "Josh, I will never forget you. And like your dad said, you will always be in my heart. Always. If I live to be a hundred.''

At last, she turned away. She started for the road where her parents, and Hunter, waited.

For a moment, the hate remained. She couldn't even look at Hunter. Then she remembered Josh's words, so real in her mind. *Don't be so hard on Hunter.*

He was still crying. She managed to walk to him and place a hand on his arm. "You tried," she said very softly.

"Oh, Darcy!" he whispered sickly.

"You tried," she repeated. "One day…one day, we can talk again.''

Amazingly, she felt better. And she knew that Hunter had tried. She knew, too, that his leg would heal. His heart never would. He would live with the night in which Josh and Mike had died all of his life. And he would fight the guilt in his soul just as long.

Her mother was waiting with outstretched arms. Her father, too. She ran to them, and let them do all the right things they thought that they could do.

That night, her mother gave her a sleeping pill, since she hadn't really slept since the accident.

And it was the pill, she was convinced the following day, that caused her strange dreams.

She was back at the cemetery. It wasn't a blue day anymore. It wasn't exactly gray, either. It seemed that there was a cast of silver, like a mist, over the day. Time had passed, and she walked through the old gnarled trees, ancient graves, and newer ones, that composed the cemetery. Josh had been buried beneath a beautiful old oak. She walked toward it, clad in black, bearing a bouquet of flowers.

And yet...

As she neared it, she saw a thin man standing by the old oak. Frowning, she came closer. And it was Josh.

He looked very handsome, dressed in the dark suit, tailored shirt, and crimson tie in which he had been buried. His dark hair was trimmed and brushed, as it had been for the prom. He was leaning against the tree, arms casually crossed, smiling as she came.

For a moment, she was afraid. Only a moment.

"Josh?"

"Darcy, poor Darcy," he said softly. His rueful smile reminded her of his father's when he had spoken to her over his son's coffin. "Darcy, you've got to know. It's okay. Honestly, it's okay."

"It's not okay, you're dead." She frowned, amazed to realize that she was a little angry with him. "You knew it, Josh! You knew you were going to die. The day that Mike threatened you...you said that maybe you'd be dead, but he'd be dead as well. And he is!"

"I know. I'm sorry. He was a true jerk, but I didn't really hate him."

"Josh—"

"I've got to go, Darcy. I just wanted you to know that I'm okay. I'm really okay. And you've got to go on."

"I will, Josh, but...I never knew how much I'd miss you," she whispered.

He touched her hair. Except that...he wasn't real, and of course, it was just a whisper of the breeze.

"I'll always be with you, Darcy. When you need me, just think of me. Here." He laid his palm against his heart.

"Oh, Josh!"

He was fading. Into the silver color of the day. Of course. It was a dream. A drug-induced dream.

He smiled. "You're special, Darcy. You'll need to be strong," he said softly.

And then he was gone.

It began the next day.

Her father had determined that he wasn't going into work; neither was her mother. They were going to spend the day with her, take a drive to the nearby mountains, and just spend time in that quite and beautiful part of their state.

He couldn't find his Palm Pilot.

"You left it on the counter of your bath," she told him.

"How on earth would you know that? Were you in our room, sweetheart?" her dad asked.

"No," Darcy said, startled herself. "I just…well, I guess it's a place you might have left it."

He went upstairs to his bathroom and returned with his Palm Pilot, looking at her oddly. "Thanks. I guess you know your old man pretty well, huh, kid?"

Of course, that was it.

But then…

Little pieces of precognition began to come to her, now and then. A few that summer, a few during her first years of college, more after that.

They were disturbing at first. Then she came to accept them. She thought that they were maybe something that Josh had very strangely managed to leave her.

It wasn't until later that she decided it was time to call Josh's father.

When the ghosts came.

1

Jeannie Mason Thomas lay in the white expanse of the four-poster bed in the Lee room at Melody House in pure bliss.

Roger was snoring softly at her side. Men, she thought affectionately. Bless 'em. Whatever came, they could sleep.

She could not. She had to keep playing over the day, minute by minute. Her wedding day.

There had been the usual hassles in the morning. Her mom had gotten all teary every few minutes, and insisted on giving speeches about sex and marriage that were totally unnecessary. Alice, her matron of honor, had clipped off two of her newly purchased acrylic nails trying to fix Jeannie's train. Sandy, another bridesmaid, had gotten too looped on the champagne they had shared while dressing for the service. The limo had been late. Her original soprano had come down with a sore throat leaving Jeannie desperately seeking a new singer at the last minute. But she'd managed to find an Irish tenor through the priest, Father O'Hara, and once she had reached the Revolution-era church just outside town, everything had gone perfectly.

Everyone claimed that it had been one of the most beautiful weddings they had ever seen. Roger had been tall, dark, and glorious in his tux. Her father had been stately, her mother beautiful. Her brother and sister, both part of the wedding ceremony, had been well behaved, joking, laughing, and wonderful. Her first dance with her new husband had been magical, but it was during her dance with her father that she had realized she was one of the luckiest human beings in the world with a tender, tight family, *and* an incredible groom.

The reception would be the talk of a number of counties for months to come. The Irish tenor had joined with the band. The music had gone from classical to rock and pop to theatrical. The food had been delicious, the cake stupendous.

Then, after fully enjoying their own reception, they had taken off at last for Melody House. And it hadn't been as if making love had been anything new for them, but making love as man and wife was new and therefore, somehow, more sensual, more erotic, and so deeply satisfying. They'd been hot and heavy, they'd laughed, they'd joked over getting out of clothing, slipping in the shower in their haste, rolling off the bed, and all sorts of little foibles. They'd had a great deal more champagne, finishing the bottle that had been left in the elegant little silver bucket on the antique table set before the fireplace. They'd dined on the delicious little snacks left for them, caviar, quiches, chocolate-dipped strawberries and more. Then they'd made love again, all lazy and slow, and it had been incredibly luxurious as well. Melody House had offered everything they had wanted. In the morning, they could go downstairs and be served breakfast in the sunny little nook off the kitchen. They could spend a day indulging in the heated pool—a recent addition to the colonial manor. They could ride the trails that meandered through miles of forest when the sun was just setting. They could have both privacy and service. Jeannie had every right to be entirely blissful, and also, patient with the fact that her new husband could sleep, while she could not.

She rose, feeling as agile and luxuriously sinuous as a cat, naked in the coolness of the night. She stretched, thinking that the strenuous exercise program she had put herself through before the wedding had been well worth it—she didn't think that she could be more than five percent body fat at the moment, and Roger had been delighted. She was glad, too, because she liked to think that she had talked Matt Stone into allowing them to use the seldom-rented room for their wedding night because she had just been cute and charming. Stone was known to be something of a hard-ass.

Walking over to the open French doors that led to the balcony, Jeannie almost pouted, then grinned instead. Roger had told her that Matt Stone had given in just because he knew the only way to keep Melody House as a private property had been to allow the house itself to earn some of the upkeep money such an estate so desperately needed. Roger had probably been right. But then again, maybe it had been a combination of Stone's needs and *her* charm and persuasion. Whatever! It had all worked, and it had come together so beautifully. She was a lover of history, and to spend her wedding night in such an elegant and historic place was like the most delicious icing in the world on the most wonderful cake—her perfect wedding day. She parted the draperies, glad to feel the breeze against her bare shin, and feeling sensual all over again as it touched her. She was married now. She was Mrs. Thomas. She could slink right on back over to the bed, wake up her slight snoring *husband,* and live out her every fantasy.

Yet...

Suddenly, the delicious feeling wasn't quite so delicious anymore. She felt a sudden, quick, bone-numbing chill. She spun around, and saw nothing in the dim night-light pouring out from the bathroom, or even from the faint glow of moonlight and property lights that seeped in from the open French doors to the balcony, just hemmed in by the drifting draperies where she stood.

She felt...

Fear. Deep and irrational.

She swallowed, stepping over to close the French doors and lock them tightly. She glanced at Roger. He kept snoring. She tried to calm herself. If she was feeling a sudden and totally irrational fear, all she had to do was run back to the bed, jump in beside him, and he would cuddle and hold her and everything would be all right.

That was exactly what she was going to do.

But she didn't. She didn't move. Because she saw...

The silvery movement in the night.

She blinked, but it didn't go away. And it wasn't the darkness, or the reflection of the lights, or a combination of the two. It was something, vague in shape, silvery-white, hovering, moving. It came from the side of the bed, where she should have been sleeping, and it was coming toward her.

She panicked totally. Her vocal cords were frozen. She stared, breathing out desperate little choking sounds, since she could find no voice. It came closer and closer. She felt ice trickles into blood and limbs and then...

It was almost touching her. She felt her hair move... pulled? Cold seemed to slap her right across the face. And she could have sworn that she heard a whisper, mocking, scornful. ''Silly little girl! He'll only kill you!''

Then again...her hair...lifting. On its own, in the grip of the vague, silvery-white substance. A substance that whispered or played havoc with the breeze. There was no breeze. She had closed the doors.

At last, she found voice, movement, and energy. She let out an hysterical, chilling scream, and ran.

She didn't run for the bed and Roger—she headed straight for the door out of the Lee room. Jeannie wrenched at the knob so hard she nearly ripped it from the wood. The door itself flew open, and banged wickedly against the wall. This had no bearing on her. She barely heard it. She kept screaming, tore along the landing, and down the elegant, curving masterpiece of a stairway to the ground level below.

Matt Stone had chosen to stay in the caretaker's cottage, fifty yards to the left of the main house. It had been his home for years before his grandfather had died, leaving

Melody House—and the responsibility for its upkeep—to him. He had only moved into the main house recently because it had become easier on the upkeep side, and, he had to admit, he had come to like it. The grand master suite he had chosen afforded a lot of comfort. Big bedroom, dressing room, office or entertainment space, and it kept him right on top of whatever was going on with the property.

He liked the caretaker's cottage, too. Since it had been falling apart so badly due to years of neglect he had rebuilt and refurbished it with every modern convenience. In contrast to the painstaking care they had used in keeping the main house historical, the caretaker's house was far more state-of-the-art.

When he had given in to allowing the Lee room to be used as a honeymoon suite, he had opted to spend the night in his old haunts.

He had been sound asleep, however, when the scream brought him bolting from bed.

Despite the quiet tone of their small town, as sheriff of Stoneyville he was accustomed to being awakened in the dead of night. Therefore, he was up, into his jeans, and streaking across the patch of lawn that separated the caretaker's cottage from the main house in a matter of seconds, the key to the huge oak front door in his hands. He burst into the house less than two minutes from the time he had heard the scream.

There was a light on in the foyer; there always was. Just as soft lights eternally flooded the front porch. He was prepared for anything when he burst through the door.

Or, at least, he had thought that he was.

Maybe not.

There was no apparent danger. Instead, there *she* was, the blushing bride, standing at the foot of the stairway, shaking and screaming in her altogether. Jeannie was a pretty girl, perfectly toned from months industriously spent at the gym in order to look perfect for her wedding day. Hard not to look, but he forced his eyes to hers first, then cast his gaze anxiously around, scanning the area for any hidden threat that might be the reason for this scene. Seeing nothing, his mind working in milliseconds, he wondered if the groom had somehow turned out to be a homicidal maniac or a simple wife-beater. Either choice seemed doubtful.

"Jeannie?" he said, his voice deep with calm and authority. Normally, he would have walked to her, set an arm around her shoulder, and patiently determined the cause of her distress. But she was standing in his foyer stark naked and screaming. "Jeannie, please, talk. What the hell…?"

By that time, her husband was rushing down the stairs as well. He was still half-asleep, and Matt would have sworn in any court that the young man appeared as bleary and stunned as anyone could possibly be. Certainly not fresh from a fight with his new bride.

"Jeannie!" Roger cried out in shock.

Matt crossed over one of the velvet cord barriers into the parlor and swept an antique throw from the fragile old love seat, striding across the room to cast it around Jeannie's shoulders. She had stopped screaming, but she was still shaking like a leaf, eyes wide, dilated.

Roger, still dazed, and definitely horrified, thanked him briefly. Then he stared at his bride again, confusion once again reigning in his eyes.

"Jeannie, what is it?"

At last, she turned to focus on him, her expression blank at first, then filled with tension. "You didn't see it? You didn't feel it?"

"Jeannie, I was sound asleep! What are you talking about?"

By then, Penny Sawyer, in a terry robe, her graying hair frizzled around her handsomely constructed face, arrived. She stood in the frame of the front door, left open when Matt had come bursting in.

"What in the Lord's name…?" she queried.

Penny managed Melody House. She kept accounts, and

ran the tours. She loved the place, probably more so than Matt himself. She had worked as an historian for Matt's grandfather, and slipped right into the role of managing the place after his death. She was like an aunt to Matt, as well as being incredibly efficient, and all but married to the place.

There was only one area in which they disagreed. And Matt silently grit his teeth then, certain that this episode was about to lead in that direction.

"Apparently, our bride has had a nightmare," Matt said quietly.

"Nightmare!" Jeannie shrieked. She must have heard the shrill tone of her own voice because she fought to control it. "I *wasn't* sleeping."

"So what exactly was the problem?" Roger asked, an underlying irritation rising beneath his concerned exterior.

"I think I should get some brandy," Penny said.

"I think Jeannie should get some clothes on!" Roger said, his anger starting to crack through.

"Clothes?" Jeannie said. She stared down at herself and realized that she was covered in nothing but the antique quilt.

"I'll make tea with brandy," Penny said decisively.

"While she's making the tea, Jeannie, you can run up and get dressed. Then we can all sit down and you can explain just what you're doing," Roger said, a thread of anger in his voice.

"What I'm doing?" Jeannie repeated, frowning. "Roger Thomas, I was scared to death, don't you understand?"

"Scared enough to run around naked?"

Matt could have groaned aloud. He shouldn't have been swayed to allow the Lee Room to become a honeymoon hangout. He glared at Penny. She had talked him into it, reminding him that they needed the money for Melody House.

Penny shrugged innocently, giving him one of her knowing looks.

Melody House was reputed to be haunted. Matt always saw the rumors as simply par for the course. The main house was well over two hundred years old. It had survived the American Revolution, the Civil War, and every manner of conflict in between. As he well knew, nothing that old went without a certain kind of history. And apparently, most of the world wanted to believe in things that went bump in the night. People couldn't just look back on the personal tragedies of the past with sorrow—they just had to make something else out of them.

Matt simply didn't believe in ghosts. He'd worked in the D.C. area long before he'd taken up working in his old home haunts, and he knew that the things that living men and women did to one another could be so violent, barbarous, and cruel, that there was simply no reason to worry about those who were long dead and buried.

"Go up and put clothes on!" Roger said, his voice almost a roar.

Jeannie, blue eyes still huge, stared at him in rebellion and defiance.

"I am *not*—get this straight!—*not* going back up to that room. *Ever!* There is a ghost up there, and it—it threatened me."

Matt shook his head, praying for patience. He looked up at the bride and groom. Wow! How quickly there was trouble in Paradise.

"Jeannie," he said patiently, "there are no such things as ghosts. Hey, I've lived here most of my life. I've spent nights in the place with no electricity, you know, in the pitch dark. I swear, there are no ghosts. I would know."

He had tried to say the last lightly. He knew, however, that his voice had an edge. He was sick to death of the whole ghost thing.

"Look what you've done," Roger said to Jeannie. "Great. Really good honeymoon we're going to have here—you've just really pissed off Matt Stone."

"Sorry, I'm not angry," Matt said quickly. "I just don't believe in ghosts. Jeannie, it was a big day for you. I'm

sure for you both...I'm not saying that anyone is totally
inebriated, but come on, now, you both had a hell of a lot
to drink. You're wired, Jeannie. Excited. Hey, it was the
wedding of the century, huh? You don't have to go back
into the room. We'll get your things. And you and Roger
can finish out your honeymoon in the caretaker's cottage,
how's that? I can clear it out in a matter of minutes, while
Penny makes tea.''

Jeannie spun around again. She looked as if she wanted
to run from Roger's side and come flying into his arms.

Don't do it, Jeannie, don't do it! He pleaded silently.

''Not one of you has suggested coming up to see if there
is something in the room,'' Jeannie said indignantly.

Matt lifted his hands. ''I'll go up to the room.''

He strode past the newlywed couple on the stairs. As he
neared the upper landing, he could hear Roger whispering
angrily to his wife. ''Ghost, hell! You're a little exhibi-
tionist. You've had a bit of a thing for Matt Stone your
whole life, you know, Jeannie. What, you just had to have
an excuse for him to see you naked?''

''Roger Thomas! How dare you suggest such a thing,
you bastard!'' she whispered back. Then her voice rose.
''We don't need the caretaker's house! I'm going home.
Home—back to my family. They're not a bunch of idiot
jerks!''

''Hey, there!'' Penny protested cheerfully. ''You know,
everyone is really tired, but we'll get to the bottom of this.
Matt, he's all he-man practical and doesn't believe in
ghosts, but I'm telling you, Roger, don't you go being hard
on your new missus! Lots of folks believe that this house
is more than a little haunted, I do tell you!''

Matt walked on into the Lee Room. As he suspected,
there was nothing there. The French doors to the balcony
were open, and the drapes were drifting in. They must have
been what scared the new bride so badly. Either that, or
she just wanted the place to be haunted so badly that she
had made it so.

He found Jeannie's peignoir robe, then discarded it as

being far too see-through for this situation. Her groom would not be happy with it, he was certain. Striding to the closet, he found a pair of robes with "Melody House" inscribed on the pockets—items Penny had insisted they needed to provide a real luxury touch for those few times when he decided to rent the room. He pulled one from the hanger and headed back downstairs.

By then, Penny, Jeannie and Roger had headed into the kitchen. It was vast. The integrity of the historical aspects had been maintained with the massive hearth and the many copper pots and herbs that adorned wall mounts, but the huge refrigerator, sub-zero freezer, and stainless steel stove were all necessary modern conveniences for the many social events, dinners, luncheons, and meetings that were held at the property.

The newlyweds were seated at the table with Penny. She had apparently moved like lightning, microwaving water and hurriedly supplying brandy, because they were all sipping out of huge earthenware mugs already.

They had been joined there by several of the other residents of the property, probably all awakened by the screaming. Matt's cousin Clint, who, like Penny, lived in one of the apartments above the stables, was seated at the table. Clint's eyes flashed with humor as they met Matt's. Sam Arden, the caretaker, old, thin, and crusty, his white hair wild, was at the table as well. He shook his head and rolled his eyes when he saw Matt. Rounding out the group was Carter Sutton. He was actually an old college friend of Clint's from the next town over. He owned a lot of local property, and had just bought a house nearby. Since it was still being held hostage by construction workers, he'd taken a room over the stables as well. It worked well. Carter made his living off his investments, and was sometimes "paper rich and cash poor," so he was happy to look after the horses and serve as stable boy and trail guide when they rented out the horses.

Matt silently offered the robe, and walked around to take a seat at the end of the table. Penny was happily talking about ghosts. Roger was convincing his wife that there had been nothing there at all, other than the excitement of the day.

"And if there was a ghost, it was probably more scared than you," Clint assured the bride.

"Hell, there are ghosts," Sam said sagely, nodding his old head.

"Sam," Matt protested.

"She meant to hurt me!" Jeannie said with certainty.

"I don't think that ghosts are supposed to hurt people," Carter said. His mustache twitched. He was as bearded as a goat, since he enjoyed a high military position in the "Rebel" unit in which he participated in many battle re-enactments.

"She meant to hurt me," Jeannie repeated.

"I've slept in that room," Clint said, "and honestly, nothing ever happened to me."

"I know the Lee Room like the back of my hand," Carter teased. "It holds the fondest memories in my heart," he told the bride with a wink.

She flushed and laughed uneasily.

"Matt," Penny said, "There's a cup of strong tea for you right there, end of the table."

"Thanks," he said. "I'll reheat it in a bit. I'm going to get a few things out of the caretaker's cottage, so you two can slip on over when you want."

"Hey, Mr. Stone, I...I don't want to put you to any more trouble," Roger said.

"I can't sleep in this house!" Jeannie wailed.

"It's no trouble," he assured them both.

All he wanted to do right then was get out—he didn't think he could bear to hear another of Penny's speeches on ghosts. He allowed her, on Friday and Saturday nights, to give a "Legends of Melody House" tour, during which she liked to go on and on about various stories involving the house, and how it was rumored to be haunted by different characters, including historical figures.

He had adamantly refused to let her call it a ghost tour.

But since she did attract dozens and dozens of paying tourists, people staying as diversely far away as Williamsburg, Richmond, Harpers Ferry, and even D.C., he had to allow the endeavor. She served cider, tea, cookies, and pastries in the middle of the tour, and he knew that she was right— they paid a whole lot of bills thanks to those tours. He still didn't like them, or anything that suggested that Melody House was *really* haunted. However, he tolerated it all, for the sake of the house.

"Go on, Matt—we'll keep them entertained for you," Clint told him laconically. Matt arched a brow. Clint could be openly lascivious. He had surely enjoyed the spectacle of the bride, wrapped in the antique quilt and nothing more.

"Thanks," Matt said dryly, and left them all to their arguments on whether there was or wasn't a ghost.

An hour later, he was moved back into his room at the main house, and he and Penny and Roger had packed up the newlyweds, who were now happily settled in the caretaker's cottage. Penny returned to her apartment over the stables.

Matt had barely gotten back to sleep before he heard a ringing sound. He fumbled around to turn off his alarm, but it was the phone instead. One of his officers was on the other end, anxiously urging him to get moving; they had a domestic violence situation threatening to turn explosive.

Matt hurriedly dressed, his thoughts half on the night gone by, and half on the day to come. There it was—the truth again. As his dad had once told him, when he had shivered at the sight of an old cemetery, the dead were the safest people around.

It was the living you had to watch out for.

That day was hell for Matt. He was so tired most of it, he could have toppled over. It began with the situation at the Creekmore house, old Harry threatening to kill his wife and kids, accusing her of sleeping around, claiming he didn't even know if the kids were really his or not. Thayer had kept the situation under control until he got there. Matt had managed first to get Harry to let him in, then pretended to share most of a bottle of whiskey with him, convince him he could do DNA testing on his kids, finally get the shotgun, and haul Harry off to jail.

Somehow, he endured the rest of the week, staying in the main house, hearing the honeymooners in the pool at all hours, day and night.

Jeannie came to thank him personally for not throwing them out. Her honeymoon, between the pool and the horses and the incredible Jacuzzi in the caretaker's house, was bliss.

She had forgotten about the ghost. She admitted that she'd had a lot to drink.

Penny kept insisting that there was a ghost, and he was being a blind fool to ignore it. Either something bad was going to happen, or—on the bright side!—were they to prove that a ghost existed, they could get so rich they'd never have to worry about the upkeep of the place again.

Finally the honeymooners departed and everything went back to normal. Then, Penny started at him again. She wanted to have a seance.

He said no.

She persisted.

He begged her to leave him alone. He had too much work on his plate at the moment.

At last, Penny backed off and contented herself with her tours. Matt thought that life was pleasantly back to routine.

Until she came to him with the letter from Adam Harrison, Harrison Investigations.

It was a month later that Clara Issy, one of the five daytime housekeepers, stopped dead in her tracks.

It was a sunny morning. The beautiful old bedroom in Melody House was as it always was. The bed she had just made with its shiny four-poster and quilted cover sat against the right wall. The polished mahogany bureau held the modern touch of the entertainment center within it. The television was off. The French doors to the balcony and the wraparound porch were ajar because it was such a nice day and the breeze was fresh and clean, causing the white draperies to stir and dance. That was natural, and she was accustomed to the smell and feel of fresh air. She loved it, and she wasn't at all fond of the air-conditioning that ran through the summer months. No, the room itself was just as it always was.

She stood near the open French doors, jaw agape, and stared.

Because she was alone in the room, yet something else was moving. Something that drifted from the bed. Something in a hazy form, something cold, something that felt threatening.

It approached Clara. She felt something touch her face, almost like the stroke of fingers against her cheek. Very cold fingers. Dead fingers. She thought she heard a whispering. Scratchy, against her ear. Something that pleaded… or threatened.

Her hands were frozen in a vise around her broom handle. Her body felt as if it had jelled into ice. Fear raced up and down her spine.

The cold…wrapped around her. Tightly. More and more tightly.

At last, her jaw snapped shut. She broke the sensation of terror. She screamed, not a bloodcurdling sound, but one that barely held a gasp of air.

Then she found life, and ran.

Out to the second floor landing; there was no one there. Down the flight of stairs to the grand foyer, where again, the house was empty. She headed toward the second doorway to the right of the sweeping stairway. Surely, for the love of God, someone would be in the house office— Penny, a tiny bastion against anyone evil, but someone, at the least.

Clara breathed a sigh of relief. Matt was there. Bursting out the doorway before she could reach it. He was in his work uniform, but he hadn't headed out for the station yet; it was still very early. Thank God.

He hurried toward her, as if he had heard her cry—being Matt, of course, he had heard it!—and had been preparing to rush to her rescue. Except that she had fled the room upstairs with greater speed than a greyhound. And so she was here, spurting into his arms.

"Clara! What is it?"

She was fifty-five. Twenty years older than Matt, at least. But he was Matt; solid as a rock. A tall man in his prime with a way about him that commanded respect which in turn offered her a feeling of security that allowed her to speak when her mouth was still all but completely contorted.

"I—I—quit!" she gasped out.

"Clara, what on earth?" he asked kindly, holding her at something of a distance from himself and searching out her eyes.

"Let me tell you, that bride was not crazy. There's a ghost in that room!"

"Oh, Clara, please. We both know the silly stories about this place! We've both heard them since we were little kids. But come on, we've also worked in this house, both of us, for years and years. Clara, I feel like a broken record here, but believe me—ghosts don't really exist. People want them to exist sometimes. Penny is dying to have a few authentic ghosts to give the place a greater reputation. Seems like being an historical masterpiece doesn't always cut it these days." He smiled, smoothing back her graying hair.

"There's a ghost in the Lee room, and it just touched me." Clara planted her hands on her hips. "How long have you known me? Forever? Haven't I always agreed with you, saying that it was just silly airheads who felt they had to make up ghost stories? But you have to believe me—there's something in that room. It threatened me. Matt, it wasn't my imagination. It wasn't a memory of ghost tales told over and over. It was real. I could see it. Come up and see for yourself!''

Matt sighed deeply. Still, there was concern for her in the depths of his dark eyes. ''All right, Clara, let's go take a look.''

Clara edged behind him, then followed as he left the office and strode with long footsteps through the foyer, up the stairs, and to the Lee room.

Naturally, there was nothing there.

Clara walked over to her broom. ''I was standing right here.''

''Clara, maybe you saw the draperies drifting in. The French doors are open.''

Clara indignantly straightened her five-foot-one frame. She could see that Matt felt as if he was living a repeat of a silly performance. He was trying to be patient; he felt like throwing his hands up as if the whole world had now gone insane. ''I know the difference between drapes and a ghost!''

Matt ran his fingers through his ink dark hair, shaking his head. ''Clara…I don't know what to say. There's nothing here at all.''

Clara sniffed. ''Matt, it's gone now. But there *was* something here! Why can't you believe me? You should. It wasn't all that long ago that we rented the room to the Thomases. She came running out of the room in the middle of the night, stark naked, and screaming! All right, I wasn't here when it happened, but I sure heard all about it.'' Clara paused, biting her lip. ''Okay, I laughed like hell, I'll admit, but…Matt, there's something going on.''

''Clara, Jeannie Thomas herself said later that she'd had a lot to drink that night. Her husband didn't see or hear a thing, and all it did was cause a big argument on the first night of their marriage. Clara, Jeannie drove me crazy and came here and specifically asked for this room, having heard that it was haunted. Don't you see? The bride wanted there to be a ghost, and so there was. History can be tragic, Clara. And there was some tragic history associated with

the place. But come on, now! You're a sensible woman.
In your heart, you know that you're just letting your imagination run riot.''

"Matt, I quit.''

"Oh, Clara!''

She knew that he couldn't afford to lose another maid.

"How about this, Clara. You don't quit, but you don't
clean this room. How's that?''

She reflected on his offer. "Who is going to clean it?''

"We'll let Penny come in here and take care of this
room. Penny thinks it's the greatest thing in the world that
the place has a reputation for being haunted.''

"You know, Matt, I can't help it. I was definitely one
of those to scoff at such absurdity, but I can tell you now—
this house is haunted!''

"Clara, maybe it's haunted, and maybe…hm.''

"Maybe what?''

"Maybe Penny is playing tricks, she wants the house to
be haunted so badly. Or maybe someone is…I don't know.
Breaking in here. Making things happen.''

"How?'' Clara asked incredulously.

"Who knows,'' he murmured.

Clara again planted her hands on her hips, her eyes narrowing. "Who the hell would break in here? Who would
have the balls—since it's *your* place—the town sheriff?''

"I don't know. But since you think there was someone
in here, I intend to find out.''

Clara shook her head. "We're the ones who have been
lying to ourselves, Matt. The whole darned house may be
haunted, but this room…this room is menacing!''

"Ghosts don't menace people, Clara.''

She sniffed. "You don't believe in ghosts, so how do
you know what they do?''

"Clara, I don't believe in ghosts, but from everything
I've seen and read, I've never heard of a ghost actually
hurting anyone.''

Clara shook her head again, appearing to be the one
wise beyond all earthly knowledge. "Well, Mr. Matt, I'll

have you know, that isn't true at all! Haven't you ever
heard of the Bell Witch in Tennessee? They say that even
old Andrew Jackson was afraid of her, that she pulled people's hair and threw the children around and even caused
the death of the master of the house. You refuse to accept
anything that isn't cut-and-dried, and you're blind to things
going on in your own house!''

Matt leaned against the door frame, smiling. "Clara,
once again, I believe that people can make things real with
their imaginations.''

"You think old Andy Jackson was an imaginative
guy?''

"You'd have to show me written proof that Andrew
Jackson was afraid of a ghost. And I don't mean any hear-
say on a Discovery program or even in a book of ghost
stories.''

Clara pointed a finger at him. "You'd better do something, before the stories about this house become so real
that no one will pay for the tours. You can't keep this
place up on a sheriff's salary alone.''

"Thank you, Clara. I'll take that under advisement. But
then again, you know, Penny is certain that a documented
haunting would make us as rich as Midas.''

Clara was startled when Matt frowned suddenly and
walked over to her. "What happened to your face?''

"To my face?'' Clara frowned as well, and walked over
to the mirror. Her cheek was red and mottled, as if she'd
been slapped, and slapped hard.

She turned and stared at him. "Ghosts don't menace
people, huh?''

"Clara,'' Matt said. "Think about it! You must have
run into something in your hurry to get out of the room!''

Clara eyed him sharply and shook her head. "Matt, the
stories have circulated for years. People have sworn that
they've seen soldiers in the downstairs rooms. They've
seen a lady in white, floating down the stairway. Ghosts
that fit in with history. It's only been in recent years, since
your grandfather died, that things have gotten really seri-

ous. Remember how Randy Gustav quit after staying a night in the Lee Room? He wouldn't even explain what happened to you. It's only in the last few years that...that the ghosts kind of threaten to get violent.''

"There are no such things as ghosts."

"Oh, yeah? One just gave me a bruise!"

With that, Clara indignantly walked out on him, calling back over her shoulder, "Matt, you're a hell of a man. That's why I'm staying. Believe it or don't, but you'd better do something about that particular ghost—that doesn't exist in your mind."

That evening, having returned home very late from work, Matt sat at the desk in his suite in the main house, going through correspondence.

There was a tap at his door.

"Come in."

Penny stuck her head in. "Am I bothering you, Matt?"

"Not at all."

She walked in and sat on the corner of his desk. "Matt, you have to do something over this latest episode with Clara."

"Oh?" He leaned back in his chair.

"Clara was hurt!"

"Penny, please. I'm sorry, I think the world of Clara, we're friends from way back, and I gave her the rest of the day off with pay. She had to have run into something."

Penny shook her head.

He leaned forward suddenly, abruptly. "Penny, you wouldn't be playing some kind of game up there, determined to convince the rest of the world, if not me, that the place is haunted?"

She gaped at him in such affront that he was immediately sorry.

"Matt, I would *never*—"

"But maybe someone would."

"Maybe," Penny agreed grudgingly. She wagged a finger at him. "You know, you are far too trusting at times. Too many people could have access to this place."

"Penny, I'm not too trusting. We're a fairly small town."

Penny shook her head decisively. "You're right, of course. But you've got to remember that even in our small town we have had a few pretty grisly murders. Why can't you just accept the fact that something strange is going on?"

"Penny, you've wanted nothing more than a real ghost for years."

Penny shook her head, suddenly troubled. "Ghosts... that cause a cold spot, or breeze by, or...I don't think this is a good ghost," she murmured.

She patted his desk, rummaging through the unopened letters. "What about that letter you got from Harrison Investigations? Call Adam. You respect him. He was friends with your grandfather long ago."

He groaned.

"Please, Matt. You've suggested that maybe someone is breaking in, or doing something to make it appear that there are ghosts. Adam can tell you what's real, and what's not."

"What he *perceives* as real," Matt muttered.

"Hey, I've followed some of what he's done. Last year, he and some of his colleagues proved that the haunting of an old mining camp was nothing more than two modern prospectors digging for gold."

"Great. I call in Ghostbusters and become the laughingstock of the town. I might as well find a new place to live."

Penny shook her head. "Matt, maybe they can just do the same thing here." She hopped off the edge of the table. "Please, promise me you'll think about it, at least."

She left him, closing the door softly in her wake.

Matt walked to his own set of French doors out to the wraparound balcony. The moon was full. In the distance, he could see the vague shape of the mountains, and the sweep of the valley. God, he loved this area. Loved the house, the stables, but mostly, just the natural beauty of the area.

He returned to his desk, reflective. Clara's face *had* been marked, as if she had been hit. He still didn't believe in ghosts, but...

He reflected on the number of people who lived on the property. Penny, Sam, Clint, Carter, even Clara now and then, and through the years gone by, various friends and relatives. Could someone have set the place up so that it appeared haunted?

He strode to the Lee Room, searched under the bed, in the closet, all around. Nothing.

Still...

He returned to his own suite, toyed with Adam Harrison's letter for a moment, and picked up the phone. He dialed Harrison's number. They spoke briefly. "Matt, good to hear from you."

"You weren't certain that you would?" Matt queried dryly.

"Nope. Not this time."

"You know I don't believe in the supernatural in any way, shape, or form."

"I'm aware of that."

"If you come down here, I'm only having you because I think you'll be able to prove that I don't have ghosts."

"Maybe," Adam agreed.

"When can you come?"

"My schedule is a bit of a mess, but...I'll arrange to see you soon."

"And according to your letter, Adam, *you're* going to pay *me?*"

"Yes. And like I said, I *am* anxious. I'll arrange something as soon as possible."

"You can usually find me around lunchtime at the Wayside Inn."

"All right, my office manager will call, set a date."

"Good," Matt said. "Look forward to seeing you, Adam."

Adam Harrison was still talking when Matt hung up the phone. He stared at it, already thinking that he had made one hell of a mistake.

On the other end, Adam Harrison, too, stared at his phone. He did so with fond amusement. He'd always liked Matt. "My boy. You're about to learn a lesson. All the courage, brain power, and brawn in the world can't cut it against a real ghost," he said softly. "Ah, well."

He had meant to warn Matt that he wasn't even sure he could come himself right away, that he'd be sending his top-notch aide.

But he didn't want to call back. Matt Stone wasn't at all pleased with this arrangement, even though he was surely having trouble.

It would all be fine. Darcy could handle any man, living...

Or dead.

2

From the moment she walked into the bar, Darcy felt at a distinct disadvantage.

It was called the Wayside Inn. It should have been called Bubba's Back-then Barn.

She was nearly overcome by the wave of smoke that almost knocked her over when she opened the door; it sat like a fog over the decades-old plastic booths and bar stools. There were two pool tables to the left, stuffed away from what might have been used, at times, as a dance floor.

There were actually still a few spittoons for tobacco chewers scattered around.

When she stepped in and the door closed behind her, the place came to a standstill. The four pool players and the broken-toothed wonders watching the games all stopped their play and stared at her. Behind the bar, a heavyset woman with teased red hair styled in something like a sixties beehive looked up from washing glasses. In what looked to be a dining area, the four men seated at one of the chipped wood tables also looked up.

She stood in the miasma of smoke and stared around, taking it in as her eyes adjusted from the sunlight. And she knew, instantly, that Adam was the one who should have come here. And he should have worn jeans and an old plaid or denim work shirt. Of course, the concept of Adam dressed that way was an amusing one, but Adam was a determined man. And for some reason, he was determined that they were getting into Melody House.

She had come in a business suit, the same attire she

usually wore when conducting business, she reminded herself, defending her choice of clothing when she was so obviously out of place. But though she hadn't imagined the Wayside Inn to be a five-star restaurant, she hadn't thought that it would be quite this…colloquial.

"Can I help you, honey?" the redhead called from behind the bar. Her voice was warm and friendly, giving Darcy a bit of encouragement. She smiled in return. But before she could reply, one of the men who'd been sitting at the table had risen.

"Miss?"

He was tall, somewhat lanky, and when he smiled, she saw that he had all his teeth, and a single dimple in his left cheek. Light brown eyes, and a pleasant way about him; he seemed to ooze accent and Southern charm with his single word.

"I'm looking for a man named Matt Stone. I was supposed to meet him here." She hoped that one of the men knew Stone. She didn't think that he was among them. She'd already pictured him in her mind. He was the descendant of a man who was practically a Founding Father. He would be tall, straight, and aging with incredible dignity. He might be one of the those fellows who sat around Revolutionary or Civil War round tables, rehashing the past. He might have a certain attitude about him, but he'd still be an incredible old gentleman.

"Hey, honey, you can meet me!" one of the pool players called out.

"Watch your manners, Carter!" one of the others said, and another sniggered.

At the table, another of the men stood.

"Come in, have a seat," he said.

She had to admit, this fellow's jeans fit him well, hugging leans hips, strong legs, and some solid length. He was wearing shades, even inside, in the cloud of smoke—maybe he thought that they'd protect his eyes from the haze. He was well over six feet, ebony hair a little too long, but apparently clean and brushed. He was clean-shaven, maybe thirty, thirty-five. Strong, solid features. While the first fellow to approach her had been polite and laid-back, his face splitting instantly into an easy grin in the first few seconds, this one looked as if he might have been chiseled on Mount Rushmore. Though he had stood courteously enough and asked her to sit, he looked as if he were entirely impatient, more like a man about to suggest that she go jump in a lake.

She walked over to the table. The first man—he with the great dimple—had drawn out a chair for her. She looked at the other two who had been sitting at the table, now risen, as she approached. One was older, white-haired, white-bearded. She kept imagining him in a butternut and gray Confederate Army uniform. The fourth in the party was somewhere around thirty as well, had a decent haircut, and was actually in a tailored shirt and chinos, and looked as if he might have a real job somewhere in a civilized town.

"What's your business here?" the tall, chiseled-face man asked abruptly, sitting as he did so. They all stared at her.

"My name is Darcy Tremayne. I had an appointment with Matt Stone. I was supposed to meet him here. I believe I'm in the right place. Do any of you know him?"

She spoke evenly and politely—she was here on business. But she felt as if hostility oozed around her. She longed to bolt from the chair and fly out the door. She knew that everyone in the bar was still staring at her.

"Know him?" the tall, lanky fellow with the dimple said.

But he was interrupted. The man Darcy had mentally begun to refer to as Chisel-face cut him off. "Are you one of the psychics?" he asked.

Darcy arched a brow. *Be pleasant with the locals, Adam had told her.*

All right, she could be friendly.

"I suppose you could say that. I'm with Harrison Investigations," she said. This was definitely a small town.

Okay, so she had come from a fairly small town herself, but this one seemed even more rural. Maybe that was because she'd spent so many years in New York, and had been living in the D.C. area for so long now. It seemed that any event regarding Melody House was news in the area, and that everyone knew everyone else's business.

"A real live ghost buster?" the fellow with the dimple teased.

"Ghost buster?" She ever so slightly hiked a brow once again, sitting back, determined that she would be cool, cordial, and dignified. "Harrison Investigations is actually a small, private company, and what we do is investigate strange occurrences in old homes and the like." She smiled. "Most of the time, we find squeaky floorboards and leaky plumbing, but when a place is as historically relevant as Melody House, the history alone could create a very old and spiritual feeling."

"Melody House is pretty damned cool," the dimpled man said, flashing another warm smile.

The old white-haired codger spoke up. "Ms. Tremayne, lots of folks have come wanting to set up cameras, tape machines, and all kinds of hocus-pocus stuff at Melody House. The owner has just flat-out told them no."

"Yes, well, that's why I'm anxious to meet Matt Stone. Mr. Harrison and he are well acquainted. Mr. Stone respects my employer, and knows that we're not sensationalist in any way. We know history and architecture, and people, and naturally, we're very discreet. I can understand any hesitation Mr. Stone has had in the past. I'm sure that many people come ready to cash in on the ghosts."

"I see," interrupted Chisel-face. "You're here to investigate some of the eerie stories associated with the house, but you're *not* trying to cash in on ghosts?" His voice was deep, the words were evenly spoken; somehow, they still dripped scorn.

"No. I've just explained. We're investigators."

"Um," Chisel-face murmured. He stared at her hard. "You said that most of the time what you discovered was creaky floorboards or leaky plumbing. What happens when it's not 'most of the time'?"

"We do our best to right matters," she said, wishing that she'd never gotten into the conversation.

"And how do you do that? Without, of course, making a bid to fascinate people—or cash in on the ghosts."

She hesitated. She didn't really need to be having this conversation with a skeptic; she was looking for Matt Stone. But they were indeed in a small town. And Adam had suggested that she do her best to get along with the locals. In such a place, they were usually full of information, and could be very helpful. She shrugged. Adam wanted it; she could try to be social.

"Some ghosts are actually a part of history, and it's the history that creates the legends that make them so fascinating to people. Some home owners and even corporations—especially those with places as significant as Melody House—want to have a resident ghost rapping on walls now and then to attract their clientele. Watch television, and you'll know that there's a huge population out there interested in being frightened. What we do is find out first if there actually is any inexplicable phenomena—or if someone is merely playing games. If there is something beyond the ordinary, we find out why, and deal with it from that point," Darcy said, staring at the man, and returning all the attitude she was being given. Adam Harrison had already spoken with Matt Stone, and apparently, done so with enough dignity that he had agreed to the meeting. Actually, Stone had called Adam, after receiving his letter. And whether or not Stone wanted his property turned into a national center for the occult, he apparently could use the exorbitant fee that Adam had been willing to pay for his team to investigate the stories circulating about the house. She knew historic mansions were incredibly hard to maintain. Especially when they were being held privately. She was suddenly angry with herself for having been intimidated by the good old boys in the bar. Hell. She'd spent enough years in a very similar environment, and that should have prepared her to deal with any form of male that pretended to walk on two feet. She had also dealt with her fair share of total, mocking skeptics. Usually, no manner of behavior bothered her. She had her beliefs, and everyone else in the world was welcome to their own. People who really wanted help usually came and asked for it.

She'd been social enough, she decided.

"Excuse me, gentlemen, but my employer has already been in contact with Mr. Stone, and apparently, he is willing to allow us into Melody House. I'll make arrangements to meet him at a later date."

"I know you," Dimple-face said suddenly. He offered her his lazy smile once again. "I could swear I've seen your face before."

Darcy hesitated. All she needed to do was tell this pack that she'd been a model for a cosmetics company for several years during and right after college and they'd never take her seriously. But then again, what the hell did she care? Her business was with Stone.

"I'm sure we've never met," she murmured politely. "Thank you for your time. And excuse me."

"'Original Sin'!" Dimple-face said triumphantly. He grinned sheepishly. "I wound up buying the men's aftershave. Your face has been on billboards all over the country."

Even in Hicksville? she was tempted to say, and then she was angry with herself, because she'd never felt that way about anything or anyone, her parents being really wonderful people who had taught her continually that people were people, didn't matter where they came from, and everyone in any corner of the country or even on the earth deserved an open mind and respect.

"So…you're a model."

Chisel-face's statement might as well have been, *So you're a dumb blonde with boobs.* Except that she was more of a redhead and certainly not overly-stacked.

"I worked for Original Sins cosmetics, yes," she said,

again forcing her tone to be even. "I also have graduate degrees in American history and sociology from NYU."

"I heard that Adam Harrison would be coming here himself," Chisel-face said.

Darcy gritted her teeth. "Yes, Mr. Harrison will come down at some time during the investigation. He's been delayed. At the moment, he is tied up with business in London." She stopped, irritated that she'd felt herself obliged to explain anything to these men.

She was about to rise when the fourth member of the party—the man with the decent haircut and store-bought clothing suddenly leaned forward, extending a hand to her. "Sorry, we should have introduced ourselves, especially me, right away. I'm David Jenner, Jenner Equipment—and someone from your office approached me about renting some recording and video equipment." He shrugged, flashing a glance across the table. "Should the project go forward."

"David, nice to meet you," she said. "Justin, our office manager, told me that he had talked to you."

"You don't have your own equipment?" Chisel-face asked.

"Of course, we have some very specialized equipment," Darcy forced herself to say politely. "But we like to rent video cameras and tape recorders from local facilities. That keeps anyone from suggesting that we've rigged anything. Mr. Stone knows how we work and what we do—he was sent information on the company."

Chisel-face inclined his head, and she wished that the idiot wasn't wearing sunglasses in the middle of a smoky bar. "It's good to hear that you think local facilities might offer you enough—you know, equipment up to the par of your…investigative techniques."

"We've worked across the country—and abroad," she said coolly, "and we have always maintained excellent work relationships in every area."

"That sounds mighty fine!"

Darcy was startled when the voice came from behind

her. She turned to see that the pool player who had been called Carter had come up behind her. He was taller than she had realized; she was fairly tall herself at five nine, and in her heels, she had another two inches. He wore a beard and mustache, and had intense green eyes. And beneath his worn flannel shirt, he seemed to be in exceptional condition. She did, however, feel as if she had completely stepped back in time. Put a uniform on him, and he might have been the cavalry general Jeb Stuart, having stepped off his horse and into the local tavern. He stared at her with a strange sincerity as he spoke. "Too many times, Yankees have come down South and thought themselves like almighty gods. But, hey, you know, this just might be the right one. Ms. Tremayne, I've seen your face all over on billboards, too. You just may be the one."

"Thanks," she murmured. *Yankees had come south?* She'd done a lot of traveling, but she'd never felt a time warp such as this before. "You know," she said quietly, "my company isn't really headquartered more than two hours away."

"A popular face," Chisel-face murmured. "Forgive me—it just seems so strange. A model. Hm. Maybe they sent you down to manipulate Matt Stone. Not a bad idea? I mean, could you possibly *really* be the business end of this deal? You are an exceptionally fine-looking Yank—even with a packet of degrees from NYU."

Darcy felt fury suddenly take root in every limb of her body. *Get along with the locals! Like hell!* She'd had it. Everything she'd learned in college, in business, and in life, fled her mind, and her temper kicked in.

"It's an excellent school," she said, rising. "And I'm afraid, gentlemen, that the rest of the world has entered the twenty-first century. The Civil War was lost during the nineteenth. We're all one big country now, you might recall. Washington D.C.—*where I'm based*—is extremely close. Busy. The world goes on there."

"D.C.," Chisel-face murmured, then grinned at his fellows. "I'll bet the old boys considered it just one and the same as this area, eh boys?"

She rose, hands planted firmly down on the table, and assessed him coolly. Words seemed to spit from her before she took the time to think them out. "You know, I did forget to return your rather backward compliment. Actually, you're not too bad-looking for a total asshole. You really will excuse me. In truth, none of this, me, my credentials, my job here—is any of your business. I need to discuss matters with Mr. Stone, and no one else." She allowed her gaze to sweep with disdain over the lot of them and she turned and walked with crisply clicking heels to the door, where she turned back. "By the way, just for your information, the South *lost* the war. If any of you happen to see Mr. Stone, perhaps you'll be good enough to let him know that I did come to meet him. I'll be calling."

As she stared at the men, they rose, staring back at her. The most friendly of them, Dimple-face, began to smile.

"What?" she demanded.

"Oh," he said, "I think Matt Stone definitely knows you were here."

"Really?" she grated. "And why is that."

Chisel-face spoke up. "Ms. Tremayne, I am Matt Stone."

Adam Harrison would have handled it all much better. He would have found a way to be both dignified and smooth. But of course, if Adam had felt that he'd cast himself into a den of testosterone, he would have had managed to gain respect immediately, no matter what.

Darcy couldn't quite diffuse the steam rising in her.

"Well, I'm sorry that I can't say it's been a pleasure, since you've done nothing but amuse yourself at my expense, Mr. Stone. And if you destroy this opportunity, it won't hurt me in the least. My employer is the man who deems your house important."

With that, she turned, exited, and let the door close behind her.

* * *

"Well, that was just great!" Mae said from behind the bar.

Matt set his sunglasses on top of his head and turned to Mae with a challenging look. "Mae, I didn't know who the hell she was at first, and since it was my understanding Harrison was coming himself, she made me somewhat wary. We don't need a bunch of crackpots thinking that they can come here and recreate a 'Blair Witch' scenario."

"He's right," Clint said, grinning in a way that made his dimple deep, amusement lighting his eyes. "A goddess walks in—and he sends her out as rudely as possible. Good going, Matt."

Clint was Matt's second cousin, but though he carried the family name, his grandfather had been born on what they called the wrong side of the blanket. Probably a good thing; Clint's commitment to enjoying life was often entertaining, but Matt was pretty certain that, had the property gone down to Clint, it was unlikely they'd be having this discussion now—the holding would have been long gone. Not because the fields might have fallen prey to plight or disease, but rather to the plague of gambling debt that never seemed to dampen Clint's spirits.

Matt looked from Mae to Clint, shaking his head. "Doesn't the concept of dignity mean anything to the two of you?"

"Not a hell of a lot," Clint said cheerfully.

"Dignity? Do you think you allowed that poor girl to feel that she had any?" Carter asked.

"She's accustomed to getting whatever she wants, I imagine," Matt said with a shrug. "And don't you tell me about dignity, Carter." He admitted, only to himself, that he might have been rude—only a bit. But at least with reason. Still, he felt obliged to remind his friend about some of his own behavior. "If I remember correctly, you were so rude to your friend, Catherine Angsley, in this very bar, in front of far more people, that she left the county, never to be seen again."

Carter shrugged. "At least I knew her first."

Mae chuckled. "And you, young man," she said to Clint. "You sent that beautiful Texan, what was her name? Salela Bennett, running all the way back to Texas!"

"Sasha," Clint corrected.

"Sasha, that's right. *Sasha.* Why can't I ever remember that name?" Mae asked. "Oh! Maybe it's because no one could possibly keep track of the women who come and go through your ever so charming lives!"

"Mae! We're just looking for true love," Clint said dryly.

"My foot! You're looking for the next great body. But I think that the two of you could be left in the dust by this new visitor," Mae informed them with a sagely spoken pleasure.

"Well, of course, because with Matt's brand of charm, she'll be heading straight back to Washington," Carter said with a sigh. He arched a brow to Matt. "I can recall a few times when you might have been a little rough on Lavinia."

"At least he married her first," Mae said.

"I was never that rude to Lavinia—even in the midst of divorce," Matt said, irritated with himself that he was still feeling defensive, and now being reminded of his disastrous marriage.

"See, Mae? You can't rush into marriage," Carter said. "Look at the whole Lavinia thing. There she was—the most gorgeous thing breathing on earth, and what a manipulative witch."

"We just didn't have the same concept of a life well lived," Matt said, wondering why in the hell he should suddenly defend even his ex-wife. Simple fact, Lavinia had been a bitch. Rich, spoiled, and heedless of anyone around her.

"We're all missing the point here," old Anthony Larkin suddenly pointed out. "Mae, seems to me the world has changed a lot since I was a young man. Hell, yes, these young people should find out if they're going to make it in an affair before tying the knot. Divorces are too easy these days, and they're still hard as hell on people. Especially on their kids!''

"Well, thankfully, Matt and Lavinia didn't have kids. A devil's tail might have shown up on one of them," Clint said. "I think Lavinia's had plastic surgery to get rid of hers, but genetically, it would have still been there."

"Lavinia is gone, and it's over," Matt said flatly.

"That Sibel, Shana, or Sheila girl Clint was dating wasn't a bitch," Mae said with a sniff. "Opinionated, and intelligent, and ready to take care of herself. But she wasn't a bitch."

Clint offered an exaggerated sigh. "Mae, her name was Sasha. Sasha Bennett. And the problem with our great affair was that she wanted me to move to Texas! And wait a minute—we're getting off the subject here."

Anthony shook his white head in a way that made his beard rake back and forth over his chest. "All right, here's my opinion from an old geezer, Matt. Let's forget about past transgressions—committed by the lot of you. Every woman isn't a potential affair. This one seems darned regal and intelligent. She was sent here to work. Matt, you're having trouble up at your place. You told me yourself, you called your grandfather's old friend Harrison after you received his letter. Key concept here—*you* called *him*. So—just why were you such a jerk to that girl?"

"She looks too much like Lavinia," Clint said.

"No, she doesn't," Carter argued. "She has the walk, the movement…kind of like a natural grace. That's all that's the same."

Matt scowled at them both. "Hey, looks have nothing to do with anything, gentlemen."

"Gentlemen?" Mae said with a sniff.

"I'm unhappy about the whole thing, I suppose. And yes, I called Adam after I got the letter, but that's the point—I expected Adam Harrison himself," Matt admitted ruefully. "And then again, maybe it all did have something to do with her appearance." He glared at Clint and Carter. "Not that she resembles Lavinia in any way."

"She doesn't. She's really much prettier," Mae put in.

"But," Matt continued. "She doesn't look like any hard-core investigator, does she?"

"Looks can be deceiving," Carter said.

"Hey, they say you're going to let Liz do a seance," Anthony Larkin reminded him. "How hard-core would that be?"

"Liz was close with Gramps, too," Matt said. "A really great nurse to him toward the end. I owe her." He shrugged. "She begged when I told her that I had people coming down who were supposedly ghost experts. She wanted first crack at a seance, before any out-of-towners took over. She also holds her Women's Town Meeting in the house once a month, and it's a big event that makes the house a good income."

Anthony shrugged. "Figured it had to be something like that. I ran into her down at the drugstore. She said that she'd been pleading with you, just for herself, since she's so sure she feels all that cold stuff, especially in the up-stairs bedroom. And she said that the writer could come in, and the new guy from the Chamber of Commerce. So…it's a crock if you're keeping out that pretty girl because she's more about ghosts than finding out if something natural is going bump in the middle of the night."

"And damn, but she is good-looking," Clint supplied.

Matt nodded slowly. They were all right—and he had been one hell of an ass to the woman. She had just hit a raw nerve with him, he supposed, looking as if she had just stepped off a fashion page, heels clicking on the floor, manicured nails expressive in the air as she spoke, her face that of a sophisticated angel—or siren, one or the other.

Redheads were always trouble.

"I'm just irritated, I guess. Maybe I do owe her an apology."

The phone rang stridently from the bar. He felt a surge of anger. She was already calling. Mae picked up the phone.

"Hello…yes, Penny, he's here. He's got his cell phone

turned off again, huh? Well, he's sitting here, sure as can be. Shouldn't have that cell phone turned off, Matt, you know that,'' she said, her hand over the receiver.

"Shirley at the station knows where I am, and that's all that matters,'' Matt said.

"Penny knows you're here now, come on over and talk to her! Please!'' Mae insisted, seeing the stubborn set to his jaw.

Matt cast Mae an evil eye, then rose to accept the receiver from behind the bar. Penny came on the line.

"Yes?''

"Matt, I heard you gave that girl from New York an absolutely wretched time!''

"Penny, I really did no such thing. And how did you hear so fast?''

Matt looked around. Sure enough, Marty Sawyer—Penny's nephew—who had been watching Carter's pool game was now nowhere to be seen. He'd slunk out already.

"Matt Stone! There is so much good to be done here! Principal Joe from the grade school was telling me how much the schoolchildren just loved the living history productions we did last summer, and you know as well as I do that you can't keep that kind of program going if we don't make sure that the house is entirely safe. And you've already agreed that we can let the seance go on.''

"Because even though I don't believe in such a thing as a 'medium,' I like Elizabeth!'' he said irritably.

"You're going to make a tiny percentage off Elizabeth—compared to what Adam Harrison is paying to investigate your property. He usually charges people for his services. Now you know that I personally think that the ghosts are wonderful, but even I'm getting nervous here. Think about poor Clara's face—and don't go telling me she bumped into a wall. We need our ghost stories, some of them are so great. Passion, spurned lovers, murders, suicides! But…there's something not at all right going on as well. Oh, Matt, please! If you really love the house and our history and want to keep the place open, not to mention in the family!—please let this girl come and get started on her investigations, no matter what it is, exactly, that she does."

He gazed back at the bar. Everyone was staring at them. Penny was speaking loudly. They could all hear. "Penny—you're right. Murders and suicides. The woman in white who's been seen floating around the staircase. You know what? It isn't going to matter what I do—the stories are going to circulate forever."

"I've seen the woman in white," Penny said stubbornly.

"Penny, you drank half the wine cellar that night," he reminded her.

"Nevertheless, this is important. Yes, we'll have stories, no matter what. But you said yourself that you were suspicious that someone was causing some of the 'haunting.' How will you ever know, or prove anything?"

"Penny, I am the sheriff. I know a few things about investigating occurrences on my own."

"Matt, where's your patriotism?"

"What?" he said incredulously.

"The house is so important. What if someone really gets hurt?"

He almost smiled. It was a new line of attack.

From the table, he heard the sound of David Jenner clearing his throat. "You know, Matt, things haven't been that great. I could really use the work."

"Right. You know, we're not all rich, kind of famous, and born with absolutely legitimate names," Clint said, grinning with a shrug.

"Matt, maybe you could do us all some good," Carter told him.

"You won't have to do a thing," Penny's voice said from over the phone wire. "Give Ms. Tremayne my number. And I'll handle everything. You don't have to come anywhere near the house if you don't want to while she's in it. But first, you go over right now and get her out of that ramshackle hotel where's she staying."

"Hey!"

Carter could obviously hear Penny. He owned the ramshackle hotel.

Again, Matt couldn't help but grin. "Hell, all right."

"Matt, honestly, you don't even have to be involved,
I'll do everything, I swear! Dammit, Matt, *you're* the one
who called Adam Harrison, why are you balking now?"

"Because I expected Adam Harrison," he said, feeling
like a broken record, his temper rising. Impatiently, he
said, "I'll talk to her, Penny." Then he hung up.

Mae grinned like a kid with a candy bar. "This is so
cool—Melody House is getting real live ghost busters."

"They're not ghost busters, Mae," Matt said.

"I've got to go to that seance!" Mae said firmly.

"You all really did hear every single word of that conversation," Matt said ruefully.

A circle of nods answered him. He shook his head.
"Hell—I guess I will start answering my cell phone," he
muttered.

"Well…?" Clint drawled. "When are you going to bite
the bullet, give that girl a call and convince her that she
is welcome here?"

"Soon. But *not* from here," he said. He slid his sunglasses back down over his eyes, and strode to the door,
taking his hat from a peg on the wall. He twisted his jaw;
he didn't believe in ghosts, spirits, haunts, or the god-
damned Easter bunny, and he sure as hell didn't believe
in premonitions.

Still, he didn't like this.

He shook his head, speaking with his back to the others.

"There's an awful lot that's bad in that place's past,"
he said.

He walked back into the sunshine of the day, letting the
door slam behind him.

There was silence in his wake for several seconds.

"He's going to let it happen, Mae, don't worry, you'll
get to go to a real live seance," Clint assured the woman

still standing behind the bar, and still staring after Matt Stone.

"Yeah, well, it's not the whole thing with the house that makes him so hostile," Mae said quietly.

"He just never should have married that bitch from New York," Carter agreed.

"Redhead, too," David Jenner murmured.

"Well, living or dead, it's always people that haunt the living!" Mae said sagely, offering a sad shake of her head. Then she brightened, sounding like a girl about to head for her first dance. "And you bet your butts, gentlemen! I'm going to get to see a real live ghost!"

"Mae, if you see a ghost, the point is, it's not 'live,'" Clint said dryly. "But what the hell? Things could get darned interesting around here."

Thirty minutes later, Darcy was back in her hotel room, listening to the voice on her cell phone.

"You want me to do what?" she said incredulously to Adam. "Not *apologize,* right?"

Darcy actually pulled the cell phone away from her ear to stare at it, despite the fact that on an intellectual level, she knew she couldn't see her employer's face.

"Don't apologize, just rethink things." Adam, far away in London, was quiet for a minute. "Darcy, I have a vested interest in the house. I'll explain when I get back into the country." He sighed softly. "Darcy, there's no one like you. I need you. Please don't sound as if I've asked you to make peace with hostile aliens or some such thing."

Darcy winced. She knew that there was something about Melody House that Adam hadn't shared with her yet. Had to be. She was often certain herself that Adam, despite his own apparent wealth, was funded as well by another source—possibly governmental. They'd quietly gone in and out of a number of Federal buildings in previous cases. This was different. He really wanted in. For personal reasons, so it seemed. Reasons he wasn't willing to share, as yet.

"Adam, if this was so important, you should have been here."

"I know. But I had to be in London."

She didn't ask for an explanation, because he was a man who always kept business confidential, and even with her, information was shared on a need to know basis.

"Darcy, are you okay?"

"I've met a lot of skeptics," she said, "I've just never had to actually work with anyone so openly hostile."

"You can do it. I know you can," Adam said.

"But," she said quietly, "you don't really want me to call this guy and apologize, do you?"

"I'd never ask you to do that."

"So…?"

"Let's let it lie for now. I'm willing to bet that you'll hear from him."

Darcy breathed out on a deep sigh. She hated the fact that she hadn't handled the situation well at all. Her affection for Adam was very deep and real.

"All right. So what exactly do I do now?"

"Just sit tight. Is the hotel okay?"

Darcy looked around the room. "Sure," she lied. As she did so, the hotel line began to ring. She stared at the phone distastefully. It was dirtier than a pay phone outside a heavily frequented gas station.

"I've got another call," she told Adam.

"Any premonitions?" Adam said lightly. "I'm willing to bet that it's Stone."

"We'll see. I'll give you a call back."

"Actually, you don't need to," he said, and hung up. Again, Darcy stared at her cell phone, shook her head, and forced herself to pick up the hotel line.

"Yes?"

"Ms. Tremayne, it's Matt Stone."

She was silent, waiting. Adam had been right.

Of course.

Apparently, Matt Stone could be stubborn, too. The silence stretched on.

"Yes?" she said again. She could almost see his teeth grate in the steel cage of his face.

"As you're aware, I own Melody House. I don't actually live in the main house all the time, though I stay now and then. However, I have a woman who manages the upkeep and the tours we allow through, and the events which are held there upon occasion. Her name is Penny Sawyer, and I'll put you in contact with her. She's incredibly anxious to have you and your company in."

"But you're not."

"I did talk to Adam Harrison," he said, not agreeing or disagreeing. "The house holds incredible historical importance," he said flatly.

"Of course."

"Look, Penny is supposed to handle everything. And she's great with the place, knows all about it, and can help you with whatever you need. When you've got your plans down all pat, I'll be back in on it, though. It's still my place. And I want final approval on what you do."

"Naturally," Darcy said. She knew that it sounded as if her words were a flat *fuck you, guess I've got no choice.*

"Penny has suggested that you move on over to the house now."

"Oh, that's not necessary—"

"You need to be in the house to investigate it, right?"

"I just meant that there was probably no need for that kind of hurry."

"Penny wants you there as soon as possible. She's very eager to have you. Also, her office is in the house. We have all kinds of documents there, so…you could get started."

Darcy looked around her hotel room. It was stretching it to even call the place a hotel. She didn't flinch at the sight of bugs, but she had gagged over the film of them she'd had to clean out of the bathtub before managing a quick shower.

Maybe Matt Stone was something of a psychic himself. His next words suggested that he had read her mind.

"Ms. Tremayne, I'm familiar with the hotel."

"Fine. I might as well get started. You're right."

"I'll be there for you in thirty minutes."

She opened her mouth to protest. She could have used a little more time just to survey the area before entering the house.

Too late. He'd hung up.

Swearing, she did the same. She looked around the small room. Not much to pick up—she'd been too afraid of getting creepy-crawly things in her lingerie to unpack much. She fished her few personal articles from the bathroom and folded the few pieces of clothing she'd had out in less than ten minutes.

Which turned out to be good. Matt Stone's concept of time was not at all precise. She had barely made a quick run-through to assure herself she hadn't forgotten anything when there was a knock at her door.

She opened it. He stood there, sunglasses in place, a lock of his dark hair windblown and sprawling over his forehead. In her business heels, she was just a shade under six feet. He still seemed to tower. She didn't like the disadvantage, even if height didn't really mean a damned thing.

"Ready, Ms. Tremayne?"

She took a breath, forcing something of a grimace rather than a smile. "Mr. Stone, somehow you manage to drawl out a simple Ms. as if it were a word composed of one long *z,* and a filthy one at that. My name is Darcy, and I'm accustomed to going by it."

He cocked his head slightly. She couldn't read his eyes because of the shades. "All right—Darcy. I'm glad you're capable of moving. I have to get back into the office so let's get going, you know, quickly. Where's your bag?"

"I can take it myself, thank you."

"Would you just show me the damned bag?"

She set her hands on her hips. "Someone ought to call the local cops on you. You may be some kind of a big landholder in these here parts, bucko, but you're the rudest individual I've ever met.''

"Sorry, but my time is limited. Please, Ms. Tremayne—sorry, Darcy, may I take your bag?'' he said sarcastically.

"Fine. Right there. It rolls—unless you'll feel that your macho image will be marred and lessened by taking an easy route.''

He offered her a dry grimace, grabbed the bag, and started out.

She followed him, exiting the spiderweb filled hallways of the place, out to the parking lot.

She didn't see any regular cars—there were a few trucks, a code-enforcement vehicle, and a county cop car in the lot.

He had a really long stride, but had paused just outside the building and removed his sunglasses, waiting for her to catch up. He saw that she was staring expectantly out at the parking lot.

"Oh, sorry,'' he told her flatly. "It's that one. I guess everyone forgot to tell you. I'm the local sheriff. Guess Adam didn't tell you, either. But then, since you're supposed to be a psychic, you should have known.'' He stared at her, a light of mockery in his eyes.

She smiled sweetly in return. "Mr. Stone, I'm not exactly a psychic. There are certain areas in which I can deduce things. There are certain things about people I don't know. But then again, there are things that people really don't want known that I can deduce very easily. I'm known for finding skeletons in closets, and I'm sure that there are dozens of them at Melody House.''

Staring back at her, he was dead still then. His eyes were dark, not brown, but a deep gray. Disturbing. They seemed to pierce right through her, and yet wear a protective veil that kept her from reading anything within them. Still, it seemed that she had given him pause.

"Shall we go?'' she said.

"Oh, yes. I'm just dying to see what bones you can dig up, Ms. Tremayne. Just dying.''

"Great. Just…"

"Just what?"

"Be prepared. Sometimes, people don't like the skeletons we find."

3

"To me, it's simply one of the most incredible houses—and historical sites—on the face of the earth!" Penny said enthusiastically.

Darcy smiled, thinking that she agreed—despite the difficulty involved with the place, and that difficulty being Matt Stone.

He had maintained something of a pleasant conversation on the drive over, pointing out Civil War skirmish sites, and telling her that at one point, on his way to battle, the great Southern general Robert E. Lee had stayed at Melody House. Then they had reached the house, and though she couldn't say he had practically thrown her out of the car, he had delivered her to the front door and Penny Sawyer as quickly as possible, explaining simply that he was on duty.

Hm. She wondered if he'd been on duty while sprawling around at the Wayside Tavern as well.

But Penny Sawyer was wonderful. Darcy couldn't quite determine her age. The woman was certainly somewhere between forty and sixty, which was quite a span. She was slender, about five-five, with an attractive shag type of short haircut in a natural salt and pepper, and had beautiful, bright blue eyes. She was also nicely dressed in a stylish pantsuit, and as friendly as her employer was rude.

"The house is quite incredible," Darcy said. "A number of historical homes—usually those owned by preservation societies—have been restored with painstaking authenticity, but it's amazing to see the integrity of this house, especially when it's been a family home all along.''

''Ah, well, the old gentleman, Matt's grandfather, really loved the place. Treated the house like a baby. He wanted it to be a home while maintaining all that it had been. He was a remarkable old fellow.''

''Apparently.''

Penny gave her a funny little rueful smile. ''Oddly enough, believe me, Matt is just as dedicated to the preservation of the house. He wants to maintain it himself, though—you know, he doesn't want it going to any societies, no matter how good they might be, because he would lose control. He knows that house has to hold its own if he's going to hang on to it. Upkeep on these places is staggering. And sheriffs just don't make that kind of money. Oh! That didn't really sound the way it should— he's a man of incredible integrity. What I mean is, no matter how he loves the place, he'd never do anything illegal. Of course, you didn't suggest such a thing!'' Penny broke off with a laugh. ''There would never be such a thing as graft involved in Matt's life. He's a great sheriff. The people love him. He can defuse the most ungodly situations, speak to the youngsters around here and all…but what it means is that he has to have tours going through here, and he has to make the house pay. That's all. So! What kind of a feel do you get from the place? Is it haunted?''

Darcy smiled again at the question, wondering how to answer. ''There's a tremendous feel of the past about the place, I can tell you that.''

''But you…well, you *see* ghosts, right?''

Darcy hesitated again. ''For the most part, I would say that, so far, the house actually has a warm feel to it. As if whatever remains of the distant past is mostly benign. But there is a feel to the house. That's natural when so much has occurred through so many years. Many people believe that since we—humans—are made up of energy, and energy cannot actually be destroyed—that trauma forces that energy to remain, when the soul should have gone on.''

Penny arched a brow to her. ''I know what most people *feel* and *think*. But you are a psychic. So—what do *you* think? Actually, no matter what you say, you won't change what I feel and believe. I know that ghosts exist. I've seen one.''

''Oh?''

Penny shrugged. They were in her office, a very nicely done room on the ground floor, near to Matt's, as Penny had pointed out.

''I've seen the woman in the white peignoir who runs from the Lee room and down the stairs. And I'm beginning to believe that she's not a benign entity at all. Oh, don't get me wrong. I personally love the ghost stories that abound around here. They're important—they draw visitors to the house. But lately, the ghost seems to be getting—physical.''

''Exactly how so?''

''Well, not long ago we had a bride and groom staying in the room. She woke up in the middle of the night and the ghost spoke to her, or pulled her hair, or something. She wasn't terribly clear. She came running down the stairs stark naked in the middle of the night, and refused to go back to the room even to pack up her things. Then, Clara Issy, one of the housekeepers, and a wonderful woman, came flying out because of the same thing happening. The ghost left a mark on her.''

''What did Sheriff Stone have to say about that?'' Darcy asked.

Penny waved a dismissive hand in the air. ''He says he's convinced Clara ran into something. Matt simply refuses to believe in anything that doesn't have full dimensions. However, he has said that we can have a seance here. None of this is making any sense to me. Matt may not know much about Harrison Investigations, but I do. Adam Harrison is supposed to be one of the most credible and influential investigators of psychic phenomena in the world! Matt knew that you all were coming—well, all right, he expected Adam himself—but he told Liz that she could carry on a seance. Go figure. Of course, he doesn't really believe that anyone will contact the spirits, so maybe he wanted to make Liz happy, and annoy those who might have been able to make a special connection with whatever is going on.''

"It will be interesting to take part in a seance here, no matter who is acting as the medium,'' Darcy told her tactfully.

"Well, it's going to be tomorrow night,'' Penny told her. "I'm setting up in the parlor, since Elizabeth says we should be using the center of the house, the heart of it.''

Darcy lifted her hands. "Sounds fine to me.''

"Well, I'm relieved. After all—*you're* the professional.''

Darcy smiled. "I'm not so sure there is such a thing as a professional in this particular area. I'm sure Elizabeth will prove to be a fine medium.'' Darcy rose. "Mind if I take a walk around?''

"Of course not, dear! Your bag has been taken up to the Lee Room—where the phenomenon has occurred. I imagine that whereas others might wake up in terror, you would wake up and try to talk to the ghost, right?''

"Something like that,'' Darcy agreed.

"Well, then, you just make yourself at home.'' She handed Darcy a pamphlet. "These are, as you'll see, obviously for the tour groups. But the little map will help you get your bearings, and there are a few little tidbits of history about the house in there as well.''

"Terrific,'' Darcy said. "Thank you so much.''

"My pleasure, and please, should you need anything, anything at all, don't hesitate to ask me. I'm delighted to have you.''

"Thank you.''

Darcy took the little map and exited Penny's office. It was one of two on the right side of the hall that connected the foyer and the grand stairway.

For a moment, she paused. This was the most important part of her work, as she saw it. Adam Harrison was excellent with machinery. Gauges that registered temperature changes, recorders that caught the slightest hint of sound. There were even gadgets that could record any rise or fall in a magnetic field. When he came, he would work with a Trifield Meter, and measure electromagnetic pollution. He also used a Trifield Natural EM meter, which measured electric as well as magnetic fields—showing disturbances where there should be none—and, as Adam was fond of telling clients—it was also a great tool for finding out if your microwave leaked or not. In his work, however, he knew that any kind of physical manifestation required a certain amount of energy, moving air, heat, cold, all and any changes that might take place in an area.

Adam worked from a seriously scientific point of reference.

But for her, it was the feel of a place. It was getting to know it.

And often, when she first arrived at a place reputed to be haunted, she would feel that Josh was with her. Ready to be beside her, vigilant, her guard in the strange world, perhaps.

She waited. But she didn't feel his presence. She waited several minutes, dead still, making an effort to clear her mind, which wasn't usually necessary. And still, she had no sense or feel of him, which was very unusual.

And yet the house seemed more alive with past energy than any other place she had ever been.

She walked back first to the entry, or foyer, and stared at the little map, getting her bearings. Not that the house was that complicated. From the wraparound porch, one entered the foyer, with the superb staircase. The house had been built like many a colonial with the hall—or what was really a massive *breezeway*—immediately to the right of the stairs. It made a straight and direct path to the back doors. At one time, before air-conditioning, such a breezeway allowed for the house to be cooled in summer by the continual flow of air, since both front and back doors would have been left open for that precise purpose.

There was one room other than the offices on that side of the house, the library. Darcy took a quick peek in at the room. Shelves lined three of the walls while a fireplace with a handsome carved hearth took up a majority of the fourth. The hardwood floor here was covered with a very fine, probably antique, Persian carpet. A huge mahogany desk sat in the room, while overstuffed reading chairs sat by the fire. She wondered if Matt Stone was aware of the value of the many ancient tomes that filled the cases— along with a lot of modern material as well.

The desk had a computer, printer, and seemed well set for any business purpose. She assumed the arrangement of the equipment here was for the convenience of the guests, since it had appeared that Penny's office was supplied with all the technology she might need to run Melody House. Matt's office was probably equally as well appointed.

Standing in the library, she closed her eyes for a moment and *felt* the room. The atmosphere was rich. A great deal of passion, emotion, and simple life had taken place within the room. But there was nothing here that seemed to hint of evil or malignance. She opened her eyes and exited the library, heading back to the foyer.

The staircase seemed somewhat disturbing, which Darcy didn't find at all odd. She wondered how many men had walked down that stairway, followed by wives, lovers, or children, only to ride away to war, and perhaps never return.

The parlor was truly beautiful. She ignored the velvet ropes that kept the area protected from the sticky fingers of visiting children, the abuse of too many feet, and the overall damage that could be caused by large groups coming through on a frequent basis. Like the library, the parlor had a feel. When she closed her eyes, it drummed with the energy of the past. But again, she felt nothing evil.

Beyond the beautifully appointed parlor were the dining room—elegantly set as if for a dinner party of twenty in the mid-eighteen-hundreds—and the kitchen, kept entirely charming while being in a state-of-the-art condition. She instantly loved the room. There, the back door gave way to the wraparound porch. The view from the porch was exquisite. It was a beautiful day and the mountains could be seen in the distance in a riot of greens, violets, pinks, oranges and golds. The season was rich with flowers and foliage.

Darcy stepped back in. Rather than return to the foyer to take the grand stairway to the second floor, she walked up the far-less-spectacular servants' stairway, winding from the rear of the kitchen up to the back of the hall on the second story. She gazed at her map again. Originally, there had been six bedrooms up here. Now, there were five, since the master suite these days consisted of a second office or sitting room as well as the master's—Matt's?—bedroom.

She assumed his personal area was off-limits to her. For the time, at least.

The rooms had apparently all been named after Southern generals, the Lee Room, or course, being the most prominent and assumably elegant, with the Stuart, Longstreet, Beauregard, and Amistad rooms being a bit smaller, judging by the map. Darcy entered each of the rooms, noting that they were all period, and quite charming, clean as a whistle, and inviting. The crew here kept the place up beautifully.

At last, she stood in front of the Lee Room, and closed her eyes. The atmosphere was heavy, cloudlike, dense, wrapping around her instantly. She opened her eyes and entered the room.

French doors were open to the porch. The breeze swept in. The room was quiet, and touched by the sweetness of the breeze.

Deceptive, Darcy thought. An aura of tremendous turbulence lay just beneath the apparent peace and serenity.

She imagined trying to explain the sensations she felt to Matt Stone.

It was not a pretty picture.

She didn't think that there was any way she would ever be able to explain her particular talents to Matt Stone. Adam would understand. He was an amazing man. He had some abilities, but his true talent was in understanding that there were people in the world with special senses. She might have gone mad, seeing and hearing what others didn't, except for Adam. First, he had believed. In his belief, he afforded her great trust. While he worked on a scientific level, proving different levels of heat and electricity, she worked purely through the visions and feelings that came to her—whether she wanted them or not, most of the time. Adam had taught her how to channel the strange images and feelings that came to her. And when she had thought herself a misfit who could live only in fear, he had taught her that she could bring peace and relief to lost souls, and given her purpose—as well as a very decent living that kept her feeling not only sane, but tremendously useful.

In this room, the feelings and impressions of trauma rushed around like a swirl of dark storm clouds.

However, it was incredible. Not a bad place to stay. Far, far, better than the hotel. Her bag was at the foot of the bed. She began to unpack, humming as she did so, yet completely attuned all the while for the slightest shift in the atmosphere.

All that touched her was the feel of the breeze and yet…

She was certain that she was watched. She could feel an unease streaking down her spine. It was as if the eyes of someone—*something*—were intently upon her, creating a trickle of sensation. An unearthly gaze seemed to reach out and touch her.

Feelings…intuitions. The hackles rising at her nape.

She paused for a moment.

But…

There was nothing solid. Nothing whatsoever. But Darcy knew.

Whatever lay within the room would wait, observe, and bide its time.

* * *

Summer hours kept the area light until well past eight in the evening.

Matt arrived home at about six and checked in at the house. He was certain that he'd find Penny and his visitor busily discussing the many ghosts they had already discovered. Maybe they'd even have the Ouija board out.

But Penny was in the kitchen with Joe McGurdy, their chef. Matt hadn't known that Joe was coming in that night; he usually arrived only when they had a function planned. Finding the two in the kitchen, he arched a brow at Penny while Joe greeted him with a friendly smile.

Penny stared at him reproachfully. "Well, of course, we're having dinner!" she said.

"We?"

"You, me, Darcy, Clint, and Carter."

"Of course. Eight-course meal?" Matt asked dryly.

"Don't be ridiculous. But you didn't want me to serve beannie-weannies on her first night here, did you?"

"Goodness, of course not," Matt said. "Where is our guest?"

"Carter saddled up Nellie for her. She's taken a ride out to see some of the country around here."

"Do we know that she can ride? There's some really thick forest if she headed west."

"Matt, she is an adult. She said she could ride."

"Maybe I'll take a ride out to find her anyway," he muttered, shaking his head at Penny. Great—they were already bringing the chef in and stretching out the welcome mat. He wondered why Carter hadn't chosen to ride with their visitor.

When he'd changed to jeans and sweater and headed out to the stables, he found out why. Carter shrugged, watching Matt as he led Vernon, his quarter horse, from his stall. "She said that she wanted to do some exploring alone, that it was important for her work. Naturally, I offered to go with her. Are you kidding? The woman is one looker.''

"One kooky looker," Matt reminded him, slipping a bridle over Vernon's nose.

"Hey, everybody's got to make a living somehow, right?" Carter said.

Matt slung a saddle over Vernon's back. "I imagine she probably had a few other choices."

"Maybe she's for real," Carter said. He thoughtfully chewed a blade of hay, eyes amused as he watched Matt mount up. "You know, I just bought the old Reed place, next county over. If you don't want her looking for your ghosts, I'll be happy to have her take a look at mine."

"I'm sure you intend to have her looking for ghosts," Matt said, shaking his head. "For the moment, just let me go make sure she's not lying on a trail somewhere with a broken leg. Whatever possessed you to let her just ride out alone?"

"Let's see—maybe the fact that she said she didn't want company?"

"She doesn't own the place," Matt reminded him.

Carter shrugged, stroking his beard. "Hell. I don't own it either, do I now?"

Matt urged Vernon on out of the stable. "Hey—don't be late for dinner!" Carter called. "Seems like Penny's got Joe cooking up something good."

Matt felt his resentment grow, and put a check on it. Adam Harrison had paid a fair price for coming in to do what he was referring to as "research." And so, hell, they had to feed the woman. Joe would be in again tomorrow night to prepare a meal for those attending the seance. It wasn't all that big a deal. And as to the horse...

He could just see lawsuits all over the place. She'd ridden out alone. What if she couldn't really ride? She'd be suing over her injuries.

The logical course was across the vast field to the south of the property, leading into trails that veered to the west. Matt could see that his chosen trail had recently been traveled; hoofmarks dotted the dirt and as he reached the field, flattened grasses assured him his instincts had been right.

Matt crossed the field, and entered into the broad riding trail that led westward, sloping upward from the valley toward the mountains.

Another twenty minutes worth of riding and he came to the narrow little rivulet that meandered its way through the woods. The area was much as it had been for hundreds of years—only the continual use of the trails kept them in such sustained and clear condition. The air was cool, the scent of pine sweet.

When he saw Nellie, riderless, drinking by the stream, he felt a twinge of fear, wondering where the mare might have thrown her rider.

But even as he dismounted, a quick search of the area showed him that he needn't have been so concerned—nor so certain that his visitor couldn't ride. Darcy was seated calmly on a fallen log, idly doodling in the dirt with a bonelike length of a broken branch. She watched him without welcome or rejection as he left Vernon to join Nellie, drinking from the crisp, cool water.

"Hello," he said, striding toward her.

There was still plenty of daylight, but in the forest, the thick canopy of trees created strange slashes of darkness, shadow, and eerie green light. Her hair seemed to shine with an exceptional depth of red, while her eyes appeared a deeper forest shade than the trees themselves. Her complexion appeared paler here, and in her jeans and sweater, she might have been something of an elegant woods nymph. Except, of course, if she were to stand, he knew she would be far too tall to be any elfin creature. It struck him again that what most irritated him about her was that tall, sinewy elegance of hers, the poise and calm that seemed to sit about her shoulders like a cloak.

She clasped her hands around her knees, eyeing him with a certain dry hostility. "Hello, Sheriff. As you can see, I've not broken my fool neck, raced your horse into the ground, or gotten lost in the depth of the forest."

"Did I ever suggest that such things might happen?"

"Only because you had no idea I might ask to ride about the area."

"You might have mentioned your intentions."

"When? As you pushed me out of your car at the entrance to Melody House?"

"I did no such thing."

She shrugged, not deigning to reply. He felt the itch of irritation again. He understood some of what he was feeling. She wasn't just tall and elegant, but almost absently sensual, her movements smooth and sleek and feline. She seemed to hint of something that smouldered, richly carnal, and yet on top, she was all wrapped up like an ice princess, lips far too often drawn tight and prudish.

"I'd expected to find you exploring the house."

"I did explore the house." The green of her eyes rested contemptuously on him.

"And you haven't found my malignant ghost as yet?"

She replied in an even, dismissive tone, eyes steady on him. "I explored the house, and then the grounds, and now, I'm exploring the area."

"Ah." He took a seat on the log beside her. He stared through the trees towards the water, caught now in the sunlight, dazzling like a thousand gems. Then he looked back to her. "The woods are supposed to be haunted, too, you know. And not because of Melody House."

"That's good to hear," she said strangely. "Just what is the legend associated with the forest here?"

"Ah, well, long ago—as far back as the late seventeen-hundreds, I believe, there was a family with a small farm a little closer toward the mountains. A father and mother, and a bucketful of kids. The oldest sister was plain, the youngest beautiful. The oldest sister's suitor fell madly in love with the younger sister. The fellow had to head back east to take care of business, and when he left, he kissed his dearly beloved, the younger sister, goodbye, and they were both deeply happy, because they would be wed as soon as he returned. Little did they know that the oldest sister was a total psychotic—a scorned one, at that. She lured her younger sister into the woods, pretending they were walking to a neighbor's. She got her to lean down by the stream…and whap!''

"She killed her with a hatchet, nearly decapitating her. And now, the younger sister's ghost has been seen running through the forest, blood oozing from the gash in her throat, screaming in terror," Darcy finished for him.

Matt lifted his hands. "Someone told you the legend!"

She didn't reply for a moment, then asked him, "What happened to the older sister?"

"Well, the young man came back and hanged himself in misery, thwarting the hopes of the young murderess. I guess they didn't have much evidence they could use at the time, so no one went to trial. But the older sister went completely insane. She was locked up in the family barn until she died, an old woman of eighty, confessing in her later years, and spending many a day screaming that her sister was coming after her in vengeance.''

"Well, there you have what one might call a truly dysfunctional family," Darcy said pragmatically.

"Yes, I guess you could say that." He looked at her. The lines of her face were truly classical, yet her sculpted, porcelain beauty seemed unique as well. She'd been a makeup model, he reminded himself, and she must have made some good money. Why give it all up for this— especially if she was really so heavily laden with academic degrees?

"The body of the younger sister was uncovered by a local dog that had been digging," Darcy said. "But they didn't find the skull, and it didn't receive a decent burial with the body. If someone finds the skull and buries it with the rest of the bones, the haunting in the forest will stop.''

"How simple. How cut-and-dried and simple. Hell, we should all start digging up the place to find a skull that may or may not be there. Hm. Then again—where, oh where, do we start? If there were such a relic of humanity remaining from way back when, animals might have carted in anywhere. The stream might have washed it down to Florida by now. But what the hell—people love the ghost stories. So what if the poor ghost goes racing through the trees, screaming and bleeding?''

"Because it's pretty damned sad," Darcy told him.

"Well, when you have time, you feel free to dig around in the forest. It's county land, but we'll try to ignore the fact that you're bound and determined to dig it all up. Just don't leave any potholes—lots of people use this area for riding, and we wouldn't want a new ghost running around with its head dangling from a broken neck."

He stood impatiently.

He must have roused her somewhat from her continual, stiff poise, because she leapt up immediately after him. "What is the matter with you? Why on earth do you have to be so hostile?"

"Because all you're going to do is feed into the idiots and drunks who should behave intelligently but go all ga-ga over a ghost story! History can be tragic. Tragic—but past. Let the dead lie, Darcy."

"You brought me here!"

"No. I told Adam Harrison that he could come here."

She planted her hands on her hips, head cast back, green eyes as dark and dangerous as the embers of a fire. "No—you signed a contract that allowed Harrison Investigations into your house. I am as much a part of Harrison Investigations as Adam."

He arched a brow slowly and was pleased to see the slightest sign of a flush entering her cheeks.

"*Almost* as much a part of the company as Adam is himself. And very good at what I do. So—since *you* hired *me* to do it, perhaps, just for a while, you could quit being such a macho jerk?"

He wanted to shout back, to put her in her place. He didn't have the words, or the intelligent argument he needed. He threw up his hands. "We need to get back. Dinner will be ready."

He turned away, starting for his horse.

"You know, every redhead isn't a total bitch."

Startled, he turned back. His voice was far rougher than he intended. "I don't know what the hell you're talking about."

"Your ex-wife Lavinia Harper," she said simply.

"I see. You know this because you're psychic?"

"You dislike redheads. One doesn't need to be a psychic to see that. Penny told me about Lavinia."

"Red hair can be bought in boxes for right around ten bucks. I would never dislike anyone for the color of their hair, skin, eyes, or anything else," he informed her, meaning to sound as calm and staid as a schoolmaster, displaying his anger nevertheless.

She gave a stiff smile as she walked by him. "Sure. Sorry, then. Excuse me."

He let her pass him while he fought his simmering temper, wondering why the hell she could get such a rise out of him, when he was usually level, sane, and careful in any judgment or assumption. Tension rippled through his muscles; he got a handle on it and turned, determined that he would politely help her mount back up on Nellie.

But before he could do so, she was already in the process of easily swinging up on the mare.

By the time he mounted Vernon, she was headed back through the forest trail.

He followed her, staying slightly behind and noticing, just as they left the forest trail, that dusk was falling at last.

Across the field, Melody House stood on its little hillock, bathed in a strange and eerie glow of crimson and gold.

The brilliance of light lasted only a few seconds; the sun dipped.

Night was coming in earnest, wrapped in shadow.

Despite Matt Stone, or maybe even because of him, dinner at Melody House was an entertaining affair, and Darcy found herself laughing a lot throughout the meal.

Matt and Penny didn't seem to agree on anything, but the affection between them was visible and real. Penny wanted to tell legends. Matt wanted to correct her when her legends became too lurid, romantic, or *too* anything.

"It was as if the entire Southern army was taking refuge at Melody House!" Penny said.

"The entire Southern army!" Matt snorted. "A company at best. Twenty men, Penny."

Penny waved a hand in the air. "They were exquisite soldiers," she said, shaking her head and dismissing Matt's correction. "They might as well have numbered thousands. They beat back the Yankees—"

"What? The entire Northern force?" Matt queried, a sparkling light in his eyes.

"There were at least one hundred!" Penny said, glaring back at her employer. "The point is, our boys wouldn't give up, and they saved the day, but their leader, a young captain, was killed. Shot in the heart by a minnie ball that whizzed right through the parlor windows. Now, he is said to be here, still guarding Melody House."

Matt leaned low across the table, amusement in his eyes as they met Darcy's. "And no one seems to have told him that the war is over, that the South lost. He's not at all fond of Yankee accents—so they say."

"Thank God, then, that I don't have one," Darcy told him sweetly. "All those years watching late-night shows seems to have paid off."

"But you trained to be an actress—of course you can get rid of an accent!" Carter applauded her admiringly.

"An actress, hm," Matt said.

"I was *going* to study acting," she corrected. "I never did. Not in college, anyway."

"That's right. She majored in everything else," Matt said.

"You can't major in ghosts these days, can you?" Clint asked.

"Don't be silly!" Penny reprimanded.

Both Carter and Clint shrugged.

Dessert had been served. An exceptional baked Alaska. Darcy was certain that at any moment, an immaculate butler was going to walk in and suggest that the ladies retire to one room, the gentlemen to another, for brandy and cigars.

But there was no butler—not tonight, anyway. They had all helped to serve the meal.

"So?" Penny said excitedly, looking at Darcy expectantly. She had a feeling that she was going to hear the word "so" from Penny a lot.

"So?" Darcy repeated, smiling.

"Do you see him?"

"Who?"

"Our captain!"

"The captain who saved Melody House from the marauding Yankees who were going to burn it down," Matt reminded her dryly.

Darcy shrugged. "I try just to get accustomed to a house the first few days I'm in it," she told Penny.

"Oh! Of course. Let all the vibrations get through to you," Penny said, nodding sagely.

"Something like that," Darcy agreed.

"So, are there vibrations?" Matt asked, seemingly polite.

She stared straight at them. "The place just trembles," she murmured.

"With?" he prompted.

She widened her eyes. "Hostility."

Clint burst into laughter. "The living give out vibes, too, huh?"

Matt stared at Darcy, the flicker of a rueful smile curving his lips. A remarkable transformation came over him. He was almost devastatingly appealing, when he looked so.

"If I'm giving out hostile vibes, it's not with intent of malice."

From him, Darcy decided, that was the best apology she was going to get.

"Sometimes it's not easy to pinpoint just where vibes might be centered," she said, surprised to realize that she was smiling as well.

And that Penny, Clint, and Carter were all staring at them.

She rose, her movement not as fluid and easy as she would have liked. "It was a wonderful dinner. Thank you all very much. I've just realized how late it has gotten. If you'll forgive me, I think I'll turn in for the night."

Matt, Carter, and Clint stood as one. A certain amount of courtesy seemed to have been bred into these men; it was as natural as breathing.

"You'll be fine," Carter told her. "I've slept in the Lee room. And I'm still here."

"He didn't even run down the stairs naked," Clint said with a wink.

"Thank the good Lord for that!" Penny breathed.

"Hey!" Carter protested. "I look good naked."

Darcy laughed softly. "Well, I imagine I'll be all right."

She was startled to see that Matt looked just a little concerned. "I'm in the house tonight, if there is any trouble, just scream."

"Ah, but you don't believe in ghosts!" Darcy reminded him.

He shrugged. "I believe in the power of men to do evil," he murmured. For a moment, his strange deep gray eyes fell on hers. "I'll be down the hall."

She nodded, bid them good-night, and headed out of the dining room and for the stairs to the second floor. She walked slowly, thinking it somewhat amazing that Matt Stone couldn't feel a thing regarding his house. Penny had asked about vibes. The house throbbed with them. Gentle, lost souls for the most part.

The only malice seemed to come from the Lee Room.

Upstairs, she decided on a quick shower, then brushed her teeth, and prepared for bed.

The room was cool, cooler than it should have been in summer. She ignored it, and the feeling of being watched.

She crawled into bed, somewhat exhausted. She fell asleep with the television on, watching a program on the history of Britain.

Deep into the night, she began to dream. She was herself, sleeping upon the bed, and yet she was not, for she moved, and moved within another persona. Fear clutched the heart of her sleeping self for a moment, for from the moment she felt the coming of the Other, she sensed the anger, a fury that was deep and dangerous. And then...

She was the Other, seeing, feeling, knowing everything he did.

A woman scorned...was a deadly one.

He came in deep thought and silence that evening, angry, but not at all sure, in his conscious mind, just what he intended. In the darkness, he stared at the house, and reflected on all that had been, and all that might come to pass.

The house...the majestic house sat as always. A place with as rich and deep a character as any living person. So it had been from the moment they had first broken ground. Time did nothing but add to the drama that must exist in such a place, as he well knew.

She was there.

He knew that she was there.

And there were things that must be said. Things that must be cleared, or ended, between them.

Still...

He stared at the house. And waited. He denied in his mind that he had come with any malice as to his intent.

His heart felt like stone. Seeds of ideas played deep down within his soul, truth and the physical essence of what must be banned from thought. What happened must happen.

At his sides, his hands flexed, eased, and flexed again, as if already slipping around the throat of the lover he knew to be inside.

Because a woman scorned...

Just might as well be dead.

*   *   *

Darcy awoke with a start, shaking. She had felt the past, as if it had entered into her. Felt not so much a person, but the fury and malevolence that had been part of a distant time.

She sat up in bed, and looked around the room, closed her eyes again, and opened them.

Whatever had been with her, whatever remnant of emotion, was gone.

And yet...

Something else was there.

Something, someone, quiet, stealthy.

Watching.

Waiting.

4

"We all know why we've come." Elizabeth Holmes' voice, though feminine, had a deep resonance. She wasn't exactly what Darcy had been expecting when she had heard that a local novice—who had found her dedication to the occult in the last year—had begged Matt Stone to allow her to run a seance. She wasn't theatrical. There was no turban wrapped around her head, and her eyes weren't dark and deep set and heavily lined with makeup to add to a mystical image. Rather, the woman was about fifty-five or sixty, slender, tall, elegantly slim, with nicely styled silver-white hair and pleasant, powder blue eyes. She looked like a typical businesswoman.

Only her voice might have fit the image of the eerie Gypsy fortune teller.

It seemed to fill the dining room at Melody House with a strange tenor, as if the walls themselves were part of a state-of-the-art speaker system.

And thankfully, the woman hadn't opted to rename herself. She wasn't going by Madame Zara, or anything like that. She was Elizabeth Holmes, a native of the northern Virginia area, and a real estate agent by day. Darcy had wondered at first if this medium wouldn't prove to be a slightly crazy friend who was convinced that she needed only to dress the part to have the powers. She seemed to be a very nice woman, and committed to what she was doing. Whether she really had any ESP or not remained to be seen.

And her opening was intriguing.

"Melody House. She has stood upon this hill since the year of our Lord seventeen-seventeen. And she has, in her years, hosted both joy and tragedy. She is one of the few such surviving grand old homes of our nation still owned by descendants of her original builders. George Washington slept here!" Elizabeth paused, smiling at the group gathered around the dining room table in the muted candlelight. "George got around, it's a wonder Martha wasn't a great deal more upset! But I digress. Washington wasn't her only well-known guest. The likes of Patrick Henry, Thomas Jefferson, and others of tremendous renown who lived in Revolutionary times came here as well, and later, she was hostess to many great statesmen and generals of another sad period of war—Robert E. Lee, Stonewall Jackson, Jeb Stuart, and then, even Ulysses Grant and Abe Lincoln were thought to have taken rest at this place. Bullets once riddled the walls, and many still remain, from battles fought on the ground. Soldiers perished within her walls. Naturally, there were other sad occurrences here, not having to do with the specific pain of battle. There is the case of the beautiful Melody herself, daughter of the builder, distraught by her suitor's argument with her father. She is said to have been rushing to his defense when she careened down the stairway, only to die in her lover's arms on the foyer floor, just feet from where we now sit. There was Eliza, the daughter of General Stone, who might well have been poisoned by her rival, Sally Beauville, who was, when accosted, shot dead by the girl's father, who then faced the hangman's noose. Those are not all the stories. There are so many more.

"Melody House has stood for nearly three hundred years, and in that time, we can only imagine all the dramas that have been lived—and the passions and dreams that have perished here as well. They say that we are energy, and energy cannot be destroyed. Just as they say that Melody House is haunted. If ghosts and spirits are those who remained, their energy still fiercely alive due to trauma or tragedy, then there would be nothing more natural than the fact that Melody House indeed be haunted! Throughout the years, many have seen, or have believed they have seen, the ghosts of those tragic souls. In the early eighteen-hundreds, the courageous Andrew Jackson, later to be president of the United States, once spent only half a night here, and mentioned to someone later that he'd rather face the British army again than spend another night at Melody House. Some swear there is a woman in white, still walking the halls. Others have seen soldiers, still, perhaps, fighting their long-lost battles.'' Elizabeth paused, something of a rueful smile on her face. "So. We shall all join hands, in the circle here created, and see what haunts or specters might wish to appear, to convey last words, wishes, or needs.''

Electricity had long ago come to Melody House, but tonight, other than the lights attached to the cameras, there was no illumination within the dining room except for a single candle burning in the center of the table.

Darcy had already felt the cold. Whether Elizabeth was able to communicate with any of the "energy" remaining in the house or not, Darcy again felt the sense of being watched. Whatever entity or entities remained at Melody House, they were watching. Across the table, she saw Penny shiver.

Darcy felt herself nudged. Hands, yes, hold hands. She set hers upon the table. She was next to Jason Johnson, a local writer and historian, and, naturally, another friend of Matt's, and Clint Stone. Carter was on Clint's other side. Clint covered her hand warmly with his own, and seemed both amused and curious, as if he might have an open mind to the happenings. Matt was across the table, seated next to Elizabeth. He wore a look of carefully restrained impatience on his hard-sculpted features. Mae, the woman who had been welcoming to her when she had first walked into the Wayside Inn, was there, attractively dressed and groomed, her round face split into a smile of excitement as she sat on Matt's other side. To round out the group, a pretty young woman with the improbable name of Delilah

Dey, newly elected to the town council, sat between Jason Johnson and Mae.

David Jenner, of Jenner Electronics, also at the Wayside Inn when Darcy had first arrived, stood a distance from the group, with video and audio running. Darcy had considered bringing down some of her own equipment, but then had decided that this was not the night for Harrison Investigations' high-tech "ghost buster" electronics.

"We have joined in a benign and caring circle," Liz said, addressing the spirits. "We wish to help with any problems, past or present. We have come in love and friendship, and wish to communicate with any presence in his house who desires a voice. Our minds and hearts are open. If there is a presence here, please let yourself be known."

Darcy felt a breeze at her nape, and she closed her eyes.

The fear had never really left her. Josh, who had been born with his unique perception, had not been afraid. But to Darcy, knowing that a very strange door was open was still a frightening experience. She knew that she had to allow the sensations in, but each time, it still seemed that cold fingers clutched her heart, and it was a fight to do what she knew she did well.

They were not alone.

Talk to me, she thought in silence.

But then her eyes popped open as she heard a rapping at the table. She frowned, then felt a very physical force as the hands grasping around the table all seemed to tighten as one. Elizabeth spoke excitedly.

"We have made a communication! Rap again, please, if you are with us."

A tap sounded.

Darcy looked around the table, doubting that any of the ghosts were tapping. Matt, too, was looking around the table.

The presence that had been so near Darcy and so apparent to her backed away. It didn't disappear; it simply receded.

"Are you the spirit we call the Lady in White?" Elizabeth asked.

There was no response.

"Perhaps a soldier?"

There was another rapping.

Matt was staring at Darcy, a certain hostility apparent in his eyes. Anger burst through her. He assumed that she was the one somehow managing to tap the table.

"Did you live during Revolutionary Times," Elizabeth asked, earnest concern in her voice.

No response. Matt was still staring at Darcy.

"The Civil War?" Elizabeth asked softly.

Another rap.

"Yes! Yes!" Elizabeth said, her eyes closed, her concentration intense. "We believe we know your story. You fought hard, so hard, for what you believed to be a just cause. You died here in this house. But you needn't stay and fight on. The war is over. Peace has come. And the outcome, in the end, was right. The only outcome that could be right, and the world has moved on. We seek now to offer true justice and equality for all men. You may rest in peace. Do you understand me? Can my words help you find rest?"

Another rap, then a number of excited raps.

Penny whispered softly to Elizabeth. "We don't want our ghosts to go away! We just want them to be happy."

"They're only happy when they're at peace!" Carter said, staring at Penny with a strange smile.

"This is so exciting!" Mae whispered.

"Hush!" Elizabeth said, moaning softly. "We'll break the very tenuous thread that is linking us to the entity."

There was a sound at the table, one of total impatience. Matt.

"Please!" Elizabeth said. "Captain…you are a captain, right?" she said, addressing the ghost.

There was nothing.

"Let us know. We're here for you," Elizabeth said.

There was another rap.

"Yes, you're a captain. A true gentleman, still fighting for his cause!"

There was suddenly the sound of a shriek. The table jumped.

The sound had come from Delilah. "Someone... something touched my thigh!"

"The captain isn't such a gentleman," Clint suggested wryly.

The table jerked again.

Matt swore, and rose, breaking the circle. "David, can you just go ahead and hit the lights?" he asked.

The room was flooded with illumination. "Okay, who was touching Delilah's legs?"

"Matt, we had contact, real contact," Elizabeth said, dismayed.

"Oh, please!" Matt said.

"By one horny ghost," Carter suggested, amused.

Matt glared at him. "Not me!" Carter protested.

All eyes naturally turned to Clint.

"Not on your life!" he protested.

"I'm telling you, we contacted a Civil War soldier," Elizabeth said stubbornly.

"Absolutely," Penny agreed. "And one of you destroyed our communication. Matt, you just can't have those two around the next time we have a seance. Delilah, we really have ghosts here."

Delilah shivered. "You do really believe that—that a captain from the Civil War was in this room with us?"

"I must say," Jason remarked, "Everyone's hands were on the table." From the way he spoke, it was difficult to tell if he was impressed with the tapping, or merely curious as to how it might have been managed.

"We're ignoring our expert," David said, his video still running as he turned the camera on Darcy. "What do you think?"

She answered slowly with a careful shrug. "I'm afraid we weren't into it long enough for me to really give an opinion."

Jason smiled at her. "But what do you think? Or feel, or intuit, whatever. Is Melody House haunted?"

"The house has a tremendous history," Darcy said. "Just being in it makes you feel an affinity for the past. Maybe that, in itself, makes a place haunted."

Clint laughed. "Boy, you can talk your way around anything, can't you, Darcy? What if this were one of those game shows and you had to give a yes or no answer?"

"But it's not a game show," Darcy said.

"I was excited!" Elizabeth said. "I know that I made contact. And we'll set up to do this again. We've only just begun. I don't think tonight would be good. I mean, I don't think we should try again so soon. Matt—"

"Forgive me, Elizabeth, but I don't want to set up any more dates right now. Bear with me. I'm sorry. My opinion is that someone here managed to tap on the table—and snag Delilah's leg in the process, whether on purpose or not."

"Matt, you are such a cynic!" Penny protested.

"Oh, my," Delilah said, and she had a half smile on her face as she surveyed the men in the room.

"He's accusing either you or me," Carter told Clint, but with no malice.

"Yes, actually, I am," Matt said sternly, but he didn't sound overly angry, just impatient. He hadn't wanted anything to do with a seance from the beginning.

"I think I'm going to step outside for a minute, if you'll excuse me?" Darcy said.

"I'll get drinks and some snacks out," Penny told them.

"Drinks!" Carter said with pleasure.

"I'll give you a hand, Penny," Mae said. "I'm still all a-tingle! I'm certain as well that Elizabeth made contact. Couldn't you feel it? The room was so cold. Oh, yes, there was someone with us. Something. Definitely. And Matt, you must do this again, please? Oh, you must, you must, you must!"

Darcy heard the last as she slipped through the foyer and out the front door. She felt a little guilty for not offering to help Penny herself, but there were others there, and she'd had the strangling sensation that she'd needed to get out.

Night could be so strange. The summer sky like velvet, and so near the mountains, a million stars showing cleanly against the darkness. She leaned against the porch rail for a minute, inhaled deeply, and smelled the fragrant, flower-filled air that marked the season.

Then she sat back in one of the rockers, closing her eyes and savoring the soft, cleansing sweep of the breeze, and wondering herself just who had done the tapping.

She was startled a minute later as she felt a presence next to her.

One that was very much alive, and carrying a low-key scent of aftershave.

She opened her eyes to see that Matt had joined her, taking the chair at her side. He watched her for a moment without speaking.

She turned back and stared at the night, not waiting for him to speak. "No, I don't believe that the tapping was a ghost."

With peripheral vision, she saw that a slow rueful smile curled into his lips.

"Thank God! I'd have lost all faith in you if you had said differently."

"Oh? I didn't realize that you had faith in me to begin with."

"That all remains to be seen."

"I've found that most people don't believe in the occult," Darcy told him. "Yet just the same, most people have a little voice of suspicion somewhere within them that suggests there might be something more between the living and the dead."

"You mean they're open-minded?" he said.

"Maybe minds aren't all open, but there's often a crack there somewhere."

He rocked thoughtfully for a minute. "We've always had a military tradition in my family. I went straight into military schools and served in the army for several years. The dead bodies I saw all stayed that way. I first became a cop in the D.C. area, and though much of the country might suggest that the main crimes there are political, I can guarantee you, there were plenty of criminals in the area who know how to kill. Death is usually ugly, but always complete. Then, again, I'm the direct heir to all those years of history, tradition, murder, and mayhem that have gone on at Melody House. If someone were to see something or have a link to the past, wouldn't it be me?''

Darcy laughed. ''Not when there's not even one of those cracks in your mind to allow the dead to try to speak to you.''

He was silent again, rocking, then looked at her with one of the smiles that suddenly sent a streak of warmth to quicken her limbs whether she wanted to admit it or not.

''When my dad died, I wanted him to speak to me somehow in the worst way. I was willing to do anything—I would have crawled into the coffin to go with him, I loved him so much. It was just about the same with my grandfather, except that I was older then, and more aware that he had lived his years, good years, and gone on.''

The emotion with which he spoke touched her deeply. Then he said, almost scowling, ''You weren't the one pulling off that tapping sound, were you?''

She stiffened, cold and indignant instantly. ''No, I was not! And come to think of it, your words just now were quite interesting. You didn't mention your mother. Do you have something against women, Matt?''

He turned to her, those strange dark gray eyes of his bearing something of a dangerous spark. ''I like women just fine, Darcy. Especially the really honest ones, and yes, they are out there. I didn't mention my mother because she died when I was a few months old, which didn't allow me a great deal of time to get to know her well.''

She turned back to the night. ''Sorry.''

''What about you?''

She gazed at him, and suddenly smiled despite herself. "I don't have anything at all against other women."

"No, I meant, how did that crack in your mind turn into a gaping hole where the dead came rushing through to speak to you at all times?"

"Oh," she murmured.

"Well?"

"I was in a car crash with a really good friend. And he died."

"And then he spoke to you?"

"Something like that." She thought that he was going to scoff at her again, but it seemed that he could be quite mercurial in his manner. She was startled when his hand lay upon hers where it rested on the arm of the rocker and his words came out soft and gentle.

"Don't you think that sometimes people see people, or hear them, just because they so desperately want to hear that person speak again?"

"Sometimes, yes."

"But not with you?"

"I wish that was all that it had been," Darcy told him.

His eyes were almost affectionate, and he watched her with an appreciation that once again sent her heart thundering, her blood racing. And she was startled to realize that she hadn't been so strongly, almost magnetically, attracted to anyone like this in years. Maybe never. There was something in him beyond his extraordinary looks, and even the sense of power and security that he emitted. Something that made her want to crawl against his skin, stroke his face, and feel the warmth burst into sensations far greater. She was almost afraid to hear him speak, because the temptation to lean closer to him was so strong and aching. He was about to speak, and she was beyond fascinated to hear what he was about to say.

Except that words never left his mouth.

The great double doors at the front of the house flew open and Delilah came bursting out, full of smiles and charm.

"Aren't you all coming in to join us for a drink and some snacks? I must say, Penny is just the most priceless human being in the world. In a matter of minutes she's created the most delightful spread in the kitchen!"

They both stared at her rather blankly for a minute.

Darcy had liked Delilah from the start. She was a nice woman, and seemed intelligent, and really concerned about her job for the county.

At that moment, though, she could have hit her.

Delilah continued, "Oh, Matty, please, don't be upset about the silly tapping tonight. Penny and Liz are right—we did come close to contact. Don't be angry with all of us!"

"I'm not angry," Matt said, rising and sounding only somewhat impatient. "We'll join you."

Delilah started back into the house. Matt reached out a hand to Darcy. "Coming?"

She accepted his hand and rose. It was as if there were sparks in his fingers. At that moment though, she wasn't sure that he noticed in the least.

"Matty?" she said lightly, arching a brow.

"It's what happens when you've lived in a small town and known people too long and too well."

"Ah," she murmured, wanting to ask, *how well?*

She refrained, and let him lead her on back into the house.

Penny *had* created quite a spread. Tea, coffee, mixed drinks, chips and dips, buffalo wings, Southern pecan pie, and other little desserts that Darcy knew she had prepared earlier in the day.

Darcy had never been less hungry, but since Penny had baked the pie herself, she toyed with a piece and opted for an Irish coffee—made with decaf, Penny explained, so she wouldn't keep anyone up all night. Clint and Carter were in rare form, accusing one another of the tapping, Delilah was flirtatious, and Mae was excited, thanking Matt over and over again for letting her come, and begging to be invited if they tried a seance again. Liz scolded the boys for being silly when she was up to something important. Penny seemed a little quiet when she wasn't being the perfect hostess. David Jenner spoke about the different qualities of tape and film, and asked Darcy her preferences for her work. As they picked up the remnants of their meal, Delilah charmingly cornered Matt over a parking problem they were having near the town hall.

Darcy rinsed plates and put them into the dishwasher with Clint and Carter bringing in the used utensils and only half helping as they flirted. She had grown to like them both, even though she did get a start, feeling as if she were speaking with a modern-day Jeb Stuart every time she met Carter's eyes above the growth of his beard. Still, she was strangely keyed, and exhausted at the same time. When she could, she left the two of them dealing with the dishwasher and excused herself to Penny, Mae, and Elizabeth and escaped up the stairs to the Lee Room.

As she prepared for bed, she didn't feel a thing in the room. Not the slightest intuitive whisper of a presence. Not even the sense of being watched. Despite the fact that it was her business to discover just what was going on, she was glad she was ready for a good night's rest.

She fell almost instantly and soundly into a deep sleep.

And that's when she was awakened.

Darcy's head jerked up, because a silent scream seemed to enter into her mind, pierce through her subconscious, and seize her attention with a start. She looked around in the night as if she had been rudely prodded by a fire poker.

And there she was, a woman in a silver nightgown, standing in the doorway, hand to her throat in terror, issuing that silent scream.

Darcy saw the image in the dim and hazy light, saw the woman trying to bolt the door, but the force behind it, trying to enter from the hall, kept her from doing so. Then the woman came racing toward the bed, and for a moment, her eyes met Darcy's. There was a terrible plea within them. *Help me!*

It was as if the woman saw her there as well, and the

plea was as silent as the scream, heard only in Darcy's head. But God, that scream! It sounded again within her mind, and the woman's beautiful lips moved, beseeching Darcy to hear her. But she couldn't understand the words; she knew only that they were desperate.

Because this wraith was running from death.

The killer, Darcy sensed, was coming from behind the woman. From the hallway. The bedroom door now burst open. Darcy could make out a hazy image of someone large and shadowy, shielded by the night, coming forward.

Toward the woman.

Then, above the woman's shoulder, she saw the flash of the knife, as clearly as if a spotlight hit the blade, and glinted from it.

The scream sounded again...more terrible than ever.

And the knife...

The knife flashed above Darcy.

She wasn't easily frightened. She communicated with the dead after all.

She sought them out.

But that night...

The malevolence was so strong, the danger seemed so real. The blade...it was threatening her, and she knew it.

She struggled for calm, for sanity, trying to convince herself that she was seeing nothing but an image from the past. There was no knife wielded by a dark and deadly murderer. Not now...what she saw was nothing but an image from the past.

But it moved again, glinting, and...dripping.

Dripping blood.

And she was terrified suddenly that if it touched her...

Darcy sprang from the bed, screaming herself. The image wasn't fading, it wasn't a whisper, a hint of what had happened. It was pure evil. And something deeper than her intuition, than her acceptance, than any peace or calm she might have garnered over the years, deserted her completely. Terror, older and more basic than any human emotion, lit into her. She raced beneath the images, and tore out of the room, shrieking herself as she tore out of the room.

Darcy ran down the stairs, mindlessly fleeing.

She came to the landing and it was there that she heard her name shouted. She had probably been called several times before the sound had made its way through to her conscious thought.

Darcy stopped dead still, sanity filling her mind as quickly as it had deserted it.

She could have kicked herself, thoroughly.

It was Matt Stone calling her name, rushing down the stairs. He was in boxers and a robe, haphazardly cast over his shoulders.

Even as she saw him appear at the top of the stairway, Penny, gray hair tousled, came rushing behind him in a pair of pajamas.

The front door burst open as Carter, Clint slamming into his back, appeared.

It was uncanny, almost as bizarre as the dream, or reality, she had just experienced, the way they all appeared so quickly, the entire household, within minutes. She almost felt as threatened, watching as Matt and Penny came down, and Clint and Carter came forward, and they gathered in the foyer at the foot of the stairs, alarmed, and then, as they saw her, saw that she was fine, disgruntled.

Matt Stone's eyes were hard and suspicious.

"The Lee Room sent you racing out in a panic?" Matt said, an edge of derision in his tone. "I thought you were the great ghost hunter."

Clint was kinder. "Are you all right, Darcy?"

She stared at Matt. "Yes, and I'm terribly sorry. I must have had a nightmare."

"Ghosts don't scare her—nightmares do," Matt murmured.

Penny was staring at her sagely. "You saw the lady in white."

Carter let out a long sniff. "Oh, Penny! I used to spend a lot of time in that room. I never saw any lady in white."

"I've seen her, Clara Issy has seen her, and she sent a bride running out of that room naked as a jaybird!" Penny said indignantly.

Matt stared hard at Penny, Carter, and Clint, one by one, then turned around, starting up the stairs. "Tapping on a table is one thing," he said irritably. "But if you two have rigged that room somehow..."

"Matt, jeez, dammit, I wouldn't do that!" Clint protested angrily.

"I sure as hell wouldn't! I don't believe in the damned spooks!" Carter said.

"I believe in them wholeheartedly. They are here," Penny said indignantly. Matt had already started up the stairs. Darcy watched as the others all rushed back up the stairs behind him. She followed, protesting.

"Look, I had a dream. A nightmare. I woke you all. I'm sorry."

Matt didn't appear to hear her. He slammed against the door of the Lee Room, causing it to open all the way. He, Carter, and Clint walked in. Where, of course, nothing was disturbed, and nothing at all was out of the ordinary.

Matt, however, appeared determined. He threw open the closet door and carelessly rummaged through her hung clothing, looking for what in the small space, she didn't know. He looked under the bed, then walked to the balcony doors, throwing them open as well. He walked out on the balcony, then came back in, arms crossed over his chest as he stared at Darcy.

"Just exactly what did you see?"

"I didn't see anything," she lied. "I had a dream. That's all. And I'm sorry. Terribly sorry."

"I don't think you should sleep in here anymore."

She felt a flicker of the fear returning, but held her ground.

"I need to sleep in here."

"Why? You can explore this room—or do whatever the hell it is that you do—by day."

Darcy shook her head. "Look, once again, I'm really, really sorry. This won't happen again. I swear it."

"No."

"Aw, Matt, you're just down the hall," Clint said, championing Darcy.

She flashed him a smile of gratitude, despite the fact that his words didn't seem to help any.

"No," Matt repeated stubbornly.

"Look, I swear to you, I'm really not a mincing little coward. I had a dream, and it gave me a terrible start. But I need to stay in that room. All right, Matt, I disturbed you. And I realize that you're the sheriff and you have a day job, and I'm really, truly, sorry."

"Matt!" Penny put in.

"We can make a deal. If I come running out again, for any reason, I'll bow to your decision and get out of the room," Darcy said. She was pleading with a man who now wore a grim expression on his face. She hated pleading with him.

She didn't intend to leave the Lee Room, though. Yes, she'd been scared out of a few years of life, but that might have been the exact intention of the malignant presence. She had lived with her gift for a long time. She could still be frightened, but she knew her own strengths.

She *wouldn't* let it happen again. She wouldn't give way to the fright.

"Matt," Carter suggested sagely, "you're one stubborn cuss, but so is Miss Tremayne. If any one of us is going to get back to sleep, I suggest you let her go back to bed in the Lee Room. Remember, you're the one who doesn't believe in spooks."

"But I do believe in the ability of man to do evil," Matt said, staring at Darcy.

"You're right down the hall," she reminded him quietly. "Actually, the next room, I believe. At least, the office part of your suite."

"All I need is something to happen to you!" he muttered.

"Bad for business?" she inquired sharply. "I assure you, I'm not going to become another ghost of Melody House," she assured him. "And I'm adult, responsible to myself."

"Yes, bad for business. And not only that, but whether you like it or not, I am responsible to Adam Harrison for you."

Just how well did he know Adam, Darcy wondered. "Adam sent me," she reminded him, outraged. "He knows that I can deal with anything that happens."

"Um. Deal with it—by being terrorized and terrified?"

"It won't happen again," she repeated stubbornly. She was disturbed to realize that they had an audience for this *discussion,* and she was beginning to feel as if she were a child having an argument with an adult.

But apparently, she was winning.

He threw up his hands and turned away. Clint gave her a grin and a thumbs-up sign. Carter, too, was smiling beneath his beard. Only Penny looked a little perplexed.

"You are sure you're going to be okay?" Penny asked softly.

"Absolutely," she assured the woman.

"Well, then, I'm going back to bed," Carter said. He gave Darcy a wink. "I know the room well. It's brick and mortar, and nothing else."

"Another true disbeliever," Penny muttered.

"Don't worry, ma'am," Clint teased, "You've got a threesome of Southern gentlemen here, not only offering charm, but all our valiant resources in whatever way you may need. We'll be happy to kick ghost butt for you at any time."

Penny let out a sound between a moan and groan. "Get out of here, go back to the stables and get to bed, both of you. You just wait until one of the ghosts does decide to make an appearance before you boys. You'll be sorry then!"

"Oooh!" Carter said.

It looked as if Penny was about to strike him.

"We're going, we're going," Clint said. He turned toward the stairway, then told Darcy, "Seriously, if Matt doesn't make it to the rescue quickly enough, all you've got to do is whistle."

"Good night, then," Darcy said, smiling at Penny and eyeing Matt. "Honestly, I'm sorry. It won't happen again."

He nodded, and walked back into his own room.

Penny was left alone to stare at Darcy. "They are real, and I know it!" Penny told her.

Darcy smiled. "We have to find out just what is going on." She hesitated. "When the dead become violent or destructive, it's because they want us to know something."

Penny shivered. "I'm here for you!" she said valiantly. But her words came with a shiver.

"Honestly, I'm all right," Darcy assured her.

"It's getting worse and worse," Penny said. She glanced at the closed door to Matt's room. "Maybe he's right. Perhaps you should sleep somewhere else, and spend time during the day in the Lee Room."

"Penny, this is what I do!" she reminded the woman. "I was taken by surprise tonight. Startled by the force of…my dream. But it's okay. Really."

Penny looked at her worriedly and sighed softly.

"I swear." Darcy gave Penny a little kiss on the cheek, and slipped back into her room.

She closed the door behind her and leaned against it. The room's temperature seemed completely normal, the air as clear as a mountain morning. She was certain that she'd experienced all she was going to for one evening. And now that the fear had receded, she was all right. Stronger, more prepared. And more determined and angry.

Melody House held many haunting secrets. But it seemed evident now that the lady in white was a victim of a deadly violence in the past, and the truth regarding her murder had never been discovered.

Darcy rinsed her face with cold water, surveyed her surroundings once again, and lay back down.

She began to doze.

Then, once again, she bolted up, wide-awake.

She *felt* the room, but there was nothing. And yet, something had awakened her.

She slipped from the bed. The doors to the balcony were open; the drapes drifted in a soft and eerie white wave. Standing very still next to the bed, Darcy searched the shadows for an visions or apparitions.

Silence, nothing…

She walked to the open doorway to the balcony, ran her hands over the drapes. As she started out to the balcony there was a shift in the breeze. The white gauzy fabric of the drapes wrapped around her as she was seized by powerful and forceful arms, trapped in a vise of merciless strength.

5

As they climbed the stairs to the apartments above the stables, Carter looked at Clint suspiciously.

"How did you do it?" he asked.

Clint looked at him, startled. "Do what?"

"The tapping."

"I wasn't doing the tapping. I thought it was you."

"Hell, no."

"Maybe the ghosts," Clint said lightly.

"You believe in the ghosts now?" Carter asked, amused.

Clint was silent a minute. "Penny," he said thoughtfully.

"Penny!" Carter said.

"She's the one who wants to prove that Melody House has ghosts," Clint reminded him.

"Yeah, but can you see Penny staging a bunch of tapping noises?"

"Why not?" Carter asked with a shrug.

"There's Elizabeth—the medium," Clint suggested with a laugh. "She needed to prove herself—especially with a real ghost buster in the room."

"Um," Carter mused. "And what do you think of our ghost buster racing out in the middle of the night, just like the young bride?"

Clint grinned slowly. "I think it's a shame she didn't race out naked like the bride. That is one exciting woman."

"Mind your manners, son," Carter said, but he was

amused as well. He shrugged. "It just strikes me as strange, all this. Darcy Tremayne is no flighty young bride. The woman is all cool sophistication—and yes, too bad she didn't come down in the buff, just like the bride. But there's got to be something going on."

"You *are* starting to believe in ghosts," Clint said, scoffing.

Carter shook his head. "Nope. I'm starting to agree with Matt that someone is somehow playing tricks in the Lee Room. And I'd damned well like to know why."

"Maybe people just feed off the fears and beliefs of others," Clint said, impatient. He grinned. "You and I have both enjoyed that room, a hell of a lot. Even Matt. Before the place was really opened up the way it is now, when Matt's granddad was still living and went in and out of Washington all the time. Hell, I had some of my best nights there. Nothing like impressing a young woman with a real historical house, a seduction in pure luxury—with the threat of a ghost to make her all warm and cozy."

Carter nodded after a moment. "Yep, I've had my share of nights there."

"And no ghosts?"

"And no ghosts," Carter agreed.

"So—forget it."

"Hard to forget when we're hosting ghost busters."

Clint shrugged. "You know, I have to admit that, over time, I've heard from plenty of people that they have seen things. Clara Issy is as rock-solid and sane a woman as you're ever going to find. And she saw something in the Lee Room. And I've heard other guests swear that they've seen a soldier walk through the parlor."

Carter laughed. "Yeah, I remember one occasion. And the couple did see a Rebel soldier walk through the room—he was headed out to take part in a battle re-enactment at Cold Harbor. Hell, I dressed up one time for a Civil War forum and scared half the people I knew."

"The point being?"

"There is usually a logical explanation for ghosts."

"All right, I grant you that. So?"

"So, I think someone is playing tricks. And if it's not you, and it's not me...then who? And why?" he asked.

"I don't know," Clint said. He hesitated. "But I'd damned sure like to find out just who and why myself."

With their guest in the house, Penny had taken up residence in the Stuart Room. It was two doors down from the Lee Room, in the ell on the left side of the house.

With both Matt and Darcy having returned to their rooms, Penny found herself standing indecisively in the hallway.

Might as well go back to bed. There was nothing else to do.

But she shook her head, staring at Matt's door. What on earth had to happen for him to realize that he had something very special in this house? Oh, he loved the house, and was a great one for historical value, she gave him that.

But they had something even...better. And more unique.

Turning her attention to Darcy's door, she folded her arms over her chest and swore softly beneath her breath. Why wouldn't the young woman just say what had happened? There were ghosts in this house. It was a fact. And certainly, it might be hard to prove it to the world, but there was no reason for Matt to fail to believe, to fail to use the experiments and happenings here to enrich the legends that already abounded. It would be so wonderful to be a real center of attention for a public that loved such stories.

Just what on earth was she going to have to do to prove her point?

She sighed and walked down the hall to her own room, opened the door, and then hesitated once again.

"I'm here! I'm listening!" she said aloud. "Talk to me, whoever, whatever, you are. I'll get your story out!"

She waited, looking around the hall.

But the ghosts apparently had nothing to say to her.

"I don't care if you pull my hair—or if you want to

slap me in the face! Hey, leave the others alone. I'm ready. I'll help you."

Still, there was nothing. The hall remained silent.

All right, seriously, just what on earth was she going to have to do?

With a disgusted sniff, she pressed the door open and went on into bed.

Darcy was caught in a terrible grip, all but smothered in the hold and the voluminous wealth of gauzy drapes tangled around her. Instinctive fear had seized hold of her as well, and she was ready to struggle, fight, and scream.

But the sound never left her lips, because a familiar voice interrupted her thoughts.

"Who are you, and what the hell are you doing?"

The voice, deep and very low, and all the more menacing for the quiet within it, cut into her mind like a knife.

And still, fear eased instantly.

She was silent and dead still for a minute, ruefully realizing her position.

Then she spoke.

"I'm your unwanted guest, and I was merely on my way out to the balcony when a breeze blew, and suddenly I found myself rather rudely accosted."

She felt the vise ease from around her. For a split second, there was the simple warmth of Matt's hold, taut muscles slackening, and a pleasant sense of just being held, of life and vibrance, masculine aftershave, and an essence of sexuality that took her completely off guard. She swayed.

His arms were releasing her.

She quickly gathered her wits about her, and found steadiness on her feet while he worked to untangle her from the draperies.

She emerged facing him, flushed, hair tousled.

"Why are you sneaking around the balcony?" she demanded.

Matt crossed his arms over his chest. "A, it's my balcony. B, I wasn't sneaking around. Your turn. What the hell were *you* doing, sneaking around on the balcony.''

''I heard something.''

''Apparently, you heard me.''

''So—why were you out here?''

''I heard something—apparently you.''

She shook her head. ''I believe that I heard you first.''

''I beg to differ.''

''Oh, this is getting ridiculous.''

He arched a brow to her, implying that the entire situation of her being in his house was purely ridiculous.

She exhaled on a long sigh. ''Look, your night has been disturbed enough. I really wasn't making any noise.''

He grunted.

''Since there's no one on the balcony except for you and me, I believe it would be safe for both of us to go back to sleep.''

''The balcony doors do lock,'' he told her.

''Do you keep yours locked?'' she asked him.

He shook his head.

''Why not?''

''Because I listen.''

''In your sleep?''

''It's a talent,'' he said dryly. ''But you should keep yours locked.''

She stared at him for a long while.

''Why should I?''

''Because someone is playing tricks with this room.''

''So you believe the danger is coming from the outside?''

''Where else?''

''Why can't you believe that there's anything in the world that isn't black or white, visible to the naked eye?'' she asked softly.

''I believe in a great big *real* world of gray,'' he said.

''If there is any danger in the house,'' she insisted quietly, ''I believe it comes from the *inside*.''

"But you want to stay in the Lee Room anyway?"

She lowered her head, praying for patience. "If you're such a serious skeptic, why did you agree to let the company in?"

"Because I know Adam. And I know that he can find any kind of sleight of hand out there."

"Adam also believes deeply in the occult. And in me," she added.

He shrugged, then brushed past her, entering the Lee Room again. For a moment, he stood with his back to her.

"I can't tell you how many nights I spent in this room as a kid. And...even in the last few years," he murmured. There was something behind his words; she didn't know what. But then he swung around, staring at her again. "Lots and lots of nights. And nothing ever materialized before me. Nothing whispered in the dark. Nothing floated by."

She twisted her jaw slightly. "I didn't tell you that anything materialized or floated by me. I merely said that I had a nightmare."

"Right. And the great ghost buster ran out screaming."

"It was a very bad nightmare."

He walked over to her and she was startled when he set his hands on her shoulders, and his eyes, very dark in the shadows of night, were hard focused on her own. She was again aware of something evocative in the mere nearness of the man. He carried a richly masculine and seductive scent, and the simple touch of his fingers seemed like a caress. She told herself that it had been a long time since she had been this close to a man so vital and arresting, and so, it was natural that her senses should be jumping. It was a hard argument. They didn't jump that easily.

"Darcy, I do believe that something is going on. But something real. And I don't want you hurt."

His words were honestly, sincerely spoken. The edge of hostility was gone between them, fallen off like a cloak.

She needed it back. She was standing in a bedroom in a flimsy nightgown, body brushing that of a striking male in his prime, clad in no more than boxers and a robe. If she moved just a little bit closer…half an inch, she'd know firsthand if she had an equal effect upon him.

"I'm…I'm not going to get hurt," she assured him. Her voice was thick.

It seemed as if eons passed in which he didn't reply. In which they just stood there. Her mind raced in a fury of thoughts. He wasn't going to let her go. He was going to take that step closer. She should, of course, step away, but she wouldn't. She'd feel the force of his arms enwrapping her again, but carefully this time, pressing her against his length. The palms of his hand would come to her face, fingers would caress her chin. Then they'd be fused together, tangled in a web of touch and taste and sensation, and—

He stepped back.

"I'm right next door. You didn't disturb my sleep. Feel free to scream at any time." He offered her a wry grimace, then took another step back. She wasn't sure his stride was as confident as usual.

Or maybe she just wanted him to be a bit shaky, too.

"Seriously, at the least disturbance, please, scream your heart out. I'll be right here." He smiled. Then his knuckles lightly brushed her cheek; for a moment, time passed again, with endless electricity and thought.

Then he was gone.

Admittedly, Matt was tired.

Still didn't help the way that the morning completely sucked.

It started out with a desperate call from one of the area's three middle schools. The sheriff's department rushed in, prepared to deal with a possibly deadly, serious situation. It turned out that Brad Middleton, tall, lanky, fighting a case of acne, but usually a decent kid, had come in to class saying that he had a gun. Not a soul in the world was going to have a sense of humor about such a situation these days, which Brad couldn't understand, since he had come in packing a water pistol. After a discussion with the psychiatric counselor, the police counselor, the principal, and then his parents, he was shaking like a leaf by the time he reached Matt, and Matt wasn't feeling much better about the situation himself. The kid was going to have to go to court, and Matt didn't lie about the fact that he was facing consequences. Since Brad seemed truly repentant, he was certain that the boy would receive leniency, and he could make him feel somewhat better. But in the middle of his conversation with Brad, there was a holdup at one of the gas stations on the highway, and when they chased down the perp, he wasn't packing a water pistol. Still, surrounded by law enforcement vehicles, the man turned himself in. Thankfully, no one, including the perp, was shot.

That was all before noon in a town where days could go by, totally uneventful.

He wondered why he had ever wanted to be elected sheriff in the first place. But he knew why. He was like one of the ancient oaks that filled the forested area, born and bred to Stoneyville. He felt the responsibility of his family's claim to the place, almost as if he was rooted there as well.

And still, though he was worn and weary, he knew how to be sheriff. He knew how to handle juveniles, gun-wielding thieves, and even the older populace who complained that their neighbors were playing rock music or rap too loud.

What he didn't know how to handle was what he couldn't see, touch, hear, or stand up against, face-to-face. The other night had disturbed him deeply.

Just as Darcy Tremayne disturbed him.

She could appear as unruffled as the most dignified queen, and yet last night, when he had first seen her after she'd fled the Lee Room, she had been terrified. She had conquered her bout of fear quickly, and with a steely resolve that truly brooked no argument. Last night he had known that he wanted her out, far away where no harm could come to her. And yet he had respected something about her determination as well; hell, he was afraid every time he faced a lethal weapon—he'd seen what they could do. Didn't alter the fact that he meant to be just what he was, and be first in line to face any situation that arose.

He didn't believe in ghosts. Didn't matter. Something had scared her badly.

He'd be damned if he could figure out just what was going on, or *who* was causing it. The seance could be chalked up to childish antics. As to the rest...

Pranks as well. Had to be. Or the imaginations of those who just wanted ghosts to exist so badly that they could create them. That worked with Penny and their streaking bride. But Clara? She was as down to earth as could be.

Why worry about it so much? He taunted himself. Half of humanity wanted to believe in ghosts, in anything that gave credence to a life after death. Let Melody House be haunted.

Ah, but there was the rub. Clara had either slammed herself into a door, or been hurt somehow. But he still had to question how the hell someone was playing games in the house. He'd gone through the Lee Room endlessly, and had found nothing. No wires, no taps, nothing.

He'd spent plenty of time in the Lee Room himself. Once, when Lavinia had been in love with the place. She considered the room exciting, for reasons he'd never really fathomed. Clint, he knew, had taken a number of women to the house. Carter, too. Maybe for the thrill of being intimate with a woman when there was an element of fear. The point was, not one of them had ever been bothered by anything in the least amiss.

He realized he'd been sitting at his desk at the station, staring down at a form, pen in hand. He gave himself a mental shake and concentrated. The true reason police forces lost so many good cops. Paperwork.

He forced himself to finish up, then called out to his secretary that he was calling it quits. It was well after six and he'd been in for almost twelve hours.

He felt a sudden uneasiness.

It was too long to have been gone from Melody House.

Stoneyville might be a small town, but it had one of the most impressive and charming public libraries Darcy had ever seen.

Mrs. O'Hara, tiny as a wren, but sprightly and quick with beautiful dark brown eyes peeping out from behind her bifocals, evidently loved books, and apparently felt a need to create comfortable and aesthetic surroundings in which they might be enjoyed. Beautiful plants and flowers adorned the numerous tables, and she proudly told Darcy that she'd found the inviting, overstuffed chairs set about the library at various yard sales throughout the county. The library was entirely user-friendly, with signs to direct youngsters to their section, and adults to where they wanted to go as well. "A library should be educational, of course," she told Darcy cheerfully. "But the point is that reading should always be a pleasure, and when one learns to read and love it, all kinds of knowledge just becomes available so easily. I do go on, but then, I do love books!" She wasn't obtrusive, however, and quickly brought Darcy to the section on local history.

Luckily, many local writers had been intrigued with chronicling events around them. In the 1870s, a woman named Murial Moore had written about the sisters Darcy and Matt had discussed on her first day at Melody House. The family had been the Claytons, and their home had been located just outside of town. A Barry Brewster had been engaged first to marry Ophelia, the oldest of the brood, but had fallen in love with young Amy, the baby of the family. Amy had last been seen with her sister Ophelia as they walked through the east forest, ostensibly to visit neighbors on the far side. Amy had not been seen again alive. Barry had returned, and on the day that the majority of Amy's bones were discovered by a farmer walking through the woods with his dog, Barry had hanged himself from a tree near the brook. Ophelia had later gone insane, but lived out her life to the ripe old age of eighty-eight, prisoner of her family, kept in the barn. The barn, and family property, had burned to the ground.

"How are you doing, young lady?"

Darcy started and looked up. Mrs. O'Hara was standing by her side. "I was about to make a cup of tea. Would you like some?"

This was definitely a different kind of library.

Darcy smiled, then glanced at her watch. She hadn't gotten very deep into the history of the Stone family at all, but she felt as if she was carefully treading water between legends, truth, and experience as it was. And she was anxious to get back to the forest.

"I'll take a rain check on the tea, Mrs. O'Hara, if I may," Darcy told her. "I'll be back tomorrow."

She handed the book she'd been reading to the librarian. Such an old volume wasn't allowed out of the library.

Mrs. O'Hara assured her she was quite welcome, and told her that she'd go through some of their old books and see what she could show her that might be important regarding the history of Melody House. "I warn you—any difficulty on research regarding Melody House and the area is not because there hasn't been a lot written. There are many, many books on the subject."

"Thanks so much for your help."

"Absolutely. I'm quite convinced myself that the area is haunted. In fact, I have a friend you might want to talk to. Her name is Marcia Cuomo. She started working at Melody House right after Matt's grandfather died. And she quit in one day. She was convinced that she was grabbed and rousted about and nearly killed when she was thrown down a stairway."

"Oh?" Darcy said. She hadn't heard a word about Marcia Cuomo.

Mrs. O'Hara was smiling wryly. "At the time, I'm afraid, she had a reputation for having a nip or two while working. She didn't want Matt Stone thinking that she was drinking on the job, so she just told Penny she'd had a fall. Apparently, when she tried to explain to a few people that there was a very physical ghost in the house, they didn't think her a credible witness in the least.''

''I see. I'd love to talk to her.'' At the counter, Darcy wrote down her cell phone number and gave it to Mrs. O'Hara. ''Could you ask Marcia to call me at her convenience?''

Darcy left the library and searched for the little Volvo she had borrowed from Penny. Twenty minutes later, she was out at the stables. Sam, the old caretaker, was working there, and she assured him that she could manage saddling and bridling the horse herself.

Daylight still dappled through the trees, but with such a canopy of green, the forest trails and copses were dark and shadowy as early evening came to pass. Darcy rode to the point where she had dismounted on her last ride out, left Nellie having a lazy sip of water at the brook, and returned to her perch upon the log.

She hugged her knees to her chest, always a little afraid. She closed her eyes, concentrating on the sense of the past that had nearly come clear to her before.

First, the cold. It settled over the forest like a blanket. An inward voice, her own, called out in silent fear as the feeling wrapped around her. ''Josh!''

''I'm here.''

It was the softest voice, or it was insanity. It was her own mind, working on different circuits, a mechanism to keep her from going mad.

She opened her eyes. The forest had darkened even further. She heard voices. One light, a girl's voice. She was laughing. Talking about the wedding, then apologizing. ''Ophelia, you've been so wonderful. He was to have been yours, but then, really, you'd never met, and then we met, and Ophelia, I really do love him so very much! We'll find the right man for you, I know it. Maybe not in this little town, but you'll travel with Barry and me, and it will be wonderful.''

She could see the sisters. They had come into view. Two ghost horses had now joined Nellie at the brook. Nellie lifted her head, snorted, shied away uneasily, seemed to get ready to run.

Both girls had a wealth of brown hair, and were clad in simple cotton dresses, petticoats beneath, heavy boots on their feet.

Amy dismounted first.

"It will be wonderful," Ophelia agreed softly from her saddle. Then she, too, dismounted.

"Why did we stop here?" Amy asked, cupping her hands to create a dipper so that she could draw a cool drink from the brook.

"Oh, I just wanted to show you something. It's in the water. You'll have to kneel down."

"I'll get soaked."

"It's summer, little goose. You'll dry."

Amy hesitated.

And watching the past replay itself in her mind's eyes in the haunted glen, Darcy wanted to cry out, to warn Amy, to help her. And instead, she sat frozen, in something of a trance, seeing the time repeat itself in the images of what had been, aware that she could only *see,* that there was nothing she could do.

"Something in the water?" Amy repeated.

"Yes, get down, you'll see!"

It was a classic execution, carried out badly, brutally foiled. Once Amy was down, Ophelia drew the heavy ax from the pouch at the back of her saddle. Her first blow merely dazed Amy, who screamed and fell sideways into the water. Ophelia instantly saw that she had botched a clean kill. She began to work arduously, swinging the hatchet again and again while Amy screamed. The thudding of the blade against flesh, bone, muscle, and sinew seemed as loud in the forest as a drumbeat.

The vision came to life far too vividly. And, watching from the log, Darcy could bear it no longer. She began to scream as well. She forgot herself, running forward to the spot, thinking that something had to stop the terror.

Neither the dying Amy nor the determined Ophelia noticed her in the least. Time had come, and time had gone, and all that vision could give was an echo of the past.

As Darcy burst upon the sisters, the images faded. Shaking, Darcy fell upon her knees in the water. Yet, as she knelt there, shaking, horrified at Ophelia's vicious cruelty to her own sister, she saw the ghost.

Amy, headless, thrashing through the brush by an old oak, not twenty feet away.

Slowly, Darcy rose.

When Matt reached the house, he saw that Clint and Carter were out by the stables, arguing over Riley, a big buckskin quarter horse. He strode over to the two of them.

"We have more horses," he reminded his cousin and their friend.

"Ah, but only one glorious redheaded guest," Clint said. He carried his usual joking tone, but there was a slight edge of steel to it.

"She's out riding again?" Matt asked.

"And I say I should be the one riding out just to make sure she's doing all right," Carter said. He rubbed his beard and grinned. "You know, give her a real feel for the charm of the Old South."

"Hell—a beard gives you Southern charm?" Clint scoffed.

"Hey, I'm a land baron, and you're…a relation," Carter reminded him.

"Right. I belong at Melody House. You've got your own property. You just like to hang out here," Clint returned.

Matt ignored the two of them and took Riley's reins, then quickly swung into the saddle. He looked down at the two of them. "I'll go."

They frowned at each other. "That's just not fair," Carter said.

"And why not?"

"You're rude to her," Clint answered.

"And she doesn't really look a damned thing like Lavinia," Carter said.

"Yeah, Lavinia is beautiful, but she's also got that pinched terrier look, you know? Like a woman who always wants more," Clint agreed.

"While this one just seems to rise above it all," Carter said.

"Look damned good in a nightgown," Clint said.

"Too bad she doesn't sleep in the buff," Carter said, shaking his head.

"Hey, the woman is working for me," Matt said irritably. "Lay off—she's not a one-night conquest here for anyone's amusement."

"Who said anything about one night?" Clint demanded.

"Working for you?" Carter said, one eye half closed as he squinted up at Matt in the dying summer sun. "Bull. You don't believe in anything she's doing."

"Neither do you."

"No, but I sure am attracted to our guest. And I'm fascinated by her work, not at all ready to mock her—the way that you are," Carter said.

"See you at dinner," Matt said, starting to turn Sam around.

"Hey!" Clint called to him.

He looked back at his cousin. For a minute, Clint looked as he sometimes had when they were kids. Stubborn, and somewhat sullen.

Matt reined in, staring at him.

"She's no one-night stand for you either, Matt."

"She's working for me," he repeated.

"Yeah. Like the air doesn't crackle when the two of you get close."

True enough. But he'd be damned if he'd have these two knowing anything and taunting him about his attraction to the ghost buster he didn't believe in.

"She's only here until she finds something...or until Adam arrives," he said curtly. Then he nudged Riley with his thighs and headed out for the forest. He hadn't asked any questions about which way she'd ridden, nor did he look for any signs.

He was certain that he'd find her right where she'd been before, near the water, probably seated right on the same log.

"Communing" with the forest.

A surge of irritation filled him, and yet he was anxious to reach her, and suddenly, deeply glad as well that he'd reached the house when he had. There wasn't a damned thing wrong with Clint—except that he was a spendthrift and a womanizer. He did have a way with the opposite sex, though. He was all smiles and courtesy, and made many an easy conquest. Carter, too, seemed to manage his share of affairs. And he hadn't seen either of them so determined in a long time. Hell, never determined enough to argue over one woman.

So?

If she was interested in one of them…?

She was working for him. Or rather, come to think of it, Harrison Investigations had paid for their exploration and examination of Melody House. It was his damned house. That gave him the right to have a proprietary feeling.

Maybe it didn't.

Hell, he had one anyway.

He reached the copse, the brook, and the place where the fallen log lay in the forest. Nellie, wide-eyed, stood in the brook. The horse wasn't drinking, just standing. She seemed to be in a strange trance, swaying oddly in the water.

Matt looked hurriedly to the log. Darcy was not there.

Then he heard a sound. A grunting. His eyes were diverted close to one of the old oaks. He stared incredulously, dismounting from his horse by rote, staring at Darcy.

She was on her hands and knees, digging furiously. Covered in mud. His austere, regal-looking guest was smudged with raw earth from head to toe, and she was totally oblivious to the fact that he was there.

She'd dug a really big hole with only the help of a club-shaped log and a sharp stone.

"Darcy?"

As he said her name softly, she gave out a cry of triumph.

And in the eerie light of the dying day, she raised a human skull high into the air.

6

She had found it!

Elation roared through Darcy.

"Darcy!"

Her name was called out so roughly that she nearly dropped the skull. She looked to see that Matt had come upon her in the woods.

"Matt! I've found it!"

But one look at his face assured her that he didn't share her pleasure in the discovery.

"What the hell are you doing?" he demanded.

"Matt, it's her skull—the younger sister's skull. The story was true. History. We all knew that she had been murdered by her older sister."

"Put it down immediately," he admonished harshly.

She stared at him, confused, frowning.

"Down, put it down!"

Slowly, she did so. "What on earth is the matter with you?" she demanded. "Look, whether you believe in any of this or not, you don't have to be such a jerk. I've found her skull. We can bury it with her body. That would just be human decency."

He hunkered down by her, looking at the skull that now lay on the freshly dug earth. He didn't touch it, but stared at her again. "Keep your hands off it."

"But—"

"You've got a human skull there. And I'm the sheriff."

She looked at him then in total disbelief. "But...this

murder took place well over a hundred years ago! What are you going to try to do—arrest someone?''

"How do you know that?"

"What do you mean, how do I know that? We both know the story."

He waved a hand in the air, dismissing her outrage. "Are you a bone expert as well, Miss Tremayne?"

Anger took slow root in her, and, along with it, a sinking feel of desolation. Dammit, he knew it. He knew as well as she did that the skull had been in the earth for eons. And there was something about the way he was hunkered down, near her, yet a million miles away. He wasn't going to admit that she had found the skull, that she was right, and that she had somehow come upon it through extrasensory perception. At the same time, he knew in his gut that was just what she had done. He drew away. He didn't believe in her power, but he was still repulsed by it, maybe at some instinctive level of his own.

"All right. There's your skull. What are you going to do about it?"

"I'm going to see that it's properly handled."

"It belongs to a poor, young, innocent girl who was brutally murdered by someone she loved and trusted. To handle it properly, you merely need to get the records out and see that her head is buried with her body," Darcy said angrily.

"You can guarantee me, beyond a doubt, that this is her skull?" he said scornfully.

"Yes."

"Well, that's not the way the law works."

"You're being ridiculous."

"I'm doing my job."

Darcy stood up and dusted her hands on the sides of her jeans. "Fine. You do what you have to do," she said, and started walking away from him.

She felt his hand fall upon her upper arm. Hard. When he swung her back, there was too much force to his touch.

She stared at his hand, stared at his eyes. He released her instantly.

"Do you go around finding body parts all the time and just burying them because you're convinced they have to be ancient?"

"No."

"No to which?"

"We both know whose head this is!"

"Whether we do or not, human remains have to be handled properly. Legally."

Her eyes fell. Maybe he was right on that. And maybe she was just dismayed by the horror she had seen in his eyes when he had watched her with the skull.

"All right, Sheriff. I bow to your very logical and legal reasoning. If you'll excuse me, though, I think I'll head back for a shower."

He nodded, those gray eyes still on her. She felt a strange hurt inside, and she was furious with herself. Matt Stone had been a hostile force from the very beginning. She'd been an idiot to let any measure of attraction form between them. And yet...attraction didn't *form*. It existed. It existed right then as they stood in the woods, as they stared at one another. Something in the air, alive, electric, static. She'd never felt such an urge to come close to another person, press against him, feel his arms wrap around her. She was certain that the sheer heat dancing in the air emitted from him. And she was equally certain that no matter what his raw desire, the static erupted from his mind, like a wild wind that pushed away, even as it pulled.

She suddenly wanted to shout that she wasn't a leper.

But in his mind, maybe she was.

She turned and walked away, striding to Nellie without looking back. She mounted, turned the horse toward home, and never turned her head.

Anger filled her. To anyone else, she might have just proven that she did have certain psychic abilities. Not Matt. He wouldn't begin to understand her job. That yes, Harrison Investigations could come in and prove if something wasn't right—if there was indeed a fake, a trickster, creating ghosts or hauntings for their own purposes—be it simple amusement or something illegal. But when phenomena were real, they tried to find out *why,* what had happened, why ghosts couldn't move on. And then they tried to help them.

She'd helped Amy. And the idiot, Matt Stone, should realize that it meant she could discover the truth about his house. And that it *should* be discovered, because it was something even stranger than she'd ever encountered before.

Something far more sinister.

And it didn't seem that even Josh could help her here, as he so often could.

When she could solve a mystery and help heal a lost soul, she loved what she did. Which was wonderful, because far too often her work was frightening, and she felt such deep sympathy so many times that it was painful. And yet, a day like today was so incredibly rewarding!

Except that it had to come with a man like Matt Stone! The great unbeliever.

She knew that he hadn't moved.

And he wouldn't move, not for a while.

He would watch after her long after Nellie took to the trail.

It was late, but it didn't matter. Matt sat at his desk back at the station, doing nothing.

He'd called out a few of his men, and the skull, and the surrounding dirt, though disturbed, had been properly boxed for forensic study.

Because he'd known that Darcy was right about the identity of the skull, he'd had it taken straight to friends at the Smithsonian who specialized in the field, and he knew that he'd get a report back in the morning that the skull was well over a hundred years old.

So he found himself sitting in his office, doing nothing. His door was closed. At first, he'd pretended to be busy with paperwork. Then, he'd given up all pretense, sat back in his chair, laced his fingers behind his head, and stared into space.

The image returned to him again and again.

Darcy, digging.

Darcy with the skull.

Her cry of triumph.

It gave him the creeps.

But not really, and it should have. She was fucking weird. No. Yes.

She was, and it didn't matter. She was still inordinately attractive to him, arresting. More. *Seductive.* He should want nothing to do with her. He wanted to be closer to her, instead. He wanted to talk to her, know what made her tick, understand her background. He loved the sound of her voice, the inflections in it. He was equally fascinated by every flick of her eyes, her slightest movement. She could have so much energy, move so quickly and fluidly, and then show such cool poise and reserve that she was maddening.

If he stayed at work, he could keep some distance. He needed distance. If anything was really *hauntingly* mysterious, it was the allure she seemed to hold for him. So she was good-looking—many women were. All right, so she was sinuous, sensual, and fluid as a cat. Other nearly-perfect people also had such seductive quality.

Not like this woman.

Maybe it was the secrets, or the knowledge in her eyes.

Why the hell couldn't he be repulsed. Christ, she'd been digging in the dirt like a gopher!

There was a rap on his door.

"Yeah?"

He pulled his feet off his desk top as he called out.

Deputy Harding, charged with the graveyard shift, opened his door and peeked in. "Everything all right?"

Alan Harding was young. A good age to keep peace between midnight and eight. Sandy-haired, blue eyed, nearly six-four, and capable of controlling the occasional rowdy drunks who called for law enforcement at that hour.

"Yeah, everything is fine. Why?"

"Just…er, checking. You don't usually sit around in here this late, that's all."

Matt arched a brow. "How late?"

"It's nearly two."

"A.M.?"

Harding grinned. "That is my shift."

"Yeah, sure." Matt scratched his cheek. "Yeah, I was just leaving."

He rose, taking his hat from the peg on the wall. "Call me if—"

"If I need you, yessir," Alan said, a cleft in his chin deepening along with his smile. "Heard you found an old skull out in the woods today."

"I didn't find it."

"The psychic found it, huh?"

He stiffened. Why the hell did he hate it when people referred to Darcy as a psychic? That's what she claimed to be.

He didn't believe in psychics. Refused to believe in psychics.

"Miss Tremayne, from Harrison Investigations, found the skull, if that's what you mean."

"She must be for real, huh?"

Matt settled his hat on his head. "She can read, and she apparently likes libraries. That's why the name of the company has the word *investigations* in it, Alan."

"Sure—sir!" Alan said.

Matt shook his head and walked out, throwing over his shoulder, "Call me if—"

"If we need you," Harding finished for him again.

Matt muttered beneath his breath. When he exited the station, a low-lying fog sat on the ground. And despite himself, he suddenly felt an intuition of unease. What the hell had he been doing at the station so late?

Deepest night.

He should have been at Melody House for hours now.

His strides were long as he headed for his car. And he was damned glad that he was the sheriff right then because he far exceeded the speed limit as he headed home.

It should have been an entirely triumphant and peaceful night for Darcy. She knew that she had done well. And usually, to go with some of the torture that her existence afforded her, she was able to feel something like serenity and satisfied pleasure at a job well done.

But that night…

Dinner should have been fun. Penny, Clint, and Carter had all been excited about her find. Clint and Carter had vied for her attention, Penny had studied her like a wise old sage who had known her stuff and was proud as a peacock herself for being the one to insist that Harrison Investigations be called into the house. Even old Sam Arden, caretaker, had seemed to eye her with a new respect. It was almost as if she had become the accepted matriarch of a village, having proven her mettle. None of them seemed ill at ease with her, though both Clint and Carter kept asking, in different ways, just how she had managed to do it. She refused to explain exactly how, just saying that she had researched the story at the library, and put two and two together. Clint, however, shook his head.

"Two and two don't naturally add up to four in a forest! You're amazing. Simply amazing. You do have a special and unique gift."

"You've got to explain how you really found the skull," Carter told her.

"Research," she told him. But she couldn't help a smile. "That's what we do—investigate."

"That ghost in the Lee Room is going to be sorry!" Penny commented.

"Maybe you've really got to be careful," Clint said, somewhat worried and subdued then. "I mean, maybe it's a ghost that doesn't want to be known, and it will be more violent, because it's afraid of you."

"What do you mean?" Carter had said, frowning.

"Ghosts only come out because they want to be discovered," Sam Arden had surprised them all by saying. And when they had stared at him, he had continhued with, "Like serial killers. They always taunt the police because somewhere, in their subconscious, they want to be caught."

There had been a few minutes of unease, but then Clint had announced that he had some special champagne. Darcy accepted her glass and slipped out to take a walk to the porch. Clint found her there.

"You know," he'd told her softly, "he's only such a jerk because he's afraid."

"What?"

"Matt. He's afraid."

"You've lost me. Matt is really afraid of ghosts?"

That brought Clint's devastating, deep-dimpled grin into play along with a spate of laughter. "Matt? Afraid of ghosts? No. He's not even afraid of whackos with guns and knives. He's afraid of you."

"Why would he be afraid of me?"

Clint had joined her against the rail. Tall, lean, charming. And very handsome. She wondered why she couldn't feel an almost painful physical draw to him.

He'd reached out to smooth down a stray strand of her hair.

"Because he really likes you—and respects you—but doesn't want to. Because you're a beautiful redhead."

That had brought a smile from her. "Thank you. That's sweet. It's also bull."

Clint shook his head. "His wife was a total bitch. She was insane over him at first, but he couldn't be deterred from the house or his work, and she just wasn't the kind who could live long without playing hard—all over the globe. Then she started to think that he had lost interest in her, and she tried to make him jealous. Wrong move with Matt. It just turned him off completely. But she did have her ways. So...when the marriage went all to hell, it left a nasty taste in his mouth.''

''For redheads.''

''A certain kind of redhead.''

''Great. I'm a *kind* of redhead?''

''Cool. Smooth. Sophisticated.''

''Sophisticated, huh?''

''A kind of sophistication that no one can acquire if it isn't just natural. So...Matt is going to act like a jerk. That's why you should forget all about him, and realize just how attractive I am.''

''You're very attractive.''

''But you're just not interested. Still...you change your mind, I'm around. Ready to rush to your defense at any moment.''

''Hopefully, I won't need any defenders.''

''Don't crush my crusading spirit!''

''If I do need a defender, I'll be delighted that you're there. How's that?''

''A crumb!'' Clint told her, but he was grinning, and he slipped an arm around her shoulder as he led her back into the house.

Penny had hot tea and scones prepared when they got inside. When it had hit eleven, Darcy had yawned, excused herself, and gone to bed. Her room had seemed cold and cavernous that night, despite the warmth outside.

She'd opened the balcony door, certain herself that nothing evil was coming from outside the room.

Whatever watched her had a place within.

She watched a late-night show on TV, giving it half-hearted attention.

Something waited within the room.

She did so herself.

Well after midnight, she was still certain that Matt hadn't returned. And still, some time after that, she drifted to sleep.

Soon after, she began to dream again, entering into the

world of another. Vaguely, in a subconscious place, she knew that she dreamed once again. This time as another…

Before, she had dreamed as a man, coming to the house.

This night, she entered the soul of the woman who had waited.

She'd not begun the evening with any great sense of fear or urgency. Indeed, she'd been angry herself, and ready to fight, argue, speak her mind—and change her life. She'd not thought a thing about going to bed that night.

She was certain that he would not come. All that raged between them was too close, too tense, too passionate.

She was furious!

By the dim light, she sat down at her desk and began to write. He could do what he wanted. She couldn't stop him.

But he was going to pay.

Yet, as she set out to write, pulling out a sheet of stationery with her personal emblem, she paused. It was a beautiful night. Cloudless, allowing even the gibbous moon to cast a serene glow over the rolling hills of the countryside beyond the window. For a moment, a sense of hesitance settled over her. There was so much here, so much between them.

Ah, but…

She had been betrayed. He had betrayed her.

She started to write. From somewhere near, she heard the whinny of a horse. A dog began to howl and bark. Oblivious she set to her task, determined. The die had been cast.

Then…

A sound.

Darcy awoke with a start. The sense of sharing another's dream, of *being* that person, reliving the past, fell from her as if she had doffed a cloak from her shoulders.

And yet, blinking in the shadowed room, she struggled to fathom what had awakened her. Had it been the sound she heard within the dream?

No…

She listened, and was certain that she had heard something.

Out on the balcony.

Footsteps, slow, quiet, furtive.

She bit into her lower lip, silent and dead still for a moment. Then she slipped from beneath the covers, stepped out of the bed and rose, slowly, quietly. Her bare feet made no sound on the soft Persian rug beneath the bed. She prayed that a floorboard wouldn't creak.

Carefully, she moved across the floor to the balcony. Standing behind the softly billowing drapes, she looked out. Nothing. Nothing, but the moon in the sky, and a gentle breeze. She moved out, one slow step at a time, and still, nothing.

With a sigh, Darcy frowned and walked to the railing.

Then she heard it again. Something…just a sound, a scratch…from behind her. She started to turn.

She saw nothing but a whir of darkness. She felt the quick whack of something hard against her head like a bolt of lightning out of the blue.

Not hard enough to knock her out. Hard enough, however, to make her stagger, fall to her knees, cry out.

And see nothing more…

She brought her hand to her head, more furious than hurt. The whack hadn't been at all deadly, and her head wasn't spinning. As she staggered up, the balcony doors next to her own burst open.

And there was Matt. Clad in Calvin Klein black knit boxers, and nothing more. Staring at her as if a lunatic had decided to knock on his door in the middle of the night.

"What the hell are you doing?" he demanded.

Perhaps it looked a little strange. She realized that she was standing directly in front of his French doors, disheveled and barely dressed. She'd opted for her favorite type of nightgown that night rather than the long T-shirts she often wore to bed. It was white, diaphanous. Sleeveless, with Victorian lace around the bodice. Her hair was all over. She might have resembled the mad Lady of Shalott.

"I...there was something out here," she said.

He lifted a brow, leaned back slightly, and crossed his arms over his chest. "The ghost is hanging around on the balcony?"

"I don't think so."

"You don't think so?"

He was mocking her, of course. Aggravated herself, she too crossed her arms over her chest and tried for a look of dignity. "I heard something out here. It woke me."

"Did it whisper in your ear?"

"Stop that, will you? I think that there was someone out here."

"Alive or dead?"

"Some*one*. Alive."

He continued to stare at her skeptically, but then stepped past her. She could hear him swearing beneath his breath, but he did at least seem willing to take a look around. He walked the length of the balcony. When he disappeared around the corner, she felt a strange sense of loss and a chill invading her. Time seemed to stand on end, to stretch out, and the cold—despite the balmy night—to seep into her bones. How long could it take him to walk the circumference of the wraparound balcony? Granted, it was a big house, but....

She stared to the left, watching the corner where he had disappeared. Hesitantly, she walked toward it herself, then nearly screamed to high heaven when she felt a touch upon her shoulder.

Jumping half a mile, she swirled around and saw that Matt was back.

"I can't find anyone," he told her, his voice polite, and still curt.

"Wait a minute here," she said angrily, planting her hands on her hips. "You're the one so convinced that there aren't any ghosts, that some kind of real, outside force is causing the 'haunting' here. So why are you so mad when I think that I've heard someone prowling around on the balcony?"

He had that chiseled stone expression one that she had learned when she had first met him at the Wayside Inn. His arms were still crossed over the breadth of his chest.

"Sorry. But I didn't hear anything. And I have really sharp ears."

"Even when you're sleeping?"

"Even when I'm sleeping."

"You still might have missed something."

"Anything is possible."

"Glad to hear you believe that."

"I think I told you to keep your balcony doors locked. If I'm not mistaken, *you* seemed to be the one totally oblivious to danger in the night."

For a moment she was still, locking her jaw as she stared at him.

"Someone hit me in the head!" she said, indignant.

"What?" His attitude changed. He stepped forward, lifting her chin, searching out her eyes. "You were hurt?"

She shook her head, still feeling his fingers against her cheek and chin. He was too close, but she didn't draw away. "I'm not...hurt. But there was someone here, and...well, I don't...it was just a way for the person to disappear."

"A real person?"

"Yes."

"Not like Clara. She said that a ghost struck her in the face. You didn't fall...trip...or bang your head another way?"

There was concern, and more. Maybe he was feeling a certain triumph, as she had that afternoon. He didn't believe in ghosts. Well, he had ghosts, whether he wanted them or not. But this time, he had been right. A real person had been on the balcony.

"There was someone—flesh and blood—out here tonight," she said. He hadn't moved. The scent of his skin seemed very rich, and ridiculously intoxicating. She didn't want to move. She wanted to lay her head against his bare chest.

He was closer, somehow.

His finger-feathered over her hair then, touched down gently on her temple. "Where…uh…were you struck?"

"I…uh…side of the head."

"Is there a bump?"

She shook her head. "I don't think so."

"Are you dizzy?"

"No." A lie, but her state of physical rubber had nothing to do with the knock on the head.

"You're all right? Really all right?"

His breath caressed her forehead. Her lips were dry. She nodded, still not moving. His hands still cradled around her head. Her lips could almost brush his flesh.

"I'm…fine."

Then he tilted her chin again, looked into her eyes. A hint of five o'clock shadow teased his cheeks. His dark hair was sleep-mussed. His body seemed to emit heat like a radiator, making the night chilly, and the length of him a beacon. Tension gripped his muscles, appeared with his every breath. She could hear his heart beat. And her own.

"This would be crazy," he whispered.

"You bet," she agreed, and yet, still, neither of them moved, and the breeze seemed to grow cooler, making the rise of tension between them a delectable, taunting warmth.

Then the warmth of his breath touched her ear and just the timbre of his voice created a cascade of hot blood rushing through her veins.

"Are you feeling crazy?" he asked.

"Totally insane," she whispered back.

His hand molded around her chin again and a moment later, his mouth covered hers. It should have been a slow and gentle kiss, a getting-to-know-you kiss, and it started out that way. But the very movement erupted almost instantly into something else, deep, consuming, passionate, ravaging. Maybe it was the way his arms wrapped around her, or that last eighth of an inch between their bodies was pressed away, the feel of the full length of his form, the sheerness of her clothing, the raw feel of the so nearly naked man. Their mouths clung together, tongues became weapons of seduction, and just standing in the night, a violent hunger seized them both, and the kiss was the most sweepingly carnal she had ever experienced, the very movement of his lips, teeth, and tongue seeming suggestive of everything that was to come. It wasn't her, Darcy thought, realizing that she responded with blatant urgency, almost awed, wanting everything and more. Life didn't usually offer her such a feast, and their exchange had been the truth, for this was lunacy. But there was no thought about tomorrow, what she did, what he did, thought, or believed. Tomorrow did not exist, for as he held her, as his mouth seared her, as the force of his arousal pressed and drummed and taunted, there was nothing she could care about except for the culmination of the storm of wonder that swept through her with such fantastic force.

Darcy felt as if she melted against him, as simply as dew against the grass when the sun rose, and she was grateful for and almost oblivious to the arms that held her, lifted her then, and carried her through the balcony doors. *His* room, not the Lee Room, she noted vaguely, too aware of the feel of his sinew in his arms, the cut of his face as he made his way to the bed. The surroundings didn't matter. The sheets were cool and clean and smelled of fabric softener, and the mattress was deep and inviting, but not even that mattered; steel at her back wouldn't have mattered because his lips had trailed from hers to her throat, and she was still in the sheer gown, which seemed no barrier. The feel of his mouth closing over her breasts, the searing wetness over and through the fabric, and his tongue chaffing her nipple sent streaks of lightning ripping through the length of her. Her fingers tore through her hair as he leaned against the bed, lowering himself against her, she was aware of his hands at her side, long, powerful, handsome hands, as arresting as...

The feel of his mouth, almost agonizingly erotic over the fabric of her gown, lowering over her abdomen, lowering still. And then those hands, those glorious hands, slipping at last beneath the fabric, and his touch on her thighs, so intimate, too intimate, and yet all that they must be for this insanity, stroking and caressing into the core of her. And then the touch of his tongue, blazing with intensity, arresting every vein and muscle within her, creating fire within every fiber of her being. And at that moment, there wasn't the least surge of hesitance, of inhibition, within her, not a thought that they were not seasoned lovers, that this kind of shattering contact should take time, knowing, caring....

There was simply response, for every action, a reaction, and she followed every law of physics, spiraling, arching, twisting, and gasping with every electric jolt of lightning that filled and awakened her. She had to touch, stroke, taste, caress and evoke in return, and in minutes, they were tangled flesh and limb. She flourished, as if long accustomed to an arid life, her world had suddenly been filled with the thrill of a waterfall, and in the end, she wanted so much that it couldn't be, that a hoarse and gasped out cry of impatience ripped from his lungs, and they were truly melded together. The shock of his body thrusting fully into her own sent another wave of climactic ripples tearing through her, and then the night became nothing but movement, urgent, yearning, fast and spinning. Man and flesh, bed beneath, the world rocking, and vague impressions of the tension in his face, the fire in his eyes, the hunger…and then…a catapult stiffness, ejaculation, and her climax, so violent, volatile, complete and almost devastating that she cried out, shuddering like leaves blown in winter, again, ripples of aftermath sweeping over her again and again until they subsided slowly to nothing more than the gasps of breath that still tore from her lungs.

And then…

The truth of shadows. The balcony doors, still open to the night. The massive size of his bed, the books on the shelves nearby, the very real feel of the person beside her, the one who had mocked her, who didn't believe in ghosts, who had stared at her in such horror when she had found the skull.

She stared at a mote of shadow dust, almost like a miniature star, dancing in a pale ray of moonlight. He stroked a hand through her hair, brushing it from her face, and despite what she had always thought of as the honesty of her life, she curled against him with a soft groan, burying her face against his chest, far from the gray eyes that seemed to see far too much within her, in daylight, shadow, and even darkness.

"Sh!" he murmured softly, and she realized that reality had come back far more quickly to him, or perhaps, it had never left him.

"What?"

"I think someone is downstairs."

"Someone…up to something?" she asked a little anxiously, and rose against him enough to see his face. He was smiling, a slow, lazy, rather self-satisfied smile. He cast an elbow behind his head to rest against it as he studied her.

"Actually," he murmured politely, only a trace of amusement in his tone, "I think that we might have awakened the living and the dead."

Shadows could never hide the flood of crimson that came to her cheeks. "Lord! I'm sorry," she mumbled quickly, suddenly thinking to escape.

His arm was around her. She wasn't moving.

"Are you?" he asked quietly. "I'm not." For a moment, he was sincere, and there was something in his face and in his tone that caught at her, heart and soul. But then he added, "Do you really think we might have awakened the dead?"

And she knew that in his way, he still laughed at her.

She pushed away from him, meaning it, and he released her. It was frustrating to discover that she couldn't find her nightgown, it had become so entangled in the covers.

"Hey!" he said softly, drawing her back. And she was

forced to meet his face, and he asked, "*Are* you sorry? Because, most sincerely, I am not."

"You do think I'm a fake," she informed him, a frost of ice coming to her words.

He shook his head. "No. Never a fake."

She arched a brow. "Are you referring to life—or sex?"

Again, that slow lazy smile that might have broken a hundred hearts. "Both, maybe."

"There's no future here," she said, somewhat primly.

"Does everything have to have a future?"

She shrugged. "No, maybe not. Could you move? You're on my nightgown."

"Going somewhere?"

She nodded firmly. "Back to the Lee Room."

"Then I'm coming with you."

She was startled, staring at him. He shifted, producing her gown. Then he rose, found the black knit boxers and a terry robe, and looked back at her. She stared at him, shimmied back into the gown.

"You don't have to—"

"Do you mind?"

"I—no."

"Then let's go."

"I'm not sure if this should be…a habit," she said.

He smiled. "Never thought of it as a habit."

"You're incredibly exasperating," she told him.

But he paused then, in front of the balcony doors, and again, his thumb and forefinger touched her chin.

"May I come with you to the Lee Room, if you find it so important to sleep there? We will, however, lock the balcony doors. I don't feel like entertaining any tricksters in the middle of the night."

"Maybe you shouldn't come. Maybe I make great bait for the trickster," she said.

Something hardened in his jaw. "You're not bait, and whatever the hell you do, don't go thinking that way." He turned, drawing her with him. Inside, he locked the balcony doors.

"You left your balcony doors open," she pointed out.

He shrugged. "No one has ever disturbed anything in my room. I simply don't want anyone in here. With us."

She was amazed to realize that just the sound of his voice made her shiver again. Thrill throughout.

Then he walked toward her. "Trust me, no one will disturb us tonight."

"But—"

She was drawn back into his arms. "Darcy, let it go, please. Give us this. Let it be normal. Not normal. Incredible. But still...let tonight be. Just be...normal."

And then...

The feel of his lips.

And then everything that was raw and real and somehow still magic started all over again, and yet, this time, a thought crept into the blindness of passion.

If only...

If only this could be a reality...

If only she really were...

Normal.

7

The day was a surprise, Penny thought, sipping her coffee and staring over the rim at Clint and Carter.

But then, all days were a bit different now, and she loved it. Darcy Tremayne had changed everything at Melody House. This, however, was amusing.

"How on earth do you think that she found that skull when no one else ever could?" Clint said, shaking his head as he added jam to his English muffin. "Creepy, huh? She must be for real."

Carter shrugged. "It's been out there for a long time. Maybe it's just that no one else ever really looked for it." Carter scratched his bearded chin. "Luck, maybe. Pure luck."

"Don't be ridiculous, gentlemen!" Penny protested. "She's the real thing."

"Oh, come on, Penny. No one really has extrasensory perception," Carter argued.

"She sure has a lot else," Clint murmured.

Carter offered a dry laugh. "But I think she's off-limits to us."

"He definitely has a thing for her," Clint agreed.

"Who?" Penny said.

They both stared at her as if she were totally blind.

"Matt," they said in unison.

"Oh," Penny said, settling back.

"And she's a redhead," Clint said, as if that made it all beyond comprehension.

"Tall," Carter said.

"Really built," Clint said.

"Regal."

"Really, really, built!" Carter repeated.

Penny leaned closer to the table. "Well, boys, I do think that you're both out of luck. Because I think that she may have a bit of a thing for Matt."

"But it's ridiculous," Carter said.

"Absolutely," Clint agreed.

"Why?" Penny demanded.

"Because she believes in ghosts," Clint explained, smiling broadly. "Matt is like old Stone Mountain. He'll never accept the idea that she might be psychic. Now me, I'm charming—and I have an open mind."

"Hell, the whole thing can't be real—can it?" Carter said, frowning. But then he forgot the main question. "Matt's still in lust, my friend," he advised Clint. "Lust can last a long time."

"Yeah, it had to be lust with Lavinia."

"Hey, we were all in lust when she first showed up."

"Lavinia," Penny intervened, "was a bitch."

"Ah, but she had us all fooled," Clint teased.

"Me? Never," Penny assured him. "She didn't have what it took to hold on to Matt."

"Well, sleeping around never did make a marriage work real well," Clint drawled sardonically.

"I don't think he cared by then," Penny said.

"Still, kind of uncanny—two redheads," Clint said.

"One a bitch—and one a psychic," Carter said amused. "Clint, surely, this field still has to be open to us."

"Matt will never really get involved with her," Clint agreed. "I, on the other hand, would not care in the least if such a woman communed with the ancients on a daily basis. I'd just thank heaven above that she was mine."

"Clint Stone, that was a lovely thought, and quite surprising from you," Penny applauded him.

"Yeah, and it's bullshit. You just think she's hot," Carter said.

"Hey!" Clint argued.

"Well, let's face it. She may be smooth, intelligent, cool, and lovely, but Matt is in lust. She's really not his type," Carter said.

"Really?"

They were all startled by the voice that spoke from the kitchen doorway. Penny actually jumped up, nearly knocking her chair over. She hadn't looked out yet, but it was nine in the morning and Matt was usually long gone by then.

Carter had the grace to flush. He shrugged. "She's a psychic," he said again, as if that explained his take on everything.

Penny, anxious to defuse a possible situation, broke in quickly. "Matt! I thought you'd left for the office long ago. I've never seen you home so late in the morning."

Clint looked down at his muffin. "Darcy does resemble Lavinia," he murmured.

"Not in any way, shape, or form," Matt said.

"Coffee?" Penny offered brightly.

"No, I'm late. I'm going in."

"Any word yet on the skull?" Carter asked.

"I'll find out when I get to the station."

"We all know that it belongs to our poor, decapitated miss of eons past," Carter said.

"Most probably," Matt agreed. "It's still a human skull, and there are laws regarding human remains."

"Of course," Carter said, looking at Matt. Then he shivered. "Scary, huh? Maybe Darcy knows things about all of us that we would just as soon no one knew."

Matt turned around and walked out.

"That is scary," Clint murmured.

"Oh, come on, why?" Penny tsked.

"Because it's quite true, we all have skeletons in our closets," Clint told her.

Shirley Jamison was, just like clockwork, at the front desk when Matt walked into the sheriff's station. She smiled at him, apparently not at all curious as to why he was late. Apparently, everyone had known that he'd worked late hours the night before.

"Hey!" She was a slim, attractive woman of about thirty-five, and truly pleasant. She loved her job, her husband, her two perfect little children. She'd been born in Stoneyville, and never had the least temptation to move elsewhere. Her husband, Ray, was a building contractor, and just as pleasant as Shirley. Matt used to wonder if there was something artificial about their constant cheer, but oddly enough they seemed to be a genuinely happy couple.

"Good morning."

"I heard you were here until the wee hours," she said. "I didn't expect you in so soon, but I was actually about to call you at home. Digger called."

Digger was actually Darrell Jordy, an exceptional osteo-anthropologist who worked at the Smithsonian museum in D.C.

"And?" Digger was a busy guy. He was given bones to study by police agencies across the country, not to mention the FBI. Matt had never expected him to get to the skull the first thing when he had walked in that morning.

She shrugged. "Just what you thought. The skull carbon dated at about a hundred and fifty years. He said he already told you it once belonged to a young woman, between fifteen and twenty-five years of age. Seems she fits right in with the old story about the jealous older sister who hacked up her younger sibling."

He shrugged. "Glad to hear it."

"They've already called from the newspaper, too. They want to know when you're planning to see that the head gets buried with the body."

"Exactly who called?"

"Max Aubry."

"Great."

Aubry would sensationalize the whole thing. Granted, they were a small town. And thankfully, in the local paper, small events were often given headlines. He still dreaded the kind of attention the skull was going to receive.

"Oh, come on, Matt! It is a great story. Sad, but now with an ending."

"Aubry will play up the ghost bit, then hone in on Darcy and Harrison Investigations."

"Well?"

He threw up his arms. Was the whole place ghost story crazy?

Crazy.

The word ricocheted in his head. He was definitely crazy. *In lust.* Who the hell had said it, Carter or Cliff? Did it matter? He wished that was the long and short of it. Every time he learned something new about her, he only wanted more. There was so much about her that was an enigma, but then looking into her eyes he could see the honesty, the fear, and most of all, the terrible wariness. As if any closeness was an enormous risk. Well, it was. She was…different. And he did have a guard up against her, it just wasn't doing him much good. The second he had risen, he had wanted nothing more than to lie back down beside her, feel the cool silk of her flesh, watch those eyes open, vulnerable if only for a second. She was truly the most sensuous and incredible lover he'd ever known, and maybe that had been half to do with him, because being with her made him just want so much more, and to be so much more himself. His world had changed because of a ridiculous chance meeting in the night.

A bizarre incident at that, because she was the ghost catcher, he was the rational man, and she had been convinced that there had been a real person out on the balcony, and he sure as hell hadn't found evidence of anyone when he had searched. When they'd opened Melody House to the public, they'd had alarms installed in the main house and the stables. Nuts. It was all simply nuts, and getting worse. And it was going to get worse. He simply would not accept the kind of sensationalism the media would try to put on this latest event. He could not accept that some kind of doorway to the dead had allowed her to find the skull.

But then, she had said that research had led her to it. Pray God she remembered that when talking to the papers. But he could see again the way she had looked, digging frantically, and then producing the skull. An image that had chilled him...

He should have thought of that before last night. But what the hell did either of them think that they were doing? It was sex in the twenty-first century. Most adults indulged on a whim now and then. He'd had his own share of too-casual relationships. Could be it was just another. Temptation and hormones and human instinct.

Except that it wasn't.

"Matt?"

"I'll be in my office," he said, a bit too gruffly. Shirley looked at him, puzzled. He couldn't explain.

Darcy woke at a quarter of eight, realized that Matt was gone, and tried to reflect on both the wonder and idiocy of the night gone by. But thinking about it merely made her head hurt.

Granted, she didn't have much of what could be called a social life, and as far as a sex life went, it certainly had been nonexistent for a very long time. That had been mainly her choice. But her college years had made her feel somewhat punch-drunk, and since she was afraid of the outcome of any involvement, it had seemed prudent to be a very private person. She had a loving family and good friends at Harrison Investigations, who understood what it was like to be different. She had never imagined such an overwhelming physical attraction to a man, and she had not envisioned that she could feel such an emotional pull to someone like Matt Stone.

The thought that last night had been a serious mistake came only this morning, when Darcy awoke. And along with it, of course, was the knowledge that she was going to get hurt, because she didn't seem able to put the relationship in any kind of perspective. She felt a tremendous aching for what happened with Matt to be something that could go on…and on. Amazing, when he had truly been such a jerk when they had met, how living in a man's house, knowing those who knew him well, could give so much insight to his life, and his true character. She hadn't felt this way since…well, maybe forever. And it was so foolish. She felt elated, having pushed so much that could be incredible between a man and a woman to the back burners of her existence, and also miserable, because a simple night had created a fantasy, a new excitement, and it was something that she well knew could never really be. Her bed now contained the simple, subtle scent of the man within it, memories of warmth and fire, passion and a closeness that remained staggering in its brief intensity.

She started to rise, then decided to screw the notion. She didn't have to be anywhere—other than exactly where she was. The day might look a little better and everything might make more sense if she just had a little sleep.

She would close her eyes for a few minutes more, and maybe get, at the least, just a bit more rest.

Yet even in a subconscious state, falling into a far deeper sleep than she had imagined, she knew when the dream state came, when the actions and emotions of the past slipped into her, almost as if she slipped into the skin of another. And she knew instantly, on that distant plane, that she had now encountered two people. First, a man, then a woman, and now a man again. And that what trauma had taken place between them had reached a heated pinnacle here, in this room, where she slept. She could see herself, below, at the door, though she couldn't make out face or form, because she was seeing from *his* eyes, as if the memories of long ago had entered her mind as completely as they had, at one time, touched his reality.

Staring up at the house, he knew that it was empty, except for her. *And so he stepped inside, quietly closing the door behind him.*

He knew the house. Knew those who usually peopled it, surrounded it, called it home, or laid a claim to the place. And he knew where they all were. Just as he was aware that she would have come here, thinking she had the right to do so.

She didn't have the right.

She had no rights.

And what she might have imagined had come to her through him!

There was nothing that night to bar his entry. As he had known. He didn't care if she had heard the door close. She would know he was there soon enough. He stood in the foyer, staring up the stairs, hands rapping idly against his pockets. He felt the bulge in the one. Ah, yes, the item he had stuffed in it earlier. A strip of leather from the stables. He pulled it from his pocket, stretched it out between his hands, tightened it until the leather was taut...

Easy to do. He was a strong man. Actually, quite strong. Stronger even than he appeared.

No...

A protest echoed in his head. A protest against himself.

He gritted his teeth, and the whole of his body was as taut as the strip of leather between his hands.

Slowly...

He forced himself to relax.

And he looked to the stairs again....

"Darcy! Darcy! Are you all right dear?"

Jostled from the dream, Darcy winced, bolting up. The rapping on her door sounded like thunder, and she rued the interruption with a deep dismay. She'd begun to see so much so clearly. And if only, she thought, she could see these images through, she would have the answers.

"Darcy!"

"Penny, I'm fine. Just overslept, that's all!" she called out.

"Thank God! I thought that maybe the ghost of the Lee Room had...well, never mind. I don't mind telling you that it makes me quite nervous, you sleeping in there alone at night!''

Darcy stared blankly at the door, wondering if Penny would feel better if she realized that she hadn't actually been sleeping in there alone last night.

''I—I'm fine,'' she repeated.

''Want me to bring you up a tray?'' Penny asked.

''No, no, I'll be right down, thanks.''

''Darcy?'' Penny persisted beyond the door.

''Yes?''

''I just had to tell you. You were so right—and so ingenuous! The skull you found was the poor younger sister. You're incredible! Well, we assume it must be her, of course, I mean, I think that's the only story we have about a young girl of that age. We have some other female ghosts, of course, but they all have their heads. You're amazing!''

''Thanks, Penny.''

''We'll get her buried—well, we'll get her head buried with her body!—and she'll be able to rest in peace, or something like that, right?''

''Something like that, yes,'' Darcy called.

''Well, I'll be down in my office if you need me. I'll leave fresh coffee in the kitchen for whenever you want it.''

''Thanks, Penny.''

She heard the housekeeper walk away as she closed her eyes. She opened them again. She wasn't going to be able to fall back asleep, and it wouldn't matter anyway, she didn't think. She had lost the slender cord of just exactly whatever it was that she could sometimes hold.

Darcy looked around the room and held still.

The presence was there, but…

In the background. Watching. Not coming forward. Waiting?

For what?

Josh, where are you? Why can't you help me in here? She thought.

No answer. She spoke aloud. "Josh?"

It wasn't that she'd ever had complete control of finding him. He was her spirit guide. John, a Shoshoni friend and another of Adam's employees, had once tried to explain to her. There beside her, with her, because he had loved her so dearly as a friend when he had lived.

And because, somehow, with his death, he had passed his strange gift—or curse—on to her.

"Josh, you helped me in the forest, why not here?"

But she knew. The sense of violence and bitterness that lingered in this room was too strong. Suddenly, she was anxious to get out herself.

Strange, Matt just being in the room had changed it so much....

She wasn't here to feel secure and safe. She was here to solve the puzzle.

She rose, unnerved, and wondering why. She had long ago accustomed herself to ghosts.

It was the living who could hurt you!

She had heard that often enough. And she had believed it, still believed it.

But then again...

She had never experienced things quite the way they were happening in the Lee Room.

There was no way not to talk to Max Aubry. Though Matt didn't return the call, Aubry caught him at one o'clock sharp, right when he was heading out to the Wayside Inn to get some lunch.

"Matt! Hey, I've been trying to get you on the phone."

"Yeah, sorry, I had a late night," Matt said. Aubry reminded him of a weasel. The guy was an inch or so taller than he was, which made him around six-four, but he was so skinny he appeared taller. Maybe because he couldn't seem to get an inch of either fat or muscle on his bones, he shaved his head for a fiercer look. Didn't help. He just looked like a hungry ferret.

"Tell me about the skull."

"I'm just heading out for some lunch."

"Great. I'll join you."

Max stared at him.

"Business appointment, huh?" Aubry said. He knew Matt didn't like him. It wasn't really a personal thing. Matt just thought that journalists were supposed to report the news, and not make up what they'd like to be the story that went with it.

"Give me something. I'm going to head out and interview that young lady working for you. I just thought that you might want to give me a word or two first."

"Sure." Matt stood still, feeling the summer sun. "Miss Tremayne is working for a firm called Harrison Investigations. They look into so-called *hauntings*. They do research on an area—and reveal when those who call themselves psychics are using fog machines to create ghostly images. We have a lot of folklore around here, which is usually based on fact. Every schoolkid in the area has heard about the headless girl in the forest. Miss Tremayne made use of the library to investigate the murder, determined where it must have taken place, and found the missing skull."

"So the ghost will no longer haunt the forest, is that right, Sheriff?"

"I was never of the persuasion that a ghost *did* haunt the forest," he said firmly. "And if you write anything different, Aubry, you'll have a lawsuit on your hands."

"Ah, come on, Matt!"

"I mean it, Aubry. You caused a poison scare here when Julie Cristopher had a stomachache one afternoon. The donut shop nearly had to shut down because you stated it was the last place she had eaten."

"It *was* the last place she had eaten."

"But she hadn't been poisoned! She told the doctor at the hospital that she'd drunk milk she probably shouldn't have because her brother had left it out on the table overnight!"

"Kids! What are you going to do?" Aubry said, brushing the complaint aside.

"I'm not a kid. And if you print a bunch of fiction, Aubry, I'll see you in court."

"All right, all right! You sure have got some hang-ups, Sheriff. Ghosts are good for a place like Melody House."

"Why in hell does everyone believe that?"

"Because the rest of the world has a sense of romance! But excuse me, go have your lunch. I'm sure your Yankee investigator will be a lot nicer. Sheesh!"

Aubry turned and walked away. Matt was tempted to call him back and somehow tell him not to go after Darcy.

But he couldn't.

Aubry had every legal right in the world to interview whoever he wanted.

He watched Aubry go, damning himself. He should have given the man some time, given him a better story, and he might have left Darcy alone. He considered calling Darcy to warn her. Tell her...what? Tell her that no matter what the hell she really believed, she had to tell Aubry that she didn't believe in ghosts?

Swearing, he headed for his car. As he slid into the driver's seat, he was startled to feel a strange urge to head somewhere, other than the Wayside Inn.

Library.

His fingers froze around the keys in the ignition. He could have sworn that he heard the word as clearly as if someone had spoken out loud to him.

Matt groaned, leaning his head against the steering wheel. They were all going to make him crazy. Had to be something on the back burner of his mind coming forward. And now, for some stupid reason, he kept hearing it echo.

Hell, no, he wasn't getting caught up in all this.

Angry with himself, he started to drive toward the Wayside Inn.

Then turned.

Darcy hadn't intended to go back to the library that day, but Penny was so determined to talk about the skull that she didn't think she could stay in the house. It wasn't that she didn't like Penny, and like her very much. She simply didn't want to try to explain just what her "extrasensory" perceptions were. She didn't understand it all herself— how on earth could she explain it all to another person?

Then, as well, both Clint and Carter had been in the house. And *they* had wanted to talk. Clint had been charming, but too curious, winking and asking her if she could help him find the cuff links he had lost last Christmas. Carter had simply wanted to talk, to know her past, what other mysteries she had unraveled. Both had seemed to want to probe her mind, and though she liked them both so very much, she had wanted equally to escape.

She had enjoyed the library and Mrs. O'Hara, and decided to take refuge there where she could research Amy Clayton's family. She was sure that someone in the area had to know where the family graveyard could be found, but the library, she was certain, would have local records.

She knew the minute she saw Mrs. O'Hara that the woman had heard she had found the skull. It was a small town. News traveled quickly. But Mrs. O'Hara didn't question her, other than to ask if she wanted tea. Darcy decided to accept a cup. Mrs. O'Hara had a nice sense of perception herself—she found the record book Darcy wanted behind the desk, as if she'd searched for it as soon as she'd heard the news.

"If you're looking for anything else local," Mrs. O'Hara told her, "just head up to the loft level." She pointed to stairs which led to the walkway that circled the perimeter of the upper floor. The intricately carved railings made it seem almost as if the library had originally been built as a grand old home, rather than as a public facility. Mrs. O'Hara grinned, seeing her look up and around. "Originally, this *was* part of an old plantation. It belonged to a man named Geoffrey Huntington, and he was very good friends with Thomas Jefferson, among other notable men. But he was a Loyalist, and the main house was burned during the Revolution. Luckily, he had this structure planned as an outbuilding, his own private retreat, and the furious Patriots were happy to keep his book collection alive and well, since he was forced out of the country. It's beautiful, isn't it? And everything is original. Except for some of the books, of course. Thankfully, the place was very large, because over the years we've accumulated many fine collections of books.''

''It's an extraordinary library,'' Darcy told her sincerely.

''On the National Register of Historic Buildings,'' Mrs. O'Hara said proudly. ''We may have to add on soon, though.''

''I imagine that it's far better for a library to have too many books than too few,'' Darcy said.

''Naturally!'' Mrs. O'Hara agreed.

With her cup of tea and the old book Mrs. O'Hara had already found for her, Darcy curled up in one of the stuffed armchairs on the ground floor and began to read.

The Clayton family had left the area in the late-eighteen hundreds. They had, however, arrived in the mid-seventeen hundreds, and had maintained a family plot in the Christ's Church burial ground. The record book—a horribly boring tome—listed family names, occupations, marriages, baptisms, deaths, and little more, but it actually offered a plot map of Christ's Church and the surrounding graveyard. It wasn't far from Melody House at all. Once the skull was deemed ancient by the proper authorities, Darcy assumed there would be no difficulty seeing that it was buried along with the rest of poor Amy Clayton.

She set the book down and looked up the stairway, noting again just how exceptionally fine the building was. Naturally, since a wealthy and influential man—who had apparently loved reading and books—had planned it for himself. But still, few towns could possibly have such a gem of a library. The stairway was winding, the wood old and polished, and it appeared that even the runner on the stairs was as old as the facility.

She decided that it was time to set the record book aside and head up to see what else she could find.

At the top of the stairway she discovered that the flooring of the loft was really little more than scaffolding. The runner extended only up the stairs, then curved into an arch at the landing, while the flooring itself then became polished wood, apparently very well tended.

Darcy began to peruse the different books. Some would be of little interest to anyone other than people who found their own family names, and yet she thought that it was quite wonderful that so many people from the area might come here and find out about ancestors. There were books with nothing more than family names on them, or titles that explained their contents exactly, such as *Marriages among the Grangers of Stoneyville,* and *The Murtons Who Attended Grace Church.* She smiled, slipping out a volume now and then, and finding most to be very old. It seemed that people hadn't kept such simple record books in a very long time. Or maybe, life just hadn't been that simple in a very long time.

A book on a high shelf caught her eye. *The Stones of Melody House.* She was delighted to see it, and once again, touched by the people of decades past who had found every little detail of life worthy of recording.

Deciding it was one volume she definitely needed to read, Darcy started to reach up for it. She was tall but she really had to stretch.

As she balanced on both toes, she heard a sudden creaking sound from the boards under her feet. Even as she frowned, the floorboard directly beneath her suddenly gave.

She grabbed frantically for the shelf in front of her. Too late, because it had all happened too quickly. For a second frozen in time, she staggered where she stood, knowing that the wood beneath her had failed, and that she was going to crash into a sheer drop. She was disbelieving, even as the simple rules of physics tore at the weight of her body.

She cried out, a whoosh of air escaping from her lungs as she felt herself suddenly plunge downward.

She grasped out desperately for any hold, all the while wondering, *How? Why? Mrs. O'Hara would never have sent anyone upstairs if it wasn't safe—*

The sound of wood crashing to the floor below came to her ears just as she managed to reach out and grasp hold of the nearest crosswise support beam. Her downward impetus was so strong that her desperate scramble for hold caused instant agony in her shoulder sockets, and yet, there was an instant of relief and incredulity when she realized that she had stopped herself.

For the moment.

For the moment, yes, only the moment, her grasp upon the crossbeam was so tenuous, and it already seemed that her fingers were slick with perspiration and slipping.

Another scream sounded, and not from her own lips.

It was Mrs. O'Hara, crying out from beneath her.

And it was then that she fully realized herself that she was dangling from the crossbeam, her legs swinging a good twenty feet above the floor below.

She rued the long-ago wealthy plantation owner who had designed such a library.

"Hang on! Hang on!" Mrs. O'Hara cried out to her. "I've called 911. Books! I'll pile some books, the cushions from the chairs, just hold on dear, hold on!"

No other thought had occurred to Darcy, but even as the woman called out, Darcy could feel the terrible pressure on her arms and shoulder blades. She hadn't really realized her own imminent danger until that minute—she had only congratulated herself on catching hold of the crossbeam.

But how long could she hold on?

Mrs. O'Hara had dialed 911. Darcy wasn't certain that help could be there momentarily. And still....

It had been seconds, surely. No more than minutes. Her arms ached as if she had been stretched on a medieval rack. She wasn't a total weakling, but neither was she ready for championship wrestling.

"Darcy, oh, dear! Hang on, dear! There's help coming!" Mrs. O'Hara called to her.

Darcy looked down. She shouldn't have. The distance between her and the ground floor seemed gaping. Looking downward seemed to create a greater burden on her arms. She winced, grated her teeth, and began to fear that her fingers would slip no matter how she strained to hang on.

"I can't imagine how this has happened!" Mrs. O'Hara cried anxiously. "Please, please…hang on." There had been no one else in the small library at that time. Too early for the schoolchildren, and perhaps too late for any legal assistants or local researchers. Darcy felt faint, looking at the distance between her own dangling body and the puny little cushion Mrs. O'Hara was trying to arrange beneath her.

She closed her eyes, in agony, wondering if she would just break most of her bones if she gave up her hold, or if she'd break her neck and die as well. Despite the pain in her arms and the fear that any second they were simply going to wrench from their sockets, it seemed as if a haze of blackness was beginning to take over. She wondered desperately if she still had the strength to try to swing her legs upward and find a hold with her ankles and calves on the torn-up floor above her.

"Darcy?" Mrs. O'Hara called.

"I always knew I should have trained for Cirque du Soleil!" Darcy tossed back, wondering why she felt that she had to sound light and okay even though she definitely wasn't. She looked up at the hole in the floor. She'd have to kick through other boards to get back up. But if the one had given, then maybe…

Fingers, hands, and arms in anguish, she gave a swing, kicking at the boards above. She nearly broke her toes.

All the other floorboards were as tight as could be. The effort nearly cost her the tenuous hold she had on the crossbeam. Black dots were forming before her eyes. She clenched her eyes tightly, knowing she would lose her grip any second.

"Darcy!"

She was startled to hear Matt's voice. So much so that she thought she was losing her grip on reality.

"Darcy, it's me, Matt. Just let go. I'm going to catch you. Trust me."

Trust him. Just let go.

"Darcy, I'm below you. Let go. I won't let you get hurt."

Trust him...it had nothing to do with trust. She couldn't hold on any longer.

Her fingers were too stiffly wound around the cross-beam, but it didn't matter. They were slipping. She never really let go.

She simply fell, because her fingers lost their grasp.

And a scream of instinctive terror tore from her lips.

In the split second in which she fell, she anticipated her bones crushing, her blood splattering across the floor, her head...

"Darcy!"

8

Matt didn't fall, but staggered back as Darcy fell into his arms. The distance hadn't been so great, but she was naturally trying to resist the impetus of the fall upon her body, and she flailed wildly, desperately grabbing him as he caught her.

For a moment, they wavered, then he lost his balance, even if he did so with a certain amount of coordination. He went down upon his knees, cradling her against him. For several seconds, she had a death grip on him, and then her eyes met his, wide, those of a startled rabbit, and a shudder of relief went through her.

"You all right?" he asked quickly.

She nodded. Then her fingers went through his hair and she smiled. "You're covered in dust."

"Your shirt is ripped and your arm is bleeding," he told her.

"Oh dear, oh dear, oh dear!" Mrs. O'Hara said, hovering over them both. They could hear a siren then. A car from the station. "This was all so impossible! We have building inspectors in regularly! I walk on that floor all the time and I know that it's sound. Was sound. Oh, my God, I had thought that it was sound. The schoolchildren go up there when they're studying. Lord, it could have been a child, a little boy or girl who couldn't get a grasp to save themselves…oh, Darcy! I am so sorry! Matt, thank God that you arrived when you did."

Thank God that he had arrived when he did.

Strange chills ripped through him, and he stared at

Darcy, still in his tense grip as they both lay sprawled on the floor.

Darcy eased her hold from around Matt's neck, stumbling to her feet, offering him a hand to rise as well. He took her hand, but stood up on his own power. She was still shaking. She might be smiling, ready to make light of the whole thing, but it wasn't an incident that could be dismissed.

"Go ahead and put a Closed sign on the door, Mrs. O'Hara," Matt said.

"Yes, yes, of course," Mrs. O'Hara said, but still stood looking at Darcy. "The police car is coming but we need an ambulance."

"No!" Darcy protested. "I'm fine."

"Your arm is bleeding," Matt informed her firmly.

"A scratch. I'm all right, honestly. I just hope I didn't break any of your bones, falling on you as I did."

· She, too, was covered in dust, or sawdust, whatever had given with the flooring. As he stared at her, Matt heard the car outside screech to a halt; Thayer Martin and Jimmy Tyson came bursting into the library.

"It's all right!" Matt called out quickly, still staring at Darcy. *But it wouldn't have been all right. By the time they would have arrived, Darcy would have been on the floor. Maybe not dead, but surely, severely injured.*

"What the hel—heck happened?" Thayer demanded, staring at Matt and Darcy and the debris, and then Mrs. O'Hara.

"Flooring collapsed," Matt said briefly. He turned to look at his two officers who were surveying the damage with amazement. "Get the building inspector in here right away."

"Will do," Thayer told him, pulling out his radio. Matt was dimly aware that Thayer was calling the situation in, and that Jimmy was walking carefully around the downed boards. He couldn't take his eyes off Darcy, and he was suddenly feeling chilled and strange himself. *What in God's name had suddenly convinced him that he needed*

*to come to the library? If he hadn't been here. But he had
been. He never just drove to the library in the middle of
the day. But despite being determined to head for the Wayside Inn, he had come here.*

Another siren, and then, Jenkins and Smith from fire
rescue were coming through the door. Thayer briefed
them, and Smith headed for Darcy.

"We'll get you to the hospital, miss," Smith said politely, looking her over with a trained eye.

"I don't need to go to the hospital, please!" she insisted.

"Show him your arm, Darcy," Matt said curtly. Too
curtly. He saw her frown, but then she opted to turn with
Smith and allow him to take a look at her.

"Let's get you into a chair and take a look," Smith said.
Fifty-five, gray, bearded and bushy, Harry Smith was as
competent a man as any to be found anywhere. He had a
manner about him that was calming under the worst of
circumstances, and Darcy accepted his pressure on her
arm, taking a chair by the library desk.

Matt could hear them speaking softly as he strode the
stairs up to the loft himself to take a look at the spot where
Darcy had gone through.

Moving carefully along the floorboards, he got down on
his hands and knees as he neared the faulty area. It looked
as if a section of the boards had rotted right through. *Only
a section.* The library was hundreds of years old, he reminded himself.

So were half the buildings in the town. They were also
sound.

"Matt!"

He walked carefully to the railing to looked down.
Smith was staring up at him. "Miss Tremayne refuses to
come to the hospital. She says she's fine. We're going to
drive her back to Melody House. She wants to drive herself. Penny's car is here. Can someone take it?"

Darcy had jumped up beside Smith. "I am fine!" she
called up to him. "*I fell on you!*"

"You're still shaken up," Smith informed her.

"Really, I'm just fine. My arm is just scratched!" Darcy protested.

"I'll get Penny's car back," Matt said. "That's not a problem. Darcy, let them give you a ride. I'll be along in a bit. I want to be here when the building inspector shows up." He offered her a grimace and a wave.

"Honestly, I can drive," Darcy protested.

"I'm sure you can. Humor us all," Matt told her.

Looking up at him, her shirt ripped, covered in sawdust, she was still stunning. Hair wild and eyes large, body stiff with indignity, she was more appealing to him than ever.

The girl is strange, he tried to remind himself.

She was ethical, dignified, beautiful, and often remote, as well. There was something about her manner that cried out to him in a way that he had never known. Lust, sure. She was supple, sinuous, elegant, and entirely sensual in her every little movement. Somewhere under it all, she was also wounded.

He could only hurt her worse, he thought. And still...

He doubted that could keep him away.

"I'll be back to Melody House as soon as I can," he said.

She set her jaw out stubbornly, looked as if she'd protest again, then accepted Smith's arm, thanking him for his care and concern.

Penny waited anxiously at the door, having received a call from Mrs. O'Hara at the library. She raced out the moment she saw Smith's rescue vehicle pull up by the front door.

"You poor, poor dear!" she told Darcy, slipping an arm around her shoulders before she had quite managed to exit the car door. "Come right in. We'll get you going in a nice hot bath. That will ease your muscles. Then I'll make you some tea with whiskey—the Irish swear that it's a cure-all. Thank God you weren't hurt worse! It's a miracle. You might have broken your neck. Or every bone in your body. My God! How could we have let such a thing happen in Stoneyville?''

Darcy smiled at her. ''Penny, I keep telling everyone that I'm absolutely fine, and no one wants to believe me.''

Harry Smith had come around the front of the emergency vehicle and stood in silence, watching the exchange. ''Would you like some coffee or tea?'' Penny asked him. ''You're on duty, so I can't lace yours, of course,'' she said, disturbed that she sounded so prim. She had always liked him. Such an incredibly kind man, always so calm and capable. Her heart had simply bled for him last year when his wife, just fifty-two, had succumbed to cancer.

''Thanks, Penny, I'm going on back. I left my partner at the library to take a quick look at Matt. I've got to get him and get back to work.''

''Matt is hurt?'' Penny said anxiously.

''Not a bit. We just wanted to make sure.''

''Thank you,'' Penny said, still standing there, her arm around Darcy.

''Well, see you both later,'' Harry said. ''Miss Tremayne, you get a headache, anything out of the ordinary—''

''I never hit my head on anything, honestly,'' Darcy said.

He nodded, waved, walked around and got into the emergency van. Penny and Darcy watched him leave, then Penny collected herself. ''Poor thing! Up, up. Clara Issy even went into the Lee Room to get your bath going. In fact,'' Penny added, looking at Darcy wryly, ''she was up there yelling at the ghost.''

''Yelling at the ghost?'' Darcy said.

Penny hesitated, then said, ''Yes, dear. We were both thinking that…well, we're thinking that the ghost should just be left alone. We know that the ghost has violent urges, and we're afraid, that for some reason, the ghost is now out to get you.''

Darcy shook her head. ''The ghost is trying to tell us something, Penny. Not hurt me.''

"Come in, let's get you out of all that dirt and saw-dust," Penny said. She looked Darcy over. Mussed, yes, daunted, no.

"Honestly," she said softly, leading Darcy into the house. "I don't want you to take this the wrong way, but…I think you should leave."

"Penny!"

"Seriously."

"The ghost is supposed to be in the house, not the library!" Darcy said.

"But maybe this ghost is so disturbed by you that it followed you."

"And maybe the floorboards are just really old, and they gave."

"Well, go on up. Everything will certainly be more logical once we've all thought about it a bit," Penny said.

Darcy stopped at the foot of the stairs and stared at her. "Penny, weren't you the one who wanted someone to come here—to prove to Matt that there were ghosts, I believe."

"Yes, I was. But that was then, and this is now." Penny was exasperated. Darcy didn't seem to understand that she could really be in danger.

"Penny, honestly, I do believe there is a presence in the Lee Room trying very hard to make itself known, and understood. I don't believe it followed me to the library. What happened to me was frightening, but I'm fine, and it might have happened to anyone. It could have been a child, and Matt might not have been there in time."

"Yes, that's strange, isn't it?" Penny mused. How had Matt managed to be there at just the right time?

"Strange, perhaps, but lucky," Darcy said. Penny was startled when Darcy suddenly put her hands on her shoulders, drew her close, and gave her a quick kiss on the cheek. "I'm fine, Penny, and I'm not afraid of the ghost in the Lee Room. And I'm very determined. I'll run up and bathe, and be back down. That tea you were talking about sounds great. But don't go treating me like an invalid. I have a scratch on my arm, nothing more.''

Darcy ran up the stairs and Penny watched her go. She stood in the foyer on the first floor landing for a very long time, still staring long after Darcy had disappeared.

She shook her head.

It would be terrible if something were to happen to Darcy.

Just terrible.

She really needed to talk her into leaving.

Dan Platt was the building inspector called into the library. Naturally, and with Matt's full agreement and support, they were closing the library until a thorough inspection could be made.

Still, Matt wanted a preliminary report.

Dan, midforties, with iron-gray hair and a muscled physique, stood in his hard hat, hands on his hips. "Right now, it looks like the boards just gave."

"Why those boards?" Matt demanded.

"Leakage, maybe."

"There are no leaks. I looked at the roof."

"Sometimes, leaks can slip down the walls and into floors without being evident. There are other possibilities."

"Like what?"

"Something spilled there, maybe. Who knows? Maybe kids came in with some kind of acidic drinks, spilled them, and were too chicken to let Mrs. O'Hara know what had happened. A spilled drink that wasn't wiped up would definitely damage this old wood. I'm not sure, exactly, Matt. But it doesn't look as if there was any tampering, though why anyone would tamper with the library to begin with is beyond me."

"I'd still like an analysis done on the boards that gave out."

"Sure. If that's what you want."

"Definitely, it's what I want."

Dan looked at Matt as if he was going off the deep end,

but he said, "We'll do a thorough investigation, and see that the rotten pieces are analyzed."

Matt nodded. "Great."

Dan started back up the stairs. Matt stood in the now empty ground floor, and waited. When Dan and his workers had finished, Matt headed back up the stairs himself. It wasn't that he didn't have complete faith in Dan Platt. Nor did he have the least suspicion that Dan wouldn't do a thorough job.

Still…

He took an evidence bag from the pocket of his jacket and selected a piece of the rotten floorboard from the area beneath the local history sections.

Downstairs, he chose another.

At last, he exited the library, saw that the building was locked, and that the notice that the facility was closed was obviously displayed on the doors.

When he left, he didn't head home. He was taking a drive into Washington. On the way, he put a call in to Shirley, letting her know that he'd be out, but to call him on his cell in an emergency.

It wasn't a long drive. Still, the day would be gone by the time he returned.

"Hey!"

Darcy was sitting in the dining room with Penny, drinking her whiskey-laced tea, when Clint came rushing in. She was touched by the way he came to her instantly, hunched down and gave her a simple, but very warm hug. Then he backed away, his hands still on her arms, his eyes anxious. "Are you really okay?" he asked.

"Perfectly," she assured him.

"I've told her she should leave," Penny said firmly, lifting her cup for a long swallow of tea.

"Because of the library?" Clint said, straightening at last and staring at Penny with a frown.

"I think the ghost is following her," Penny said.

"Following her?" Clint repeated incredulously, sliding into one of the chairs at the table. "Penny, that's insane."

"Is it?"

Clint let out a long breath. "I'm not convinced there is a ghost."

"Then you're an idiot," Penny said primly.

Clint arched a brow to Darcy, smiling in amusement. "Penny, in the old days, I spent many a night in that room. You know it."

"How old are you now, Clinton Stone? Over thirty, right?"

"Penny—"

"You should have been married long ago, with a family of your own."

Clint sat back, his brows raised in surprise. "Penny, some people just aren't the marrying kind."

She shook a finger at him. "Some people just aren't mature and responsible!"

"Right. I should get married—like Matt did."

Penny looked abashed. "Lavinia seemed right for him at the time."

Clint sniffed, then grinned at Darcy. "See, there's always a way out of a tongue-lashing by Penny."

"Penny? Darcy? Where is everyone?" came a call from the foyer.

Carter. The household was all arriving, so it seemed.

"Dining room!" Darcy called out.

Carter came striding in. Like Clint, he made his way straight to Darcy, bent down on a knee, and took her hand. He looked earnestly into her eyes. "Are you all right?"

She smiled. "I'm fine. And I'm going to take out an ad in the newspaper soon, swearing that I'm fine." She looked at Penny and added softly. "And that I'm not leaving."

"Leaving? Why should you leave?" Carter asked frowning.

"Penny thinks the ghost followed her to the library and pushed the floorboards through."

Carter tried to hide a smile. "Why would the ghost do that? I thought that she was here to talk to the ghost."

"Go ahead, make fun of me, you ruffians!" Penny said indignantly.

Carter found a chair at the table as well. "Penny, I'm not making fun of you. My question is why? If there is a ghost, and I'm not at all convinced myself, one would think that the ghost wanted to talk to someone. Clear the air. Be released from its terrible curse of haunting, moaning, and chain dragging!"

"Our ghosts have never dragged chains around—or even moaned, for that matter," Penny said, a hard edge in her voice.

Carter was trying very hard not to smile. "Penny, I'm sorry, honestly, I'm not mocking you. I just can't see any correlation between old floorboards giving out and a ghost that should be relegated to haunting a single place. I mean, what ghost have you ever heard about that travels around the countryside haunting different places?"

She stared at him hard. "You want my opinion?"

"Well, not really," Clint murmured softly, playfully.

Penny cast him a baleful glance. "You two and Matt think that it would be an unmanly—un*macho*—thing to believe in ghosts, and therefore, you won't accept anything. Even though Darcy found poor Amy's skull in a day when it had been missing for over a hundred years! She won't admit it, but I say that the ghost told her where to find it."

"*Did* the ghost tell you where to find it?" Clint asked Darcy.

Despite herself, Darcy felt a flush rising. Penny needed backing, but she didn't want to get Clint and Carter going.

"Research, intuition, and maybe some energy from the past," she murmured uncomfortably.

"So there!" Penny said.

"Yeah, so there. Darcy looked up the history behind the legend," Carter said. "Penny, come on! Even Matt spent a lot of time in that room, remember? Lavinia was crazy about the place. She thought it was so historic and fascinating.''

''Yeah—he spent time with his charming *wife*,'' Clint reminded Penny, smiling.

''I spent some really great days in that room, too,'' Carter said, grinning at Clint.

Penny glared at him.

''What?'' Clint said, staring at Penny. ''Doesn't Carter get a tongue-lashing on his wild, womanizing ways as well?''

Penny set a hand on Carter's. ''At least this poor boy was in love with Susan Howell.''

''Susan Howell?'' Clint said. ''What about Catherine Angsley, Tammy what-ever-her-last-name-was, Gina Danson, and that Glynnis-something woman?''

''Eh!'' Carter said to Clint.

''He, at least, cared very deeply about Susan.''

''Penny, the point here,'' Carter said, ''is that all of us so-called longing-to-be-macho men stayed in the room many times—with nothing happening. A scared little bride who wanted the room to be haunted panicked in the middle of the night. Clara Issy freaked out while cleaning. And Darcy claims to be a ghost buster. Sorry, Darcy,'' he said quickly.

''Maybe it's a ghost who only dislikes women,'' Clint said, grinning. ''You know, some horses are like that. Dogs too. They have definite preferences for male and female people. Remember that German shepherd we had years ago? Gracie was her name. She absolutely despised men, but became a kitten anytime a woman was around.''

''Yeah!'' Carter agreed. ''And remember that little white mop thing Lavinia had?''

''Lhasa Apso,'' Clint told him.

''Whatever. The dog was the cutest little pile of white fur in the world—until a guy went to pet it. Then it was all teeth and obnoxious yaps,'' Carter recalled.

''Matt should have known not to marry her once he saw that dog,'' Clint said.

"Ah, hell, we all thought she was the hottest thing since fire had been invented," Carter reminded him.

"You're getting off the subject," Penny said.

"I didn't realize we were really on a subject," Clint said.

"But, Penny, there you go, we were on the subject, we simply found a solution to the dilemma," Carter said with a laugh. "We have a ghost that isn't fond of women. Maybe it's a she, and she is simply jealous of good-looking girls."

"Clara Issy would be delighted that you called her a good-looking girl," Penny said tartly.

"Clara is adorable," Clint argued.

"But hardly a girl," Penny pointed out.

"It comes down to this, Penny," Carter said. "It's quite ridiculous to associate an accident in the library with a malignant ghost from the house, should one exist."

"And it also comes down to this," Darcy interjected firmly. "I'm not leaving. Unless I'm thrown out." She stood. "Thank you, all of you, for your concern. Penny, since the public library has now become off-limits, may I crawl through some of the old house records?"

"Yes, dear, of course. Make my office your own," Penny told her. She looked at her wistfully as she rose. "I still wish that you'd leave."

Darcy smiled. "I'll be all right, Penny. I promise."

"Dinner at seven," Penny said.

"I'll be there," Darcy assured her, and headed for Penny's office.

The woman was a wonderful organizer, Darcy thought. As she studied the bookshelves, Darcy saw that records, histories, legends, and books related to ghost stories were arranged first chronologically, and then alphabetically. She sat in the chair in front of Penny's desk for several minutes, just studying the shelves and musing over what had happened at the library. She didn't believe that the entity haunting the Lee Room was truly malevolent—

merely frustrated. And Carter and Clint had made an interesting point that afternoon—it had been all women who had been troubled by the ghost.

Meaning?

She wasn't at all certain.

She needed to get moving.

She rose and selected a history that chronicled the early days of Stoneyville. The first pages were dry and bland, recording a great deal about building materials. Darcy skimmed the information. Then, there was the sad story about poor Melody, who had died in her lover's arms.

Melody was given a loving, Christian funeral. Her parents mourned her loss until their dying days. The poor girl did not seem a good candidate for such a haunting. Besides, she hadn't slept in the Lee Room. The Jackson room had been hers.

Reading further, Darcy again skimmed a great deal of mundane material dealing with births, deaths, baptisms, and marriages. However, moving forward to 1777, she found mention of a strange mystery. Apparently, the Stones had done a fair amount of procreating outside the bonds of marriage. Arabella Latham, the great-granddaughter of the builder's brother, Malachi Stone, born on the wrong side of the blanket, was furious with her family's decision to side with the Patriots during the Revolution. Malachi Stone had died before the house had been finished, and it was said that he had loaned his brother large sums to have the house completed. His heirs—legitimate and otherwise—were left penniless.

Arabella, however, had been engaged in a passionate affair with Regan Stone, a legitimate cousin of the current master of the house, Ryan Stone, and spent endless days there, basking in the admiration of both cousins. Perhaps she had designs on the legal heir to the house, and was using Regan to get close to him. Ryan, however, was in love with a young beauty of the region, Mary Anderson, who defied her own family, strong Tories, to elope with him.

Arabella, hearing of the wedding, was furious, but perhaps more convinced that she must snag her errant lover into marriage. Ryan was heading off to battle, and against the British, no one believed that the pathetic little American army had a chance. To be close to her new husband, Mary followed him around the country as he went to war.

But somewhere in those days, the ambitious Arabella disappeared. Regan himself was finally drawn into the battle, and killed at Monmouth. Ryan Stone survived the war and returned with his beloved Mary who produced no fewer than eleven children for him, ten daughters and one son, who then proceeded to inherit the house in his turn.

"Arabella!" Darcy murmured aloud.

She closed her eyes, and waited, trying very hard to open her senses and her mind. She thought of the dreams or visions that had plagued her.

The man, outside the house, coming in.

The woman, waiting.

It would make sense, she thought. Since apparently Arabella wanted marriage and legitimacy, and Regan Stone wanted nothing more than a mistress, they would have definitely argued. If their affair was as passionate as claimed in the history, they would have argued with a fervor.

Arabella probably knew intimate secrets about her lover. She could easily have become a burden to him.

A tap at the door made Darcy jump.

"Yes?" Darcy said, drawn from her musings.

Carter stuck his head in the door. "Hey, you've been at it a long time. Dinner is ready. And you've had a long day. A rough fall. Maybe it wasn't quite a Humpty Dumpty thing—you're not in pieces and you're certainly all together nicely—but still, you need a break."

"Thanks, Carter," she said. "And you're right. I'm coming. Dinner sounds great."

He waited for her at the door. When she rose, put the book back, and joined him, he slipped an arm around her in a brotherly fashion.

"You're not scared off, are you?"

"Not in the least."

"Good. There's no way that a fall in the library had anything to do with a ghost here."

"No, of course not," Darcy agreed. "They were just old floorboards."

As they walked through the breezeway to the foyer, the front door opened. Matt was back, in uniform. Darcy felt a bit strange, noticing the way he looked over her close proximity to Carter. Maybe Carter noticed Matt's look as well. His arm fell from her shoulders.

"Hey, hardworking lawman," Carter said. "You made it back just in time for dinner."

Matt nodded, glancing at Darcy. "You feeling all right?"

She made an effort not to grit her teeth. "I'm really feeling terrific. You were the one who hit the floor, remember?"

"Ah, yes, the valiant, manly man of a sheriff!" Carter teased, and yet, Darcy thought that there was just a slight edge to his voice." Of course, Darcy is fine. She fell on all that terrific muscle and sinew, eh, Matt?"

"Something like that," Matt said dryly.

Penny appeared in the foyer. "Matt! Great. I'm so happy you're back in time for a real dinner. Where did you get to? You weren't answering the cell, and Shirley said that you'd left the station."

"I had some business out of the county," Matt said simply, still looking at Darcy. Then he turned to Penny at last. "Go on and start dinner without me. I'm going to take a quick shower and change. If you'll all excuse me?"

It wasn't really a question; more of a statement. He headed up the stairs.

"Well, ladies?" Carter said. He offered them both an arm.

Penny smiled and took one. "Honestly. You and Clint can be the most wretched young reprobates in history, but then, you can be the most darling men I know."

"We strive for 'darling'!" Carter said. "Come along." He looked at Darcy, wiggling his free arm. "I'm working so hard on being 'darling,' Darcy. Give me a hand here!"

She smiled and accepted his arm.

"You should shave, Carter," Penny told him.

"I've worked long and hard on this beard!" he told her.

"You're still such a handsome fellow without it," Penny argued.

"But I don't look like Jeb Stuart without it!" Carter protested.

Penny sighed and looked around him to tell Darcy, "They called Jeb Stuart 'Beauty' when he was at West Point, and not because of his good looks, but because they thought that he was ugly as sin. So he had to grow a beard! Carter, it's just the opposite with you. You have a great face. The beard should really go. What do you say, Darcy?"

Put on the spot, she shrugged. "I think he has to do what makes him happy with himself," she said.

Carter studied her, slowly grinning. "That's the whole crust of life, right in a nutshell, don't you think? We all have to do what we all have to do—to be happy with ourselves."

"While we're living—and when we're dead," Penny said. She shivered suddenly. "Oh, Darcy! I like you so very much, but I sure do wish that you'd leave. I'm so worried about you."

"Penny, there's an expression that's not very nice, but it fits the bill, I think," Darcy told her, then quoted, "It's not happening. So live with it."

Penny grimaced. "That's just the point, Darcy," she said, and there was a real shiver to her voice. "I want you to live!"

Clint came striding to the foyer from the dining room. "Excuse me, people, but dinner is served!"

Penny walked ahead, touching Clint's cheek. "We're coming! But stalling a minute is fine, too. Matt's home, showering and changing."

"Well, then, Ms. Penny, you come and tell that to the cook!" Clint said.

Clint and Penny moved on. Darcy started to follow.

Carter pulled her back. "Darcy, something there just gave me chills, and I don't believe in chills. Maybe you should think about this."

"What are you talking about?" Darcy asked him.

"I don't know. Just a feeling of discomfort. I don't think that I believe that a ghost could be after you. No, I definitely don't believe that. But still…"

"Still…what?" Darcy asked.

"There does seem to be some danger here for you," Carter said, his words slow, as if he was struggling to understand his own feeling. Then the look of worry left his face. "You're just too gorgeous. Which means, of course, we'd like to have you around forever. But not as a ghost! We want you to remain among the living. Oh, what the hell am I saying? Come, my beauty! The dinner table awaits."

Caught in his arm, Darcy walked with him toward the dining room.

Then she was startled herself.

An icy chill suddenly swept up around her. Cold, so cold.

And she felt a strange tug….

As if someone was trying to get her away from Carter.

Keep her back.

Have her there…

Alone.

9

"So, our skull proves to be that of poor Amy, who has been running around the forest looking for her head for years," Clint said, helping himself to more mashed potatoes. "This means we have to have a nice little ceremony and bury her skull, right?" He looked at Matt.

"Oh, but of course!" Penny exclaimed, before Matt could speak.

Matt arched a brow to her.

"We should bury it quietly," he said. "If we have a ceremony, every idiot journalist from here to Alaska will be in the place, making a big deal out of it."

"Matt, really!" Penny said with disgust.

Matt might be exaggerating, but he also had a point. People loved stories like this one; the *New York Times* might not pounce on it, but small papers and sensationalist rags from all over would jump on that kind of a story.

"Actually," Carter said, "it wouldn't be so bad. It would be a nice thing. A tidy end to the story. And the journalists would have to write up the fact that the ghost had been put to rest. Once put to rest, there would be no more hauntings. Right, Darcy?"

Darcy set her fork down. "The skull should be buried with the rest of the body. Having a minister officiate would be nice. Exactly what goes on other than that probably doesn't matter."

"None of it really matters anyway," Matt said. He sounded irritated. Naturally. He didn't believe in ghosts.

Darcy chose her words carefully. "Whether Amy's

ghost ever actually ran around the forest or not isn't the point. We bury people out of respect for the lives they led, and for those loved ones left behind. Granted, Amy doesn't have any remaining relatives in the area—that we know about—but she was still a living, breathing human being. A pitiable one, considering the way that she was murdered. In all due respect, we should see that her skull is buried with her body.''

Matt hesitated, then said, ''Her skull can go near her body. She was buried more than a century ago. God knows what shape she'd be in now. The coffin was probably simple wood, long since deteriorated. There are different laws regarding burial now. We can do our best—since I suppose you're right, that it would be proper.'' He looked around the table. ''Go into any major museum, and you'll find bones and skulls coming out of the woodwork. Dead is dead. If there truly is life after death, I'd say it's pretty well confirmed that we don't need our physical bodies once we get there.''

''Matt, there's not a bit of the romantic in you!'' Penny moaned.

''What is romantic about a tragic murder?''

''The simple rightness of seeing that she is whole again, at least in her final resting place,'' Penny said firmly.

Matt shrugged. ''Penny, we'll see that the skull is interred near the body, all right?''

''And we'll have a little ceremony?'' Penny pleaded.

He threw up his hands. ''Whatever you wish, Penny.''

''Hey,'' Darcy asked, determined to change the subject. ''Did any of you all ever hear of a woman named Arabella?''

''Yes, there is a story about Arabella,'' Penny began. ''She was supposedly the bastard child of a far distant Stone who tried to seduce the legitimate heir, eons ago. Scheming, conniving, and all. But he married someone else. And she disappeared from the legend. Why? Were you reading about her?''

''Yes, just now.''

Penny was excited. "There's no story about her dying a violent death."

"But she disappeared. Maybe she was murdered. She could be the haunt in the Lee Room."

Matt pushed back his chair. "Excuse me, ladies, gentlemen. I hear the night air calling to me."

"But Matt!" Penny said.

He didn't reply. He pushed his chair in, then looked at Darcy. "You're sure you're all right?"

They had managed to go through the entire meal without referring to the episode in the library.

Darcy sighed. "I'm fine," she said.

"When you're tired, go up," he warned.

"Darcy, he's right," Clint said, looking at her worriedly.

"I'm fine," she persisted.

"I agree. You looked darned good to me," Carter said lightly.

Matt turned and walked out of the dining room. Penny folded her hands and looked at Darcy excitedly again. "Arabella! I can see what you're thinking. She disappeared from the records and the area—because she was dead. Murdered by her traitorous lover. In the Lee Room!"

"Something like that," Darcy said.

Carter groaned. "There wasn't a body."

"Oh, posh! A man who knew the area—years ago, before forensic sciences were so advanced—could easily dispose of a body," Penny said. She looked earnestly at Darcy. "I watch all the forensic shows, so I know about these things."

Darcy looked down, hiding a smile. Then she looked at Carter. "I'm afraid that even today, with all the police work and forensic technology available, lots of bodies still disappear, and many murderers go unpunished."

"I suppose," Carter said. With a shrug he added. "I'll let you ladies play, *Murder, She Wrote*." He stretched and yawned. "If you'll excuse me. I think I'm going to head out to play some pool. Anyone want to join me?"

He looked hopefully around the table.

"Not tonight," Clint said.

"You sure?" Carter asked. "Darcy?"

She shook her head. "Thanks. Maybe tomorrow night."

Clint laughed. "Carter, you don't need to look like an old hanged dog. I heard that our lovely new young city commissioner, Delilah, plays pool a lot of evenings. Ah, hm. I'll bet you knew that. Makes the Wayside Inn so much more appealing, huh?"

"She may be there, she may not," Carter said.

"Why don't you just ask her out?" Darcy suggested.

"Well, since I'm barking up the wrong tree following you around like a coonhound with his tongue on the ground, I might as well."

Darcy smiled at him, certain that he was joking, but feeling just a little bit uncomfortable anyway. But Carter's smile deepened and he winked. "So I should just ask her out, huh?"

"Sounds like a plan to me," she said.

"I'll give it some real thought. Meanwhile, I'm going to go play pool and see if I run into her. Night, all."

With a wave, he left the room.

Penny stood. "Heavens. I forgot to make those fellows help clean up!"

"I'd like a little busywork right now," Darcy told her. "We'll get this all picked up in a matter of minutes."

She stood, gathering plates. Clint rose with her. "I guess I didn't run out fast enough," he said, moaning to Penny, giving Darcy a quick grimace.

"Young man, work is good for you."

"I'll have you know that I actually have lots of irons in the fire. I'm just not sharing my activities until I have something really sound to say."

Penny eyed him skeptically. "Hm." Then she took a casserole plate and moved on into the kitchen.

Darcy rinsed dishes while Clint put them into the dishwasher. He was amusing as they worked, finding a way to break into a song regarding every comment Penny made as she put leftovers into containers and then into the refrigerator.

By the time they had finished, Penny was groaning, Darcy was laughing. And yet, Penny was very fond of Clint, and not half as dismayed by his antics as she tried to appear to be.

Matt didn't come back in.

When they finished, Darcy excused herself, anxious to get up to the Lee Room.

She turned the light on as she closed the door behind her. She looked around the room, then closed her eyes, and tried to let any sensations ease into her.

The room seemed extraordinarily still and quiet. And empty.

"Arabella?" she murmured softly aloud. "If there was an injustice, we can at least let it be known. There's no need to be so hostile. We're trying to help you."

No response. No whisper of a breeze, no hint of a voice on the air. No coldness. Nothing.

The ghost was lying dormant. Darcy didn't even get her usual chilling sense of being watched.

She hesitated a few minutes, then went out on the balcony, gripped the rail, and stared into the night. So beautiful. Surely, this area of Virginia was blessed.

After a few moments, she went back in.

She turned on the television, and was surprised to realize that the late-night talk shows had come on. Idly, she began to strip down for bed, started to choose a T-shirt for sleep, then hesitated.

Matt would come. She was certain.

She opted for a light-blue silk peignoir.

Seated upon the bed, she watched the television for several seconds, waiting. But that night, the Lee Room seemed to be giving her nothing.

"I don't understand at all," she said out loud. "You obviously want help. Let me help you. Or are you simply angry with the Stones for what happened to you, Arabella,

and eager to hurt them? They are not the same people now.
Matt Stone is not the man who did this to you.''

Still…nothing.

With a sigh, she turned around and curled up with her
pillow.

Matt wasn't sure why he stayed out on the porch so late.
But then again, there were times when he did just sit out
there, doing nothing, feeling the light, watching the land
beneath the moonlight. There was something calming and
reaffirming about doing so. He did love Melody House.
More than that, he loved Virginia, especially his county.
It was as if the heritage and history were ingrained in him,
and as if his love for the land returned to him sometimes
on nights like this, strengthening.

Either that, or he didn't want to listen to any more non-
sense from Penny.

Carter had gone to play pool. After a while, Clint, too,
had decided to head into town claiming he was feeling a
little edgy and might as well go to the Wayside Inn and
play some pool.

Matt lingered outside a bit longer, then went in.

The house was silent. Those who hadn't headed out rab-
ble-rousing had gone to bed.

He went to his own room first, but didn't stay more than
a few seconds. Walking out on the balcony, he paused a
few minutes again, staring at Darcy's door. It was closed.
She probably hadn't locked it, though, and he didn't know
if he'd be relieved or angry once he made certain that he
was right. She should be locking it.

But then again, maybe she had left it open for him.

He tried the door. Open.

He should go in and yell at her.

Matt stepped into Darcy's room, closed and locked the
balcony doors behind him. For a few moments he stood
where he was, thinking that she had been through a traumatic day. Except that a near-death experience hadn't
seemed so traumatic to her.

He should leave.

He wasn't about to do so.

The television was on, but the lights had been dimmed. And Darcy was soundly sleeping.

He walked to the bed, treading softly.

She looked like a heroine of old, red hair splaying out like an elegant, fire-touched shawl. She was long and lean, slender legs visible beneath the gauze of her nightgown, feet just peeking out. The way she slept…her position enhanced her cleavage. And the way her arms were curled around it…he wanted nothing more than to be her pillow at that moment.

"Darcy?" he said softly.

"Um?"

She stirred, turning. Her eyes, heavy-lidded, opened slowly. She stared at him, a slow, seductive smile curling her lips.

"Why, Sheriff Stone," she said softly.

"You left the balcony doors open," he said, sliding down to sit beside her.

Her smile deepened. "Not to be too presumptuous, but…I assumed you might arrive here," she said. Heavy with sleep, her voice was husky, the sound of it eliciting drumbeats in his veins that echoed into his mind. And beyond.

"You're sure…you're fine? After today?" he queried.

Her smile deepened. She lifted her arms, curling them around his shoulders as she halfway rose to him. Head cast back, throat at an incredible arch, voice richer than carnal sin itself, she assured him. "Really, truly, fine. Better than fine. Want me to prove it?"

She had come to him completely, hot breath of her whispered words against his ear, causing the drumbeat to shudder down to a mambo in his groin. He wrapped his arms around her, finding her lips, her mouth, depth and heat and wetness, and locking her into a kiss that seemed to fuse his body to hers. He had to press her back to struggle in his haste to remove his clothing. Bared to muscle and sinew and pure lust, he rose above her, fingers finding the hem of the gauzy gown, dragging it up before he settled, flesh against flesh, arousal spiraling with the first brush of the senses. He could drown in the sweet aroma of her soap, perfume, and self. The feel and taste of her were seductive, intoxicating, and he ran his palms over her flesh again and again, savoring the feel, bringing his lips against her next for a taste of the texture of her skin. The impact of their bodies against one another created an arousal within him that he fought, not just for the desire to be a giving lover, but to prolong the excruciating promise of climax and pleasure.

Yet that night, she was the aggressor, pressing against him, pushing him away and forcing him to his knees, fingers radiating over his chest, a flutter of kisses and the tip of her tongue drawing exquisite lines against his flesh caused it to burn, chill, and burn again. Her hands aroused and caressed, encircling the fullness of his arousal, before her lips moved again, the liquid fire of her tongue creating an agony of hunger, the energy within her a lightning storm that catapulted around him until it was unbearable and she was in his arms again, bodies fused and fitted and moving in an ever increasing, staccato beat that drove ever upward, wild, sweet, and all but blinding to every thing but the needs of the senses, in the end, totally raw, and then explosive. The force of climax left them both breathless, veins still thundering, hearts pulsing, arms and limbs entwined. He held her against him, loathe to let her go even as satiation seeped throughout him. There were things he wanted to say, and could not. In a distant corner of his mind, he longed not to be entangled, because his world was real, and she believed so fiercely in all that was not.

And yet…

Impossible. He harbored a fear of her. Not because she was an elegant redhead. Because there was something—

Something, perhaps, that challenged all his beliefs, and therefore, his strengths.

He thought of all the lies that passed so easily between men and women. And she was far too fine to be told lies.

And yet...

"It's all right, you don't need to say anything," she told him.

His muscles inadvertently flexed.

Shadow and light filled the room. "I've never expected forever," she told him.

"Darcy—"

"It's all right."

"Darcy—"

"I'm telling you—"

"Don't. Don't tell me anything," he said, and added, "Just be with me."

He cradled her against him. Neither tried to speak again.

In the dream, or somewhere in the deep recesses of her mind, she knew she was someone else.

The woman in the room.

She had known the woman in the dream before, sat within her entity, and she had known the beginning of the scene from both sides, for she had entered into the energy or entity of the man involved as well.

But tonight...she saw it all from the woman's eyes.

Felt the spasm of fear as she heard the sound.

Near. Within the house. A creaking of old floorboards.

The woman hesitated, straightening, listening, wondering why an ordinary sound should elicit such an instinctive sense of fear.

So often, the house was filled with people. Not that night. And at first, she had been glad that it would be so empty.

Now...

She rose, exiting the room, hurrying to the second-floor landing of the staircase, and looking down. Her breath caught as her eyes focused on the figure at the foot of the stairs.

He had entered the house. He had the right, in his own

mind, at least. He had the right to everything. She did not. Strange, he had stood there, looking up at her, dozens of times before. Then, he had smiled. Admired the way that moonlight played through the white fabric of her nightgown. He had instilled within her an intoxicating sense of anticipation, pleasure…excitement. He was so many things that a man should be, physically arresting, sensual, exuding a sense of power that was all but an aphrodisiac.

But tonight…

He did not smile.

They stared at one another for several long moments. Maybe an eternity.

Then…

She saw what he carried. What was in his hands. And the way that he held it…she knew what he intended to do with it.

A scream rose to her throat; she held it back, for there would be no one to hear. Then words, disjointed, tumbled from her lips, for she still couldn't believe what appeared to be his intent.

"You…you loved me," she murmured. "You must still…love me. Somewhat. You can't mean to…to…you *can't!*"

The last was whispered. It was a plea. It was a tone that called forth all that had come between them…before. All that had been shared.

His eyes remained upon hers. He didn't reply.

He started up the stairs.

And she ran.

First, back to the room where she had been writing, setting down words, her own revenge. But even as she attempted to close the door, she felt the force of his weight against it. As he burst in, she saw the metal bed warmer hanging on the wall, and she grabbed hold of it firmly, dashing him against the side of the head. He cried out, staggering back.

She took flight, forcing her way past him, tearing down the stairs, her white gown trailing in a diaphanous cloud behind her.

Blackness, a cloud of shadows, arose around the vision.

Darcy's visions were often so crystal clear in dreams. Sometimes, the fact that they were fading awakened her. And sometimes, the fact that she awakened ended the dream. Perhaps, some instinct inside caused her to awaken so that she wouldn't witness too much. Maybe innate fear kicked in. But she didn't want any natural defense mechanisms kicking in on her now.

But…

She was losing it. Losing touch of the vision. Awakening.

No! She knew that she had to see the end. She cried out silently in fierce frustration, knowing she was close…so close…to knowing the end.

Knowing that she felt…what the woman had felt.

She fought both the fading of the dream, and the terror that was washing over her. She leapt to her feet, crying out, racing to the door. She thought that it was opened. It was not. She slammed against it, woke completely, and stood, facing the door, shaking off the aftereffects.

"Darcy?" She heard his voice, startled, deeply concerned.

She was aware that he was looking at her, though her back was to him. A wave of misery swept over her; she was certain that there would be revulsion in his eyes.

She turned quickly, grabbing her robe from the foot of the bed, slipping into it and heading out the balcony doors. She inhaled deeply, breathing in the night air.

She was startled to feel his hands fall upon her shoulders, his presence, warm and strong behind her.

"Darcy, are you all right?" His voice was deep, resonant, husky, and deeply concerned. She wondered just what she had done in her sleep.

"Yes. Look, I'm really sorry—"

"Don't be. What—happened?" he asked. "What was it? The house? A sound?"

"No, nothing. Nothing at all. Just a dream."

"Tell me about it."

"I—can't," she lied. "It's faded already."

"Darcy, please, tell me—"

"I can't. It's gone."

"All right, then just—"

"You don't want anything to do with this...with me, and it's all right, honestly—"

"Honestly, Darcy, even knowing you as I do, seeing what I've seen...I'm not sure what I believe. But I wish you'd try to tell me more about it."

She swung around, startled to see that the eyes she expected to be so filled with wary distaste held nothing but gentleness. Strangely, his manner made her a bit more determined to pull away. He really didn't understand the half of it. He still didn't believe. If he really did, he would pull away.

She lifted her hands. "It's very difficult to explain what you don't understand yourself."

"All right. Let me help." He smoothed back a lock of hair that the night breeze had sent drifting over her forehead. "Did you always...have visions?"

She shook her head. "No."

"Then?"

She had to turn away from him. She gripped the balcony. In the distance, the mountains were deeper indigo shadows against the rich deep blue of the moonlit night sky. The entire world might have been at peace. The struggle was within herself.

"I was very good friends with Adam Harrison's son, Josh, when we were in high school. He was bright, funny...charming. But most of the kids stayed away from him. They thought he was strange. He didn't run around giving out prophesies or anything, but there were moments when it was a little eerie. He knew when it was going to rain or snow, when the ponds had frozen over solidly, when the ice was going to break. There were other little things. He would be cramming for a test when we weren't supposed to be having one, and then we'd walk into a class to find out that we were having a pop quiz. He knew when Mrs. Malone was going to be out for an extended time, because he had known when her husband was going to die. He didn't know everything—it wasn't as if he had a crystal ball that offered up any image he wanted to conjure. There were just times when he did know things that there was really no earthly way he should have.''

"I think I did know that Adam had a son. He was actually my grandfather's friend. They were both tremendous history buffs,'' Matt offered, his voice soft as he spoke behind her. "Where is his son now? Does he work for Adam as well.''

Darcy shook her head slowly. "Josh is dead.''

"I'm sorry. Truly sorry.'' Then, a moment later, "What happened?''

Darcy shrugged and inhaled again. "We were in a car accident. I'd been dating someone in high school forever, but we had a huge breakup just before senior prom. I asked Josh to go with me. He was great, but Hunter had a real jerk of a friend, and he decided to chase after Josh and play chicken with the cars after the prom. Hunter's friend was killed as well. I survived. And…''

"And?'' he said, prompting her after a moment.

She turned around at last, her eyes meeting his. "At the funeral, I felt as if I was talking to Josh, as if I saw him. And it had been very strange, because he had known he was going to die. But he told me that it was all right. After that…well, I began to know the little things as well. Where something was when it had been lost. At first, it wasn't so bad. There were just little things, the day-to-day things. Just the way it had been with Josh. And I thought—and even the therapist I went to thought—that I was creating conversations with Josh in my mind as a way to accept his death.''

"But you weren't?'' He was still soft-spoken, watching

her with curious eyes, and not those that as yet condemned and warily shut her out.

"But then, I started seeing other ghosts," she said flatly, watching for his reaction.

A slight smile twitched his lips, but he was making a serious effort not to mock her. "What ghosts?"

Again, she shrugged. "I went to NYU, as I told you."

"Yes?"

Darcy kept watching him. "I was walking by one of the very old Episcopalian churches near my dorm and I ran into a woman in front of the church. She was pacing, looking really nervous and distraught, and," she added wryly, "though my folks had warned me when I went to school not to talk to strangers, she was so upset that I stopped and asked her if she was lost, or if there was anything that I could do. She looked at me as if she had seen a ghost, and said, 'You can see me?' I told her that yes, of course, I could see her. She touched my shoulders, and looked as if she was about to cry, and at the same time, she looked incredibly relieved. Then she said, 'I beg of you, find my granddaughter, Charisse, and tell her that the diamonds are in the Shirley Temple doll. Please, please, do this for me. She's in there now, in the church, and I can't seem to reach her, no matter how hard I try. She just can't see me.' I thought then that she might be seriously unhinged and I tried to reassure her, to tell her that, of course, her granddaughter could see her, and that she just needed to talk to her. But the woman shook her head violently, becoming so distressed that I told her I would go in and tell Charisse that the diamonds were in the Shirley Temple doll, whatever that meant. I left her on the sidewalk and started to walk into the church. I turned around, and I couldn't see her anymore. When I opened the door to the church, I saw that a funeral was taking place. Since I felt like an intrusive fool, I walked back out and looked for the woman again. I couldn't find her. I went back to my dorm. That night, when I was sleeping, I woke up to the sound of sobbing. I nearly had a heart attack. The woman who had been in front of the church was sitting at the foot of my bed. I had chills that went straight into my bones, goose bumps broke out all over my flesh. I couldn't even scream, I was so scared. But then, the fear just kind of locked in on me. She was sobbing in such horrible pain that I did manage to reach out and touch her. And she looked at me and said, 'You told me that you'd tell Charisse. You don't understand, she supported me, and she had nothing, and I knew that I was dying, but that it would be all right, because when I died, she could sell the diamonds, and she and the children would be okay. Please, she cared for an old woman when no one else cared, she with Ben dead in that awful train accident, with two jobs and three children. You've got to help me, help her, you have to, she can't hear me, though I try so hard.' I knew, I just knew then, that she was dead, that she was a ghost, and that I was somehow communicating with her just as if she were real, and sitting with me, talking to me, in the middle of the night.''

"Perhaps you were dreaming,'' he said. His tone was logical and matter-of-fact, but he wasn't looking at her as if she were insane.

"Perhaps I was. But it gets even better.'' She paused just a moment, watching him carefully. "You see, Josh was there again. It was as if he had come in behind the woman. And he seemed as natural about being there as if we were back in school, and he had met up with me in the cafeteria. 'Darcy, please, she just needs a little help. She can reach you, and she can't get through to her granddaughter. Darcy, it's a little thing. Just find her granddaughter,' he told me.''

"So…'' Matt said, and the word was elongated, betraying a hint of doubt. "You told Josh that you would find the woman's granddaughter?''

She smiled. "No.''

"Then what?''

"I don't really remember. I woke in the morning, certain that I'd had a dream myself. But I couldn't quite accept

that. I went back to the church, and I found the minister,
and I asked if there had been a funeral the day before that
might have involved a woman named Charisse. He said
yes, that a young woman named Charisse Whittaker had
been the one to make arrangements for the funeral of her
grandmother, Lanie Beacon. He asked if I was a friend of
Charisse's. I told him not exactly, but that I had known
Lanie. He seemed surprised, since apparently, Lanie had
been very ill for some time. I asked if he could get a note
to Charisse for me, so I wrote suggesting that she look in
the Shirley Temple doll for the diamonds. He promised to
get it to her for me.''

"And he did?'' Matt queried.

Darcy nodded. He wasn't touching her. He just leaned
against the balcony, listening, as if she was telling him
about any event in her past.

"And then?''

She hesitated. "Three days later, Charisse called me.
She was practically hysterical with gratitude, she had been
nearly destitute, paying off her grandmother's bills.
Though Lanie had been sick for a long time, apparently,
she hadn't been in her right mind before she had died, and
so she hadn't told Charisse much of anything about her
jewelry. She had known that her grandmother had a few
pieces, and had hoped to sell them to be able to pay off
the funeral and medical bills. As it turned out, Lanie had
actually had quite a small fortune in jewelry, gifts her
mother had given her from her family, who had been some
kind of Russian nobility. At any rate, Charisse was grateful
to me, and sadder than ever about Lanie, because her
grandmother had been so careful to hold on to the gems
so that she might have them when Lanie died. She asked
me how I knew, and I told her the truth. She didn't seem
to doubt me at all, she just kept saying thank you and
asking me if I needed any financial help or if I wanted any
kind of reward. I told her that I was fine and that I hoped
everything would go well for her and her children.''

"She didn't want to meet you to say thanks?" Matt asked.

Darcy smiled wryly. "She couldn't have been nicer or more grateful—on the phone. She expressed no desire to meet me. I think the whole thing was quite…creepy for her."

"After that?" Matt asked.

"There were more…happenings. I was a theater major at the time. When I first went to college, despite what had happened on prom night and after, I thought I had the perfect life. I was in school in New York City. There was competition coming out of the woodwork, but I was also in the land of opportunity. I had wonderful film classes as well. An opportunity to work part-time for MTV. And, yes, I had some work modeling and I was making really decent money for a student. Then, I dreamed one night that I was at a funeral with a friend whose brother had died. It was so real that I told her how sorry I was the next day. She wanted to know why I was sorry. I realized that I had been dreaming, but then a week later her brother was killed in a boating accident. Naturally, I went to the funeral. And she accepted my condolences then, but I could see in her eyes she didn't want me anywhere near her, it was almost as if…as if I had somehow caused it to happen. I was seeing someone at the time too. Fairly seriously. We broke off that night. I felt terrible. As if I were some kind of a pariah. I went out to Queens the next day, to the cemetery. And I didn't actually see Josh then, but it was as if I could hear him. I wasn't exactly suicidal—but I was feeling fairly desperate. But while I was just sitting there, I felt as if Josh were by me, telling me that I needed to go and see his father. I remembered Adam, how very kind he had been to me at Josh's funeral. While I was having that thought, I could swear that I saw all kinds of ghosts walking around the cemetery. One man in particular. He was wearing some kind of a uniform, but I didn't know what it was. I walked over to the gravestone where he was standing, and saw that he had died in 1780. The gravestone was hard to read, it was broken and untended, but I finally made out the words 'Revolutionary Hero.' So...I started telling him how grateful the nation was for all that had been done to give us our freedom, that we were far from perfect, but a truly great nation in the ideals for which they had fought and died. Anyway, he smiled, and disappeared, and I didn't feel quite so terrible, and the next day, I looked up Adam Harrison.''

"And he told you that you weren't ill, or insane, but that you had a special gift?" Matt asked. She couldn't tell if there was skepticism in his voice or not.

"Not that day," Darcy told him, smiling. "He broke down crying, and asked me about Josh, and I told him that Josh was just as he had always been, kind and there to help. And he asked me, next time I saw or heard his son, to tell him how much he had loved him, and cherished every day that he'd had him with him. Then he asked me to come back. That's where we began. I did go back. I submitted to all kinds of tests, and I met other people who worked for him. People who experienced events the way that I had, and people with different forms of...extra-sensory perception. I wasn't going to go back to school at first, but Adam suggested that I should, that we would keep close contact, and that he would be ready for me full-time whenever I was ready to come back. My interests had changed, however. I wanted to study human psychology, to help me deal with the people who had a bad time dealing with me. And I was fascinated then with history, architecture, old homes...." She paused, shrugging again. "And I'm a good student. I don't think my IQ is off the board or anything, but I'd always had a good bent toward the academic. So I studied, acquired the degrees I wanted...and then went back to Adam. Full-time.''

He was quiet, watching her, waiting, perhaps, for her to say more. The night breeze continued to drift gently around them.

There was no more to say. And she was disturbed to realize just how anxious she was for him to say something that would show he wasn't so disturbed by her that he would turn away. Not now, perhaps. He was, in his way, a true gentleman. Raised to courtesy.

She didn't want to care. She knew better than to care. She shouldn't have gotten involved in any way with him, because she had studied so hard, learned so much about the human psyche. When she frightened people, they turned away. By the nature of her existence, she frightened people.

"So...?" she murmured, wishing she didn't sound quite so desperate. She had longed to sound casual. Things were the way they were. She couldn't change the way that she was—God knew, she would have done so years ago were it possible.

"There must be a certain satisfaction in feeling that you've helped someone," he said. "Even if it does happen to be someone dead."

He sounded polite, courteous, and even gentle.

"Are you making fun of me?" she asked very quietly.

"No."

"But I know that you don't believe in ghosts, or the occult, in any way."

He smiled. "I can't say that I'm convinced. That I can suddenly fall on my knees and say that I'm a true believer."

"Then?"

"I believe in you," he told her.

The breeze moved.

She must have heard him wrong.

"What?" she whispered.

He made a move toward her, taking her into his arms. His thumb stroked her chin in a way that made her incredibly warm. His eyes touched hers.

"You are quite different."

She arched her chin upward. "If you're not convinced that there is a world beyond that which most people know, you must think that I'm a liar. Or insane."

He shook his head. "There are often rational explanations for what doesn't seem rational at first."

"A scientific explanation for anything?"

"Maybe."

She smiled. "But you do believe in God, in a greater existence."

He hesitated. "Yes."

"How would you explain God, then?"

A slow smile curled his lips. "Hey, we could get into a whole thing here on the missing link, Darwinism, and more."

"But you're missing my point. Belief is not tangible. God is not tangible. So…if there is a greater being, then there can be a much greater reality than the one we see daily, that most people accept."

"How about I say that I'll try to keep an open mind?" he asked her.

"I say that you're incredible!" she breathed softly.

"There is one thing of which I am convinced," he told her.

"Oh?"

"You are a force of nature!" he said. She smiled. He swept her up. She slipped her arms around his neck.

"Manly muscles and sinew, you know," he teased.

"Totally appreciated," she assured him.

He walked back into the bedroom.

By the time Darcy slept, it was so deeply that she wasn't so much as nudged by a vision or a dream.

10

"Adam!"

Darcy was stunned and delighted when she came downstairs the next morning to find that Adam Harrison was in the dining room, sharing tea with Penny.

"There's my girl!" He stood, straight and dignified as ever, a smile creasing his features as she hurried forward to greet him with a warm hug.

She pulled away from him, searching his eyes. "I didn't know you were coming. I thought you were really involved with the situation in London."

"Indeed, but apparently, that will be solved at another time," he told her. "I hadn't heard from you, young woman!" he told her sternly.

She laughed. "Adam, you're the one with the international cell phone. You could have called me, too."

He shrugged. "I leave you alone, unless you call to say you need me. You know that."

She arched a brow. "Did I send out a psychic distress signal of which I'm not aware?"

"Can you really do that?" Penny inquired with awe.

Darcy laughed, looking away from Adam to smile down at Penny, at the head of the table where she remained seated. "I'm not sure," she told Penny.

"Anything is possible," Adam assured Penny. "But no, I simply came because, as I said, the situation in London is complex, and must be handled at a later time. And since Matt's granddad and I were such great old chums—not to mention the fact that I paid Matt, rather than having Matt pay me, a most unusual experience, I do assure you—I thought that I should add my moral support to Darcy's work here.''

"Moral support?" Penny said. "But you're the head of the company—"

"Ah, but not nearly as gifted as my very special associate here," Adam assured her. Darcy realized that he was looking at her with concern. "I hear you nearly had a terrible fall yesterday."

"Boards rotted, Adam. It was nothing. I didn't really fall at all. And it probably wasn't a life-threatening situation. I might have broken a few bones."

"Any kind of a feeling about it?" he asked.

"Did a ghost in the library shove me through the boards?" she queried ruefully. "No. No feeling whatsoever. Boards rotted. Period."

"Ah, but Penny has been telling me that you made an excellent discovery in the woods," Adam said.

Darcy had to smile. "Adam, I'm not sure that everyone would refer to a skull as an excellent discovery."

"A poor, brutalized girl can now be put to rest," Adam said, and his tone was both sad and serious.

"We will have a church ceremony, no matter how Matt feels," Penny said.

"Matt just doesn't want a circus, I'm sure," Darcy murmured.

Penny leapt to her feet suddenly. "I'm sorry, I've just been so charmed to see Adam that I've completely forgotten my manners. Let me get you some coffee, dear."

"Penny, I'm a big girl. I know where to get the coffee," Darcy assured her.

"But Penny is a Southern hostess of the most gracious variety," Adam said, staring at her in a way that said, *Let Penny get the coffee!*

"It's absolutely my pleasure," Penny said.

"Then I will most graciously accept a cup of coffee, thank you, Penny," Darcy said.

With a brilliant smile, Penny went off to get the coffee.

"So?" Adam said, frowning. "What's going on here?"

"Adam, honestly, I don't know. Usually, a wounded spirit is pleased to be eased. There's just something...I don't know."

"Josh hasn't been able to help you?"

It had taken a very long time, but Adam had accepted his son's death. He had even known it was coming, though he had never really sat down with Darcy and explained how, if Josh had talked to him, or if he had intuited the short life span of such a special young man. She thought for many years, though he had kept his own counsel on his feelings as well, that Adam felt a certain pain that she could communicate with his deceased son, while he could not. But whatever his personal pain, kindness had always been one of Adam Harrison's greatest virtues. His son had inherited the trait. For the good or the bad of it, she was sure it was why she and Josh had been best friends, and why he was still so often with her, even now.

She shook her head slowly. "It's very strange. It's almost as if he can't enter this house. As if there's a block...he helped me find Amy's skull, to see what happened in the woods, picture her murder. But I've tried to reach him while I'm in here. I can't."

"Very strange," Adam said.

Darcy shrugged, opened her mouth to agree, then shut it again. Penny was returning with a mug full of coffee for her.

"Did you see Matt?" Darcy asked Adam, after thanking Penny.

"Briefly. He was hurrying off to work when I arrived," Adam said.

"He's a very good sheriff," Penny said proudly.

"Um. And you might have mentioned that fact to me when sending me out here," Darcy said.

"Come now. I'm sure you two have managed to get along okay," Adam said.

Darcy was glad that he wasn't blessed with a true second sight, but she began to suspect he did have a special intuition, he seemed so amused as he spoke.

She merely smiled. "I imagine he was quite glad to see you. I told you that he found me a poor substitute when I first arrived."

"He was glad to see me," Adam said. "Naturally—his granddad and I went way back." Adam hesitated, studying her. "He's also anxious about you being here now."

"Oh?" Darcy said carefully.

"He's afraid you're going to get hurt."

She couldn't help the flare of anger that went through her. She'd bared her soul to the man the night before, and he'd claimed—at least, she thought that he'd claimed—to have something of an open mind. But now day had come and Adam had arrived, and he wanted her out. "I fell through some old floorboards, and didn't get hurt. And he doesn't believe in ghosts, so...?"

Adam arched a brow to her just a hair, his eyes indicating the fact that Penny was listening. They never discussed their progress—or lack thereof—in front of others.

"Matt is convinced that someone very much alive is pulling pranks," Penny said.

"Attempting to kill or injure someone is a prank?" Adam said.

Penny waved a hand in the air. "Floorboards do rot. Matt is just being Matt. Suspicious. Because he thinks someone has been causing the disturbances at the house— again, someone alive, and not a ghost."

Darcy was silent, uneasy for a moment. Because that one night, she had been convinced that there had been someone, alive and well, playing tricks as well.

"Having you attempted using sensors, photography, or tape as yet?" Adam asked Darcy.

"No. You know me. I like to spend time without equipment first."

"Right. But don't you think it's time to bring it in?"

She lowered her head slowly in acknowledgment, thinking that it was actually a damned good thing that she hadn't set up sound or videotape in her room *as yet.*

"I'll call Jenner later—I understand his company is our contact," Adam said. "For the moment...Penny, would you excuse us? I'd like Darcy to show me the woods."

"Of course!" Penny said. "You two go right on and get to work."

"Thanks, Penny," Darcy murmured, and started out of the dining room, and then the house, Adam Harrison behind her.

They'd passed the stables and walked some distance from the house before Adam spoke again. "Just what do you think is happening in the house?"

She glanced at him, smiling ruefully. "It's crawling with ghosts. There is a Civil War soldier in the place, definitely. A benign fellow, I believe. And perhaps he's happy, watching over the place. Most of the time, the feeling is quite good."

"Except for in the Lee Room."

Darcy shrugged. "Mostly. I had a pretty strange chill in the living room once." She shook her head. "I don't know what's going on, Adam. It doesn't make any sense. I've done a lot of reading. There was a young woman who was having an affair with the heir to the house many years ago. She was supposedly an illegitimate relation from a few generations back. The young heir then married a proper young woman and his mistress, Arabella, disappeared. At least from the record books. She's not among Penny's known 'haunts,' or those she tells about on her legends tours. But I've tried connecting with her...and I get no response. It seems as well that Josh isn't able to connect in the house, or in the Lee Room. As I said, it's very strange. Arabella should want to communicate, to let me find her, wherever she is, and perhaps bring to light the fact that she was murdered—if, indeed, she was."

Adam was quiet as they moved down the path. "Do you feel as if you're in any danger?"

She stopped, staring at him. "Adam, you know that,

sometimes, I experience the fear of what went on years before. And I've woken here shaken and frightened—but it's nothing I haven't lived with before, and I'm really determined now that I am on to something, that I can get to the bottom of this. I do believe that someone was murdered in that room. I've gotten snatches of what happened in my dreams. Several times. You understand how that works with me. I'm asleep, and somewhere in my mind, I know that I'm dreaming. But I also become that other person in a way, and see and experience the situation from their point of view—*as it happened.* I've slipped in to the past life of a woman in the room—and into the life of the man who came after her.''

''Can you see their faces?''

She shook her head. ''Not yet. I've seen him reach the house. I've seen her as she's been here, alone first, then realizing that he's come.'' She shrugged and let out a long sigh. ''Last night, I saw him race up the stairs after her, and he was furious. He's carrying a stretch or broken rein—long enough to wrap around her neck, which is what I believe he eventually does. But the dream eluded me before I could see the end of it. Or even make out faces.''

''So you're close.''

''Very close.''

''I should keep watch while you sleep,'' Adam said.

Darcy hesitated. She shook her head then. ''I'm more frustrated than frightened. Honestly. I want to see this through. We should set up equipment, yes, and I probably should have done so a few days ago. But we're not going to get anything on tape—maybe a little mist. I need to get to the bottom of the dream. I need for the entire sequence of events to play out for me.''

''I understand you had a seance here.''

''Yes, and there was definitely a feeling of spiritual presence—but not through the medium. The ghosts were probably laughing at us all that night. Except...''

''Yes?''

''The malignant presence. I felt it that night, as well.

But someone was definitely playing tricks that night. Parlor games. Rapping on the table.''

"Who did it?"

"I don't know."

Adam paused on the walkway. "Ah-huh!"

"Ah-huh?"

"We're going to recreate the seance."

Darcy grimaced. "Adam, the woman who came was earnest and all that, but not a real medium."

"Don't be silly. Your 'medium' will be here for the seance, of course. We need to recreate it with everyone present who was here that night. Except for this—you'll be the medium this time."

"You're going to try to figure out who was rapping on the table? I can tell you right now—both Clint and Carter can be pranksters. And Penny is so determined that Matt believe in ghosts that she might have done it herself."

"I'll be watching for the table rapper myself," Adam said. "To get to the bottom of the story with the ghost, we're going to have to find the mischievous living soul first."

Darcy arched a brow. "There's something not right. Most of the time, spirits just want us to tell what happened in the past—see the evil culprit named, the truth known. This is all so very strange."

"Let's see what happens at a seance when you're doing the communicating and I'm doing the watching," Adam said. He turned back toward the house, then cast his face back in her direction again. "Enough of a walk for me," he said cheerfully. "Come along. We've a lot of communicating with the living to do this afternoon."

"You want to have the seance tonight?"

"Why let grass grow beneath our feet?" he cross-queried. "Sure. Absolutely. If it can be arranged, we'll plunge right in tonight!"

Matt hung up the phone, groaned, and put his head down on his desk.

Naturally, Shirley chose that moment to tap, and walk into his office.

"Matt?" she cried with concern.

He lifted his head, shaking it, and lifting a hand quickly. "I'm fine. Just ready to jump in a lake."

"Oh?" Shirley was still frowning, disturbed.

"It's nothing. Adam Harrison has arrived, and wants to repeat a seance at the house tonight."

Shirley made a thoughtful face, taking up a perch on the corner of his desk. "What's so bad about that?"

"Shirley, you know that I don't even believe that there is a ghost. I think I've got a real live person playing tricks around the place." He scowled. "Serious tricks."

Shirley shook her head slowly. "Any reports back on the wood from the library?"

"Yeah. Soda."

"What?"

"They were weakened by soda. Some kind of cola spilled into them."

Shirley was silent for a minute. "Matt, sounds as if some kid was in the library and spilled a drink that they weren't supposed to have in there in the first place."

"Yeah, that's what it sounds like, isn't it?"

Shirley was silent. "Matt, do you think you're protesting this a little bit too much?" she asked. "I mean, really, does what happened at the library have to have something to do with anything else going on at Melody House?"

"No, it doesn't."

"And yet you're still convinced that it does?" Shirley asked softly.

"Yep."

"Why?"

"Hunch, I guess."

"Mm," Shirley said thoughtfully.

"What the hell does that mean?"

"Let me ask you another question. I heard that your arrival at the library was incredibly opportune. You arrived just in time, before Miss Tremayne gave up her grasp on the wood. How and why do you think you arrived in just the nick of time?"

He scowled. "I probably knew that Darcy was hanging around the library and just wanted to check up on her."

"Oh, Matt, come on. You went there on some kind of a hunch, too. And how is a lot of police work done? Hunches!"

"Gut reaction, from what we've learned over years," Matt corrected.

"Ah, come on, you're doing that Shakespearean thing, protesting too much."

"Shirley, please. You don't believe in ghosts."

"I don't know what I believe in," she told him earnestly. "I certainly wouldn't say oh, yes! There are ghosts, I know it. But I've seen far too many strange coincidences not to believe that there may be some form of ESP out there. Experts say we only use a very small section of our brains in our day-to-day lives. Maybe the human mind, or spirit, is capable of far more than the normal person ever gets to know. Hey! Can I come to your seance?"

"Shirley, I'm really sorry. Adam Harrison wants to re-create the last seance we had down to the last man and woman, with only himself there as well, observing. But I tell you what—the minute I hear they're going to pop out a Ouija board, your name is first on the invitation list."

By eight that night, all those who had attended the first seance had arrived at Melody House. David Jenner had his video set up, and Adam and Darcy had also arranged a small slew of instruments throughout the room, including a gauge to determine the temperature in different parts of the room, as well as an electrometer and magnometer which Adam explained were to measure electric and magnetic forces within the room.

Matt had stayed late at work, hoping to avoid most of the hoopla. Still, it was his house, and nothing was going on in it without him being there. He managed to shower and change and be down for eight, just as Adam was arranging the table to his liking.

Tonight, Darcy was to be the star of the show.

He had tried to behave no differently toward her. After all, Adam was the one who had come to take things over. And he had been entirely earnest the night before in his efforts to understand just what made her believe in all that she did. Try as he might, though, by daylight, he couldn't help but think that she was living in a world of her own mind, no matter what results she might be able to achieve. He knew that he was offending her with his brief words and marked distance.

But he didn't like having the seance, and that was that.

Elizabeth Holmes came to him and spoke softly but reproachfully. "Matt, I really did know what I was doing. I was close, so close. I wish you would have let *me* try again."

"They're professionals, Liz," he told her.

Her eyes scanned him. "But you don't believe in any of this."

"Lizzie, I brought them in to find out what was going on."

Mae strode up, giving him a kiss on the cheek. "Oh, Matt! I do thank you for having me again. This is so exciting."

"I had contact! I know I had contact!" Liz continued.

Jason Johnstone was carrying a scotch as he joined their circle. "I admit I'm intrigued. Hey, Matt, it has been pretty different and amazing since Miss Tremayne arrived. I'm going to cover the ceremony when you bury poor Amy's skull."

"Great, just great," Matt said, trying not to sound aggravated.

"See, Liz, *you* never found a skull," Mae said.

"But you were here! I did contact the dead," Liz insisted.

Carter sauntered on over, hand in hand with Delilah Dey. "Our councilwoman is a bit nervous," he said.

"So spooky!" Delilah said with a delicious little shiver. *So asinine!* He almost retorted. Somehow, he refrained.

"Shall we begin?" Adam called out.

They all began to gather.

"Darcy, you'll take the middle seat," Adam said. "Clint...Carter, if you would take seats at her side. David, you'll be filming. Miss Dey...Delilah, if you would sit at Carter's side? And Matt, next to Delilah. Mr. Johnstone, we'll put you next to Penny over there, who will be next to Clint. Matt...you and I will take the ends of the table down here, with Mae and Elizabeth down here, between us."

They all filed into the chairs as Adam directed. Penny jumped up then, though, to lower the lights.

Adam remained cordial and cheerful throughout his instructions. Ever calm, casual, down-to-earth. He didn't advise that the house be darkened to a point of shadow—evidently, the man wanted some light on the situation. Matt had to admit a tug of admiration for the old man, but then again, he knew that Harrison would allow for no charades.

Wasn't that why he had allowed Harrison Investigations in from the beginning?

Not really, he admitted to himself.

He'd hoped that Adam would show up, and immediately prove that there was a hidden mike in the Lee Room or some such thing. Something Matt just hadn't seen.

But then...

He was a cop. A good one. He should have found any bugs by now.

"If everyone will take hands, we'll begin," Adam said.

Obediently, hands were held around the table.

Matt wasn't sure what he was expecting then. Adam speaking with a Vincent Price spookiness to his voice, maybe.

But Adam was as casual as if they were gathering for a picnic on the beach. "Please remember to keep contact with one another, hands on the table at all times. If anyone should become really frightened, just cry out, and we'll stop the proceedings.''

"Oooh, I'm scared!" Clint teased, wide-eyed.

"Me, too," Carter said. "Thank God I'm hanging on to Delilah."

"Carter, you rake!" Delilah said with an appreciative giggle.

"Really! However can we expect anything?" Liz demanded indignantly.

"Oh, Darcy's fine, whatever," Adam said mildly. "But... are we ready?" He wasn't really asking the crowd around the table. Just Darcy.

Her eyes were on his. She was as casual as she might be herself, in an attractive green blouse and jeans. She certainly didn't look like a medium.

"Darcy?" Adam said.

She nodded imperceptibly, and lowered her head.

Silence reigned for several long seconds, then Adam said. "Is Josh with you?"

"He's calling to me, but says that he can't enter," Darcy said.

"Why can't he enter?" Adam asked.

"He doesn't know exactly why. The spirit within is too strong now, the emotions remaining are almost overwhelming. There's terror...and mistrust."

"Tell Josh to be himself. Gentle, kind."

They waited. Darcy shook her head, and once again, there was silence.

"Ask the spirit itself to speak with us," Adam directed her.

She nodded, moistening her lips. "Please, we're here for you," she said. "We don't understand, but we're here for you. We need to understand."

Jason Johnstone shuffled his legs. Penny frowned. They all stared at Darcy.

Matt didn't know what to expect next.

What did come caused the hair to rise at his nape.

"Help."

It was Darcy who spoke the word, but it wasn't really Darcy at all. The voice wasn't hers. Her eyes were closed, her head was slightly lowered. Her lips moved, and sound came from them, but the voice that spoke wasn't Darcy's at all.

"I never thought…as bad as it got…a killer, my God, a killer. That he could do such a thing…"

Penny gasped softly. Adam frowned at her sternly.

"Do what? Who are you, please? We can't help if we don't—"

"Oh, my God!" Darcy suddenly called in the strange voice.

"What, please?" Adam said.

"Can't, can't…can't breathe, don't you see…the danger is…here, danger is with us, oh, God, you must see, must see, must…"

"Who are you?" Adam inquired again softly.

There was silence for a minute. Penny's grip on Matt's hand was so hard that it threatened to break bone. Her eyes were open, her mouth was formed into an O. Mae, too, was just staring at Darcy, jaw slack with amazement. Clint and Carter were trying to appear skeptical, yet Matt was certain that his cousin was feeling a jolt of fear.

And as for himself…

Yes, he felt the sense of fear, too. A deep, strange unease. He didn't *want* to believe. Logically, he *couldn't* believe. And yet he felt it. Something very eerie. Something that created a chill, deep in his bones.

Elizabeth Holmes, the ex-medium of the moment, was simply gaping. And Delilah Dey looked as if she would cry out at any second.

Then a scream sounded. Gasping, high-pitched, rising to a shriek loud enough to shatter glass. It was Darcy, and yet, it wasn't Darcy at all.

They all jumped.

"Maintain your handholds!" Adam directed, and he spoke to Darcy. "Please, we're here, trying to help you."

Darcy shook her head wildly.

"Why are you so afraid?" Adam asked.

"Here, here, here…" Darcy mouthed.

"But we're here, to help you."

"No!" The voice that wasn't Darcy's, but coming from her lips, cried out.

"Please, we need to know—" Adam began.

"No, no!" The voice cried again in terror and anguish.

Once again, the sound of the scream shattered the night.

"Help me, God help me, help me!"

And then, something worse. Choking, gasping, a desperate struggle to breathe. Sounds so terrible, and so real.

The sounds of a murder…

The sound of death.

11

This time, it was too much for Delilah Dey. She jerked free from the handholds around the table.

"My God! That's horrible! Please, turn on all the lights, please, make this stop!"

To Matt's amazement, he felt the same way himself.

Hands were released. Darcy's eyes were wide and on Adam's again. She had a questioning look in her eyes.

"We have to give it up tonight," Adam Harrison said, staring at Darcy.

"Drinks!" Penny gasped out. "Drinks. Would you all like drinks? I know I want one!"

She leapt up. The circle was definitely broken. Delilah was shaking like a leaf blown in autumn. Jason Johnstone was white. Even Clint and Carter were looking unnerved.

Matt found himself staring hard at Darcy. Still so beautiful. Something inside him had to deny her, though. Deny what he had seen.

It must have been…theater!

A sham, all a sham. She was beautiful, smooth, cool, dignified…and a charade artist. Or half-crazy herself. How the hell had she done the voice? Because it was good, oh, hell, yes, he had to admit, it was good, really good, he had goose pimples rising on his own arms.

Dead was dead. He had seen the dead too many times. The dead did not come back to life.

No matter what he had seen, heard. No matter hints of something more played with his mind.

She knew. Although Adam had locked his gaze with

hers, Darcy knew that Matt was looking at her. She turned to him. Distant, challenging, cool, and even contemptuous. As if she knew he was a liar. All the gentle words and tenderness he had offered were false. He might be madly infatuated with her elegant beauty and sensuality, but he was the one who was a sham. He couldn't handle it.

He was angry with himself, angry with her. He never gave away anything with his expression that he didn't mean to. He was a sheriff; he'd been a cop too long. But Darcy could see right through him.

She turned away, dismissing him. She rose as if she hadn't been speaking in a different voice, as if she'd never let out a scream that had just paralyzed an entire room.

"Penny, let me help you. I'd love a drink, myself."

"I'll help, too!" Delilah said quickly.

Adam looked at David Jenner. "You got it all on tape?"

"Yes, Mr. Harrison."

"I think I'll take it to my room," Adam said. He looked around at the others. "If you'll excuse me."

No one actually answered him. He took the tape from David, and left them.

"I think I should go home," Mae said, still just sitting, staring blankly in front of herself. "Oh. I didn't bring my car, Delilah picked me up." She focused then, looking at Matt. "I…well, I'll just have a drink, too, then."

"If you want to go home, Mae, I'll be happy to take you," Matt said. He rose so quickly he could have knocked the table over. It was his house.

He couldn't wait to leave it.

Mae said a few quick goodbyes, and Matt led her out to his car. She was silent as he started up the engine, then she said, "Mother Mary!" Matt knew that she stared at him. "That was the scariest thing I've ever seen in my life."

"Yeah, she's good," Matt said. *Good! What was he saying, admitting? Good. There were many ways to be good.*

He realized that he was furious with himself, but he was

furious with himself because of Darcy. And it couldn't be real.

"She can really contact the dead!" Mae said with awe.

Matt found himself barking back at her. "No—I mean that she's good as an actress. A damned good actress. That was her major before she came up with all those other degrees, you know."

"Oh, Matt!" Mae said with dismay. "You can't believe that."

"I do," he said stubbornly.

"Granted, I haven't gotten to know her anywhere nearly as well as you—"

"Right, you can bet on that," Matt said, a double edge of irony in his voice.

"But we both know she's not the kind of flimflam artist who would go around…giving people false hope, or making a mint on a pretense."

Matt stared at Mae. "You can't really believe that someone can just talk to the dead at will, can you?"

"I sure believe what I saw tonight."

"What did you see?" Matt said angrily. "You saw Darcy speaking, answering questions that Adam asked her, screaming like a banshee, and that was about it. Did she come up with any answers? Did she give us a name? A reason why this woman would be screaming and asking for help?"

"Delilah jumped up," Mae reminded him. "She broke the circle, the communication."

Matt sniffed audibly. "Darcy has been here some time now. And she hasn't the least idea of what is going on in the house."

"Yes, but she found the skull in the woods," Mae reminded him. "And she went through the floorboards in the library," she added frowning.

"God knows, she probably spilled cola all over the floor herself."

"Matt!" Mae protested.

"Okay, so that was coincidence," Matt said.

Mae shook her head. "Oh, come on, Matt. I know what you think. You believe that maybe even Penny is making things happen, because she's so into the concept of the house of being haunted. Or maybe someone else, for God knows what reason. You thought that if you had Adam Harrison out, he'd find some immediate proof that everything that has happened was bogus. Well, that's just not true. And I always thought you were so smart. That you listened better than anyone I knew, which made you such a great sheriff. You could handle the really bad guys, and keep young pranksters from going down the wrong path. Well, now you're just being stubborn and stupid. And you know why? You're afraid. You're afraid to let go of any preconceived notion you have. You've believed something forever, so it must be true."

Matt stared at her. He'd never heard Mae so fierce.

"Every word I'm saying is true. And I can tell you what other people won't because I knew your folks, and I'm way too old to flirt with you, or any of that rot. I'm just an old barmaid with a good eye and a good ear, but I care about you a lot, and I hate to see you act like an idiot!"

He almost laughed, Mae was so determined to speak her mind.

"Mae, please."

"Hey, no! Matt, *please*. What, are you letting your past slip into some of this? Darcy has red hair. Besides that, she isn't a thing like Lavinia, yet you automatically distrust her. Your ex-wife could stab someone in the back and smile while doing it. Darcy isn't a thing like that."

"Hey! May I remind you, when Lavinia first came to Stoneyville, everyone thought she was the most beautiful, sweetest thing to ever walk the earth."

"We thought that for all of about two seconds. We were horrified by the time you two married. But hell, none of us had a right to say anything."

"Thanks for the lecture, Mae," he said dryly.

"How is Lavinia these days?" Mae asked, smoothing her hair back. "Clint told me she used to call you constantly, even after the divorce. That she was jealous as all hell, even when she went back to her old social whirl.''

"She must be happy, because I haven't heard from her in quite some time," Matt said.

"She must have found herself a new young stud somewhere," Mae said.

"I hope," Matt said absently. Lavinia was the last thing on his mind at the moment.

"Right, I know you mean that. But what you haven't gotten down right is the fact that Darcy Tremayne isn't anything like her.''

"Thank you, Mae.''

"Ass!" Mae muttered.

"Mae, look, I'm damned sorry, but I do think this is all bull. Hey—maybe it's even bull in her own mind. Hell, that's not a maybe. Because you're right. I'm uptight, all right. And maybe that's why I've been such an ass, and I'm sorry. Darcy…is very different. Beautiful, and a wonderful person. She means to be decent. She believes all this herself. But she has dreams, wakes, and thinks they're real. She wants to conjure up a spirit, and so she does. Excuse me. It's just a little too creepy and ridiculous for me.''

They'd reached Mae's house. She slammed out of the passenger door and came around to peer into the driver's window, despite the fact that he had just started to back out.

"Anyone could see the way it is between you two, Matt. Fire and ice. She makes you mad as hell, and hot as hell. Just like Lavinia. So, if you're really going to be such a pigheaded jerk, keep your pants zipped, huh?''

"Mae—" he began angrily.

She quickly retreated from the window. "Thanks for the ride, Matt. Good night.''

She turned to walk up the path to her house. He swore, slammed his hands against the steering wheel, and backed out the driveway.

* * *

Darcy was always vaguely aware of what had gone on, even though she didn't know the particulars. The way everyone was behaving, she was certain that, if nothing else, there had been one hell of a show.

She had apparently done Carter a favor though, or so it seemed. Delilah Dey—whose eyes remained huge with fear and unease every time they fell upon Darcy—was clinging to him.

Actually, they made a cute couple, Darcy thought wryly.

Cute couple, yeah, but the way that Delilah stared at her was surely as unnerving as anything she might have done during the seance.

Drinks had been served all around. David Jenner seemed the most blasé, while Clint appeared to be sympathetic as he looked at her, Elizabeth Holmes in awe, Penny concerned. Carter? Hard to tell, he was so busy being supportive to the lovely Delilah Dey. Jason Johnstone was reflective as he watched her, and appeared to be entirely open-minded. Unnerved perhaps, but not to the point of staring at her as if she were an alien.

Not as Matt had done.

Matt, gone now, naturally. Sure, he needed to give Mae a ride home.

"Have you always been like that?" Delilah asked her.

"Like…?" Darcy said, arching a brow. She knew what Delilah meant. She just wanted clarification.

"Well," Delilah said, hesitating.

Creepy? Is that what you mean? Darcy didn't say it out loud.

"Able to…really get to dead people?" Delilah said.

"No," she said. "I had a friend once. He taught me," she said simply.

"Okay, okay," Clint said. "Darcy gave us all a start. We've all been so freaked out that we haven't stopped to wonder just what it meant." He was looking at Darcy expectantly.

She shook her head. "I'm going to have to see the tape, Clint."

"So you, like, black out, when that happens?" Jason asked her.

"Not really. But I don't have a clear vision of what happened."

"You really had a different voice," Delilah told her.

"A very frightened voice," Carter said.

"The point is, what was the voice so frightened of?" Penny said.

"Right. How can someone dead be so terrified?" Delilah asked.

Darcy shrugged and answered slowly, carefully. "Hauntings are usually caused by a spirit's inability to get past certain moments in life. Maybe they haven't accepted the fact that they're dead."

"Say this is Arabella," Penny chimed in, excited, "and she was murdered. Maybe she thinks that she can get help, and it won't happen."

"There's probably a line," Liz put in excitedly. "A delicate, fragile line, between life and death. But those who died violently or in painful circumstances can't quite find the line. So they're in limbo. And still afraid, perhaps, of the things that frightened them in life."

"That may be the answer," Darcy told her.

"We have to find out what that poor creature is afraid of!" Liz said.

"I agree," Penny said, swallowing down the last of her scotch. "Adam should have let us start over. Maybe we could try right now."

Darcy shook her head. "She won't come back now."

"How do you know that?" Carter asked.

"Fine lines," Darcy told him. "She's retreated."

"Is she watching us?" Clint asked.

Darcy hesitated. "I don't…feel…anything right now. Whatever ghosts reside here, they've all stepped back."

Delilah turned to Carter. "I have my own car, but I think I'm afraid to drive home alone." She looked abashed at Darcy. "It's so dark around here. These roads at night are creepy on their own, and I'm going to think there's a ghost at my shoulder all the way home.''

''Delilah, it will be my pleasure to drive home with you in your car,'' Carter told her.

''I can pick you up,'' Clint told him.

''I'll just take a cab,'' Carter told him.

''I don't mind coming to get you,'' Clint said.

 Carter stared at him, smiling over clenched teeth as he tried to make a point. ''No, Clint, thanks. It's all right. I'll just grab a cab.''

''Oh. Oh!'' Clint said, quickly lowering his head to hide a smile.

Liz yawned. ''I'm exhausted. But so excited! Darcy, what you do is so incredible. Can you teach me?''

I don't do parlor tricks! Darcy thought. *What I have can be a curse as much as a gift, and painful as well as rewarding!*

''I'm not sure I know how, Liz. It's a matter of keeping your mind open, I believe. I'm sure you'll get there,'' she said aloud. It was a lie. But there really was no truth to tell that could be understood. She rose. ''Excuse me, I think I'll go up with Adam and take a look at the tapes.''

She made a hasty retreat up the stairs.

Adam was in his guest room, the Longstreet Room. When she tapped on the door, he bid her to enter absently. He was deeply engrossed in the tape when she went in.

Darcy watched it with him. She listened to the voice, and the fear in it.

''What do you think?'' she asked him.

''I think it's strange, as we've all noticed, that a ghost can be so afraid.''

''Think it can be Arabella?'' Darcy asked.

''I don't know. I haven't had a chance to do the research that you've done,'' he said.

''I'll show you everything that I dug into tomorrow,'' Darcy assured him.

Adam sat back, looking at her. ''Matt is still convinced that there's a living human creating most of his problems.''

"I don't know," Darcy said. "I heard noises one night and I have to admit, I was convinced myself that there was certainly someone living and breathing making them. But Matt was there, and he walked around the balcony, and found nothing."

"Someone could have slipped back in the house, right?"

"Sure. But that doesn't account for the dreams, visions, and other phenomena."

Adam grinned. "I know that, and you know that, but Matt is a skeptic. Still, it's an interesting situation. Why would someone pretend to be a ghost?"

"I thought that maybe Penny wanted a ghost so badly that she was helping to create one," Darcy said. "Or maybe one of the guys was just having fun at Matt's expense."

"Tell me more about those two—Clint and Carter."

"Clint is a cousin from the wrong side of the blankets, as they say. Carter is a friend. Heavily into real estate, I believe."

"And Clint? What does he do?"

"Hang around, mostly. Penny is often despairing of him," Darcy said.

"What does he survive on?" Adam asked.

"I'm not sure. Maybe Matt's goodwill," Darcy said.

Adam nodded. "I'd like to spend tomorrow doing research. Get some things settled in my own mind. After that…maybe hypnotism?"

Darcy was not fond of being hypnotized. But it often worked.

"We'll never do anything you don't want to do," Adam said as she hesitated.

"Oh, I know. I guess, sometimes, still…" she sighed. "Adam, am I really such a freak? That's how people react to me, you know."

He smiled. "Elizabeth Holmes is green with envy."

"Yes, but I saw the looks in everyone's eyes tonight."

"You saw the look in Matt's eyes," Adam corrected softly.

She waved a hand in the air. "It's just the look...I get it from far more people than Matt."

Adam sat back. "I think he's falling in love with you. What do you say?"

"I say that he's entirely repulsed."

"I say that he's afraid," Adam told her.

"Matt Stone? You know, his name fits. He's chiseled. He's like coming up against a rock. Hard. And unchanging."

Adam laughed. "Even the hardest stone can be eroded. And maybe you've shaken him to the core, which always make a man or woman don a facade as quickly as possible. He's a decent man. Give him a chance."

"A chance for what?"

"A change of thought. That's difficult to come by, you know."

Darcy fell silent. Difficult. Impossible. If a ghost walked by in pure daylight, oozing ectoplasm, Matt would think he was seeing sunspots.

"By the way—he's worried about you. He doesn't think you should be here.

"I'm fine."

"He says you woke up terrified last night."

She frowned. "I just can't get a handle on this. I'm more frustrated than terrified, Adam, really. I see this event unfolding. I've taken on the persona of the man coming to the house, and that of the woman inside, waiting. I know that she's frightened, and I know that he has deadly intentions. When I have it, the dream goes a little further each time. Then...I lose it. I know that I'm seeing the past, but something in the dream bothers me every time. There's something that I should see, but just don't."

"That means that there is an end out there. We are getting somewhere, Darcy. You're seeing the event. We know that there is an entity, trying to tell us something. She's been reaching out, but she's still terrified herself. Poor thing. It's the depths of the fear she was feeling when she died. We have to make certain that we know who she is—you believe it's this Arabella. So, we're getting close, very close."

Darcy smiled. "Adam, I actually believe that this place is swarming with ghosts."

"Probably. But the rest of them seem to be happy ghosts. Just watching over the place. Arabella, or whoever she is, has the greatest power. And that's because she's so desperate to say something to us all. We'll get to it. By the way, I've asked David Jenner to set up a few of the cameras and some tape equipment in your room. Is that all right?"

"Of course," she said. She's seen Matt's face that night. He wouldn't be coming back to visit her in the darkness of the night.

"I'm right here, not a stone's throw away. Call me if you need me. Call if you think you may need me."

"I know, Adam." She gave him a kiss on the cheek.

"Are you all right, Darcy? I haven't seen you this shaken since…since the beginning."

"I'm fine," she assured him.

She wasn't. She was hurt. But then she'd known better than to fall for Matt Stone, to become emotionally involved. The truth of it was that she *wasn't* normal, and there just weren't many men out there willing to deal with her circumstances.

Adam was still staring at her. He knew her too well. "Adam, I'm fine," she said firmly.

"Maybe Matt Stone is right."

"About what?"

"That's it's dangerous for you to be here."

"Adam—"

"What about the library?"

"Adam, this I know—a ghost did not follow me into the library. I was alone when I stood on those boards. What happened was a coincidence."

"Still—"

"Adam, I'm close. I know I'm close. There's some little thing there that I'm not seeing, and once I know what it is, the situation will be solved. I'm certain. Good night, and please don't worry about me."

He nodded. Even as she left the room, he was rewinding the tape to study it once again.

Darcy walked to the Lee Room. It seemed very quiet. She didn't feel that the eyes watched her. Then she wondered if maybe the ghost was simply exhausted. Maybe the seance was as hard on their entity as it was on those living souls who had been involved.

"Let me help you!" she said aloud. "You don't need to hurt me or anyone. You have to get the courage together to let us know what happened."

There was no response.

Darcy locked the balcony doors. There would be no one slipping through them to see her tonight.

Weary, she got ready for bed, and crawled in.

The emptiness around her seemed absurdly loud.

Matt arrived back at Melody House, but for several long minutes, he remained in the car, staring at the house. Brick, mortar, and stone. It was a house, nothing more.

It was living history.

He thought about it and knew that he loved his house, no matter what.

And he was falling in love with Darcy.

No.

They'd shared some time together. She should be perfect, soft-spoken, clear-eyed, dignified beyond belief, beautiful in her every movement. Kind to others...

And just plain damned weird.

Shaking him and everyone else straight down to their foundations.

He thought about Mae's words with irritation. Whether she meant to do so or not, Darcy was perpetuating ridiculous beliefs. Maybe she really believed everything she said. The power of the imagination was tremendous. He knew that. But to believe that ghosts could come back, or even that a ghost could be causing dangerous events, even come back as a killer....

He'd known killers; too many of them. Men who killed in the pursuit of gain. Men and women so hung up on drugs they'd stab their own mothers for a dollar. Even those killers who thought that God or dogs ordered them to kill. And then there were those who killed for the sheer pleasure of it.

Flesh, blood, real. More terrifying than anything imagined that could go bump in the night. And he had dealt with them so many damned times that to believe that brutality could exist in some fifth dimension was preposterous.

And yet....

How the hell had he known to go to the library the other day?

He swore softly and exited the car. He'd taken his time getting home.

And to his great pleasure, his house was empty.

He locked up and climbed the stairs to the second landing.

He paused there. Darcy's door...the Lee Room. She wouldn't be expecting him. He knew that. It had nothing to do with ESP or instinct.

He had seen the way that she had looked at him.

He went into his own room and closed the door.

The dream came again.

She had dreaded that it would, but she had been anxious as well, desperate to experience what had happened, and *see*. See clearly, know exactly what had happened.

She entered into the mind of the man in the past. Saw what he saw.

The woman.

She was, the man knew—beneath the rage that had risen within him—always urgent, obsessive, beautiful. He had seen in her again everything that he had desired when she had appeared at the upper landing. He had seen the structure of her face, the shadow and light of the night, enhancing the sculpture and curves of her body, granting moonlit magic to her hair. She could create a fire with a single glance, whisper words that could drive a man to pure frenzy.

She could touch a man....

And do so many things. Bring arousal to life in seconds, manipulate the senses, tear into the mind.

Ah, yes, and she could do so much more.

His head was spinning, torn with pain. And she was running, but it appeared she did so in slow motion. He rose in much the same way, seeing the wall, the bed, the clock, ticking away the seconds, minutes, hours.

Ticking away the night.

He staggered to his feet. She was running; he had to run, too. She was so gorgeous in flight. Her appearance so fragile, so innocent. She ran....

As if she could escape.

She wasn't so fragile, and certainly not at all innocent.

Still, he was far stronger. He followed her out the door.

And faster.

She was captured in the replay of the past, yet her own resources blindly guiding her, Darcy rose in her sleep, anxious to catch up with the specters of time gone by. She moved like a wraith in the night, sliding across the floor, opening the door—that through which the spirit images had so easily drifted.

She came to the landing, to the rail, and looked down the stairway.

But a sound behind her startled her back to life. She felt a fierce shove, slamming her hard against the railing where she teetered precariously for several seconds.

She came to full wakefulness in a split second, realized her position, and instinctively fought to right it. She was strong enough herself, and quickly maintained her grasp and equilibrium, her mind working quickly and with outrage.

Someone real, alive and well, had been on the upstairs landing. She had heard a real noise. And real hands had attempted to push her over!

Righted, she spun around.

Matt's door was moving.

Opening? Or closing?

She stood against the rail, her heart in her throat, staring. The door seemed to close another inch, and then to open.

In boxers and a robe, Matt emerged, striding out on the landing, eyes touching on Darcy, then looking up and down the second level.

"What are you doing out here?" The question sounded like a bark.

She swallowed hard. She knew him—didn't she? *Or did she think that she knew him because she had been so tempted to sleep with him?*

No. Whether they ever spoke two civil words again to one another or not, she didn't believe that Matt Stone was the type of man who would push a woman over a railing to her death.

"Darcy! What's going on?"

Still, she hesitated. *She couldn't tell him.* She didn't believe that she had been accosted by a ghost, but then…it hadn't been until she had heard the noise, felt herself in extreme danger, that she had really snapped clearly from the force of the vision.

And whether she told him that she believed she had been attacked—by either a ghost or a living being—he would start insisting again that she was somehow in danger. He would force her from the house. And her instincts were good—she really could protect herself.

She hoped.

"I couldn't sleep," she lied. "I was just trying to… imagine what might have happened here."

"You should never lean against a railing like that."

"No? I suppose not." She pushed away.

He was tense. His hands were knotted at his sides, his

features drawn. She was certain he had no idea he looked
so fierce.

"You shouldn't run around the house at night," he said.

"Why not?"

"You know that I believe there's a person behind all
this."

"Oh? Who, Matt? You, Penny? Or do Carter and Clint
slip into the main house at night? Or could it be the
groundskeeper, that great guy, Sam, who works out
there?"

"I don't know," he said flatly. "The point is, you, of
all people, shouldn't be running around the house at
night."

"Why me, of all people?"

"Because you've got an imagination that would put any
child to shame."

"Really?" she inquired icily.

"Oh, come on, Darcy, that's the point. You really do
believe everything that you say."

"Ah. Damn, I really need a psychiatrist."

"Maybe you do."

It seemed as if the words pained him. His fingers were
still balled into his palms. A pulse throbbed at his throat.

"Why are you so ridiculously angry with me?" she demanded.

"Because you've let this happen to you!" he exclaimed.
"Darcy—"

He started to take a step toward her. She shook her head
vehemently, backing away. "No, Matt, I haven't let anything happen to me. *You* should see the psychiatrist.
You're so set in your ways it's amazing that you even
agree to daylight savings time. Excuse me, will you? I'm
going back to bed."

She walked by him, heading for the door to the Lee
Room. As she passed him, it was almost as if he touched
her. He didn't move. She could still feel the heat emitting
off him in great waves. She could somehow feel his vital-
ity, his tremendous strength, and his emotions.

Was that what remained? Such emotion, passion, laughter, love, anger?

She walked on by, breathing the scent of him. *Beloved* scent of him. Not to be. She wasn't the possessor of an incredible imagination, and she wasn't acting, from either anything made up, or anything believed.

Fuck him.

She could bend.

Matt Stone could not.

She wanted to cry. Spin around, beat against his chest. To what end? She had no power to change what lay within a man's mind. What she knew, what she did, had no tangible proof.

"Darcy?" Her name sounded somewhat strangled on his lips.

"Good night, Matt."

She walked into the Lee Room, and closed the door.

The dream didn't come to her again that night. She slept easily, yet awoke, a strange sense of fear slipping into her thoughts.

The sense had nothing to do with ghosts.

She had slept on through the night; she had not been bothered.

And yet, by day, her vision seemed clear, and her mind entirely rational. *Someone* had been out there on the landing with her last night.

Living, breathing.

And with deadly intent.

12

Downstairs, Darcy discovered Adam in Penny's office, going through the many volumes of history and legend there. When Darcy tapped on the door and entered, he slid his reading glasses from his nose and smiled at her.

"Good morning."

"Good morning, Adam. What have you found?"

"Well, I've read through the information on Arabella, and she does sound like a likely candidate, but then again...nothing conclusive. I'd like to do a great deal more reading here, and then, this afternoon or early evening, around dusk, I'd like to try hypnotism, if you don't mind."

"I told you last night. It's fine."

He nodded and waved toward the door. "Go get yourself some coffee. Matt is at work, Penny is off shopping...I think Clara is around working somewhere. Do you have any plans?"

Adam liked to do his reading alone. She knew that. He was politely suggesting that she make some plans, if she didn't have any, and let him get on with his work alone.

"Actually, there is something I'd like to do today," Darcy told him.

"Oh?"

"I'm heading back to the library."

"*Oh?*" Adam said.

"Mrs. O'Hara told me about someone else who had an encounter here. A maid who was working right around the time that Matt's grandfather died. Marcia Cuomo. I'd asked Mrs. O'Hara to have her call me, but as yet, she hasn't done so. I think I'll stop by and ask Mrs. O'Hara for Marcia's phone number or address, and see if I can't speak with her.''

"I think the library is still closed, with inspectors checking out stairways and floorboards everywhere," Adam advised her.

"Ah. Well, then, I'll see if Mrs. O'Hara is answering the phone there anyway," Darcy said.

Adam nodded his assent, already turning his attention back to the tome in his hands.

Darcy wandered into the kitchen. As always, coffee had been left for her. She helped herself to some and then started back up the stairs to the Lee Room.

As always, she paused when she was in the room, and waited. But this morning, the ghost was remaining still.

The information operator connected her with the library, where an answering machine picked up. But Mrs. O'Hara left her home phone number on the service, should anyone have an emergency.

It was hardly an emergency, but Darcy was beginning to feel a sense of urgency in regards to the ghost and whatever else it was that was going on at Melody House.

Mrs. O'Hara was not upset at being called, and was happy to give her Marcia Cuomo's home phone and address.

Since Marcia Cuomo's phone rang and rang, Darcy thought she'd drive by the residence just for something to do. She could hope that Marcia would return in the interim.

Penny had taken her car, but Adam had driven down from D.C. in his Navigator, a car Darcy loved. She ran downstairs to ask him if she could take it, and waved a hand in the air, she hurried back upstairs to grab her purse and Adam's keys.

Someone had been up cleaning her room in her absence. The balcony doors had been left open. Darcy started to close them, then paused, tempted to walk out and feel the sunshine and the breeze. As she did so, she was startled to hear sound from Matt's room. She walked over to the doors that opened to his room. They were locked. She peeked in a window.

There was someone in the room. She couldn't see clearly because the sun was so bright outside and the shadow so deep within.

Matt? Back from work for some reason? She raised a hand to tap on the window, then thought better of it.

Why speak with him?

Yet, as she stood there, the man at the desk looked up. She could see nothing but his form in darkness, nothing at all of his face. He stood stiff and rigid, staring back.

Matt, and he wasn't happy to see her, peeping through his window.

She turned, walked back into the Lee Room, grabbed her purse, and started out. Halfway down the stairs, she turned around and walked back up the stairs. At Matt's door, she paused a minute, but heard a rustling sound within. Firmly, she rapped on the door.

No answer.

"Look! I'm sorry. I didn't mean to stare in your window!"

Nothing.

Beneath her breath, she called him a few names.

"Matt?"

Still no answer. But she was certain someone was in there.

"Fine. Sorry, I'm leaving," she called out.

She ran on down the stairs, but at the landing hesitated. There was a phone on a little marble table beneath the arch of the stairway. She walked over to it, and flipped through the index on it, easily finding his number at work. She dialed, and a woman answered the phone.

"Is the sheriff there, please?" Darcy asked.

"He's not available right now. May I take a message?" the woman asked.

"Um, when will he be in?" Darcy asked.

"Oh, he is in—he's just not available. He's in a meeting

with the county code inspectors. Can I have him call you?''

''No, thanks, I'll just talk to him later.''

Darcy started to hang up, then hesitated.

She could have sworn she heard an extra click on the phone, as if someone had been listening in on an extension.

She hung up the phone slowly. She stared up the stairs, then walked up them resolutely. She lifted a hand to knock at Matt's door. The door swung inward; it hadn't been securely closed. ''Matt?'' she said, stepping into the room.

She looked around his office area, then walked into the bedroom. She knew that the place was empty.

Whoever had been in there was definitely gone now.

Her heart thudding, she once again walked down the stairs. It was all very, very, strange.

Far stranger than communicating with the dead, in her opinion, she thought wryly.

''Did I have any calls?'' Matt asked Shirley, exiting the conference room.

Since the accident in the library, he had gathered the council to suggest that a number of their civic buildings be given a thorough once-over.

Except that he was still having a hard time believing the truth that he had learned from both the local building inspector and his friends in Washington—the rot had been caused by the simple spill of soda. ''Imagine what it can do to a stomach, huh?'' Shirley had marveled. He had known then that her kids were going to be looking at straight water and milk for a long time to come.

''One call, and she didn't identify herself,'' Shirley said. She wiggled her brows at Matt. ''Great voice, though. Think it was Ms. Tremayne.''

He shrugged. ''If it was her and she wants something, I'm sure she'll call back. I have to be in court. Niles Walker was running around naked again last month, and I want to see that his family takes care of him humanely. Call me on the cell if you need me.''

"Sure thing."

Matt started out, then stopped, swearing silently to himself.

"Shirley?"

"Yep?"

"If Darcy Tremayne calls through and needs me in any way, make sure that she gets the number, okay?"

"Certainly, Matt." Shirley watched him, somewhat covering a smile of amusement. Then she frowned. "Do you think she's in some kind of danger?"

"Why should she be?" he asked.

And realized that he was thinking, *Yes! Definitely, yes. And why...*

Damned if he knew. Gut feeling. Except that he was determined he just wasn't going to have any more gut feelings.

He suddenly wished that he didn't have to be in court. No gut feeling—he was just worried. Darcy had acted so strangely on the stairway last night.

She had stared at him, as if *he* frightened *her*.

Worse than that, she had looked at him with something else in her eyes.

Suspicion?

Damn the whole thing.

"Later, kid," he said to Shirley.

"Later, Matt," Shirley agreed, and went back to her paperwork.

Adam sat back, puzzled. Darcy was right—it certainly sounded as if Arabella was the prime candidate for such a haunting. A woman who had considered herself a rightful heir to the property, thrown over so that her lover could marry a proper spouse. Yes, she sounded just right.

He sat back.

And yet...

He tossed his reading glasses on the desk and rubbed his eyes. Darcy had told him that there was something else, something she just couldn't touch.

Yet.

She would.

He rose and walked to the window, worried himself.

Was he putting Darcy in danger? Shouldn't he, at the least, explain why he had been so determined that they get into Melody House?

He couldn't, he thought with a sigh. Not yet. He couldn't color her opinions in any way, make suggestions, or even give hints that could throw her into the wrong direction. He just had to wait. This afternoon, under hypnosis, she might reveal a great deal.

He glanced at his watch. An anxious tick pulsed in his throat.

He should have gone with her.

Darcy was glad that she had driven out. When she knocked on the door of the old Victorian house near the small, lazy downtown section of Stoneyville, the door was instantly answered.

The woman might have been young. She was medium height, with dark hair, blue eyes, and a nice figure. But her face had a haggard appearance, the type that came from a difficult life. For some, it was bearing the burden of a house, husband, job, and children while struggling under a mound of debt. For others, it was the abuse of alcohol, drugs, and tobacco. Once, this woman had been very pretty. Now, she just looked exhausted.

But she was very pleasant, smiling at Darcy. "Yes, can I help you?"

"I hope so," Darcy said. "I'm sorry to disturb you." She hesitated, then explained. "I'm a psychic investigator."

The smile on Marcia Cuomo's face disappeared. She started to close the door on Darcy.

"Please! Wait, hear me out. I—I got your name from Mrs. O'Hara at the library, and I need your help. You definitely weren't crazy or anything of the like." She bit her lip. "Please, I'm not here to mock you or malign you, others have had experiences at Melody House and I really need your help!''

Marcia hesitated, then opened the door. "Come in, please."

Darcy stepped into the house. It bore a look of genteel poverty.

"Coffee? Or iced tea? This is summer, huh? I don't keep anything stronger in the house." She stared at Darcy, still stiff. But then, she sighed, as if believing in whatever empathy she saw in Darcy's eyes. She made a complete turnabout, admitting, "I joined AA—I never wanted to give anyone a reason to doubt my credibility again. Then, of course…there was just life to deal with." Marcia offered Darcy an ironic shrug. "One good thing about Melody House. I left there and went straight to a meeting. How's that?"

"If you're an alcoholic, a very good thing," Darcy said earnestly.

Marcia smiled, all her defenses seeming to melt away. "Iced tea, then?"

"I'd love some."

A few minutes later, they were seated in the Victorian parlor with tall glasses of iced tea. Marcia pointed out a few of the antiques, and told Darcy the house dated from the 1870s. "Not very old, not in these parts, anyway. But a great-grandfather of mine built it, so…well, I try to hang on to it. I've been learning a lot about carpentry myself, and my son comes down from New York to help me now and then."

"You have a grown son?"

Marcia smiled again. "He's twenty-two. I'm afraid I was one of those young ladies who had a high-school affair, and finally ended up with a four-year-old by the age of twenty. I screwed up a lot, I'm afraid. Danny's father helped out somewhat, but we never married, and he was killed in an industrial accident a few years after Danny was born. So…anyway, life is good now. Danny is great. Went to school on scholarships, and he's got a great job with NBC now. So...he helps out. I won't accept any of his money, not yet. It's too hard to live in the big city. But he brings a few buddies down now and then and we all paint and do odd jobs.''

"How wonderful," Darcy said.

"You're sweet. But you're here for a reason."

"Yes." Darcy stared steadily at her. "I believe with my whole heart that there is a ghost in the Lee Room, and I'd like to hear about your experience there."

Marcia stared back at her, and then shrugged. "You see, the thing of it was, I was drinking that day. I went to work with a little flask all the time. I loved the place, too. I'd worked for Matt's granddad now and then, knew all the guys around the place, even pretended I didn't know about a lot of the fooling around going on there, you know what I mean? Lots of women thought it was hot to let guys like Carter, Clint, and even Matt pick them up, you know, then screw around in a supposedly haunted room as truly historic as the Lee Room. The old man was tolerant of Clint, of course. And even Carter. Matt was gone a lot—he was working in D.C. before his granddad got sick, but when he was home, well, you meet a pretty girl, you get to tell her that you live in an incredible mansion like Melody House... Well, that's all beside the point. I was cleaning up there one day and suddenly it feels as if my hair is being pulled. Not tugged by a breeze, or anything. Pulled! Hard. I whipped around, thinking I was losing my mind. Then I hear this voice. And it's soft and moaning and going, 'Help. Help me! Please, for the love of God, help me!' I thought at first that one of the fellows was just kidding around. So I yelled at them to stop. Then...I thought I saw something. Like a little glimmer of light, heading out of the room and down toward the landing of the stairway. So I followed...peeked down the stairs, and the next damn thing I knew, I was lying at the foot of the stairway! By the mercy of God, I didn't break my neck. Penny found me there, and I suppose I reeked of alcohol. Still, I started raving, told her what had happened, that I'd been shoved down the stairs by a ghost. Penny is just dying to have ghosts there—I would have thought she would have believed me. But then again, I don't think she'd ever realized before that I did drink on the job. She didn't fire me. Only Matt could fire me then—his granddad had passed away. But with the way Penny looked at me, all disgusted over the way that I smelled, I knew that no one would believe me. Not even Penny. And Matt…if he knew, he'd say it was the alcohol for sure.'' She let out a long sigh and shrugged. ''I told Penny that I was leaving, to please tell Matt. And she told me to get help, and she'd never tell him the real reason that I left. So…some people know now. Cathy O'Hara, over at the library, is a saint. She had a run-in with vodka in her twenties, and was my mentor at the meetings. So…she knows all about me. And my experiences. The thing of it is, though, I don't talk about it, even when I hear about new episodes at Melody House, because I wouldn't be credible in any way to most people. Hell, I'm not sure I would have been credible to myself at the time.''

''Well, alcohol or not, I think you did meet up with a ghost. A dangerous ghost, so it seems. But at least, it did do something good for you,'' Darcy said.

Marcia smiled. ''Yes, the occasion did change my life. But I can tell you one thing—I'll never step foot inside Melody House again. Ever.'' She studied Darcy. ''Psychic investigator…so? Have you seen the ghost?''

''I know that there is a ghost in the room, and that she's trying very hard to make us understand something. I think she may be a woman who lived there hundreds of years ago by the name of Arabella,'' Darcy told Marcia.

''Yeah, maybe,'' Marcia said.

''You have another idea?'' Darcy asked her.

''No…no.'' Marcia shrugged. ''I don't know—I had worked there before, that's all. Been in and out of that room dozens of times. And I'd never felt anything before.''

''Really?''

Marcia nodded. ''It was about…I don't know, five years

ago, I think. You could check the records. But I'd done parties in that house, worked part-time, forever.'' She grimaced. ''Arabella sure has taken her time getting around to whining, huh?''

''I guess she has,'' Darcy said, then asked, ''Is there anything else you can remember that might help me?''

''I wish. Like I said, I was drinking back then. I wish that I could help you more.''

''Believe me, you've helped me a lot,'' Darcy told her. ''I guess I'd better get going. It was a pleasure to meet you. And thank you so very much.''

''My pleasure,'' Marcia assured her.

''And—'' Darcy began.

''If I do think of anything else, I promise, I'll call you right away. Hey! Tell the gang hi for me, will you? Clint, Carter, Penny—and Matt.''

''I'll do that,'' Darcy said. She waved as she walked out to the car, feeling as if a bunch of puzzle pieces were in front of her.

Their positioning should have been obvious, and she was certain, if she just tried hard enough, they would all fall right into place.

Just what was it that she was missing?

There was time to go back to the office when the judge adjourned the court for the day. Matt realized that he simply didn't want to go back.

Adam had never told him how long he and Darcy planned to be at Melody House. He could remember Adam telling him, ''It's not a paint job. I can't really estimate the hours we're going to need. But don't worry about it. You'll be able to go about your day-to-day business with no interference.''

Hah.

All right, so they didn't really interfere with his life. Not by just being there.

But there was this ridiculous tug. Not a hunch, or a gut feeling. He was anxious to be at the house.

Anxious, sure, because there were people in it.

There were always people in Melody House. They hadn't rented any of the rooms for now, and they hadn't scheduled any tours. But if they really needed to, they could. He was just loathe to do so until…

Until whatever was happening was solved—and not happening anymore.

He turned his car toward home, then poked the speed dial on his phone for home. Penny answered. "Hey," he told her.

"Hey."

"What's going on there?" he asked.

"Nothing much. I'm in the office, calling a few people. Juggling some Christmas parties—do you believe we have to book this early? Of course, it's exciting, but—"

"Darcy around?" he broke in.

"Yes, she and Adam were just having tea, and they're going up to the Lee Room soon."

"She's all right?"

"Perfectly."

"Has she been in all day?"

"No, actually, she wasn't here when I finished shopping."

"Where did she go?"

"Honestly, Matt! I don't know. I don't give her a third degree every time she walks in or out of the house."

"Maybe you should," he muttered beneath his breath.

"What?"

"Never mind. By the way, call the appropriate minister and see if we can't have a little rite and get that skull buried tomorrow."

"Tomorrow, Matt? That's too fast! We won't be able to invite people, to have the press."

"That's right."

"Matt!"

"Penny."

He heard a huff so loud the wind from it almost came through the phone. "All right, Matt. As you wish."

"Thanks, Penny. You're a doll."

"And you're a tyrant."

"Sorry."

"What on earth was that?" Penny murmured.

"What?" he asked, frowning.

"I don't know…a thudding sound. I'll go see. Bye, Matt."

"Penny, don't hang up—"

His answer was the dial tone. He tried to call back, and got the answering machine. Swearing, his lowered his foot on the gas pedal.

Adam knew that he was a good hypnotist, but there was also no subject in the world quite like Darcy.

They had talked awhile when she'd returned that afternoon to tell him about her visit to Marcia Cuomo. They had gone over the various events that had occurred in and around the house, and both agreed that there was something very peculiar about the ghost's desperation—and fear.

Most of all, Adam was disturbed that Josh didn't seem to be able to enter the house, the realm of onetime violence. He had always been Darcy's spiritual guide, and he knew that she sometimes felt lost without him.

"There's a force that keeps him away, and I can't understand it," Darcy explained, shaking her head.

Adam was silent for a minute. There were still so many things that he would never understand. He had never had the abilities Josh had possessed, now passed on to Darcy, but he did have a tremendous skill with the occult and it saddened him that he couldn't reach his own son, not the way that Darcy could. He had always recognized an extra sense in others, and he had known how to mentor and lead those who were confused and horrified by their own gifts.

He had begun Harrison Investigations when his wife, Carol, had died, and Matt had only been a child. His son had told him then, at the funeral, that his mother was there, trying to make them both understand that she would never really leave them, that she would be with them forever. He had wanted to contact her himself so desperately, for the pain of her loss had been devastating. And yet, he'd known that Josh had spoken the truth when he talked about seeing his mother, for he had told Adam things that only Carol had known, and in the time that followed, he had discovered himself incensed by those who claimed to be mediums and merely took the bereaved for all they were worth. In his pursuit of lies, he had stumbled upon truth, and found his own fascination with the sixth sense and the powers of the mind—and spirit.

Death had not been a terrifying prospect for Josh. He had known that his mother would come to take his hand, just as he had known that he was not meant to have many years on earth. Josh's certainty regarding his own early demise had chilled Adam, and yet Josh's calm acceptance of the fate awaiting him and the knowledge that he would reside again with his beloved mother had been a strange comfort for Adam.

And though his son wasn't with him, there were times when Darcy could make him feel as if Josh were in a room, joking with them, helping them.

In the realm of the world of the dead, however, Josh was not an old soul. And there were barriers he could not cross, forces he could not best.

Adam thought that pure malevolence was something Josh couldn't touch. He had been far too decent to know evil. Perhaps, one day, he would gain the strength to go against such a force. Not yet. He was a spirit as kind and patient as the human he had been, able to touch pain, sorrow, regret, and loneliness, simply not a lingering wall of brutality.

"Adam," Darcy said softly. "Josh doesn't come in this room."

Adam nodded. "If I'm frightened for you, Darcy, I'll bring you right out."

"I trust you completely, Adam," she told him. And he knew that she did. He reached out and squeezed her hand.

"Let's begin," he said, and she settled back.

They were in the Lee Room together, she lying on the bed, he in the chair by the little secretary against the wall.

Adam had suggested that they work alone, quietly, without having the household around. There had been too much disruption at the seance.

"Relax, breathe. In and out, in and out. Think of cool mountain streams, the sweet sound of the trickling water. Let nothing disturb the sweetness of the moment, the absolute calm and tranquility that seep into you with every breath." He didn't dangle chains in front of her face; he talked her into a state of calm, cleared her mind, and left it open to possibility. "Think of nothing, just feel the peace of the water, of the wind. Ease all your muscles, stretch, release, relax, and feel the air, fresh, clean, free...you'll enter a state like sleep, totally open, and let those who would speak come through, but you'll be safe, because when I say the word 'redhead,' you will awaken with ease. Follow my voice, and listen to the breeze, the water, and let the voices enter in...."

His voice droned on. He could see the changes as Darcy entered a stage of consciousness that was neither sleep, nor wakefulness.

"There is someone here," he said then. "Someone who resides in this room, and perhaps roams the house upon occasion. Someone hurt, brutally hurt. I'm here to listen."

He waited.

For a moment, there was nothing. Then, he started as the phone book flew off the secretary and landed with a hard thunking noise on the floor.

A moment later, Darcy's lips moved.

"Help, God help me."

The voice they had heard at the seance left Darcy's lips. The spirit spoke in a desperate moan through Darcy.

"We must know who you are."

"There's danger...danger."

A strange sound, a moaning, a keening.

"You've got to explain," Adam said patiently.

' "Afraid…"

"You mustn't be afraid." He hesitated. "You've gone on. Nothing can hurt you now."

"No…still here. He's still here."

"Who? We must understand who you are, and who he is, and why he is still here. You're not the one hurting people, he is—is that right?"

"No."

Adam was startled and silent.

Darcy was beginning to breathe harder and harder. He needed to keep talking. "Are you hurting people?"

"So…hard. So hard…to touch. I'm tired…exhausted. They won't see."

"Are you hurting people?"

"No. Showing them, trying to show them…they don't know."

"Are you Arabella?"

Darcy's lips began to move. She said something, but Adam didn't hear what. The door to the room flew open, and Penny was standing there.

"My God!" Penny said. "What on earth was that?"

Adam frowned fiercely, shaking his head.

"Oh!" Penny said softly, staring at Darcy, who still lay on the bed, eyes closed, breathing coming deeply, shallowly.

"She's all right?" Penny asked.

"She's fine."

"Are you sure?"

"Penny, please be quiet," Adam said.

"Must…be careful. More than me, I'm certain. I knew…the girl. I thought…for the power, for the money," Darcy said in the strange voice.

"Who? Please, you've got to be more specific," Adam prodded gently.

"Afraid…"

"You don't have to be afraid," Adam said.

Darcy began twisting in distress.

"Adam!" Penny said.

Another voice interrupted them from the hallway. "Hey, what the hell?"

Clint had come up the stairs, and was standing behind Penny.

Adam kept his voice low, his tone even. "I need you two to either go away, or stand there silently."

"But—" Clint began.

Adam waved a hand at him and Penny, trying to shoo them away. Darcy was becoming more and more mired in the emotions that had once raged her, but Adam was certain that they were very close to a breakthrough, and he didn't want to break the tenuous thread that was connecting them to the spirit.

"She's…she doesn't look well!" Clint said, deeply concerned. "You should stop."

"We will," Adam said calmly. He stared at Clint. "When I'm ready."

Clint was unhappy, and uncomfortable, but he locked his jaw and was silent.

Darcy murmured something low.

"I can't hear you," Adam said, rising, and going to sit on the bedside.

Darcy's muscles were tensed like bowstrings. A sheen of perspiration had broken out on her face. She tossed on the bed, hands going to her throat.

Clint rushed into the room. "You've got to stop this!" he told Adam.

"Here, here, here…" Darcy murmured.

The door slammed inward with force. Adam saw that Matt Stone had arrived on the scene.

"What in hell is going on here?" he demanded.

A sudden breeze blew and the balcony doors flew inward. Distracted, Adam looked toward the balcony. He heard something scrape against the wall, just beyond the doors.

"Here, here, with us, run…go, no, no, there's no help, I have no help, alone, oh, please if you could hear me, if you could just hear me…help!"

Darcy screamed, clawing at her throat.

"Stop it!" Matt snapped.

Darcy was contorted, her back arched. For a moment, it appeared that she had been dragged straight upward, almost off the bed.

"Stop!" Matt shouted with thunder in his voice.

Darcy started to let out the terrible choking sound they had heard the night before. Her face was growing more and more flushed, beginning to resemble the red of a boiled lobster.

"Redhead!" Adam said.

She didn't respond. It seemed as if there were a rope, suspended from the ceiling, drawing her ever upward.

"Here, he's here! Are you blind!" she garbled out.

Here? Adam thought. *Was that it? Both specters lived on in this room, with the poor girl reliving her own death every time she tried to cry out for help?*

"Here!" Darcy shouted, then began choking.

They heard her breath, rasping, ridiculously loud in the room. Shorter, shorter…she ceased to fight, her body was falling….

As if she were dying.

"Jesus, stop this, stop it instantly!" Matt said.

The sound continued.

"Adam!" Matt shouted.

"Redhead!" Adam stated loudly.

Darcy fell back on the bed like a rag doll, every bit of tension eased from her body, the color fading as quickly as it had come.

Her eyes didn't open.

Matt pushed his way over to the bed, slipped his arms around Darcy, dragging her up.

She lolled, still like a doll…broken.

He pressed his fingers against her throat, feeling for a pulse.

"Darcy!"

She began to blink, then stared at him blankly, not even aware of the way he held her.

''Darcy!''

''Yes!''

He was shaking. ''Darcy, are you all right?''

''Fine, I'm fine!''

His eyes had been filled with anxiety and fear. They seemed to take on a clouded edge. He swore angrily, still shaking, set her down, and strode from the room.

As the others watched him leave, Adam became aware again of a scraping sound against the outer wall.

13

Penny and Clint were staring at her, Darcy realized, as Matt Stone left the room. Adam could bring her out of a state of trance quickly and completely, but that time, she had felt a little disoriented, the more so because it seemed that she had opened her eyes to see Matt staring down at her like a raging bull. The force of his emotion sent a sinking sensation throughout her, then a rise of anger. She didn't know what had happened, but it must have been something that clearly demonstrated there was something beyond their known world. Matt simply didn't want that to be the truth, and so he continued to deny it, no matter what he saw or heard.

Darcy looked to Adam, but he was the one person in the room not paying any attention to her. Adam was heading out the balcony doors.

"Darcy?" Clint said hesitantly. "Good God, Darcy! Do you feel faint, ill? Should we call a doctor? Do you need something?"

"I'm fine," she assured him. "I'm really, truly, honestly fine. If there's any sense of danger, Adam gets me out of a trance. And once I'm out of it...I'm fine. Please believe me."

Clint kept staring at her, but then nodded slowly. "What...what happened?" He asked.

"I don't know," she told him.

"You don't know anything?"

"I'm afraid not. Did we learn anything?" she asked anxiously.

"I...don't think we learned anything more," Clint said, looking at Penny.

"It was like last night," Penny said. She added softly, "Very scary. You're...not scared now?"

Darcy shook her head. "I'm sorry. I must have been very deeply under. I don't remember anything. I was listening to Adam...and then looking into Matt's eyes."

She was surprised by the look of anger that flashed across Clint's face then, and she thought it was for her. But it wasn't. "I'm sorry that Matt can be such a jerk," he said. "But, hey, that's his problem." He walked forward into the room, offering her a hand. She accepted it, rising. "I think we should get out of here. How about it?"

"Go out? The two of us?" she said. She really didn't remember anything, and yet she was still a little slow as she made the transition back into the world of the living. Hypnotism was very different. Sometimes, she knew snatches of what happened, as if she had been a distant observer. Sometimes, as on this occasion, she had no recollection at all of anything that had gone on.

He smiled. "Not a date—you'd turn me down. I mean, I think we should go out. You, me, Adam, Penny, Carter, if we can find him. Clara, if she's around, even old Sam. Anyone we can round up. We need to get out of this house for a while."

Adam walked back in from the balcony, wearing a frown of deep introspection.

"Adam?" Darcy said.

"Yes, what?" he said, as if startled by being drawn from thought.

"Would you like to go out?" Darcy said.

"Out where?" Adam asked.

"Anywhere away from the house. Heck, even the Wayside Inn," Clint said.

"It'll be fun," Penny said, but didn't sound entirely certain.

Adam smiled. "Sure."

"I'll see who I can round up. We'll meet downstairs in ten minutes?"

"Sounds like a plan," Adam said.

Penny and Clint turned to leave them. When they were gone, Darcy walked to the door, closed it, and turned to Adam.

"Well?"

He grimaced. "We're close."

"Is it Arabella?"

"I don't think so," he said slowly.

Darcy frowned. "Then…?"

"I don't know. But I agree with what you've been feeling, that we're very close, that the ghost is afraid, so afraid that she can't quite tell us what she is so desperate to say. We have to figure it out."

"But it seems that we're hitting a wall at the same place every time," Darcy said. "And I'm afraid that I'm going to be thrown out of here any minute now."

Adam waved a hand in the air. "Matt would never force you to leave."

"You haven't seen the way he looks at me."

"I know Matt."

Darcy arched a brow.

"Scared ghost—scared sheriff," Adam said, shrugging.

"Neither makes much sense, does it?"

"When you're dealing with matters of life and death, faith and belief, things don't have to make sense, Darcy. You know that."

"Maybe we're letting this all go too easily. They're gone now. You should hypnotize me again, we should pursue this with greater intensity—"

"Darcy, no. Whether you want to admit it or not, there's too much stress in what we do to repeat it with that kind of frequency. And I'm not sure we could make contact again. Spirits seem to possess only so much energy themselves. Clint has the right idea. Let's get out, do something. Are you ready? Do you want to change or anything?"

She grinned. She was in jeans and a tank top. "For the Wayside Inn? No, I think I'm formal enough."

He offered her his arm and started for the door.

"Adam," Darcy said suddenly.

"What?"

"What were you doing out on the balcony?"

"Oh…nothing. Looking around."

"Why?"

"I thought I heard something out there, while you were under. But when I went out, there was nothing, no one. Must have been birds, or a squirrel or something. Heck, maybe the old place even has a rat population."

"Charming thought," Darcy said.

"Hm. I was just thinking. What do they do in these old places when they have rats?"

"Traps," Darcy said. "Or exterminators. Or maybe even they bring in a cat."

"Cat! Precisely."

"Then…"

"Oh, I'm just thinking out loud at the moment," he said. "Come on, I'm anxious to see this Wayside Inn, the heart of society in Stoneyville!"

As it turned out, Clint's idea was not a bad one.

Matt had disappeared, but Clara Issy had been folding sheets in the laundry room and Carter had been working on his real estate papers in the stables; both were eager to spend some time out. Even Sam, the caretaker, joined them. Adam and Clara did the driving, since she was heading on home after and Adam never drank alcohol. Whether Darcy wanted one or not, he was determined that she had a drink—a big one.

When they arrived, the Wayside Inn was jumping. A band was playing a cross between rock and country and there were a number of pool players in action. Mae and a few younger barmaids were bustling about. Carter instantly challenged Darcy to a game of pool. She imagined that he was certain he could best her in a matter of minutes, but he was to be sadly mistaken. She could play the game with a decent skill.

David Jenner was playing at one of the tables when they arrived, and Delilah Dey was there as well, sitting at the bar. Since Carter had challenged Darcy, but David had possession of the table, Darcy suggested she partner up with David. That way, Carter could ask Delilah to be his partner.

Delilah was very pretty, and certainly, she was intelligent and savvy regarding Stoneyville.

But she was no pool player.

Darcy had thought that she might be somewhat distracted from the afternoon events, but she wasn't. She sank three balls on the break, and within a matter of minutes, she and David emerged the winners.

"My turn!" Clint challenged.

"Who's partnering who?" Carter asked.

"One on one. Darcy and me," Clint said.

An "Ooooh!" went out through the bar.

Darcy laughed, feeling her competitive spirit rising.

"What's the bet?" she asked.

"Winner takes all, of course," Clint said.

"Oh? And what would that be?"

"Let me think," Clint said, then brightened. "I know. You and me. Dinner—somewhere other than here. And a movie."

"Go for it, Darcy!" Adam told her.

"I can beat you, you know," she told Clint.

"Maybe. And then maybe, hey, the South shall rise again!" Clint teased. "What can you lose? A night out."

"That's if I lose?" she said, laughing.

"If you win, you get to pay," Clint told her.

She grinned, and bent down to slide her cue.

This time, the game was tough, and it seemed that it went on and on. The entire bar seemed to tune in, and even the musicians went on break to make comments, call out encouragements, and monitor the game.

Darcy was caught up in the contest, enjoying the chal-

lenge. Clint was good, very good. When she took the first
game, he called for two out of three.

She lost the second.

They started the third.

Clint made a shot which left her with a dangerous play.
Her only shot would set her dangerously close to the eight
ball. As she walked around the table judging angles and
distances, she became aware of the sensation of being
watched.

It was strangely familiar, and yet...

Not at all unearthly.

Of course, she was being watched. Everyone in the bar
was watching her.

And still...such a strange feeling.

She hesitated, straightened, and looked around.

She was startled to see Matt at the bar. But he was the
only one in the room *not* watching her. He was on a stool
between Adam and Penny, talking to Mae, who was behind the counter.

She gave herself a shake, unnerved by both the sensation, and the fact that Matt was there.

"Ms. Tremayne...?" Clint prodded, grinning.

"You think you've got me, don't you?" she said.

"I think you're in a tough spot," he said.

"Check—but not checkmate," she told him.

She would not let Matt ruin the good time she'd been
having here tonight. Very carefully, she gave her attention
to the game, focusing.

She made the shot, setting up the eight ball so that she
could easily call the side pocket. A second later, she sank
it as well, and victory was hers.

Her effort was met with thunderous applause, and a
round of congratulations from the friendly folk around her.
She smiled, and saw that Adam was watching from the
bar, and that he seemed very pleased to see her having a
good time.

Matt still hadn't glanced her way.

Clint set his cue down and walked away, but came right

back, bearing two beers, one for her, one for himself. He clicked his bottle to hers. "I concede. With tremendous graciousness, of course."

"Thanks."

They both leaned against the table. He looked at her, smiling ruefully, shaking his head. "So you can play pool, too. Who would have known?"

"My dad liked pool," she told him.

"I'm supposed to be pretty good, you know," Clint said. He leaned closer to her suddenly. "Don't look now, but Carter is putting the moves on Delilah at last."

"Good for him," Darcy said.

"Not a bad match," Clint mused. "He prefers to hang around Melody House, but Carter's quite a mogul. He needs to clean up a few of his holdings, but, hey, he has invested in a number of good land and property deals. And there's the young councilwoman. Should work out well, don't you think?"

Darcy nodding, sipping her beer, studying Clint. "What do you want out of life, Clint?"

He laughed suddenly. "Am I nothing more than a sad reprobate, living off the largesse of my far more responsible family member?" he said.

"I did not ask a question anything like that!" she protested.

"I've actually been working very hard on a project that should come through at any time," he told her. "But don't give me away, huh?"

"I can't give you away. I don't know anything about it," Darcy told him.

"Hm." He studied her. "You can't read my mind?"

"No."

"And…" He hesitated. "You really don't know anything more than what you're saying about the ghost at Melody House."

"No. I can intuit things, sometimes, but I can't read minds," she told him.

His grin deepened. "That's good."

"Why?"

"Because you'd probably want to slap a lot of people a lot of the time, if you knew what they were thinking."

"In a strange way, I think that's a compliment."

"It's meant as a compliment—even if a strange one." He lowered his head to whisper against her ear. "What do you think old Matt is doing here?"

"Having a beer."

"I don't think he can let you out of his sight."

"I think he'd be delighted for me to be permanently out of his sight."

Clint shook his head. "No. You've gotten under his skin. Big time. He's just being a jerk. Want to make him jealous?"

Darcy smiled. "Thanks—but no."

"He's nuts about you. And he should just admit it."

Darcy touched his cheek affectionately. "Clint, I'll agree that he was attracted to me. But nothing will go beyond that."

"Why?"

"He can't deal with me."

Clint weighed that for a minute. "He can't deal with his fear for you."

"Why should he be afraid *for* me?"

"Darcy, you should have seen him last night. Of course…"

"Of course what?" she demanded.

"I'll tell you myself. It was damned scary. And this afternoon was worse."

She didn't answer him, but took a long swig of her beer.

"Darcy," he said, "could you take on a past experience with such reality that you could die?"

"I don't think so."

"You don't *think* so?"

"No. I never get into a trance or allow myself to be hypnotized unless Adam is running things. I trust him implicitly. So…it never gets that far. He says a single word, and I snap out of it."

''Not today.''

''What do you mean?''

''He spoke to you twice before you recognized his command.''

''He probably didn't speak loudly enough,'' Darcy said.

''He spoke loudly,'' Clint told her. ''Darcy, I have to admit, this afternoon was scarier than last night. I know how determined and confident you are, but...maybe you ought to just drop this case. What if you wind up being in the soul or spirit or whatever it is of the ghost—and unable to get out? Today it was as if...as if you *were* dying.''

''But I wasn't.''

''Still, Darcy,'' he said, ''Aren't you ever scared yourself?''

''Terrified, at times,'' she assured him.

''Then why do you do this?'' he asked.

''Why do people become cops, or firefighters? What I do is nowhere near as dangerous as anything like that.''

Clint exhaled, shaking his head as he looked at her, and yet doing so with a certain admiration. ''You are a good kid, Darcy. Still, you should give this one up.''

''I can't,'' she said simply, and determined to change the subject. ''What about you, Clint? What is it that you really want out of life?''

''I think I'm going to get it very soon,'' he said.

''What?'' she pursued.

''I'm afraid if I tell anyone, I'm going to jinx myself,'' he said, laughing. ''Hey, but I'm not the old ne'er-do-well you think I am. Ask Matt. Penny runs the household, Matt is the sheriff. Sure, he has final say. And, of course, we have Sam to run the grounds. But who do you think makes sure that the little things get done on a day-to-day basis? I find the right roofers and carpenters, I see that the outbuildings are repaired. I'm not such a bad guy, really.''

''I didn't suggest that you were,'' Darcy said. ''I was just curious about what you really wanted.''

''Um, sure, because the house is Matt's.'' He laughed suddenly. ''Don't look at me like that. I don't have any plans to off my kin so that I'm the only Stone left to inherit the place. I'm not sure I'd want Melody House. The place can be a damned headache. The upkeep is exorbitant. But don't worry about me. I have a few college degrees of my own—I taught for a few years, did you know that?''

''No. What did you teach?''

''English. Hey, don't look now, but the sheriff has been watching us suspiciously. Want to make him jealous?''

''No,'' Darcy said, smiling as she shook her head.

''Too bad,'' he said, but lightly.

''Well…what shall we do now? Want to order some food? I'm ravenous.''

''Sounds good.''

''And there's an empty table over there. Let me see if I can gather the forces.''

They headed for the table Clint had indicated, gathering their group as they did so. Adam had been deep in conversation with Matt, but the two of them joined them. Whatever his anger had been earlier, Matt displayed none of it at the Wayside Inn.

Neither did he come particularly near Darcy. When the conversation at the table started to veer toward the haunting at Melody House, Matt stepped in to ask Carter about some of his properties, and Adam kept the ball rolling, wanting to know more about the general area. The meal passed pleasantly, and when it was over, yawns around the table indicated that it was time to go home.

Darcy drove back with Adam, Penny, and Carter. They reached the house first. Darcy went straight up to the Lee Room. Adam went with her, taking the video and audio tapes that had been running from the recorders, and resetting them.

''You are all right in here?'' he asked.

''Absolutely,'' she assured him.

''I can stay in the chair, if you want,'' Adam said.

''Adam, if I don't let these dreams come, I'll never see it out to the end.''

He nodded. ''But you're sure you're all right?''

"Yes! Get out, Adam. Go to bed," she told him.

He kissed her cheek, and left her.

Darcy had just started to doze when she thought she heard movement on the balcony. She lay in bed for several seconds, listening.

After a moment, she got up and went to the French doors, but didn't open them. She paused, and listened. Sound…movement. She moved the draperies, her heart seeming to pound in her throat.

There was someone on the balcony. Matt. He was at the rail near the door to his own bedroom suite, looking out at the night.

She hesitated, wishing she could go out. There was no reason to do so.

Painfully, she turned, and went back to bed.

The woman in white.

That night, Darcy saw her, standing at the foot of the bed. She was in a haze; Darcy saw no details in her face, no colors, just the woman, in sheer white, standing at the foot of the bed.

Then, she faded.

And the dream came. Somewhere inside herself, Darcy knew that the woman was growing more desperate, determined that Darcy understand.

Darcy slipped into the entity. Into the woman. And into the past.

She ran.

She made it out of the bedroom, and to the landing. And it was there that he caught her, falling upon her.

She struggled briefly, aware of his heat and strength as he grappled her down.

Once…

It had been so different. But now, she knew.

Still, she fought fiercely, struggled, desperate, aware that her life was at stake. The very urgency gave her a burst of power she might never have known that she possessed. She scratched, swore, kicked, punched, and fought to gouge out his eyes. She caught him with such a blow against the jaw that he went immobile, and she took full advantage, shoving wildly against his body, casting him off. She crawled to free herself from the sprawled weight of his limbs. She staggered up herself, and made the first step, but his fingers entwined around the hem of her gown, dragging her back down. She fell atop him, the breath knocked from her, and for a moment, they both lay panting. The pain in her temple dazed her; she realized she had hit her head on the second step. At her side, while she remained paralyzed, he rose up to a half-seated position beside her. And again, their eyes met. Something within his softened suddenly. He reached out a hand. She flinched, but his fingers felt as gentle as raindrops against her cheeks. ''I did love you so much,'' he said.

She touched him in return. He came to his feet, reaching for her hands, drawing her up and against him, and it might have been as many another night, when they had melded together, when passion had reigned every thought, when she could not bear to keep her hands off him, or he her. The room continued to spin, the pain in her temple was deep...but it seemed that he was whispering now, the words that could so arouse...and his hands, they were on her, his lips...nuzzled those whispers against her throat.

It was a fight, surely, nothing more. His eyes could not have been so deadly.

His whisper came again, against her lips, throat, her earlobes, her mouth, hard then, crushing against her. And she was falling...into his arms. She was aware of the sound of his footsteps against the hard wood floor, aware of his movement as he bore her weight.

They returned to the bedroom, and he set down upon the bed, tenderly. She closed her eyes, thinking that the affair was too passionate, ruled by the senses, nothing more, and yes, so totally wrong. But he moved away, and she knew. Knew that he had left her only to shed his clothing so that he could return, and flesh could burn against flesh.

But...

Silence. Nothing.

The moonlight pouring into the room, but no touch of his warmth, no vibrance and heat as he crawled atop her for he did not do so.

A dog howled, a cry to heaven, to the night, mournful, pathetic, prophetic.

Perhaps a storm was coming, and there would be thunder outside, like the rage of desire that was all that had ever really been between them. But a storm could mean a tempest, and that would be fine, for she still felt the adrenaline racing in her veins, but what she had seen before could not be, for he had loved her, loved her more than she had loved him, wanted her first without thought of consequences.

The wind blew...

But his silence continued.

A howl sounded again, eerie in the night. A rage of wind? The baying of the hound. She didn't know. She merely felt her heated flesh began to chill.

She came up on her elbows, searching for him.

He stood still at the secretary. He had not moved, not cast off his clothing in fevered abandon.

He was reading, reading what she had written. He stood dead still, his eyes riveted on the paper, and the words that she had written.

Then he turned to her, slowly. She saw the tension build in his hand, and rock through his arms and chest. She felt his gaze fall upon her with fury, greater than that she had ever seen before, even when he had first come that night.

Fear, like icicles, ripped into her.

Terror curled around her heart.

His eyes, oh, God, his eyes.

"You wasted no time," *he said aloud.*

She had to escape. But perhaps, her only chance lay in playing a game. Pretending that she didn't see the death in his eyes.

"I was angry. You meant to leave me."

He walked slowly to the side of the bed. "A woman scorned," he said lightly.

She would never know what the outcome might have been if she hadn't sat down to write that evening. Perhaps, no different. She had seen her own destruction in his eyes when he had first come; this look was only a compound of that, and when they had struggled in the hallway, it had been a reprieve and nothing more. She had seen him when he had first arrived, seen the way he had looked up at her from the first-floor landing, far below, staring up the stairway, to see her at the railing.

"A woman scorned," he repeated. "Is deadly. Deadly, deadly...dead."

She didn't scream. She didn't bother. She cursed him as he came toward her then. Cursed him, and the house, for all eternity. Her hatred was deep. She was about to be silenced. No one would ever know the truth about him, what had really happened. The truth would die with her, and in time, she would be...

Nothing more than legend.

If that much.

She started to spring to her feet once again.

She didn't make it. He fell upon her.

His hands...those hands which had brushed against her with the greatest tenderness and ardor...now closed around her neck.

Tightened, and tightened.

She strangled out curses. Swearing. With the darkening of the light that was her life, she still swore that he would pay, that come hell and damnation, somehow, sometime, through all the powers of existence, dark and light, she would come back, she would find her revenge.

Choking, gasping, lips turned blue, breath fading, blackness before her eyes...

"You'll pay," she swore.

"But no one knows that you're here," he told her.

The vise constricted, thumb pressing into her throat.

Black pinpoints joined together. Her lungs were bursting.
She longed desperately to keep fighting.
But light was fading…fading.
And then….
She was history.

Darcy woke, drenched with sweat, gasping for air. She sat up. A late-night show was still playing on the television. A coolness hummed throughout the room, soothing to her flesh, for she had been so hot, tossing and turning, twisting the bedclothes into piles of knots.

She had come to the end. She had seen the spirit die in the flesh. And yet…

She'd seen nothing clearly. No detail of face or form. She had felt the hands around her neck, but she hadn't seen the face.

She smoothed back her hair, and stopped.

She was there again.

The woman in white. Standing at the foot of Darcy's bed.

Then, she turned and started for the door. Darcy slipped from the bed. The woman turned back in her unearthly haze of white and beckoned.

She opened the door to the hallway and beckoned again.

And Darcy followed.

14

Matt lay awake, the picture of Darcy, contorted and gasping, replaying in his mind, over and over again.

She needed to be out of this house.

So why didn't he just make her leave?

He couldn't deal with it, he knew he couldn't deal with it, so why let her stay? *Figure it out.* Because he couldn't bear to see her go. So, what? Was he waiting to see if she'd wake up one morning and admit the whole thing was an act, their way of bringing the culprit to justice who was rigging the house to make it appear haunted?

It wasn't going to happen. And though it might be in her own mind, what she thought she saw and felt was real to her.

He was afraid for her, and he didn't know why. He didn't like being away from the house when she was in it. He didn't believe that ghosts could hurt people. But the living could. Why should he be afraid for her then when those she was chasing were ghosts?

He tossed, and turned, and then...

He thought he heard her door open.

He lay still, listening for a minute. Nothing. Nothing he could hear.

He rose anyway.

The wraith moved out of the door, and along the landing, heading for the stairs. Darcy followed. The ghost misted down the stairway in a white haze. Darcy paused at the landing.

The spirit stopped, looking back. Beckoning.

Once again, Darcy followed.

She scampered down the stairway, and became suddenly aware that she wasn't just in pursuit of a spirit. She resembled the spirit. She was in a long white cotton nightgown, chasing a specter. They were both puffs of white, the ghost floating, she actually setting her feet upon the steps. Bare feet. She hadn't bothered with slippers.

It hadn't occurred to her that the ghost would lead her beyond the house.

But that was what the specter intended.

She drifted through the foyer, straight to the front door, and then through it.

From somewhere within the house, Darcy heard a door close. She hesitated, then hurriedly began playing with the alarm and the complicated locks on the front door, opened it, and rushed out.

The spirit moved across the lawn and started drifting toward the stables and the outbuildings beyond.

Darcy followed. There was a moon out, and floodlights illuminated the entry to Melody House. But once she passed the stables, the lights dimmed. The ghost was headed toward the old smokehouse.

Suddenly, the apparition went dead still. Darcy, too, paused.

The spirit began to fade, slipping behind the building. Darcy ran after it.

She came around the side of the smokehouse and discovered that the wraith had indeed disappeared. As she stood there, puzzled and frustrated, she heard the snap of a twig. Something warned her not to make her presence known.

She flattened herself against the smokehouse, listening, waiting.

Footsteps fell…slowly, furtively. She held very still.

Closer…

She let her fingers crawl down the wood of the smoke-house door, seeking the handle. She gripped it, and tugged, but it refused to give.

The moonlight was casting curious shadows. Shapes that formed and reformed, billowed and withered, like the rise and fall of branches from the neighboring trees. But then one shadow became distinct.

It was that of a man.

She heard a strange, soft, snapping sound.

The man was carrying something. A cord...a strap...of some kind. An end was held in each hand and he tightened it, eased it, tightened it, eased it.

She'd seen the motion before. In a dream. When a killer had been contemplating murder.

He stood very still in the moonlight. Darcy ceased to breathe, watching, waiting.

Then the shadow moved.

And Darcy did, too.

She shoved away from the smokehouse, coming around the other side of it. She ran as if all the demons of hell were after her, heading back toward the house. At first, she heard thundering footsteps as well, footsteps that fell in hot pursuit.

The porch, blackened by shadow despite the floodlights, was directly before her. She raced up the steps, wincing when her bare foot fell upon a small pebble. She started to hurtle herself toward the door, then tried to halt her impetus, a scream rising in her voice as a massive shadow moved between her and the entry.

She crashed hard into the rising shadow, gasping out rather than screaming, but in a frenzy and ready to rip away and scream.

She couldn't do so.

Arms wrapped around her, fingers bit into her shoulders.

"Darcy!"

She froze. Matt.

"Darcy!"

Matt. Had he been behind her? Had he been the shadow

she had seen? Impossible, he'd still be behind her. Unless he had doubled around, leapt the railing, and sped around the porch. She was fast. That didn't mean that he might not be faster.

She had heard footsteps, and then...

Nothing.

"Darcy!" He gave her a little shake.

"What?"

"What?" he echoed. "What the hell are you doing out here?"

Chasing your ghost! She thought.

"Sorry, I was just out on a moonlight stroll," she said aloud.

She was close to him, and yet startled when his palm fell against her heart, a touch far too intimate, and though platonic, an aching reminder of other nights.

"Your heart is beating a thousand miles an hour."

"I thought I'd jog."

"In your bare feet and nightgown?"

He was looking sterner than a turn-of-the-century schoolmaster.

"Matt, what are you doing out here?" she demanded.

"Trying to find out what you're doing. And don't tell me about moonlight strolls."

"Why? I'm sure you'd believe that far easier than the truth," she challenged dryly.

"The ghost invited you out?" he quizzed skeptically.

"Yep."

"And where did she go?"

"She disappeared behind the smokéhouse," Darcy said. "Look, what good is any of this? You think I'm practically psycho, and it doesn't matter what I say. So—will you excuse me?" He was still blocking her way. "May I go back in?"

He hesitated. She was afraid for a minute that he'd tell her no, that he'd get her things, and drive her into town.

Then, she felt an unwilling tinge of fear. Maybe he had followed her. And maybe he had leapt the railing and raced around to accost her on the porch. Maybe whatever it was going on in Melody House somehow related back to him.

No.

"Matt, please, let me by you," she said softly.

He didn't budge. "I don't want you running around here at night like this," he told her.

"May we go back in?"

"Did you hear me? I don't want you around here in the dark like this. Barefoot. Half-naked."

"I am not half-naked!"

"In the moonlight, Miss Tremayne, you might as well be entirely naked."

"Sorry. I'll try not to excite the bugs and bats too much," she said. "May I please go in?"

"Once you've listened to me!"

"Fine, I understand. You don't want me running around the place at night."

"I don't care if the ghost sits down at your bedside and asks you out for a barbecue, do you understand?"

"Your words are incredibly clear," she assured him.

He stepped aside, and opened the door. She slipped on in, hoping she could tear back up the stairs and elude his questions and orders for the rest of the night at least.

But the stairway lights were on and Penny was standing at the landing. "What's going on?" she demanded, wide-eyed.

"Darcy felt like a stroll."

"The woman in white!" Penny said. She gripped Darcy's shoulders. "I told you before—I've seen her, too."

"You might want to notice that Darcy is wearing a white nightgown," Matt pointed out.

"Not tonight!" Penny said. "I'm not saying that I saw her tonight. Matt, I've told you this before. I've seen her. She runs down the stairway. As if…"

"As if she wants someone to follow her," Darcy finished.

"Moonlight plays tricks on the eyes, Penny," Matt said,

shaking his head. His voice had a grate in it. "And I don't think you all are crazy. I think you want this to happen so much that you do see and feel things." He swore softly beneath his breath. "Look, it's over now, right? Over for the night. Isn't it, Darcy?"

"Yes, it's over," she agreed.

Penny nodded, turned, and started up the stairway. "Good night then. But you're going to eat your words, Matt Stone. Trust me. You're going to eat your words."

"Good night, Penny," Matt called to her.

Darcy headed for the stairway. She was startled, and oddly frightened when Matt's hand fell on her shoulder. He pulled it away as she turned back to him.

"Darcy, I'm seriously afraid for you. I saw your face, at the seance and this afternoon. What happens if you see this thing all the way through? What happens when the murderer goes all the way, and the ghost is strangled to death in your vision?"

He had the ability to speak with a tone that gave nothing away, and to look at her with eyes as shielded as if clouds formed to cover all emotion. She didn't know if he was mocking her, or seriously concerned.

"I've seen the dream to the end," she said. "Tonight, before the ghost led me down the stairs and then outside."

It seemed that he drew away from her. Not physically. And yet…there was a new distance between them.

"So then, she's told you her story. Shouldn't this be like the discovery of the skull? Doesn't it mean that she'll be at peace?" He asked, and she thought that he wanted it to be over, he wanted Harrison Investigations out of his house.

He wanted her out of his house.

"There's something more, Matt. There's something more she wants us to know."

"And is she. this Arabella you read about?"

"I don't think so."

"Then…?"

"I don't know. But I almost know. I *will* know." She

turned again with precision and started up the stairs. He stayed at the landing, watching her for a minute. She had almost reached the door to the Lee Room when she realized that he had come behind her.

Once again, she felt his hands on her shoulders. She felt force in them, and anger. But once he had turned her into his arms, she saw his eyes again, and she was startled to realize that his anger was directed more at himself than at her.

"Darcy, you can be the most incredibly stubborn fool. You're playing with fire. You're going to wind up hurt!"

She opened her mouth to speak, but never did so. His fingers left her shoulders, fell upon her cheek, and the tension left his touch. He pulled her against him with a volatile emotion that sent shards of shimmering crystal desire racing through her in a matter of seconds. She wished she had the strength to know that it was all a loss, to push him away, but she didn't offer so much as token resistance, but slipped her arms around his shoulders, opened her lips to his, and pressed her body close, savoring the hard feel of muscle, heat, and life, and the extent of his arousal. They clung together there, in front of the door to the Lee Room, entwined in a building passion, kisses wet, searing, open-mouthed and desperate, until Matt at last pushed at the door. He walked into the room, his fingers then braided with hers, until he reached the recording equipment and yanked the plugs from the walls.

Then he turned to her, wrapping his arms around her and tilting her chin upward. "If anything happened to you…" he breathed.

"Nothing will happen to me."

"How can you be so damned certain?"

"Matt!" she stared up at him, drawing her fingers through his hair. "I know what I'm doing, honestly. And you mock me, you don't believe any of it, so why…"

"I have a feeling," he said, and mockery sounded in his voice, bitterness against himself, "I have a feeling. One

of your fucking intuitions, if you want. I have a feeling,
and the feeling is fear. Darcy, you should just let this go!''

    She didn't have a chance to answer, because once again,
it seemed, the desperate need to meld together swept over
him, and his mouth crushed down on hers, almost violently, but it didn't matter. His hands were on her shoulders, still a little rough, the white gown that might have
belonged to the spirit fell from her body to the floor, and
she felt the fire and ice of his heat and the room's coolness,
and she found her own hands on his chest, found that she
was pressing him back until they both fell on the bed and
she was in a fever to touch and kiss every inch of his
length, sinking into the heat, into the fire, into the need
which had become stronger than any sensation which had
ever touched her before, in either the physical or meta-
physical sense. Insanity might have even created the
depths of the hunger just to touch, the knowledge that there
was so much hostility between them, in all that their
thoughts ranged in such disparate patterns. His flesh was
vibrant with life, a heartbeat pulsing against her lips wherever they fell. His fingers ravaged her hair as she moved
against him, and his whispers were hoarse and taut and
curt, sound, shadow, light, anger, need, determination, all
creating the most vital sense of arousal. She dragged the
length of her body against him, fingers, lips, tongue, a
starting point, an ending point, and a need, somehow, to
make him realize that she was a part of him, within him,
burned against him, never to be forgotten. He swept her
beneath him with a surge of power that caught her breath,
thrust into her with raw and vivid drive and emotion, and
seemed to take her flying into a world of heat, of dampness, where everything physical, the scent of him, the feel
of his arms, brush of his palm, ragged, searing, movement,
cotton of the sheets, seemed extravagantly wild and real,
and still, somewhere else, she was soaring, and the ecstasy
for which they arched and pounded was far beyond earthly
pleasure. The world exploded and rocked, and she felt the
depth of him like fire and steel inside her, and a slow

withering that remained, for they were loathe to part from one another. And yet, all in the same moment, she found herself thinking of the dream, of the near-desperate passion that had ranged between the two....

And then, how the man had killed the woman.

Chilled, she almost threw him off her.

She closed her eyes, fighting the sudden wave of recall. *This was Matt. She had lived a past life, seen murder, and the memories lingered, and still...*

All that anger. All that passion. All that hatred.

"Darcy?"

"Matt." She lowered her head against him, chin against his cheek, not wanting him to see her eyes.

"Is something wrong?"

His knuckles brushed down the side of her face. Featherlight. Erotic, sweet, tender. Her breath caught again. The lightest movement caused a quickening in her.

"Everything is right," she murmured.

His arms tightened around her. She was startled when he said, "I'm afraid now, when I leave you alone."

"Matt, I can take care of myself."

"Then why am I so afraid?"

"You don't trust in me."

"Maybe I do. More than I imagine. And maybe that's why I'm so afraid."

"There is a ghost, Matt." She was quiet for a minute. The thought of the violence done in this room, in this bed, still haunted her. She fought the memories. This was Matt.

"You scare me, Darcy."

Tonight, for a moment, you terrified me, Darcy thought.

"Some things never can be," she said flatly. "But I'm glad I've known you."

"Darcy—"

"Please, let's not talk. Not tonight. Just hold me."

"Trust me. I'll be here. Holding you. Until I've gotten you out of this house," he said, his tone harsh, hoarse, and determined.

But his touch belied his tone.

A touch, a whisper, a breeze.

As seductive as a dream.

And yet, later, as she moved against him, she found herself asking, ''Matt...did you follow me out as far as the smokehouse?''

She thought that it took him a while to answer.

''No. When I reached the porch, you came flying into me. Why?''

''I just wondered,'' she lied.

He didn't say anything more.

She lay awake, absurdly afraid to sleep, afraid that the dream would return, and that it would be relived....

All that passion. All that hatred.

She would be the woman.

And he would be the killer.

Somewhere in the wee hours, she slept, and she did not dream. When she woke, Matt was gone. The hour was still early.

Darcy rose, showered, dressed quickly, and hurried down the stairs. She was in time. Matt was at the breakfast table along with Penny, Clint, Carter, and Adam. Clara Issy saw her, smiled, and poured her a cup of coffee.

''You're still sleeping in that awful room?'' Clara said.

''It's actually a beautiful room,'' Darcy said.

Clara sniffed. ''Anything eventful happening in it?''

Darcy looked at her for a moment, praying that Matt wouldn't say anything, and that her cheeks wouldn't flood to a brilliant red.

''There is a ghost there,'' she said, ''and we'll understand her problem soon enough.''

''Tell her to quit hitting people!'' Clara said.

''I'll try,'' Darcy assured her.

''We're burying the skull in the churchyard today,'' Penny said. ''Poor Amy! At one this afternoon, she'll be all together again. Well, in a way. One ghost down. But then, this place is riddled with ghosts, really, right, Adam?''

Adam set his coffee cup down. "Benign ghosts. Some aren't miserable, you see. They linger because a place meant something to them. And only those with truly acute senses ever know that they're about. So...actually," he said, and paused, winking at Penny, "some should be more than welcome to remain."

"Do you think they ever party together?" Carter mused.

"The ghosts?" Clint said.

"Well, I was wondering, if they all haunt the place, do they become friends? And do they talk to one another? Like, 'Hey, Beau, you there, Civil War guy? You spook out the parlor today and I'll take the upstairs rooms?' Whoops, sorry, Adam," Carter apologized. "I know how serious this is to you."

"Maybe they do correspond. I don't really know," Adam said, hiding a smile.

"Hey, I wonder if any of them can beat Darcy at pool," Clint said, smiling at Darcy. "Boy, kid," he told her. "Can you play pool."

"Thanks." She was grateful. It seemed that he was trying to take the attention away from a subject that always turned uncomfortable when Matt was in the room.

"I have to admit, I was amazed," Carter told her. "Who knew? She's gorgeous, she sees the future and she's a pool shark!"

"I like the game," Darcy said, sliding into her seat.

"You should play Matt. He's the best," Penny said.

Matt set his napkin on the table. "We'll have a tournament one day," he said, rising. "I've got to run into the office. I'll see you all at the church. And Penny, please tell me you didn't call every newspaper in the state."

"No, Matt, I didn't," Penny said.

"See you there," Matt said, waved a hand, and left them.

"I only called a few of the newspapers," Penny said softly when he was gone.

"Penny, Penny, Penny!" Carter chastised.

"They weren't that interested, I'm afraid," Penny said.

"Except for the obnoxious guy that Matt already hates. And Jason Johnstone, of course, will do a piece. But the town will be gearing up. The reenactment of Stone Gorge is this Saturday. Carter, are you taking part in that?"

"Definitely," Carter said.

"A battle reenactment?" Adam said with interest.

"I'm not so sure it was a battle. It was a major fight, not like Spotsylvania or the Wilderness. But there was cavalry involved, and a few companies, North and South, fought a desperate battle for a little hillock on the water, just off the main road. This year, the anniversary falls on Saturday, and the land is available—privately owned, but rented out to a living history company—and so people are very excited about it. The Wayside Inn is completely booked for the weekend, as is everything near here. It's great fun."

"And educational for the kids," Penny approved.

Carter grinned at Penny. "Wow. She likes me."

"Silly boy," Penny said.

"That does sound interesting," Darcy said. "Where do we go to watch?"

"The main road, just the other side of the forest. Clint and I will take you around. Clint has agreed to be a private in my company this year. We're short a few fellows."

"Yeah, they're all dying off," Clint said.

"So, we had a few old geezers. Armchair history buffs who have gone on to that great battle in the sky. It's still living history, and pretty cool," Carter said.

"Yes, and I agreed to join your company," Clint said. He stood. "One o'clock for the skull burial, huh? Adam, mind if we take your car? We can all go together that way. That Navigator is great."

"Sure," Adam said.

"Where are you off to?" Penny asked him.

"I'm a busy man, Penny—I've just had you fooled all these years," Clint told her.

"I've got work to do, too," Carter said. "We'll meet in the foyer, say twelve-thirty?"

They all nodded agreement. Both Carter and Clint started to leave. Penny cleared her throat, causing them to pause.

"Dishes. Kitchen," Penny said.

"Yes, ma'am!" Clint said quickly, saluting her with precision, as if he were practicing for the battle to come.

Darcy leapt to her feet, anxious to get Adam to herself. She picked up her own plate, and a number of the serving platters, telling Adam, "Meet me in the Lee Room."

Within fifteen minutes, they had extricated themselves from Penny and the kitchen and were sitting together in the Lee Room.

"I saw it all the way through, Adam, last night."

"Good. So…?" He moved around the room, hunkering down, picking up the plug to the video, which was not in the outlet. "You decided not to tape?"

"The plugs came out after the dream. We might have something on the video."

"Tell me about it first," Adam advised, taking the chair in front of the secretary.

"I've been in it from both sides," she said, "that of the victim, and that of the killer. I've felt their emotions, but I haven't seen their faces. Not clearly. But in life, they were very hot and heavy lovers. Then something went wrong. I think that the man did care about the woman, or, at the least, he was absolutely sexually fascinated with her. When he arrived at the house, he was contemplating murder. He arrived, she saw him, they struggled…and he almost stopped. But she had been angry when she'd been in the house alone. Angry, and writing something at the secretary. The murder may have been averted by lust, but then he saw what she had written. And then killed her. Here, on the bed. He had brought a strap of leather with him, but he wound up doing the deed by hand."

"So, we still don't know who, but we do know what," Adam said.

Darcy hesitated. "The ghost beckoned to me after that.

She led me out of the room, down the stairs, and outside. I got as far as the smokehouse. Then she disappeared.''

Adam was silent for a minute. ''We'll have to get Matt's permission to do some digging. And,'' he added, wagging a finger at her, ''we're going to have to set a few parameters for you, Darcy. You're telling me that you followed the ghost down the stairs—and outside?''

She hesitated, then nodded.

''But you didn't think to get me?''

''Adam, I would have lost her.''

He shook his head. ''I'm right down the hall. I should have heard you leaving.''

''It was all right.'' She hesitated. ''Matt came out.''

''Good.''

''Adam, there was something more. At the smokehouse, when the ghost disappeared, she didn't slip into a wall or anything. She just…faded. And I felt her sense of fear. Then…I saw a shadow. The shadow of a man, as if he were following, too, but lost her at the smokehouse as well. Either that, or…''

''Or?'' Adam demanded.

''He was following me,'' Darcy said flatly.

''This shadow was ethereal—or real?''

''I don't know. Yes, maybe, real. Because I heard footsteps. I felt…stalked.''

''So?'' Adam prodded.

''I ran.''

''To the house?''

''To the porch. That's where I ran into Matt.''

''Are you certain that Matt wasn't the one who had followed you out? Maybe he came partway to the smokehouse, then turned back,'' Adam suggested.

''He said that he wasn't out there,'' Darcy told Adam.

''You don't sound certain.''

''I am certain—I think,'' Darcy said, causing him to smile. ''Adam, how well do you know Matt? You were friends with his grandfather, right?''

He smiled. ''Yes.'' Then he looked a little sheepish.

"Once upon a time, Darcy, I was fascinated by history to the extent that I joined a reenacting group. A Pennsylvania group, of course. I was Yankee. Captain of a company that was involved in the skirmish here, at Stoneyville. I met Matt's granddad then. We would spend long nights on the porch, talking about 'what ifs.' He didn't have a strong belief in the occult or ghosts, but he was willing to admit that things happened in his old place that he couldn't quite explain. But nothing bad. Never anything that could be construed as dangerous. There were lots of stories about guests seeing a Civil War soldier in the parlor. Now and then, a door would open and close. There would be a chill in the room. He didn't believe that anything ever happened in the house that couldn't be explained. As in the one woman who was certain she had seen a soldier probably did see one. It was this time of year, and lots of folks were preparing for the annual reenactment. And the cold…well, it's an old place. There are drafts. As to the doors opening and closing, it might have been the wind as well. So he enjoyed the stories, but didn't feel that the place was in any way haunted."

"Is that why you were so anxious that we get in here? The fact that you were friends with the Stones, and you're so familiar with the place?"

"More or less," Adam said.

Darcy was slightly troubled. Adam never lied to her, and she didn't think that he was lying then. She just didn't think that he was telling her the whole story.

But she didn't press the point because he said, "When you returned to the house, you came back to this room with Matt, I take it."

He took her by surprise, and she was certain that she instantly blushed. "Right," she said.

"And then…nothing else?"

"Nothing else," she said, and it was only a small lie. There had been that awful feeling for a moment that she was going to relive history in more than a dream. The passion…

Then the violence.

Except that Matt wasn't violent.

"Adam, I need to get back into that dream. I need to see more clearly. I don't have any faces, and yet something that I do see but don't recognize is nagging at me terribly, and I think that it's the answer to the dilemma."

Adam nodded. "Hypnotism is the best tool. But before we go into it, I want to run through the video and sound tapes. I'll take them to my room and take a look—there's probably nothing, if you were in a dream state. Why don't you take a little break? Watch television, read a book, go for a walk."

He wanted to study the tapes alone, that much was obvious. And she agreed with him. There wasn't going to be anything on the tapes.

"Sure." Darcy went to the machines and got him the tapes. "Whatever you do, don't forget that we're meeting downstairs at twelve-thirty."

"I won't."

When he left the room, Darcy headed back downstairs. Penny must have been in her office, and there was no sign of Clara, either.

She walked on out to the stables, just to see the horses. As her eyes adjusted to the light, she was startled to see a form, a man standing by one of the stalls.

"Hey, Darcy, did you want to go riding?"

It was Carter. She exhaled, amazed to realize that she had been frightened.

"No...I just thought I'd come and give the fellows a few pats," Darcy said. She walked over to him. The nameplate on the stall where he stood identified its occupant as Midnight Blue. Naturally, the horse was so deep an ebony in color it might have been blue.

"This your guy?" Darcy asked.

"I don't own any of them. But when I ride here, he's my fellow," Carter told her.

"He's beautiful."

"Yes, he is, isn't he? You wouldn't believe it, but Matt

found him working on a hack line up in the mountains. He was underfed, and pathetic looking. But a fine horse, and Matt knew it. Brought him here, and Sam looked after him. That was a few years ago. Look at him now! Old Midnight is a gorgeous fellow, great riding horse.''

"Well, I'm glad he's here," Darcy said. She leaned against the stall, studying Carter. "Thought you were busy this morning."

He shook his head. "I was supposed to meet with the construction boss over at some property I bought. The man bailed on me."

"Ah," she said. "It's strange to think that you have your own property. You seem so much a part of Melody House."

"It's easy to become a part of Melody House," Carter said. "There's something about that old sense of Southern hospitality here. And it's true, I've been around a heck of a long time. I like Stoneyville."

"And Delilah Dey?" Darcy teased.

He shrugged, smiling. "She's darned cute. She's not you, of course, but I knew right off that you were a loss. Matt beat me out, again."

She shook her head. "Carter, I can't see where you feel you have any problems in life. From what Penny says, you've had a major run of love affairs."

"But the right one hasn't come along," he said.

"That's hard in life for everyone, huh?"

"Um." He leaned against the wood, studying her. "People can be so deceptive, as well. Take Lavinia— Matt's ex. She was stunning, sophisticated, and sweet as molasses when she first arrived. She was down with friends to do some antique hunting, met Penny in town, and Penny dragged her here for a ghost tour. Lavinia met Matt, and suddenly, she wasn't leaving. Lord, but they were gorgeous together. Then she turned into the Witch of the West, thinking Matt could drop anything at any time, and take off with her. All he had to do was be polite to another woman, and Lavinia went into a tantrum. They were something, though. Hot as fire one minute, ready to kill one another the next. Funny, though, right after the divorce, it seemed they'd become friends. But now…hell, we haven't heard from her in years. Strange, she was going to come down to arrange some big financial social party here…but then she never did. And we never heard from her again.''

"Sometimes it's best when the past is really behind us," Darcy said with a shrug.

"Don't worry, you're nothing like her, not really," Carter said, rubbing his beard, and studying her with an amused smile.

"I wasn't worried."

"You do have her hair."

"Hey—there are lots of redheads in the world."

"She was tall and elegant, too."

"But I'm not a socialite, by any stretch of the imagination," Darcy said. "And anyway…I like Matt. I like you all. But I live a strange life. And few people can really handle it."

"You really can see what others can't?" Carter asked.

"Carter, it's impossible to explain. I don't have a crystal ball. I can't really conjure any visions. Sometimes I see, and sometimes, I don't."

He was silent, then said, "Darcy, I wish that you'd leave here."

"Carter, I can't believe that you're not on my side!"

"I am on your side. I think you're gorgeous and adorable, and you don't really freak me out at all. But…I don't know. I just don't feel that you're…safe here."

"Why not?"

"Well, it's just not a good place for redheads. Matt is a great guy, but…maybe he's not good for you. And maybe Melody House does have some kind of evil in it, but since we don't see it, we're not hurt by it. And you may be."

"Carter, please, I'm not afraid of ghosts."

He turned to her, setting both hands on her shoulders.

"Darcy, you're a very brave young woman. Truly. Beautiful, assured, absolutely incredible. But Melody House...I have to say it. I really believe you should leave. Because...because you've become too involved, for one."

"Too involved?" she echoed. He seemed so sincere, despite the fact that he had mocked the idea of ghosts so much himself.

"With Matt. Darcy, you can only get hurt," Carter warned softly.

She nodded, and placed both her hands over his where they lay on her shoulders. She gave them a squeeze, then extricated herself from his hold.

"Thanks, Carter."

"Don't get me wrong—he is a great guy."

"Just not for me, right?"

"There is that Lavinia thing," Carter said. "Too bad you couldn't have met her. But then, well, you know. She's disappeared."

"I'll be fine, Carter. But thank you so much for caring." She turned to leave.

"Darcy!"

She turned back.

"I don't mean this strangely, but...I love Matt. I think he's basically one of the finest men I've ever met. I think you're pretty great, too. And maybe...maybe this place just isn't very good for you. Please, like I said...I just care about both of you."

"Sure. Thanks, Carter."

She left then, without him calling her back. The conversation had been very strange, and unnerving.

He'd talked in such a strange, roundabout way. Not that his words hadn't been evident. Matt was his friend, his very good friend.

So...

If there was something wrong about Matt, he'd never come out and say so.

Just how loyal was he as a friend?

Had he been making implications that something had gone seriously wrong with Lavinia, even after the divorce?

That was too far beyond ridiculous. To suggest that Lavinia hadn't been heard from—*because something had happened to her!*

And yet...

As she walked back to the house, she couldn't help remembering the strange sensation she had felt the night before.

Passion...

And then violence.

15

The ceremony for the skull was sadly beautiful.

The minister's name was Todd Bellamy, and he was a tall trim fellow with graying hair, and a voice that was clear, resonant, and soothing.

Despite the fact that the family had moved from the area eons ago, and the old family stones had eroded with time so that they were almost impossible to read, records had set the workers digging in the right area. Matt told them all that the original wooden coffin had decayed, and so the skull had been given its own twenty-first-century metal box, and would be lowered to join the bones at what would be approximately head level.

And so, as it was lowered into the ground, Reverend Bellamy said a prayer, and gave a small speech.

"May all the sins of the past find forgiveness, and as she sits in the warmth and glow of her maker, may Amy find the grace of forgiveness herself. Her time on this earth was brief and fragile, and stolen from her in the sadness of betrayal. In His grace, Amy must surely find peace, and in that peace, grant it to the one who so cruelly wronged her life. So it is that those who faced evil on earth will face the greatest rewards of Heaven, and there, surely, Amy has found her happiness and love. If you will all bow your heads…?"

Bellamy went into a series of prayers for the dead. Darcy bowed her head, but found herself looking around the cemetery.

It was a beautiful old place that was still attached to the

church. There were majestic angels guarding tombs, while many of the seventeenth- and eighteenth-century head-stones offered up grim carvings of death heads and grim reapers. By night, she was certain, the place would carry an ethereal atmosphere, and most people would certainly consider it eerie.

Even now, though it was a summer's day, storm clouds were moving down from the mountains. When they had first arrived, the sun had lit the place, and it offered the historic charm that brought many to such churches and cemeteries.

Now, the darkening sky changed it to a brooding atmo-sphere, reminiscent of many a Hollywood horror film. Still, no one seemed to notice too much—those in this area were well accustomed to the old and historic.

With her head slightly bowed, Darcy felt a small twinge, noting that to her side, farther from the church, there was a canopy. A velvet liner remained beneath it, and chairs still surrounded an open grave.

The dead were still being interred in this cemetery.

Darcy found the idea traditional and charming.

"Dust to dust, ashes to ashes..." the reverend intoned.

Matt had planned the ceremony with determined haste, and so, the crowd was small. Naturally, the household was there. Sam, Clara, Penny, Carter, Clint, Matt, Adam, and herself. Delilah Dey had come, naturally representing the city council, Jason Johnstone had come—specifically at Matt's invitation—and a tall, skinny fellow—an Ichabod Crane look-alike—who claimed to be a writer was there as well. Mae had come, delighted to be part of the event, and even Mrs. O'Hara had come from the library. There were a few people in attendance that Darcy didn't recog-nize, but somehow, Matt had managed to keep it all very low key.

"Amen!" the reverend said. "Go in peace, and may the blessing of God be with you and yours."

The ceremony was officially over. The last word had

barely left the reverend's lips before the Ichabod-man turned to Darcy.

"Miss Tremayne?"

"Yes?"

"I'm Max Aubry from the local paper. First of all, welcome to Stoneyville. We're delighted to have you. It's my understanding you found the skull. Would you mind talking to me for a few minutes?" he asked.

Darcy didn't get a chance to answer. Clint was suddenly behind her like a bulldog, hazel eyes flashing. "Aubry, she minds."

"What is this, the Stone kingdom?" Aubry said. "Clint, this is America. We've got freedom of the press here. Let the lady answer herself."

"I can talk to him, Clint, I'll be all right," Darcy said.

"There, see? She wants to talk," Aubry said.

Clint looked at Darcy, as if offering her a warning, but he lifted his arms, shrugged, turned and walked away.

"Darcy, dear!" Penny called. "We're going to head down to the Wayside Inn for some lunch."

"Go ahead, I'll be along," Darcy called. She saw that Matt and Adam were both talking to the minister; Carter had Delilah Dey by the arm and they were reading old tombstones.

"Perhaps we could move over by the old oak, and your Dobermans won't be nipping at my heels," Aubry said.

She smiled, confident that whether or not this fellow was a sensationalist journalist, she could handle him.

"Careful, the ground is rough around here," Aubry warned.

The oak was near the open grave. Darcy found herself curious about its intended inhabitant.

"Mrs. Morrison," Aubry said.

"Pardon?"

"Old lady Morrison. She was a hundred and one on her last birthday. Died a few days ago in her sleep, surrounded by loving family. That's the way to go, I do say," Aubry said.

"Certainly."

"So!" They stood behind the oak. "You're a psychic investigator. Did you see the skull in a vision? How did you do it? Do ghosts talk to you? People are fascinated by such phenomena, you know."

"Actually, Mr. Aubry, I was able to find the skull because I looked up the history of the legend at the library. After that…it was a matter of deducing where the murder took place, and how far a skull might have moved through time and the elements."

"So you don't talk to ghosts?" he said, disappointed.

She would never let this man quote her as saying that she did. "We all have incredible minds, Mr. Aubry. And we don't use all of our mental power that often. Harrison Investigations is a company that does a great deal of research. We ferret out shams, and we can say that there aren't always answers to the unexplained. They may be there somewhere, not just in our current knowledge of science and technology. So, if you want to write up what happened, I discovered the details of the story at the library."

"You fell through the floor there, too," Aubry told her. "You weren't hurt?"

"No."

"The sheriff saved you, huh?"

"Yes, luckily, he was around."

He was staring at her, trying to get to something. Darcy didn't feel daunted; just challenged.

"That was odd, don't you think?"

"What was odd?"

"That the sheriff was there," Aubry said impatiently.

"Why would it be odd? He knew I was doing research there. It was natural that he might check in to see how I was doing. And luckily, the timing was good."

"Do you think that a ghost, afraid of what you might discover, followed you from Melody House to attack you at the library so that you would cease your meddling?" Aubry asked.

She laughed out loud. "Mr. Aubry! The floorboards gave because someone spilled a cola on them! The acid ate into the wood. I hardly think that a ghost drifted over from Melody House, sneaked a soda into the library, and spilled it all over the floor."

Aubry blushed.

"Weren't you scared, though?"

"When the floorboards gave? Of course."

"Aren't you scared now?"

"Why would I be scared now?"

"Because the ghost must think that you're meddling."

"Mr. Aubry, I don't remember telling you that there was a particular ghost. And there would be no reason for a ghost to be disturbed that I was meddling, as you say."

"This is just ridiculous," Aubry argued with her. "Obviously, Matt Stone called you because of a ghost!"

"Mr. Stone allowed Harrison Investigations in because of a few reported incidents that had occurred in his home. We're investigating those incidents, doing research, just as I did when I heard about Amy's murder, which is how I found the skull, Mr. Aubry. And that's it. I've talked to you, and I'm afraid that I really don't have anything else to say."

"What do you think about the fact that so many of these incidents have only started cropping up in the last several years? Think the Stones are trying to invent ghosts in order to bring in the tourists?"

"Since Matt Stone doesn't believe in ghosts, he'd hardly go about inventing them."

"He doesn't believe in ghosts, but he'd do just about anything in the world to hold on to Melody House," Aubry said. "He was married to Lavinia Harper, you know. A very wealthy woman. Since they divorced he doesn't have her money behind him anymore. She'd once wanted to put all kinds of money into the house. We haven't seen hide nor hair of her for ages, though. So there you go. Money problems. You don't have to believe in ghosts to invent them."

"I definitely don't believe that Matt is inventing incidents at his house, Mr. Aubry. If you need to ask any more questions, my associate—and the founder of my firm—Mr. Adam Harrison, is here. Perhaps you should talk to him."

"Where is he?" Aubry asked sharply.

"He was over by the minister," Darcy said, pointing toward the church.

"Thanks!" he told her.

Darcy leaned against the oak, feeling oddly drained, and once again, uneasy. Aubry pretty much came right out and said what he was feeling.

Matt Stone had married for money. Then he'd divorced. He needed money.

His wife had disappeared.

If he'd murdered his wife, he wouldn't need the money, would he? But she was his ex-wife. They'd been divorced.

She gritted her teeth, furious that she was allowing people to let such suspicions seep into her mind. Especially when they didn't make sense. Matt was simply impatient and angry with the whole ghost concept. And yet, even Matt thought that something was going on.

He'd loved Lavinia at one time. Been enamored of her. Their relationship had been one of passion—and hate.

Just like that she had witnessed in dreams, from both sides...

"Ridiculous!" she said aloud. Just as she did so, the threatened storm came. First, a few raindrops fell on her head. Then the wind kicked up as if the hand of God had indeed reached down to stir up a tempest. The raindrops suddenly became a deluge.

Darcy started away from the oak. The cars were around in front of the brick wall, but if she leapt over it, she'd reach them far quicker than if she were to walk around. She headed toward the wall, and in doing so, needed to skirt by the open grave awaiting Mrs. Morrison, the centenarian who had passed away in her sleep.

She wrapped her arms around her chest, lowered her

head, and started to run. She shot through the area where the chairs had been arranged around the grave.

She didn't hear anything behind her. Nothing at all. But the rain was pounding and the wind was whistling. Footsteps would have been washed away.

The wind was strong. Very strong.

And still, she didn't know what kind of force seized upon her with such strength as she ran by the grave. She only knew that it rocked her to the side with such vehemence that she lost her footing, teetered precariously on the uneven ground, then slammed over to her right.

Flailing...

Falling...down. Down, into darkness.

Six feet down, to be exact. Into the deep, damp earth of the freshly dug grave.

The rain was pounding hard. Matt saw Penny, her summer shawl over her head but doing little good, come running toward the passenger door.

He leaned over to open it.

Penny slid in, moving the shawl, and apologizing. "Oh, Matt, I've gotten the car all wet. You would have thought we'd have been prepared for this kind of summer storm! Oh, well, thank God it's summer. You can go for lunch, right? We're all supposed to be meeting at the Wayside Inn."

"Yeah, I can lunch," he said. "Where are the others?"

"In Adam's car. He drove."

"Darcy?"

"She's probably with Adam. Or else..."

"Or else what?" he asked sharply.

"Max Aubry cornered her. And you know Darcy. She was confident she could take care of herself. I never had a chance to tell her that he was a headline-grabbing monster. Clint tried to come between the two of them, but...Matt, don't worry. Darcy doesn't like to tell anything, she hates it when people turn her kind of perception into ooh-aah parlor tricks."

Darcy was with Max Aubry. Great.

He gunned the motor with greater force than he intended.

"Matt, it will be all right."

"Yeah, sure."

"That was a beautiful ceremony!" Penny said. "Wasn't the Reverend Bellamy just wonderful?"

"Yep."

"Matt, come on. Sure, it will be in the newspapers. They'll say that Amy was put to her final rest with tender words. What else can they say?"

"Let's see—they can say that the sheriff of Stoneyville has become a complete nutcase, bringing so-called ghost busters in to solve problems in his jurisdiction because he hasn't the skill to makes discoveries beneath his own nose."

"Matt, Aubry would never write such a thing," Penny said.

He stared at her.

"Trust me, Darcy won't give him anything to add fuel to the fire. Isn't this weather just terrible? Can you see where you're going?"

"Yes, Penny, I can drive. Are you sure we're supposed to go straight there? Everyone is going to be soaked."

"It's summer—we'll dry," Penny assured him.

It was still pouring when they reached the Wayside Inn. Matt gave Penny his umbrella, lowered his head, and ran through the rain himself.

They were the first to arrive. Not even Mae had returned as yet, but Sim Jones, standing in for her, assured him that they had a number of tables ready, and could put their party together. "Hell, Matt, you all are our regulars anyway. No problemo," Sim said.

He and Penny ordered coffee and sat, awaiting the others.

Darcy's temple thundered. She had struck hard earth when first going in, and she might have blacked out. For how long, she had no idea, though with the rain flooding over her, it couldn't have been more than a few minutes.

She was quickly becoming engulfed in a mud bath. The rain and earth were already past her ankles when she made it to her feet.

"Help!" she screamed as loudly as she could. A sinking feeling told her that no one would hear her—even if they were still around.

She bit into her lower lip, hugging her arms around herself, and feeling the chill of the rain. The sun had gone completely. In the deep hole in the earth, it was darker than she could have possibly imagined, the sky above her offering nothing but gray.

What the hell had happened? A massive gust of wind? Or a hand with a tremendous force? And why?

"Help!" she shouted again. She dug at the earth around her, trying to get a hold on anything. But the grave had been deeply and cleanly dug. There was nothing to grasp.

She tried to claw her hands into the earth, but it merely crumbed away at her touch. She jumped, trying to reach the perimeter of the grave. She got one handhold, and slid back.

Gasping for breath, trying to move her soaking hair from her eyes, she paused for a minute. Someone was going to realize that she was missing.

Weren't they?

"Help! Help! Help!"

An unbidden sense of panic seized her, and she began to shout and try desperately to crawl from the grave again herself. The sky rumbled with a fury. There was a flash of lightning, and then the sky seemed darker than ever. Already shivering, drenched, and exhausted, she lay back against the earth of the tomb, trying to reason.

The darkness, the depth of the grave, the scent of the earth around her entered into her instinct and made her afraid.

"I talk to ghosts!" she whispered aloud to herself. "Why on earth would I be afraid, *now,* in a cemetery?"

But she was afraid. The mud at her feet was getting deeper and deeper, rising now to her calves. She imagined she felt creepy, crawly things sliding up her flesh. She was cold; it might have been a summer's day, but she was thoroughly wet and the wind kept sweeping down. Her teeth were chattering, and she felt hemmed in by the darkness, as if she was locked in a coffin as well as a grave.

Cell phone.

The two words popped into her mind, and she almost smiled, thinking she'd been an idiot. Except, of course, that she'd hit her head, and it was spinning.

She dropped down to the ground, trying to find the small black purse she'd carried for the occasion. The ground was pure mud.

So were her hands by the time she opened the purse.

And so were the contents of her purse.

She found the phone easily enough, but it was caked with mud. She pressed on the keys, talked to the phone, tenderly tried to clean it.

No good. The water had gotten inside. The water—that kept rising around her, joining with the earth, making her pit more and more of a slushy, mucky, mire.

In fury she threw the phone across the pit. It thunked sickly against the side. The rain was still falling. The day was getting darker and darker. The wind whipped around, creating an eerie noise, as if all the banshees in Ireland howled at once.

She closed her eyes, hoping for a word from someone, a sense of security, of comfort. She was desperate for an assurance that everything would be all right, she would find her way out of the grave.

What if…

She was supposed to have knocked herself out completely when she fell? What if she was supposed to remain there, silent, lost, while everyone assumed that she was with someone else. And what if it had been a real hand that had pushed her, forcing her into the grave?

And that real person was coming back.…

"Help!" She screamed the word again.

She closed her eyes. Visions of floating bones swept by her mental vision. Darkness seemed to sweep around her, touching her. The way that panic was setting in, she saw so much more. Rotting corpses, floating to the surface, finding life, swaying before her...darkness, the mud sucking her down, hands of the dead curling around her ankles, pulling her deeper and deeper into the muck.

"No! Darcy, no!" she chastised herself aloud.

They would come. Someone would come for her, soon enough.

"Josh?" she whispered softly.

She didn't see him. But she felt as if a brush of warmth came over her. "Josh...help me!"

Again, a sensation of warmth, of comfort. In her mind, a whisper, *You'll be all right.*

"Stay with me, Josh. I'm afraid," she said softly.

But then, a huge bolt of lightning flashed across the sky. She heard an explosion, and didn't know what it could be until she heard a cracking sound.

"Josh!" she cried.

But there was nothing. No whisper of assurance. No sense of warmth. She was alone, entirely alone.

A massive creaking filled the air then, and she realized what had happened.

The oak, the giant oak had been hit by the lightning.

A second later, she screamed as it came crashing down, right on the spot of the open grave that jailed her.

Adam arrived with his carful of people.

Clint, Clara and Sam.

"Where are the rest?" Matt asked Clint.

"Carter's driving here with Delilah—they should be right behind us. Mae is parking her truck around back. Jason Johnstone was helping David Jenner with his equipment. Reverend Bellamy couldn't come—he's busy making new arrangements for a funeral that was supposed to be this afternoon. Mrs. O'Hara had her own car, and—"

"Darcy. Where the hell is Darcy?" Matt asked.

"She didn't come with you?" Adam demanded, walking over.

Clint sniffed out a sound of distaste. "That screwball, Max Aubry, probably coaxed her into driving with him."

"She left with him?" Matt asked.

"Oh, yeah. Well, she walked away with him, at least," Clint said.

Matt nodded, rose, and walked over to one of the pool tables. He set up the balls with precision. Aimed to break them, and sent the cue flashing so hard that they distributed across the entire table.

"Matt? Want me to order for you?" Penny asked tentatively, watching the game he was determined to play by himself.

"Sure."

"What do you want?"

"Food."

"Matt?"

"Just get me a burger, Penny. Thanks," he added after a second.

Clint walked over to the table. "Matt, I can call Aubry's paper, get his cell phone number."

Matt stopped playing and leaned on his cue stick. "For what? So I can demand that he bring Darcy back to us?"

Clint grimaced. "I should have stuck with them."

"It's all right. The guy's a jerk, and there's no way out of it. And hell, Darcy is over twenty-one, and in her right mind. At least, mostly," he added wryly.

Clint stared at him for a minute, trying to think of something to say. Then he lifted his hands, and walked away.

Matt sank the balls, one by one, with the first shot. By the time he finished, he had somewhat cooled down. He remained angry, though. And he wasn't sure if he was most furious with himself for not being more vigilant, with Max Aubry for being an opportunist, or Darcy for being...

Darcy.

He set the cue stick down and returned to the table.

Penny was at his one side, and old Anthony Larkin had joined them. Good. Anthony wasn't talking about the ceremony for the skull. He was excited by the prospect of the battle reenactment.

"I'll be riding old Geyser, and though we may both be long in the tooth, I promise, we'll give the young 'uns dragged down to the battlefield a damned good show," he advised. "You riding for your homeland, Matt?" Anthony asked.

"You bet. I'll be in my best sheriff's uniform, making sure the crowds stay under control, and that none of you blows yourself up!" Matt told him lightly. Looking around the room, he saw that everyone he had seen at the cemetery had arrived.

Carter and Delilah were there. Mrs. O'Hara had made it, and was deep in discussion with Adam Harrison. They were both such history buffs. They seemed like a team made in heaven.

"Hey, Matt!" Carter called. "Where's Darcy?"

"I don't really know," he replied.

"Is she still with that wretched Mr. Aubry?" Delilah asked from across the room.

"Darcy hardly turned traitor, the way you're all making it sound," Adam said. He stared across the Matt, perplexed. "Wait a minute—I don't think she's with him at all. He accosted me, right before I headed for the car. And actually, I had assumed she was with you, Matt."

"I'll bet she just wanted to tell Reverend Bellamy what a lovely job he did," Penny said.

Darcy needs you.

Matt nearly jumped a mile, jerking around quickly to see who had whispered at his ear.

There was no one there. No one. The person nearest to him was Penny, and she was a good three feet away.

"Who said that?" he demanded.

Penny, wide-eyed, turned around to stare at him.

"I just said that Darcy probably went to talk to the Reverend Bellamy,'' she said. "Why, is that bad? Why do you look so angry?''

"Maybe that reporter went back to her,'' Adam said, as if he was trying to assure himself. "The rain had started, and I was anxious to get away, but he had just left Darcy, so he probably went back to her, and maybe got her into his car.''

Darcy...Darcy...

Her name was like a whisper in Matt's head. An urgent whisper. He stood so quickly that his chair fell behind him. He gave no notice.

"I'm going back to find her,'' he said, and started out of the room.

Adam Harrison rose as if he would accompany him. Matt gave him no notice, he suddenly felt such a sense of urgency.

Alone, he ran out of the Wayside Inn and hurried for his car.

The old oak's heavy branches covered the entire opening to the grave and protruded down into it. After her initial terror at the fall, Darcy had tried to use the tree to crawl out. But every time she got a grasp of a branch, it split in her hands, sending her splashing back hard into the rising mud.

She was soaked clean through, cold, miserable, freezing, and wondering if she could survive an overnight stay in the stygian pit. The afternoon had waned, and real darkness was setting in. Something slithered by her in the water and she choked back a scream. A snake.

Virginia had rattlers, right?

Not a rattler. Rattlers rattled.

A moccasin? What deadly venomous creature might roam the dryness of a cemetery by day, and swim through the flooding of the rain by night?

She had to get out. She was too cold, trembling throughout her limbs. She was imagining too much again. Ghostly dances before her eyes. Bones reaching out from the ground. Yes, she spoke to ghosts. But none of them were speaking to her. They were just playing tricks with her mind, adding to the terror of her situation.

The water in the hole was almost to her waist.

"I'll be able to swim out soon!" she told herself out loud.

Once again, she tried to get a grasp on one of the tree limbs. Her fingers curled around what seemed like a sturdy branch. She braced a foot against the side of the hole.

Her foot slipped on the mud and the branch snapped at the same time. She plunged all the way down, her head going beneath the surface of the rising water.

She rose, sputtering, gasping.

And then, a miracle.

"Darcy!"

Had she imagined it? Or had she really heard a voice?

"Here, here! I'm here! Help!"

Nothing then, she heard nothing at all. She hadn't shouted loudly enough, not to combat the wind and the rain. Her voice had grown hoarse, almost nonexistent.

"Darcy!"

She wasn't imagining it. Matt's voice.

She jumped, throwing herself as high as she could. "Matt! Here, Matt, here, please!"

And then, at last, the limbs were ripped from the top of the grave, piece after piece. "Oh, God, yes, thank God, thank you, thank you!" she heard herself gasping.

The last of the oak was pulled away, and she was standing in the mire, looking up. The sky was dark.

She saw only his form.

Huge, hands on hips, glaring down.

And for a moment she felt a twinge of panic.

Matt. How had he known that she was here—unless he had pushed her in. Maybe he hadn't come to save her at all. Maybe he was about to reach down and use his imposing size and strength to press her down, down into the muck and mire, where she couldn't breathe, where she would slowly struggle and fight until she....

He hunkered down by the side of the grave.

She'd thought it before. Maybe she'd been pushed, just shoved into the grave, so that someone could come back....

And finish her off.

"Jesu, how in the hell...?" he said. "Take my hand."

He didn't give her a chance. He reached for hers.

Inadvertently, she pulled back.

"Are you hurt?" he asked anxiously.

"No."

"Let me get you out of there!"

She swallowed hard, let him get a good grip on her hand.

A moment later, she heard a strange suctioning sound—she hadn't even realized that the water had turned the earth to such a grasping muck. And still, it gave her up. He reached down to slip an arm beneath her right shoulder, pulling her out.

They both fell to the side of the grave. The rain continued to sluice down upon them. He stared at her a moment before righting himself, and reaching to help her up.

"You're like a goddamn ice cube!" he said. "How the hell did you manage to fall into a grave? Never mind, let's just get you back to the house."

She was shaking, trembling. Her knees weren't holding her. He picked her up and carried her to the car, setting her into the passenger's side.

He found a blanket in the back and drew it around her shoulders. "How could you have missed a hole that damned big?" he asked her, turning the key in the ignition, and hitting the switch for the heater.

I didn't fall in—I was pushed!

But she didn't say the words. Yes, she had been pushed. But by a *who* or a *what,* she didn't know.

Matt himself?

"The rain...I was running from the rain. I thought I could just leap over the brick wall and reach the cars faster," she stuttered out.

"Oh, man, Darcy, look at you. Are you hurt? No broken bones? Sprained ankle?"

A crack on the temple. Maybe one that made her mind wander too fiercely.

"I'm fine."

"Are you?" he murmured. He glanced at her, his look concerned and anxious. "This place isn't good for you, is it?" he murmured, more to himself than to her.

"I'm all right," she repeated. They were driving through rain, but at long last, it seemed to be slackening. "Matt?"

"Yes?"

"How did you know where to find me?"

"What do you mean?"

"How did you find me? That oak had covered the entire grave. And actually...it did take you a while."

He scowled, cast her a glance, and looked back to the road. "We all thought you'd gone off with Max Aubry."

"Gone off with him?"

"Clint said you were determined to talk to him, that you could handle yourself."

"I did handle myself, very well, thank you."

"There were so many cars, as well. I didn't realize you were really missing until Adam said that Max Aubry approached him when he was leaving."

"I see," Darcy said.

He drove fast. They reached the entry to Melody House, and he swung hard into the drive, halting the car abruptly, coming around the side for her. He opened the door in haste, then paused, staring at her suspiciously.

"You're not going to tell me that a ghost reached a bony hand out of a grave and wrenched you down into it, are you?"

"Nope. Absolutely not," she assured him.

"Come on. I'll help you."

"I can manage on my own, thanks."

She slid quickly out of the car, and up onto her feet. But the world seemed to waver before her. She gritted her teeth hard, feeling the pounding at her temple where she'd struck the earth hard as she'd catapulted into the open grave.

"You're going to slip in the mud!" Matt said impatiently. He swept her up.

Her limbs still felt frozen. She couldn't fight. He walked up the steps to the porch, fumbled with his key, and opened the front door.

A moment later, they were on the stairway.

They passed the spot where, sometime in the past, two lovers had battled viciously, before the man had swept the woman into his arms...

And into the Lee Room.

Just as Matt now carried her.

And, just as in the past, he laid her down upon the bed, and turned away.

And once, in the past, a man had realized just what a woman knew, and what she could tell the world about him. He had turned back to her, wound his fingers around her throat, and strangled the life from her.

Matt turned back to her.

"Damn you, Darcy!" he said softly.

And came toward her.

16

"They're taking a really long time," Penny said, looking at her own empty plate and the untouched hamburger she had ordered for Matt.

"Yes, well, we can order coffee," Delilah said. "I'd really love some coffee."

"I just wish we all knew where Darcy was," Penny murmured.

"But, surely, nothing could have happened to her!" Delilah said.

"I'm certain that everything is all right," Carter said firmly.

"Wonderful," Delilah said, smiling. "We'll all order coffee, and hopefully, they'll arrive along with it."

"So what's taking so long?" Clint demanded.

"I think that I should get back to Melody House as quickly as possible," Adam Harrison said.

They all stared at him.

Penny jumped up. "Adam! Do you have a feeling, a hunch? What's wrong? Should we all be running out of here?"

"Penny, I'm so sorry, calm down," Adam said. "I don't have a feeling about anything. I just assume that, if Darcy had been caught in the rain or anything, Matt would have taken her straight back to the house."

"Of course!" Penny said with a sigh of relief. "Mae, would you get the check for us, please? Or better yet, can you just bill the whole thing to Matt?"

"Naturally," Mae said.

"I really think we should order coffee!" Delilah said, somewhat plaintively. "What if Matt is bringing her here? Then we'll all be in cars going in different directions."

"Who could drink coffee at a time like this?" Penny said, glaring at Delilah.

"Delilah has a point," Carter said.

Adam let out something of an exasperated sigh. "I'll head back to Melody House, and the rest of you stay here. That way, we'll be covered."

They all stared at him.

"Good idea, right? Miss Dey, you go right ahead and order your coffee. When I get to the house, I'll call."

He started toward the door. The bar phone began to ring. Sim picked it up. "Hello...yes?" He held the receiver away from his mouth. "Hey! Mr. Harrison. You don't need to go anywhere. He's got her. Matt's got her. She fell into a grave, can you imagine that?"

He was answered by silence. And in the bar, one by one, they all looked at one another.

Darcy ran the water in her shower, feeling like an idiot. She'd almost cringed when he turned to her, but he hadn't even glanced at her then. "Can't believe this—I forgot to call and tell them that I'd found you. You're really all right? Feels like I'm always saying that to you, Darcy. It's why you shouldn't be here," he added somewhat harshly. "Grab a shower. Then, if you want, we'll drive on over to the Wayside Inn. I'm sure the others have finished their meals by now, but I don't know what we've got around here right now, and since you're the lost lamb at the moment, the others are going to want to see you. I'll be in my room. I think I could use a shower and change, too."

So Matt was gone.

No violence, and no passion, either.

And now, out of the hole, away from the terror, she was at a complete loss. Had she been pushed, or had it been the wind?

She dumped her clothes straight into the garbage—the

summer silk black tank and skirt were never going to be the same again. She thought she'd hate the outfit the rest of her life anyway, always associating it with an afternoon in an open grave. Before hopping beneath the shower spray, she opened the medicine chest and downed several ibuprofen tablets, anxious to avoid the headache that threatened.

A shower had never felt so good. She had the water steaming, the pressure hard, and she stayed far longer than she should have. But she emerged mudless, hair squeaky-clean, and feeling far stronger than she had when she had first emerged from the pit.

The rain had turned the warmth of the day into a cool-ness that didn't quite fit with the Virginia summer and she had been chilled to the bone. She found a light knit sweater and jeans, and dressed quickly.

She paused for a moment, wondering if the ghost was being recessive, hiding, but watching. She felt as if the room were warm, not at all cold. If the ghost was there, and watching, it was with sympathy, and no other emotion.

She exited her room just as Matt left his.

"Ready? We don't have to rush. If anyone wants to move on, they can. Your hair is still wet."

"It's all right. It will dry."

He nodded, and lifted an arm, indicating that she should precede him down the stairs. She was irritated to realize that she was afraid to do so.

She hurried down each step, anxious to keep a distance from him. When he opened the front door, they saw that the rain had stopped completely. But evening was there, and the darkness seemed more ominous than ever.

Matt didn't seem to notice. He walked ahead of her, and opened the passenger's seat door of his car. She slid in.

He didn't speak on the drive to the Wayside Inn. But she caught him glancing at her frequently.

"What wrong with you?" he asked her.

"Nothing. Really. I was pretty shaken up, of course. No

one likes to fall into an open grave. And, of course, I was soaked. But now…I'm fine.''

He didn't reply, but she knew he was still watching her, as if not believing a word she'd said. But they reached the Wayside Inn, and she jumped out of the passenger's seat before he could walk around. Darcy hurried toward the door and was startled when it was flung open.

Clint was the first one out, reaching her, picking her up, swinging her around, and looking at her anxiously.

"Poor baby! We all walked off and left you in a grave!'' he said, dismayed.

"Clint, you can set me down. I'm fine. Just fine.''

"Darcy!'' Adam was the next one out. He didn't lift her, and she offered him a warm hug before he could crush her.

"I'm fine. Thank God Matt came to get me out. Otherwise, I'd still be there, screaming.''

"Matt! Good going. But how did you find her?'' Carter asked, bursting out the door behind Adam.

"Hardly brilliant police work,'' Matt said dryly. "We'd left her in a churchyard. I went back to it.''

"Naturally!'' Penny said, poking her head out of the door. "Darcy, dear, I ordered you a hamburger along with a new one for Matt. I hope that's okay. I mean, you've been with us long enough for me to know that a ghost buster isn't necessarily a vegetarian. Why one would assume such a thing anyway…never mind. Is a hamburger all right?''

"Lovely, Penny, thank you,'' Darcy said.

"And we've nice hot coffee on the table for you already!'' Mae called loudly from within.

"Bless you!'' Darcy shouted back.

Clint held the door open. Carter ushered her on through. Mae caught her, hugged her, and Mrs. O'Hara came up to her as well, eyes huge. "Poor, poor, dear! You are accident prone, Darcy. But I hope you don't think that it's Stoneyville. We're really a wonderful little place. I'd never want you to go away thinking otherwise.''

"Great!" Clint teased, grabbing Darcy's hand and leading her to her place at the table. "Don't be fooled. They all thought you'd gone over to the enemy. Okay, so maybe I did, too."

"The enemy?" she said.

Clint made a face. "Max Aubry."

"Of course, I didn't go off with Max Aubry."

"Did you tell him that you were a psychic, and that you can talk to ghosts?" Penny asked anxiously.

"No," Darcy said. She was aware of Matt watching her, arms crossed over his chest. "I explained to Mr. Aubry that our firm worked through solid research, and that was that."

"Clint! This is horrible. We're worried about what poor Darcy might have said, when she just spent an hour in a grave," Penny protested.

"I would have died," Delilah said. "I would have flat-out died of the fear. But then, you are you, and I imagine that you just told the bones or ghosts what they could do with themselves!"

"No," Darcy said pleasantly. "I was frightened. Truly frightened. It was an eerie experience—even for me."

"Let's hope you don't catch your death of cold!" Mae piped in. "Drink up that coffee, it's nice and warm. Soup! You should have some soup. And I made chicken noodle from scratch. Sim! Get a bowl of that chicken noodle for Darcy."

"I could go for a bowl myself," Matt said. "Sim, would you mind?"

Carter left Delilah's side long enough to grab the chair next to Darcy's. He touched her cheek. "Thank God!" he said softly. He shook his head, amazed, looking at Matt. "She was inside the grave! And you still found her."

"Inside, covered by the old oak. It went down, lightning," Matt said. He looked at Darcy. "She's a fighter. She was still screaming. She was easy to find."

"Hey, why didn't you call someone?" Clint asked.

"The cell phone is dead."

"Better a phone, than a person!" Mae said cheerfully.

"Of course." Darcy laughed.

"You're really not hurt?" Clint asked.

"I'm really not hurt," Darcy said.

Clint offered her an ironic half smile. "Hm. Well, I will say—you are accident prone. But thankfully, you bounce right back."

"Thankfully," she agreed.

Delilah sighed. "You're certainly much braver than I. And I was under the belief that I was a highly competent woman!"

"I'm sure you are," Darcy murmured.

"But, at least, you did have to be dragged from the grave," Delilah said.

"Couldn't get out myself," Darcy told her.

"But you tried hard, huh?" Clint said, picking up her hand. "Look at what you did to your palms."

She gently extricated her hand. "Naturally, I tried."

"We'll get some aloe on those palms," Penny said firmly.

"They'll be fine," Darcy said.

Sim brought them bowls of soup. They smelled wonderful.

"Oh, my, what a story!" Delilah said. "Thank the Lord that Max Aubry isn't here now. Can you imagine his headline? 'Psychic thrown in a grave at ceremony for skull she discovered!'"

"You're right, Delilah, let's be glad he isn't here," Matt agreed, obviously irritated.

"I'm here," Jason Johnstone said, "but don't worry, Matt. I have no intention of writing up the incident."

"Actually, why not? It is news," Mae commented. Matt glared at her. "But then again, the ceremony was so beautiful. That's what should be in the news."

Matt looked at Jason. "Hey, write what you see as the truth," he told him.

Delilah let out a long sigh. "Well, I'm afraid I'm going to have to get home. Make some of the calls I should have made during the day. I'm actually not my own boss, not the way Matt is.''

"I'll be going in, too, tonight, Delilah," he informed her.

She smiled at Carter. "Thanks for the escort through the graveyard. I admit, any time I was in that place on my own, even for just a few minutes, I felt creepy.''

"Delilah!" Penny chastised. "It's a beautiful cemetery and church.''

"Sure. Of course. And that's how I always make sure we write it up when I work with the tourist board! Darcy, I truly hope you suffer no ill effects. Bye, all!''

"I'll see you to your car," Carter said.

Adam yawned. "Sorry!" he apologized. "It's not the company. But I'm not a young man. Now that I know Darcy is safe with you, Matt, I'm heading back for a long, hot bath. Anyone with me?''

Clint nodded, rising. "I guess I should be getting back, too. Since you're together, of course, and no one is left dining alone!''

"I've work to do, too," Penny murmured.

"We're fine, right, Darcy?" Matt said.

"Of course," she murmured.

The hamburgers had come. She was famished, she realized. And once she had eaten, she knew that she would feel much stronger. And far more sane.

Far less suspicious.

The others left. Even Sim went home. Mae was there to handle the bar.

As they finished the hamburgers, Darcy and Matt were alone. They didn't talk, but ate. He consumed his last bite a minute after Darcy had given up.

He set his napkin on the table, eyeing her. "Let's play pool.''

"Pool?''

"Yeah, come on, since you're a shark. Let's see if you can beat me.''

He rose, catching her hand, dragging her to her feet. "I don't know if we should play right now," she protested.

"We should definitely play. You keep insisting you're fine, so let's play."

"All right."

"What's the bet?" he asked, but he wasn't expecting an answer, nor did he want one. "I know, we'll make it a truth or dare."

"What?"

"When you sink a ball, you ask a question. I'll tell you the truth. When I sink a ball, you answer a question. And you have to tell the truth."

"That's ridiculous!" Darcy said.

"Why?" he asked, his eyes dark. "Are you incapable of telling the truth?"

"No. I've never lied to you."

"I think that you have," he said flatly. He racked the balls, but then stepped away. "Ladies first."

"I really can play, you know," she told him.

"I believe you."

She was afraid that she'd be uneasy, and off. She wasn't. She shot a clean break, sinking the three.

"Ask a question," he told her.

She hesitated. "Who wanted the divorce, you or Lavinia?"

He arched a brow, as if surprised by her choice of question. "I filed."

"That didn't really answer the question. Who wanted the divorce?"

"I did. Shoot." He indicated the table.

She sank another ball.

"Did you ever really love her?"

He shrugged.

"Come on, you called it—truth or dare."

"I was absolutely infatuated with her. Did I really love her? I don't know. We didn't give ourselves time."

Darcy sank another ball.

"Did you ever hate her?" she asked.

"Yes. Go on, play."

This time, Darcy missed. Matt picked up his cue. It didn't seem that he even took the time to check his angle; he sank his first ball with an absolute minimum of effort.

"My turn. You swear that you aren't feigning when you take on another voice?"

"I swear that I'm not feigning," she said flatly.

"Maybe without even knowing it?"

"Excuse me, I answered the question, shoot!" she said.

He sank another ball. She wasn't even sure he looked at the table.

"Why were you so strange on the porch last night?" he demanded.

"Strange?"

"You were afraid of me."

She hesitated. "Yes, because I—I thought that I'd been followed out."

"Why did you lie?"

"That's another question. Shoot another ball."

He started to protest, then shrugged. Again, his ball seemed to slide into the pocket effortlessly.

"Why did you lie?" he demanded again.

She shook her head. "I don't know. I supposed I thought that you'd followed me. Maybe to scare me, or something. I don't really know."

"That's the truth?" he demanded.

"We are playing truth or dare," she said dryly.

A flicker of something passed through his eyes. To her amazement, he missed his next shot.

She quickly took up her own cue, and made a shot.

"Where is Lavinia now?" she asked.

He looked puzzled. "How the hell should I know? Maybe Paris, maybe London. If she's in D.C., I haven't heard about it. Why?"

"It was my question, not yours," she informed him, and made another shot. She stared at him a long moment.

"Well?" he said impatiently.

"Did you kill your wife?" she asked quietly.

"What?"

"My question!" she grated.

"No, I didn't kill my wife."

She looked at the table quickly, took aim, and missed her shot. Matt walked past her with his cue. He made his shot, but didn't ask a question. He cleaned the table, and set down his cue.

"Last question. So that's it. You think that I killed my wife. You think that the ghost is Lavinia—*that I strangled her in the Lee Room?*"

Darcy opened her mouth, and closed it. "I...no, not really. I just thought that I should make sure. Matt...did you...did you push me into that grave today?"

"What?"

"You keep saying that!" she told him, irritated. "I asked you—did you push me in that grave today?"

"No. No, a thousand times no. And why the hell didn't you tell me you were pushed into it?" he demanded.

Her eyes fell. "Because I don't know that I was pushed."

"What the hell does that mean?"

"It could have been the wind, it could have been a hand."

"Darcy, that's ridiculous."

"No, it's not. The rain had started. The wind was howling. I was running, not watching where I was going, and suddenly, I was toppling into the grave."

He walked around to where she stood, crossed his arms over his chest, and leaned against the table. "Great. You think that I would push you into a grave, and that I killed my ex-wife."

"No...not really."

"But the suspicions rose in your mind?"

"A little."

"Want me to call you a cab?"

"What?"

"I think that we actually both hear each other just fine.

I said, do you want me to call you a cab. Meaning, are you afraid to drive back with me.''

She shook her head, swallowing hard. ''No.''

''Are you afraid of me?'' he demanded.

Again, his eyes seemed very dark, very intense. She shook her head. ''No.''

A small smile crooked his lips. ''But you think that if you weren't somewhat taken with me, you would be. You don't want to be a fool, right?''

''I'm not afraid of you, Matt.''

''Hm,'' he murmured, still watching her. ''The suspicions tore at the back of your mind, but they were just teasers, huh?''

''More or less.''

''Come on, then. Let's see if we make home.''

He took her cue from her hands and set it on the table.

''Mae!'' he called out.

''I know!'' she shouted back. ''Bill you!''

''Thanks, good night!''

Every once in a while, the very idea that Darcy had even so much as an inkling that he might have actually *killed* Lavinia made Matt so mad that he was tempted to stop the car, get out of it, and slam a fist into the windshield.

Somehow, he refrained.

He had the feeling that she wanted to speak, but she didn't.

Not until they reached the house.

''We're here,'' he said.

She nodded, still not making a move for the door.

''Whatever it is, say it, Darcy?''

''How did you find me?'' she asked, and it wasn't an accusation, but a question.

A little voice whispered in my ear.

He couldn't say it. He just couldn't.

''Darcy, you weren't with us, and the last place we saw you was the churchyard. You have to admit yourself, it was the obvious place to look.''

"I guess...but you found the freshly dug grave—even with the tree over it."

"You shouted out. I heard you."

She nodded, then flashed him a sudden smile. "Sure."

He shook his head. "Darcy, that was no great mystery."

"Right. I agree," she told him. She was still smiling.

"Darcy, don't go getting weird ideas that you don't share with me. Why on earth would you suddenly have a suspicion that I had killed Lavinia?"

"I don't know."

"She left here alive and well."

"Wasn't she supposed to do some kind of a fund-raiser or something at Melody House, even after you two divorced?" Darcy asked.

He sighed, and looked at his hands. "Darcy, it's really so cut-and-dried it's boring. We met, we were attracted, whirlwind, we got married. She thought that I was ready to enter her world. Here I was, the heir to a small Virginian dynasty, founding fathers, all that rot. She thought that she could turn me into what she wanted. I had mistakenly believed that she was done with party after party, and so on. We argued like cats and dogs, and then I knew I'd made the biggest mistake in the world. She'd thought she'd get me into politics, with my heritage and the house, and being a cop and a sheriff. At this particular phase of my life, my interest is here. Keeping the place afloat, taking the town into the future. My fund-raisers are for this place, and then civic—we need money to keep the kids off drugs, even here, and for awareness, and everything else that society faces. We were finally amicable, both realizing that we'd made a mistake, seeing what we wanted to see in one another, and not what was really there. But I really don't hate her anymore. I feel rather ambivalent toward her. That's all. Hunt her down, if you feel the need."

She shook her head. "I didn't mean to pry so much... sorry, yes. Maybe I did."

The front door to the house opened while they were still sitting there. Penny came out on the porch. "Matt? Everything all right? There's a phone call for you on the main line. Jason Johnstone. Should I tell him to call back?''

"No, we're coming in," Matt called.

Darcy quickly exited her door, asking Penny where Adam was as she walked by her into the house. Matt followed more slowly, telling Penny he'd pick up the line in his upstairs office.

Darcy had disappeared by the time he reached the second-floor landing. He walked into his own room, to the desk in the office area of the suite, and punched in the line on the phone.

"Jason, hi, Matt. Sorry to have kept you waiting."

"That's all right. I could have called back. I just wanted to let you know that I did write up what happened today. But I think you'll like it."

Matt inhaled on a deep breath. "Look, Jason, I know I have a chip on my shoulder about the whole ghost thing. But I mean it—you are a journalist, and a good one. Don't let me influence what you write."

On the other end of the line, Jason laughed. "Matt, honestly, I wrote what I saw. I think you'll be fine with it. The only thing is, of course, Max Aubry will see it, and write what he wants to the following day. We are at rival papers."

"Doesn't matter, Jason. Don't worry about it."

"I thought you should be forewarned."

"Thanks."

"I'll see you at the reenactment."

"I'll be working."

"They're not making you play your famous ancestor?"

"Can't. I'm still the sheriff here."

"Great. I'll see you, then."

"Thanks, Jason."

As he hung up, he thought he heard another click that preceded his own.

He frowned. Who the hell would be listening in on his conversations?

And *why?*

* * *

Darcy dropped by Adam's room and was dismayed to find him sneezing. Since he had been old for a parent when Josh had been born, she feared for his health now that he was twenty-five years older.

"You caught a cold today!" she said.

"Never mind me," he said, waving a hand in the air. "What on earth happened to you in that cemetery today?"

"Believe it or not, I really don't know."

"How can you not know?" he asked.

"Because it was pouring, and the wind was howling as if a sudden hurricane had popped up. It was really strong, and you know it. What I said in the Wayside Inn this afternoon was the truth, the whole truth. I was running to jump a wall and get to the cars, and suddenly I was in the hole."

"So the wind blew you in?"

"Maybe," she said.

"You were pushed?"

"I might have been, but I really don't know."

He sneezed again.

"Adam, you're getting sick."

He shook his head, but he looked worn and tired as well.

"I've taken some cold stuff, and I'm going straight to bed," he told her. "I was just waiting up for you to come in."

She smiled. "I swear to you that I'm just fine. But I am worried about you."

He shook his head. "There was that incident in the library. And now this. I don't like any of it, Darcy. We've had problematic ghosts before, but...there's something here that's just not right."

She shrugged. "Adam, did you ever meet Lavinia Harper?"

"Once or twice. Why?"

"Just curious, I suppose."

"Ah, the ex-wife. Rich, stunning, always throwing parties for some cause or another, but underneath it all, not a truly generous or nice woman," Adam said.

"But a living one, right?"

He frowned. "You're suggesting she might be dead?"

"No," she said quickly. Too quickly. "I mean…Matt is truly a decent guy. Hardheaded and heavy-handed at times, but ethical, I would swear. Still…"

"You think your ghost might be his murdered wife?" Adam sounded very skeptical.

"No. I really don't think that. But I don't want to be an idiot, either. People say she was supposed to show up here…but that no one heard from her."

"I see what you mean. And very difficult when you're so infatuated with Matt," Adam said flatly.

She cast him a frown.

"You don't believe in him?" Adam asked, a slight smile curving his lips.

"I do."

"Ah."

"Too much, Adam."

"We'll check into Lavinia's whereabouts," Adam promised her. "Oh, ye of little faith!"

"I do have faith!" she protested.

"Cover all the bases, Darcy. I'm teasing you. I've always told you to cover all the bases, right?" Adam said, smiling at her.

"Adam," she began, then hesitated, and started again. "I've seen too many women fall…fall in love. And lose their minds and their senses because of it. I don't want to be an idiot because…" She shook her head and threw her hands up. "Because I am so infatuated!"

"Good girl!" he said. Then he sneezed again.

"Get in bed!" she chastised, giving him a kiss on the cheek and then walking to the door. "Good night!" she called to him.

"Darcy."

"Yes?"

"Don't worry. We'll find Lavinia," he told her. "And Darcy, you'll get me immediately if you need me!" he commanded. Then he sneezed again.

"Absolutely," she promised.

In her own room, she paced awhile, wondering if Matt would come that night.

Probably not. He was offended that she had suspected him of foul play in the nonappearance of his wife. She started to put on a T-shirt, then opted for her lacy white gown instead, thinking wryly that, if she did go down the stairway that night, she could convince any onlooker that she was the lady in white.

Restless, she watched the late show. But then she fell asleep. She tried very hard to clear her mind before she did so, since the day's events had prevented Adam from trying hypnotism again.

The dream came again.

Not the violence of it, or the murder.

Just the woman, a haze of white, staring down at her at first where she lay in the bed. She heard a single whisper. *"Please!"*

Then the woman moved to the door, and slipped through it.

Awake, Darcy rose, and hurried after her.

Once again, she waited on the stairway. Halfway down, she waited again. Darcy followed. At the front door she hesitated, remembering all the warnings she had received, and the fear she had felt herself.

But she wanted so desperately to get at the truth.

There were umbrellas in an old stand near the door. She took one, then let herself out.

The ghost waited on the porch steps. Then she started moving again, drifting toward the smokehouse.

Tonight, she went in.

The old building was in sound repair, and from the scent within, was obviously still used. Darcy opened the door, and stood there, looking into the darkness.

Great. She had an umbrella. No flashlight.

And still, with only the moonbeams hurtling down for illumination, Darcy could see the ghost. Standing in the middle of the small space.

"Please!" she said again.

A rustling sound came from behind Darcy. She swung around with her umbrella, ready to strike. She thought that she saw a shadow, disappearing against the stable wall.

A feeling of cold wrapped around her shoulders and she heard the whisper again, right against her ear, urgent and quick. *"Please!"*

Suddenly, she knew. Exactly what the ghost was trying to say, and exactly what she wanted. There was an old call bell for the plantation hands on the porch. Darcy ran like a maniac to clang it, then raced back to the smokehouse again.

She ignored the darkness, burst into the center of it, and began to dig, using the point of the umbrella. She'd gotten down no more than a foot, and was so involved in her task, that she screamed when she felt hands on her shoulders.

She spun around.

Matt.

"What the hell are you doing?" His words sounded like an angry growl. She took a step back, aware of his size, and of the darkness.

But she had rung the bell loudly enough to wake the dead. Naturally, he was out here. And yet, in the small room, it seemed that he was staring at her with malignant eyes.

"What's going on?" The shout came from the house. Penny was running on out. Adam, with a slip cap and robe on, was hurrying along behind her.

"She's here!" Darcy said. "She's here, I know it!"

By then, Sam Arden, Clint, and Carter had come from the stables. They were all barefoot, dressed in nothing but hastily thrown-on jeans.

"What the hell...?" Clint demanded, rubbing his five o'clock shadow.

Carter stared at the scene. "She thinks she's found something," he murmured to Clint. "Hey, should I get a shovel?"

"Yes, please!" Darcy said.

Matt threw up his hands. "Hell. Sure. Get a shovel. Let's dig in the middle of the night."

Sam disappeared with Carter. They were back in a minute with two shovels, a portable floodlight, and a pick.

"Darcy, move, let me at it," Carter said, entering the little room, and starting right off with the pick. He loosened the earth, and Matt joined him to start digging, swearing beneath his breath as he did so.

The others looked on. Minutes ticked by, and mounds of dirt came out of the smokehouse.

Sweating despite the coolness of the wee hour, grimy with dirt, Matt wiped his brow. He glared at her. She forced herself to stand firm, wishing that she didn't note that his physique remained exceptionally imposing, tanned biceps and chest glistening with sweat, streaked with mud.

"Darcy, we're down several feet."

She let out an impatient sound and started for the smokehouse herself. He raised a hand to her. "All right, all right!"

He went back to it with a vengeance.

Still, it was Carter who gave a sudden cry.

"Damn!"

"What, what?" Darcy cried.

"He probably shoveled his own toe," Penny murmured.

Matt hunkered down with Carter. Clint nosed his way in. Darcy couldn't get past them.

"What is it?" she cried out.

Matt rose, tossing down his shovel, glaring at her once again as he started to walk by her. "Don't anyone touch anything else. I'm getting a team out here."

"A team?" she said.

He stopped walking, hands on his hips, eyes like ebony as he stared down at her. "A forensics team, Darcy. Yes, we found bones."

"Could be an animal," Penny suggested softly. "It is a smokehouse."

Matt glanced over to her. "It's human. It appears to be complete, or nearly complete."

"But do you really need a team in the middle of the night?" Penny said, perplexed. "Poor thing has probably been there for hundreds of years."

"Maybe not, Penny. We don't know that."

Darcy felt her breath catch. That was it, of course. She'd assumed, they'd all assumed, that the ghost had to have been there for years. She had never really thought that Matt might have killed his ex-wife, and yet...

The suspicion had been there.

She stared at Adam. He stared back at her, and she knew that they were both hoping that they hadn't found Lavinia Harper Stone.

Matt was still staring at Darcy. She felt his eyes and looked back at him.

"We don't know anything about this skeleton—*yet*," he said. "But we will."

With that, he walked on by.

And all eyes turned on Darcy.

17

It was approximately one in the morning when they first dug out the bones.

It was four by the time Matt's team had carefully dug out the surrounding dirt along with the skeleton and sealed off the smokehouse for further excavation. The box containing the remains was locked into the morgue at the Mahoney Funeral Home by four-thirty, and Matt was back at the house by five and finally showered and in bed at five-thirty.

He was exhausted, and should have slept easily, but he lay awake staring up at the ceiling. *How the hell had she done it?*

He was tempted to go to her. Knock on her door, the hell with whoever might hear the sound. He felt a greater need than ever to be with her. He tried to tell himself that he was an idiot—she had suggested that he might be capable of murder, for God's sake! And there was still that thing…tonight, once again, seeing the look in her eyes, the set of her jaw. It was creepy, and if he was failing to realize it, it was all because he was blinded by emotion, he was letting his dick, rather than his mind, rule his thinking.

Didn't matter, he realized. He felt the same way about her, no matter what. Except…he was damned indignant. He looked at his watch. Six. He groaned, then rose, went out to his desk, and began shuffling through his papers. Somewhere, he had the cell number he wanted. Not in his phone, it was too new.

At last, in the bottom drawer, with a stash of old pictures, he found the number. He punched it in, expecting an answering machine.

She didn't answer with a simple hello. After all these years, she must have recognized the house number on her caller ID.

"Darling!" Lavinia cooed over the wires. "Darling, do you know what time it is?"

"Six-o-five, I believe," Matt said dryly. "Sorry, I thought your machine would pick up, and you'd give me a call back."

"That's quite all right, although really, you should know better than to call me at this hour, unless, of course, you have some kind of incredibly hot proposal to make?" she teased.

"No. Actually, I just called to see how you were doing."

"At six in the morning?"

"Like I said, I didn't expect you to answer."

He heard Lavinia's low, husky, rumbling laugh. Once, the sound of it had been sheer aphrodisiac. Now...

"Things are going wickedly down there, so I hear," she told him. "Believe it or not, I was going to call to see if you were all right."

"Oh?"

"An article made it into the New York papers by that local walking-stick you've got down there. All about the occult. You'll just have to see it, darling. All about the world's most beautiful ghost hunter finding a skull, then being cast into a grave."

"That just happened yesterday!" Matt said.

"Darling, it's only 'news' because they get it out quickly."

"Good point, Lavinia."

"Is she that beautiful?" Lavinia inquired.

Matt wondered if there was a touch of jealousy in her voice, and even, a touch of pathos.

The past was long gone. And Lavinia was alive and well and in New York. He was suddenly feeling very generous.

"Lavinia, she looks a great deal like you. A tall redhead with all the elegance in the world."

"Should I come down and meet her?" Lavinia asked. Matt wasn't sure if she did so with mischief, or the best of intentions. "I mean, it sounds as if you could use a little help. You know...actually, I wasn't all that fond of the Lee Room myself, but...the article this fellow wrote tells about all these weird events at the house, how a ghost has pulled hair and slapped people, and all that kind of stuff. If you need help...?"

"That's sweet, Lavinia. I think we're fine." He hesitated. "Miss Tremayne led us to a skeleton last night. Once the remains are identified, I think we'll be fine."

She was silent for a minute, intuitive, then she said, "Oh, Matt! I am so sorry. I haven't been there in years, of course, and I had said that I was coming back. I had an offer in Paris I couldn't refuse, and there was no point in pursuing that lovely affair between the two of us...."

"A marriage isn't the same as an affair, Lavinia," he said.

"But someone there thinks the bones are me!" she exclaimed.

"Lavinia, look at that! If you tire of the social whirl, you'll be perfect for Harrison Investigations. What intuition."

"Don't tease, Matt. I'm between events right now. Summer can be so droll. If you need to prove that I'm alive, I'll be happy to come down."

"Lavinia, I know you're alive and well, and I'm grateful. That's all I need."

"Ah, well. You do have my number." The last was filled with sexual innuendo. It didn't mean anything. Lavinia was incapable of anything else.

"Thanks, Lavinia. And hey, if you need me, I'm here."

"Oh, darling, on nights when I'm alone, I do need you."

"Good thing there aren't many nights like that, eh, Lavinia?" he said, his tone light. "Sorry to have awakened you. Take care."

"You, too. I'll love you a little, Matt."

"Yeah? Thanks. Take care."

He hung up, feeling remarkably smug. Maybe he should have asked her to come down. Make sure everyone saw her.

He nearly jumped when the phone started to ring again. Thayer.

"Thayer, what's up? Didn't you get anyone to spell you yet?"

"Matt, you're not going to believe this."

The pleasure he'd felt at hearing Lavinia's voice evaporated in a flash. "Try me."

"The bones are gone."

"What?"

"The bones are gone. There was a break-in at Mahoney's place. And the box with the dirt and the bones has been stolen."

"Anything else missing?" he asked Thayer.

"The office drawers were trashed, some petty cash was taken," Thayer said. Then he plunged in with, "But if you ask me, they broke in for the bones. Someone has chalked a few of the walls with Greek letters as if it were a fraternity prank, but...who knows? College kids have been known to do more than steal bones on a lark."

"You've got the area sealed?" Matt asked, a little too harshly. But he'd be damned if he'd lose fingerprints or any other important evidence on this one.

"Matt, you know that we're capable of protecting the integrity of a scene," Thayer said.

"Sorry, I do know that," he said. "I'll be right there."

Darcy woke to the sound of an ear-shattering scream. She'd had to shower again last night, after her bout in the smokehouse, and she was wearing a knee-length sleep T-shirt. She didn't bother with a robe or slippers, or care in the least about her appearance, not at the sound of a scream like that one.

She tore out of her room and to the railing, looking downward.

Penny was standing in the foyer, her hand to her throat.

"Penny!" Darcy cried, and came racing down the stairway.

She came up abruptly against Penny's back, and stared past her.

There was a soldier at the front door. He was wearing worn butternut and gray, his sash tied perfectly around his hips, his sword swinging at his side. His hat was low slung over white hair, and he wore a regal silver beard. He was ready to march to battle.

"Harry Smith!" Penny chastised, her finger falling from her throat.

Harry Smith. Darcy smiled, recognizing the medical technician who had come to her aid when she'd crashed through the floor at the library.

"You scared me to death!" Penny told him.

"Penny Sawyer, why I'd suddenly scare you after all these years, I can't begin to imagine!" he said gruffly, shaking his head. "But I sure am sorry." A smile was tugging at his lips, and only barely hidden by his growth of beard.

Darcy started to laugh herself, and then Penny eased completely and laughed as well. It was easy to see how Penny might have thought that she had indeed come across a ghost from the past. Harry Smith was the perfect image of a long-ago soldier.

"Harry, you look great!" Darcy said.

He inclined his head toward her. "Thank you, ma'am. The uniform belonged to my great-great-grandfather, who was captain of one of the units that fought here. The sword is authentic, too."

"Harry, this is all well and good, but did you forget the concept of knocking?" Penny asked. "If you'd knocked at the door, I might not have come so close to having a heart attack!''

"Penny, now, you're the one who's claimed to have seen ghosts in the past, anyway," Harry told her. "I did knock. No one answered, and the door was open."

"That's odd—we've been careful about locking it lately," she murmured, then challenged Harry again, her eyes sparkling. "And we had a rough night. Darcy led us to a stash of bones in the smokehouse, so you see, Harry Smith, there is a ghost!"

Harry looked at Darcy. "I heard," he said. "Good work, young lady. Except, it seems that you ladies haven't heard the latest."

"What happened?" Darcy asked.

"The bones have been stolen."

"Stolen!" Penny repeated. "Who on earth would have stolen old bones?"

"Are you sure?" Darcy said. "They were just dug out in the very early hours of this morning."

"I'm sure. This is a small town, Miss Darcy. I'm with the fire department, and we know the minute something has happened down at the sheriff's office."

"So Matt is down there already?" Darcy said.

"He's been down there for hours now," Harry Smith said. He smiled. "It isn't exactly morning anymore. It's almost one in the afternoon."

Darcy hadn't had the least idea it could be so late. But then, she hadn't gone to sleep until very late—or very early.

"Who would want old bones?" Penny said again.

Harry shrugged. "Looks like a fraternity prank. Like a challenge, even. Thayer told Bill Jenkins that there were some Greek letters chalked on one of the walls. And some money was taken, too. Not a lot. Maybe a hundred dollars. Anyway, Matt is livid. Don't blame him. We make a discovery, hold the bones overnight in a mortuary so that they can be brought up to Washington the next day—and they disappear. Bad business. Makes us small-town folk look like real hicks. Anyway, he's on it. Don't you all worry.''

But Darcy was worried. She didn't think that it was any kind of fraternity prank. "That's very strange. The bones must have been stolen during a very small window of time.''

"Yep," Harry said.

"How would fraternity pranksters even know they were at the funeral home?" Darcy asked.

"Ah, the kids can listen in on the police radio," Harry said, waving a hand in the air. "Had to be kids. Who else would want old bones?''

The front door had remained open when Harry had come in and Clint came up behind him then. "Hi, Harry. Why, you old geezer! You look like a million bucks.''

"Thank you, young sir," Harry said, and went on to explain that they were discussing the bones—and the fact that they'd been stolen.

"That's friggin' bizarre," Clint said.

"Clint, mind the language," Penny said.

"Yes'm," Clint said, rolling his eyes. "You should hear her swear when she's got a bee in her bonnet.''

"Not true at all.''

"What's not true?" Carter had arrived as well. Entering behind Clint, he too looked Harry Smith over, and whistled. "Man, you look like the real thing.''

"So do you, once you're in uniform," Harry reminded him.

"So what's going on? Why would Penny be swearing? What bee is in her bonnet?" Clint asked, and once again, Harry Smith went through the explanation.

"Probably was frat boys," Carter said, shrugging. "And those bones will show up somewhere again. Maybe on the field on one of the college campuses.''

"Matt isn't taking it as a prank," Harry said. "He's going after the offenders, with a vengeance.''

"Sure, right now, because he's really pissed off," Clint said. "But I know Matt. If he doesn't get them right away, he'll know that it's more important to protect and serve the living, and go after the real criminals. Then the bones will show up."

"I don't know," Carter mused. "I can see how a thing like this might make him look bad to all the big boys he knows up in the D.C. area."

"He must be running on empty, too," Penny said. "After last night...well, the rest of us have all slept really late. He has to be exhausted."

"He'll be fine, you know Matt," Clint said. "That is something, though, isn't it? We're all feeling this incredible elation, this triumph, because Darcy found the skeleton. And here we are—bones all gone in just a matter of hours. Easy come, easy go. Sadly, that's life. Hey, Harry, what are you doing all dressed up today? The reenactment isn't until tomorrow."

"I came to take out old Tannenbaum," Harry said. "I haven't been out on him for a while. I just want to make sure that he and I are still real good friends, before we get out in front of the crowds tomorrow."

"Sure. I'll go saddle him up for you," Clint said.

"I lead one of the cavalry charges," Harry told Darcy. "You ever been to one of these things?"

"No. I've been to a lot of the national parks, but I've never really seen a reenactment," Darcy told him.

"Well, want to take a ride with me, young lady? I'll show you where it's all taking place. Sorry—you do ride?"

"I love to ride. And if you'll give me a minute to get dressed, I'd be happy to go with you. Unless..." She hesitated and looked at Penny.

"You can go to the mortuary if you want, if you think you can help," Penny said. "But I'd be staying the hell away from Matt myself this morning. Let him handle things the way the police would do it, first."

"Hell! Did you hear that? My, my, Penny Sawyer swearing!" Carter teased. "But seriously, I'd stay away from Matt right now, too."

"You saddle Tannebaum for Harry, and I'll get Nellie ready for a ride," Clint said.

"There's really nothing else you can do at the moment," Penny told Darcy. "Go with Harry. You'll enjoy it."

Darcy nodded. "Give me just a minute, then."

"Hell, I think I'll go for the ride, too," Carter said.

"Hell, I'll join you, too," Clint said, grinning at Penny.

"I'll be right down," Darcy said.

"No hurry," Harry Smith said. "I'm off the next three days. Take your time."

"Yes, dear, take your time. I have muffins in the kitchen—how rude of me. Harry, come on in and have some coffee and muffins." She looked both Clint and Carter up and down. "And when you ne'er-do-wells with all that time on your hands have saddled the horses, you can have coffee and muffins, too."

"Ne'er-do-wells!" Carter protested. "I'm a hardworking entrepreneur!"

"And I even have some work this evening," Clint said. He winked at Penny. "You wait and see. You'll be eating your words."

Penny sniffed. "Coffee when the horses are saddled. Darcy, you take your time. Harry, you come with me."

Darcy ran back up the stairs, but didn't head straight for her room. She tapped lightly at Adam's door.

He told her to come in, and she found him still in bed.

"I might be getting a cold," he told her sheepishly. "Anyway, Penny brought me some cold pills and tea and toast awhile ago. I'll just hang out in here for a few hours."

"Adam, the skeleton was stolen from the mortuary," she said.

"I know. Matt called."

"Oh?"

"Don't worry. He's on it like a hornet."

"Adam, doesn't it seem really suspicious to you?"

"Of course."

"They all seem to think it was a fraternity prank," she said. "They—Clint, Carter, and the rest of the town, I imagine."

"Sure. They all think that you discovered a skeleton that was hundreds of years old."

"There was nothing there, right? No jewelry, no remnants of cloth…nothing?" Darcy asked.

Adam shook his head. "The remains, from what Matt said, were purely skeletal."

"Still…there would be teeth," she said.

"Yep."

"Adam, do you think it's possible that the skeleton isn't so old, and therefore someone really wanted to get it back?"

"Darcy, I told you I'd find Lavinia Harper."

"I wasn't particularly implying that it would be Lavinia Harper."

"Darcy, let's give Matt a chance to be a sheriff, okay?"

"Right, but…if there was a break-in…"

"Yes?"

"Wouldn't it be most feasible that it was done by someone who definitely knew that the bones were there?"

"Darcy, give Matt a chance."

"Of course." She told him then that she was going riding, and she would check in on him later.

A few minutes, she was dressed, and she ran downstairs. Penny had a plate with corn muffins set for her, along with juice and coffee.

"Did you check in on Adam, dear?" Penny asked her.

"Yes, he's just going to sleep for a bit. Hopefully, he'll feel some better by this evening."

"Let him get some rest today," Clint said. "He'll want to enjoy the show tomorrow."

"The reenactments are fun," Carter told Darcy. "You'll see today when we go riding—there are already a bunch of encampments set up. Wives come along and dress in antebellum fashion and cook on the battlefield. Some women dress up as laundresses…and those who just kind of follow armies, if you know what I mean.''

"Prostitutes," Penny said impatiently.

Carter grinned and laughed. "Right. Prostitutes. Since General Hooker gave his name to one of the current labels for such ladies, we know that they were in abundance in the Civil War. And, hey, do you know how many soldiers came down with sexual diseases?''

"No, and we don't want to know," Penny said.

"Well, that's good. I don't really know the number. But a lot," Carter said.

"Shall we ride?" Harry asked.

Darcy gulped down the last of her orange juice and stood. "I'm ready, whenever. Penny, did you want to join us?" she asked.

"Heavens, no! I watched these boys play soldier far too long. Have a lovely afternoon.'' She waved them all away, and they headed out to the stables.

Despite his absolute faith in his own people, Matt recognized that they were a small-town force. Before he ever reached Mahoney's himself, he'd put through a call to Randy Newton, the friend at the FBI who had tested the library floorboard for him.

While he waited for Randy and his team to arrive, Matt followed Thayer around the mortuary, seeing where a screen had been broken in the basement, allowing the thief—or thieves—entry. Mahoney's desk had been rifled, but it looked like a sloppy job. Nothing had been taken but the hundred dollars from the petty cash box, while Mahoney's Rolex, a Christmas present from his wife the year before, lay untouched right on top of the desk.

The wooden evidence box, filled with dirt and bones, had been left in one of the viewing rooms, where one of Matt's men would have picked it up from to drive it on in to Digger at the museum.

Mahoney was concerned, convinced that they were making far too much out of an ancient skeleton, and was concerned that the police would still be around when the Thompsons arrived for their great-aunt's funeral that night. Matt could only assure Mahoney that he'd do his best to collect what he needed, and be out.

Randy Newton was a tall, well-built guy who had made some of the top scores when he'd been in the academy at Quantico. He'd met Matt while working on a serial killer case in the outskirts of D.C., a truly psychotic fellow who had preyed on impoverished prostitutes. They'd worked together well, and remained friends. Despite the usual peace and tranquility to be found in Stoneyville, northern and central Virginia provided havens for criminals who struck in the bigger cities, and hid out in the countryside. Matt and Randy had kept up a communications system which had served them both well in the past.

Randy looked like FBI. He wore the inevitable suit, and sunglasses, and with his height, build, and dark hair, he emitted an aura of authority. Even Mahoney welcomed him with something like awe.

But when they were alone in the viewing room where the box had been, Randy shook his head. "I don't get it, Matt. I mean, I can see where you're angry, but hell. This probably is a fraternity prank. Who the hell would want a bunch of old bones?"

"Randy, there is no guarantee that they're old bones."

"I thought that your psychic had been led to them by a ghost in a long, flowing white gown."

"Yeah—and there are still lots of white flowing night-gowns out there."

"Really? I don't remember. I've been married too long. Rita wears T-shirts." He shrugged. "She used to wear nothing at all, and that was pretty cool, but then we had the kids…. hey, Matt, you're not smiling."

"Because I think this is serious."

"Do you know how many known murders I have on my plate right now, Matt?"

"I can imagine. But Randy, help me out on this. Get your guys to do the fingerprinting, look for any shoe marks…anything." He hesitated. "And do me another favor."

"What?"

"Run your files for me. Look for anyone in your missing persons files who…who just might have disappeared from this area."

"Matt, I think a bunch of kids stole the bones of a woman murdered so long ago, there's not a damned thing we can do for her."

"Randy, help me out here anyway."

"Did your psychic tell you to bring me in?" Randy asked suspiciously.

"Randy, no. I'm asking a favor."

"All right. You've got it."

"I need the files as quickly as possible."

"Drive up to my office tomorrow. I'll give you everything I can get."

"Thanks."

"Hey, you're looking frazzled as hell."

"Haven't slept."

Randy cocked his head to one side. "Ghosts, ghosts, ghosts. Hell, I guess they can keep you awake. Go home. Go to sleep. We'll take over here. And get out before the funeral. Trust me. Go."

Matt didn't argue. He left Mahoney's, and headed straight home. He could hear Penny in her office when he stepped into the foyer, but he quickly slipped up the stairs, and crashed straight into his bed.

In a matter of minutes, he was sound asleep.

The ride was incredibly pleasant.

They headed out toward the north, following the main road for several miles, then riding into pasture land where canvas tents dotted the fields. They dismounted from their horses and walked around the various living history exhibits, visiting the blacksmith, an officer's tent, a seamstress, a common soldier's little plot, and the field hospital. Harry Smith introduced her to dozens of people, but when they came across those who had read about her in the newspapers, he politely but firmly found a way to steer her away.

Carter and Clint were old friends with many of the men as well, and with a few of their friends, they rode on over to the Yankee camp, where they all teased that she belonged.

Naturally, she reminded them who had won the war.

"Of course," Carter said. "The North had to win. I mean, what were those fellows thinking, that any man had the right to own another? It's crazy now. But history."

"And history we shouldn't forget," Clint said. "Things that were horrible have to be remembered. Hopefully, we learn from our mistakes. What is that saying? Those who cannot remember the past are doomed to repeat it?"

"Very true," Harry Smith said. "I fought in the very early stages of Viet Nam. Any man who has really gone to war knows how terrible it is. Generals usually do their best to avoid conflict—politicians are the ones who are most eager for it. Anyway, don't get me started. Dusk is coming soon. We ought to get back. Let's take the back fields."

"Sure you want to do that? We may have some fences in the way," Clint reminded him.

"I know the way," Harry said.

The ride back was far more beautiful. They never touched a main road, but traveled around farm fields and pastureland. After one massive cornfield, they came up a lovely little stream, with the water dancing over small rocks and boulders.

"Some of the heaviest fighting took place there, in the cornfield. Just like it was at the battle of Sharpesburg, men and corn alike were mowed down," Harry said. As they rode, the stream widened. They came upon a beautiful whitewashed wooden bridge, spanning the stream between fields and the dirt trail they rode.

"The bridge is new. The original was destroyed during the fighting. Dozens of men crashed through it, and died, broken and battered, on the rocks below,'' Harry said sadly.

Darcy could well imagine. There was an aura here, one of great sadness. She closed her eyes for a moment, and heard the heartrending cry of a wounded man. The lucky ones died instantly, she thought, because the others had lain with broken bones, in agony, while the fighting had continued.

She quickly opened her eyes. The memory of pain here was deep.

Harry winked at her. ''There's some activity in this area tomorrow. But we don't destroy the bridge anymore. Too expensive.''

''I can imagine,'' Darcy said.

''Still, you'll enjoy it, I promise!'' Carter told her.

''Darcy, you should dress up,'' Clint said.

''I'm not a native,'' she told him.

Clint waved a hand in the air. ''Half the Southerners today are from New York. Who cares? And there's still a romance about the Southern Cause. Oh, don't get me wrong. I have great friends who are true loyal Yanks! But it doesn't matter, we're reenacting history. Dress up, and ride with us. Not in the actual battle, of course. But you can be one of our wives. It'll be great.''

''Or she can belong to all of us,'' Carter said with a wink. ''Camp follower, you know.''

''Carter, really!'' Harry said with indignation.

''I'm sorry—prostitute. Penny did correct us, right?''

''That's not the point. Darcy is far too...dignified to be a camp follower!''

''It's a reenactment!'' Clint said, laughing. ''We're not really going to put a 'for hire' sign on her, or anything.''

''We'll see,'' Darcy said, laughing. ''I think I'm fresh out of camp follower clothing, though.''

''Penny can set you all up,'' Clint said cheerfully.

''Let's ride on,'' Harry said. ''It's getting dark.''

* * *

Matt had been soundly sleeping when he felt the fingertips moving down his cheek.

Then he woke with a vivid start.

The room was mostly in shadow, with dusk upon them, and yet he knew, instinctively, who it was.

"Lavinia!"

He bolted out of the bed and turned on the light. She was still seated on the side of the bed, smiling.

"What the hell are you doing in my bedroom?" he demanded.

She pouted, something she did very well. "What a greeting! When I took the first plane down from New York just to show myself."

"That was great of you, Lavinia, really. But did you ever hear of knocking? Who let you up here?"

"No one let me up. I told Penny I'd run up and see if you were awake."

"You could have knocked."

She waved a hand in the air. "I know my way around." She smiled. "Look at that! I think you're getting a touch of gray in your hair."

"Time does go by." And it had. It had been years since he had seen her. With the initial shock of her arrival over, he had to admit, it had been pretty decent of her to come. He was actually going to enjoy seeing Darcy's face when she met Lavinia. "But you," he said magnanimously. "You look great."

She did. Her hair was still long, red, and shining. She seemed to have acquired more of a lithe, hourglass figure.

She stood. "You think so."

"Yep. You're even more…voluptuous than ever."

She grinned. "Okay, so I had a boob job. They did great work though. Want to see?"

He laughed. "No, but thanks."

"Ah, so there's something going on with the ghost chaser, huh?"

"Did you come because you were bored, Lavinia, or to help me out?"

She reflected the comment honestly for a minute. "Okay, maybe I was a little bored. But I did come to help you out."

"Want to really help me?"

"Sure."

"Get out of my bedroom. I'll be right down."

Lavinia rose regally, stretching like a cat. She walked by him, rising against him, planting a kiss on his cheek. "Maybe I'll still be bored if the little ghost chaser goes away."

"Lavinia, we've been that route before. Let's be friends, huh?"

She shrugged and started toward the door. "Your cousin still hanging around here? And that handsome friend of his?"

"Clint—and Carter."

"Carter, yeah."

"They're still around, Lavinia."

"And they've gone through women like toilet paper, I take it. But then again, I'm not the usual country fare, am I?"

"If you're trying to make me jealous, Lavinia, I told you, we've been that route before."

Her smiled deepened. "I'm not trying to make you jealous. I'm just bored."

"I'm sure that both Carter and Clint will be around for dinner."

"Good. I am hungry," she said, and at last departed his room.

Darcy insisted on taking care of Nellie when they returned to the stables, though Sam was waiting for them, and managed to remove the horse's saddle the minute she had crawled out of it. "They're waiting for you, up at the house," Sam told them.

"Waiting for us? Are we late for dinner? It's early," Carter said.

Sam rolled his eyes. "We've got a visitor." He turned his back on them, leading Tannenbaum back to his stall.

"A mystery. How cool," Clint said.

"What is it?" Carter asked Sam, frowning.

Harry linked an arm with his. "Let's just go on up and see."

It looked as if Carter still wanted to protest but he was dragged along. As they walked up the porch steps, Darcy knew that she was curious herself. They walked into the foyer, and saw a group sitting in the parlor.

Adam, up and dressed and looking very regal. Penny, flushed and a little flustered. And Matt, casual in jeans and a knit polo shirt.

And a woman.

A really gorgeous woman in tight black pants and a blue silk shirt that enhanced her assets to a T.

She stood with the others as they entered.

"My Lord!" Clint breathed.

Matt smiled broadly at Darcy across the room. "Darcy! I think the others have all met. This is Lavinia Harper. Lavinia, Darcy Tremayne."

18

Matt might have been mad as a hornet that morning, but now, he was as smug as the Cheshire cat. He somehow refrained from shouting, *"She's alive. See, see! My ex-wife is alive and well."*

And stunning. Smooth, elegant, and with perfect poise and sophistication, though her eyes were still curious and judging when they fell upon Darcy.

"Miss Tremayne! I've been reading about you all the way up in New York." Lavinia took her hand in a truly decent shake.

"Have you?" she said dryly, then, "It's a pleasure to meet you."

"Well, of course, it is," Lavinia said. "With bones popping up all over, I'm happy to prove that they're not mine. But if you're a psychic, shouldn't you know that?"

"I've been trying to explain to Lavinia that dealing with the mind is not always such an obvious thing," Adam said.

"Lavinia, you are gorgeous!" Clint told her.

"Clint! I haven't given you a hug yet." The woman flashed Darcy a smile. "If they wanted to be honest, they'd all tell you that it's not such a thrill to have me here, but these are true old-time Southerners, determined on the old hospitality!"

"Lavinia, really. We're certainly pleased to have you," Penny said stiffly.

Lavinia broke into laughter. "Her words a lie, her tone the truth! Oh, Penny, don't go getting all flustered." She offered her smile to Darcy again. "The boys, however, really don't mind too badly, hm? Clint, I'm still waiting on the hug."

She walked toward him. Clint winked at Darcy and mouthed, "Yow! Come to me, baby!"

She turned. Matt was looking at her. Still smug and pleased.

"Hey, any luck finding the bones?" Carter asked Matt. He shook his head. "But we will find them."

"What can I get you all to drink?" Penny asked.

"Beer for me, thanks, Penny," Clint said. Lavinia had gone on to hug Carter and Harry.

"Ditto!" Carter said, over Lavinia's shoulder.

"A Coke for me," Harry called, next in line for the buxom hug.

"Darcy?" Matt asked politely.

She met his eyes and smiled sheepishly. "A big anything," she told him.

"Not too big. I just found out myself that Adam bought you a present today," Matt said.

"Oh?" Darcy looked at Adam.

"I've been thinking about it a long time. Sam helped me out after I made it out of bed," Adam said.

"How are you feeling?" Darcy asked him.

"Much better. Sleep helped a lot," Adam said.

"Yes, it does," Matt said. "Darcy, I'll get you a beer. Better yet, come with me to the kitchen—if that's all right with you, Adam?"

"Certainly," Adam said.

"What's going on?" Darcy asked.

"Your present is in the kitchen," Matt told her.

She followed him, and as he walked to the refrigerator, she looked around. Then she heard a sound and solid bark. Matt grinned, handing her the beer.

"A dog?" she said.

"Adam thought that, since you didn't seem able to stop yourself from running around in the middle of the night, you should have a big dog. She's around the counter in her crate, waiting to meet you."

Darcy walked around the counter. Her tail wagging away, one of the most beautiful German shepherds Darcy had ever seen was waiting impatiently.

"She's gorgeous!" Darcy said.

"You can let her out."

"She full-grown?"

"Almost full-grown, and fully trained. And once she gets to know you, she'll be your most loyal fan, and most ardent protector. Hopefully, you won't send her after me. Now that you know that Lavinia is alive and well."

Darcy had slipped the bolt on the crate and the dog was sniffing and licking her hands. She looked at Matt. "I never really thought—"

"Yes, but now you don't even have to suspect, huh?"

Darcy gave her attention to the dog.

"I'm sorry," she said softly.

"I'm sorry, too," he said.

"For?" she asked, looking up at him.

"For the times I have tried to convince myself that you were just too eerie to get really close to," he said flatly.

"I'm still eerie."

"Not to me."

She smiled, but wondered if she really believed him.

"Lavinia is really as gorgeous as everyone said."

"Yes, she is," he agreed, but he shoved his way close to her, despite the dog. "So help, huh?" he asked.

"Help?"

"Stick close."

"You need protection from her? Do you doubt yourself?"

"Not for a minute. But she's really the touchy-feely kind."

"Um," Darcy said, studying his eyes. "But you really do seem to be in a good mood tonight. And I was warned that you were in a real temper this morning. You must be happy to see Lavinia."

"I'm happy for you to see Lavinia," he said.

She smiled, then became serious. "But the bones were stolen," she reminded him.

He ran his fingers down her cheek, the touch gentle, his voice like lead. "You mean more to me than the bones, but trust me, I'll find them. I have the best forensic help you can get anywhere in the world."

"Oh? Is that why you're not still down at the funeral home?"

"I've asked a friend in the FBI for help."

"To find old bones?"

"Do we know that they're old bones?"

She shook her head in response to his question, still studying his eyes. He shrugged then. "You don't have to mention that fact. Everyone will know soon enough. It's no great secret. But for now…"

He was interrupted by a bark. The shepherd stood looking up at them, wagging her tail.

"What's her name?" Darcy asked.

"Oola."

"Oola?"

"According to Sam, her breeder was very fond of the play *The Producers,*" Matt explained with a smile.

"I see. Oola! Come on, let's go and tell Adam thanks!"

Darcy returned to the parlor with her beer and her dog. Matt followed behind with the two bottles of beer for Clint and Carter and a Coke for Harry.

"Thank God I wasn't drowning!" Carter said.

"A dog!" Clint exclaimed.

Darcy hunkered down with Oola, smiling at Adam. "She's beautiful and a great gift, thank you so much, Adam."

"I've had a dog in mind for you for some time now," Adam said. "Sam just happened to know the right folks. She's housebroken, six months old, and she'll bond to you like glue, so he assures me."

"Great animal," Clint said.

"Great protection," Matt said.

"Do ghosts get dangerous?" Lavinia asked.

"Apparently, the pursuit of them may be," Matt said. He was staring at Harry. "That uniform is great on you," he said.

"Well, you'll be in uniform tomorrow, too," Harry told him.

"Not me. I've got business out of town," Matt said.

"Matt Stone!" Penny protested. "You can't go out of town."

"Penny, I wasn't going to ride with a unit, no matter what. I was going to be crowd control, you know, act like the sheriff. Thayer can handle it all, though."

"Matt, Penny has a point," Adam said. "You should be here. After all, this is Stoneyville."

"Clint is a Stone. He'll have to do."

"Wow. Great. Thanks," Clint said.

"Sorry. I didn't mean it that way," Matt said sheepishly.

"You're the one so big on tourism, Matt. On showing folks our little piece of Virginia. You're so gung ho on opening historic houses and buildings. How can you fail to be part of a reenactment?"

"Yeah, Matt!" Clint said.

"I have really important business," he told them.

"Darcy is going to be part of it," Clint told him.

"Oh?" Matt arched a brow to her.

She shrugged. "They think I should dress up, at least."

"What fun!" Lavinia put in. "I'd love to playact."

"You are more than invited to join us," Carter said graciously.

"I'll be there."

Oola barked, as if agreeing that she'd participate as well, causing them all to laugh.

"Even Oola will be there," Penny told Matt.

Darcy was surprised to see him suddenly hesitate, which seemed strange. He'd been so definite. "You know," he said, "there was a General Stone. But he was nowhere near Stoneyville during the fighting. He was surrounding Richmond at the time."

"Matt, you've always taken part before," Clint reminded him. He looked at Darcy. "He's usually Ian Ripley, a cavalry captain, like Harry."

"We'll see," Matt said. "I have business, like I told you. But I'll see how far things have progressed by the morning. Hey, Penny, is something burning?"

"The roast!" Penny said with dismay. She leapt up.

"I'll help you," Darcy offered.

As she ran after Penny, Oola followed.

She didn't go after the food; she just sat in the kitchen. And when they left the kitchen, she sat by Darcy's feet at the dining room table.

The meal was light, and fun, with everyone talking about the reenactment, and Lavinia bringing them all up to date on her social whirl, while flirting outrageously with every man at the table, including Harry. Still, after the nights they'd been having, it seemed a blessing.

Later, with the place cleaned up, the hour getting late, Matt at last rose to break up the group. "I slept all afternoon, but I'm still bushed. Harry, did you want to stay?"

"Nope, got to go home, thanks," Harry said.

"There's lots of room in the caretaker's cottage," Lavinia told him. He blushed to the roots—the exact effect she had intended.

"I have to go," Harry said, "but thanks."

Matt walked Harry to the door, then came back by Darcy's chair. She thought she was going to blush herself when he said, "Ready to go up?"

"Um, sure," she said, trying to sound very casual.

"I'll just let myself out," Lavinia said.

"Never! I'll escort you," Carter said.

"Hey, I'll walk with you. He's dangerous," Clint teased.

"Really?" Lavinia said. "I like dangerous men."

Darcy gave Adam a kiss on the cheek and followed Matt up the stairs.

Oola followed her.

She started for the Lee Room.

"Not tonight!" Matt told her. "My place," he said lightly. "Oola can have the office area. We'll take the bedroom. Alone. No ladies in white or any other visitors tonight."

"This house does give new meaning to the term, 'your place or mine,'" Darcy murmured. With the dog at her heels, she accompanied him.

The minute they locked the dog out of the bedroom area, and turned to one another, she began to whine. They looked at one another and laughed.

"I'm prepared," Matt told her.

"For a whining dog?"

"You bet."

He disappeared, then returned smiling. When the door closed, Oola was quiet. Darcy lifted a brow to him.

"Pig's ear," Matt said.

"Pardon?"

"She came with a supply of pigs' ears," he explained. "Chew toys. And now…well, you really do owe me an apology."

"I do?"

"For thinking I might have done evil to my ex-wife."

"I didn't really think it."

"Um. Humor me." He walked to her, embracing her, offering a kiss that was electric and fevered, lips tugging upon hers, tongue all but savage in its raw seduction. The same fevered urgency came damply down the length of her throat, while his fingers, at their most nimble, tugged at buttons and the zipper of her jeans. She ran her own fingers around his waistband, finding his zipper as well, and finding that just the sound of it, and the promise there given was erotic. She might have been the one who owed the apology, but he was creating an arousal and urgency in her that was high-pitched and searing. The stroke of his fingers down the bareness of her back seemed to elicit a burning in the core of her sexuality, and she moved against him wantonly, wondering only in a very distant place in her mind if he might be determined to forget that Lavinia was on his property. Then even the whisper of such a thought eluded her, for his lips were everywhere, a caress that swept over and into her. The scent of him invaded her, and whispering a soft penance, she returned each brush of a fingertip, every steam-tipped stroke of the tongue, every intimacy, until at last they were arching, writhing, straining, and pulsing together toward a maddened crescendo that burst upon Darcy violently, climax racking her body with delicious shudders, loathe to let the least touch, taste, or scent of him leave her. And for the longest time, he did not. She lay against him, hair splayed over the vital dampness of his chest, deliciously drowsy.

She must have been exhausted herself, because she drifted to sleep.

When she woke, she was alone.

"Matt?" she said his name softly, but he wasn't there.

Puzzled, she opened the door to the office area. And then she could see him. He'd thrown on a robe and was out on the balcony, just staring into the night. He looked like a man in torment. The dog was at his side, and Matt was absently stroking the shepherd's ears.

Darcy wanted to go to him, but she didn't. Instead, she stood there watching him, and thinking that if they did or didn't find the bones soon, it wouldn't matter. It was time to go. She had allowed this involvement, and encouraged it, lost herself within it. But she was certain that she knew what gave him such anguish.

He did care about her. He really cared.

But no matter what he tried to tell himself, what she was, what she did, mattered to him. He would never be able to look at her without remembering her tearing through the dirt for a bone, or falling into a trance, and not feel repelled.

She determined to leave him in peace. She closed the door and slipped back into bed.

Later, when he returned, she was the aggressor, laughing and teasing at first, then telling him how sorry she was.

Truly, how sorry she was.

* * *

Darcy was still sleeping when Matt awoke. He quietly slipped from the bed, showered, dressed, and took Oola downstairs so that she could take a run outside.

Penny was already up; coffee was already on. Matt accepted a cup, slipped into his downstairs office, and called Randy Newton. He didn't know if he was relieved or impatient when Randy apologized profusely, but between working the crime scene at the mortuary and handling a political death that was suspicious, he hadn't been able to pull all the records he could find as yet.

"Give me a day, Matt. Hell, that's nothing in most cases, you know."

"It's all right, Randy. I appreciate your help."

"Hey, tomorrow is Sunday, but I'll keep working until I get it. My wife is going to hate you, you know."

"Tell her your workload is my fault."

"Hey, I have to blame it on someone, huh?"

"I guess," Matt said. "Honestly, thanks. If you do get anything, anything at all, call me."

"I can tell you this—whoever broke in to the mortuary wore gloves, and even slipped plastic bags over his shoes. We went over the window screen and the rest of the place for fibers, and came up with zilch. Anyway, I'll get on those records, though I think you're barking up the wrong tree. The bones haven't shown up anywhere, have they?"

"No, not that I know of."

"Go deal with your battle buffs. I'll call you, I promise, the minute I've got something."

Matt thanked him again and hung up. He drummed his fingers on the desk, feeling antsy, and thinking there had to be something more that he could do. He'd called in the FBI. Best help he could have, and he knew it.

There was a tap at his door and Penny stuck her head in..

"Are you going to have to leave town today?" she asked.

He wished that he could lie.

"No, Penny," he said honestly.

Her smile lit up her face like a Christmas tree.

"And you've already got Thayer in charge of crowd control, right? I mean, of course, I know the society manages things really well, but that you put out the officers as well."

"I should oversee it all."

"Matt! Thayer is the best deputy a sheriff ever had. You leave him in control. Come on now, please? I've got your Captain Whittaker uniform all ready."

He groaned. "Penny, I'd told you I probably wasn't going to be here, and that if I was—"

"But you are here, and Thayer is in control. Oh, Matt! It means so much to everyone when *the* Stone of Stoney-ville takes part!"

"All right, Penny, all right. Where's the uniform?"

"In the laundry. I'll bring it right to you."

Penny's excitement and enthusiasm regarding the day was contagious. Darcy had barely emerged from the shower when Penny arrived with a surprisingly complicated costume. "Naturally, it's the real thing, corset, pantalettes, hoop, chemise...it's a little hot, being summer, but not so bad. We're going to have a breeze. Of course, in a way, that's bad. There will be black powder everywhere, but it's great, really, because you get the true essence of how horrible battle was and just what the poor men faced. It will be great. Now, the chemise goes on first, corset over that, then the dress. It's not an elegant evening gown, but a typical day dress. Nice one, and it will look great on you. Deep blue. It will do wonders for your hair."

"Thanks, Penny," Darcy said, and she meant it until Penny tried to tie her too tightly into the corset.

"It's how they really wore them!" Penny told her.

"Hey, that was then, this is now. I'm not passing out on the battlefield, okay, please?"

With a sigh, Penny eased her hold on the ribbons. "Lavinia will let you tie her up until she's just about dead."

"I'll just bet she looks great then," Darcy said. "I want to breathe through the show."

When she went downstairs, she discovered that Matt had already headed out—as a last-minute participant, he had to fill in his registration papers for insurance purposes. But Carter and Clint were waiting for her.

"Wow!" Clint told her. "It's a look—it's a look!"

"The best that money can buy, huh?" Carter teased.

They were alone with Penny in the foyer. "Is Lavinia coming with us?"

"Lavinia, ride? Are you kidding? Adam is driving her down the road to the field. We'll go the way we came back yesterday."

"Great," Darcy said. She felt a cold nose touch her hand. Oola. She stroked the dog and looked at the two men. "Can she come?"

"Sure," Carter said with a shrug.

"Maybe we should leave her in the house," Clint said. "All the commotion out there…she may not be used to it," Clint said.

"There will be all kinds of dogs around. People bring their pets," Carter said.

"I guess you're right. All right, Oola. Let's see what kind of a cavalry dog you'll make. Of course, you won't really be riding with the cavalry," Clint said. "We'll set you up with Penny, Lavinia, and Adam, and whoever else is around, during the battle."

"Sounds good," she said.

When they arrived at the field, they could see it was already crawling with people. Darcy was startled when the three of them were asked to stop a dozen times for tourists to take pictures.

Carter grinned at her. "See, you look great."

"Thanks. I'm glad I make a good camp follower."

"The dress is too good," Clint said. "You get to be my wife today."

"Your wife? Why not mine?" Carter argued.

Darcy could see that most of the people were arranged

behind a makeshift fence. There were officers in sheriff's department uniforms patrolling the lines, while those in Civil War attire were on the other side of the fence. "Where's Matt?"

"With his company, probably," Carter said. "We'll find them later. We'll position you back here—you can see better."

"Where will Adam and the others be?" Darcy asked.

"If they get here soon enough, we'll bring 'em back with you," Carter said. "If not, they're going to have to join the rest of the tourists." He tipped his hat to her, then dismounted to offer her a hand down. "We'll tether Nellie right here. Don't you love that—a perfect historical image, until you see the hot-dog stand!"

"Ah, well, progress, what can you do?" Darcy sympathized.

"I have to go down on the first volley," Clint told her, "so I'll get back to you as soon as I can reasonably crawl, noble and injured, off the field."

"You get to go down with the first volley?" Carter asked him as they rode off.

Darcy grinned, and was then surprised when a Robert E. Lee look-alike rode out to the center of the field on a beautiful white horse, dismounted, and lifted a megaphone to speak. He introduced the day of the battle, the circumstances that brought about the skirmish. Yankee troops, cut off, were trying to wind their way back to Meade, while the Southern troops were riding to catch up with Lee before the battle at Sharpsburg. A militia troop had recently held up a Northern baggage train, and, realizing they had a small force of the enemy in their sights, decided to turn the stolen guns against their enemy. It had been a bitter day of fighting, some of it house-to-house, but the majority of the action had taken place here, when the guns had sent the tattered Northerners fleeing. And yet it had not been a victory for either side as far too many lives had been lost. When he finished speaking, he gave a flourish of his hat, mounted his white horse, and left the field in a flurry of hooves and dirt. The moment he was gone, the first cannon sounded. The battle commenced.

Darcy was spellbound. She had never imagined what such a battle must have been like. Within minutes, the powder produced by the cannons and guns filled the air. Officers roared out commands from both sides of the field. The cavalry came in first, and it was an incredible show, horses rearing, swords flying. Men advanced, went down, retreated.

She saw Matt, riding with his sword swirling in the black-misted air, all but standing in his saddle. A pang touched her heart.

He disappeared into the field of black powder.

Foot soldiers advanced behind the cavalry. From the hillock where Clint and Carter had left her, Darcy was in perfect position, and she was enthralled.

Suddenly she felt an odd sense of real pain and nostalgia sweep over her. She closed her eyes, and the shouting seemed to change.

She opened her eyes to true horror.

There were twice as many men on the field. And there were no spectators. Broken, bleeding, riddled with bullets, soldiers in blue and in gray lay littering the field. A horse whinnied in terror and went down. Bullets flew hard and furious...she heard the whap of one as it struck the tree near her.

Darcy had closed her eyes...and opened them to a vision of what had once been real. It was appalling, horrifying. Northern soldiers and Southern soldiers, praying to the same God, dying...praying that they headed for the same heaven. For a moment, the image, and the pain it awakened, was almost unbearable.

At her side, she heard a whining sound. She shook her head and blinked.

And she was drawn back to the present.

She heard the crowd yelling in appreciation. Oola pawed her, huge brown eyes wide with distress as they fell upon Darcy.

"It's okay, girl," she said, hugging the dog. "I'm back."

Suddenly, Oola barked excitedly. Darcy looked back to see a soldier emerging from the powder that now seemed to blanket the entire scene.

"Darcy?"

"Clint!"

She rose, dusting her hands on her skirt. "That was truly magnificent. So sad, of course, but it's true, the reenactment really makes you appreciate what it must have been like."

He grinned at her. "Hey, Matt is off the field, too. Let's mount up, and we'll find him."

"Where's your horse?"

Clint sighed. "I told you, I had to go down at the first volley. My horse is with the Yankees now." He grinned. "We'll get him back later. My buddy, Aaron Swenson got to capture him. I'll hop up with you on Nellie for now, if it's all right."

"Of course, it's all right," Darcy said.

She mounted first. Clint leapt up ably behind her. Oola stared at them, barking furiously.

"Oola, what is the matter with you?" Darcy said. "Clint, which way?"

"That way," he said, and pointed ahead.

"Are you sure? Isn't that back toward the house, through the fields?"

"You're disoriented, Darcy. It's the powder. Trust me, I know where I'm going."

He'd had a hell of a good time, Matt had to admit. Riding off the field in triumph, laughing with James Arnold, head of one of the Union companies, he congratulated his friend on the excellent fake sword fight they had waged, and their speed and prowess in getting off the field.

"Hey, Matt, never give it up!" James told him, giving him a thumbs-up sign as they left the field.

Matt nodded and grinned, then realized that his cell phone was ringing.

"Hey, did you guys have those back then?" James teased.

"Hell, no. We'd have won the war if we'd had 'em," Matt said. "Sheriffs have to carry them," he said in something of an apology.

He urged his horse a distance from the field as he punched in to answer.

"Hello? Matt Stone."

"Matt! Jesus! I've been trying to get you for hours."

"Randy?" Matt said, his muscles tensing instantly at his friend's tone. "You found the bones?"

"No, but I found something else."

"What?"

"You know you asked me about missing persons?"

"Yep."

"There are at least five women last seen in or around your area who've been reported missing."

A strange freeze settled over Matt.

"I can change and get right up there."

"No need. I can fax you this stuff. But get this—none of them were really from the area. Just passing through. But this one, Susan Howell, twenty-six, five-five, one-hundred-twenty pounds. Professional girl, no family, last seen at the gas station right by the highway exit to Stoney-ville. Here's another. Catherine Angsley, last seen at the drugstore on the town line. She came from Stamford, Connecticut, folks deceased, another professional, a biochemist, made good money, and was reported missing months after that incident by a grandmother, who has since passed away. Then there's—"

"Stop!" Matt said. "Give me the names again!"

"Susan Howell, Catherine Angsley. There's a Tammy Silvera—hey, have you ever heard of these women?"

"Yes," Matt said dully. "They dated a friend of the family. A man named Carter Sutton." He looked anxiously around the field. He could see nothing but powder. Darcy had left the house that day with Carter and Clint. He hadn't seen any of them since, except for Clint, when he lay on the ground after the first volley.

"Randy, I've got to go. We need APBs out on Carter Sutton, right away. I've got to find him. I need you to get to my own men for me—I've got to get searching through this crowd."

He rang off, not waiting for Randy's reply; he knew the man would take it from there.

Right then, he felt a sense of sheer panic.

Carter had dated the women, yes. Didn't mean that Carter had made them disappear.

Clint, and Carter. They both went through women with total nonchalance.

He felt ill, thinking that Darcy still might be with either of them.

Activity was spinning around him. Where the hell were they?

This way.

He almost fell off his horse. The whisper again. He looked toward the trees. Nothing.

This way!

The whisper, urgent, fierce.

He started to ride.

"Wait a minute—maybe I am going the wrong way," Clint said. "I don't believe this! I'm disoriented myself. Hang on a minute."

Clint dismounted and disappeared into the smoke. Darcy waited. At her side, Oola began growling.

"What is it, girl?"

A moment later, a man emerged from the trees. But it wasn't Clint. It was Carter.

"Hey, lady! You're going the wrong way!" he called cheerfully.

Oola growled again.

"Shush, girl! It's only Carter. Where's Clint?"

"I was riding his horse. I gave it back to him. Let me mount up and show you the right way to go."

"Come on up."

"Turn her around," Carter said. She did so, and they started to trot.

"My God, that smoke carries!" Darcy said.

"I know. It's blinding, right."

"Big time!"

"Hey, pull up ahead for a minute, will you?"

"Sure." Darcy frowned, trying to see clearly. They had come to the area where the bridge spanned the rushing stream. "Why are we here?"

"Sorry, it's on the way back to the house. We're meeting up there. But I had to run over and do duty on the bridge after the first engagement. I lost a glove. Do you mind? It will only take a minute for me to feel around for it." Carter smiled at her, and slipped from the horse's back. "Hey! How about giving me a hand. It will go faster."

"Sure."

Carter helped her down.

"Go on. Let me just tether Nellie to this tree."

Nonchalantly, Carter started toward the bridge. Darcy tethered Nellie to a branch, then turned back. To her amazement, Oola started to growl again and went rushing toward the bridge. She heard the dog yelp.

"Oola! Carter, what happened?"

Halfway to the bridge, she came to a sudden halt. She could see Carter, standing there, waiting for her.

She could also see a strange white form through the mist.

"Darcy? What are you waiting for?"

"What happened to the dog?"

"I don't know. Maybe she stepped on a sharp stone or something."

Darcy didn't move. The white mist was next to Carter. She couldn't believe that he didn't see it, especially against the smoky tinge the day had taken on.

"Darcy, what on earth is the matter with you?"

"The ghost is there, Carter. Right next to you," she said.

He jumped, staring around. But he still didn't see. He turned back to Darcy, his eyes narrowing. "Come here, Darcy."

"Not on your life, Carter."

But she wasn't prepared. He ran like a bat out of hell, so suddenly and swiftly that she had barely screamed and turned to run before he was on top of her, grappling her to the ground. "You're going over the bridge, Darcy. This time, you're going over. I meant business at the cemetery—but again, I thought you'd be smart enough to get away from here. No, not you. So…before you find the bones again, Darcy, you've got to have a real fall."

He held her down. But her fingers were grasping in the dirt. She managed to get a handful. She got a good grip, and threw it in his eyes. His hold on her eased as he shouted in pain, instinctively bringing his hands to his face as he tried to clear his vision.

Darcy took full advantage. She brought her knee to his groin with all her strength. He howled with pain. She shot to her feet.

But before she could run, his fingers wound around her ankle, and he jerked her hard, back down to the earth.

The world spun in black. She felt him picking her up. She knew he meant to take her to the bridge and throw her over. And she would break her neck, or smash her skull, and she would die there, and when they found her…

Well, it would look as if she had gotten lost in the black powder. Wandered over the bridge, fallen….

"You killed her, the girl in the smokehouse," Darcy said, praying her strength would return.

"Her? Yeah, I killed the girl in the smokehouse." He looked down at her. "Kind of a sad thing, really. You're terrific, Darcy. You really are. But you just had to go and find the bones. And open the whole can of worms. I really am sorry, Darcy. But…hopefully,'' he said softly, ''it will be quick.''

She had gathered her senses again. The world had ceased to spin.

She raised her fist with all her strength against his eye. He grunted, doubling in pain, and she raked her nails down his arm, escaping his hold and falling hard to the ground.

They had come to the bridge.

And he was scrambling to get ahold of her again.

19

Matt raged inwardly at himself for being a fool. Even as he carefully rode Vernon through the crowds of people, he flicked open his phone again and called Thayer. The phone rang and rang. He knew his deputy was in the midst of the throng, and swore, praying that Thayer would hear the call. He had about given up when he heard, "Thayer here."

"Thayer, it's Matt. I can't explain but get all our men looking for Carter Sutton. Hold him."

"Hold Carter? On what charge?"

"Suspicion of murder."

"Murder? Carter?"

"Damn it, Thayer, just do it. Get him, and hold him. And keep an eye out for Darcy Tremayne."

"She murdered someone?"

"Thayer, I don't have time. Just do it."

"I'm right on it, Matt."

He clicked off, swearing that he should be in the midst of so many people. With the exhibition over, they were thronging over the fields.

Thayer had been alerted; whether his deputy thought he had gone off the deep end or not, he would see that every man they had was looking for Carter. And just because women Carter had dated were missing did not mean that Carter had murdered. *But a number of women Carter had dated were missing, and a skeleton had been discovered on property Carter knew like the back of his hand. Then the skeleton had disappeared. And he didn't know where*

Carter was, and he didn't have Darcy. Carter didn't know that his game might be up anyway, that Matt had asked the FBI to run a check of missing women. In Carter's mind, Darcy must surely be dangerous. If he had stolen the bones from the morgue, he must be afraid that Darcy could find them again, wherever he had taken them.

And there was a voice in his head, telling him which way to go. Insane, but hell, everyone had instinct. And instinct was telling him to follow the voice.

He ignored the sound when he first heard his name called, he was so intent on following his intuition, or the voice.

Then he realized that it was Adam Harrison, and he pulled in on the reins.

"Matt, there's no sign of Darcy," he said. "Clint went to find her. He'd left her in the rear for a better view. Now Clint hasn't returned. I'm not Darcy, Matt, but I have one damned bad feeling."

"Adam, I have that feeling myself. But don't worry. I'm going for Darcy."

He nudged Vernon and moved on. He had cleared the battlefield when he was blocked again by someone on horseback, hazy in the black smoke, but solidly on the trail.

"Matt!" she cried.

Lavinia. On a horse. Lavinia, who hated horses.

"Lavinia, what the hell are you doing? Get out of my way."

"Matt! Please, you have to listen to me," she said.

"Not now, Lavinia."

"You have to listen to me. I told Carter I wanted to be with Darcy to watch the show. He said sure, then disappeared. And I can't find her now. Or Carter. Or Clint! Matt, there are a few things that I never told you. And when I was going through the crowd, I saw some guy in blue with Clint's horse. They've all disappeared. Matt, there's something I never told you—"

"You're too late, Lavinia, whatever it is. Get out of my

way." He urged Vernon forward, heedless of her presence there.

"Wait, Matt!" She grappled for the reins as Vernon forced her horse off the side of the trail. "Please listen to me! I was certain I was wrong, that I had to be wrong...but I'm afraid for Darcy."

"Damn it, I'm afraid for her, too! That's why I'm trying to find her."

He went on past her, nudging Vernon into a lope.

She was following him, swearing as she clung to the saddle.

"I'm coming with you!" she called out to him.

"Go back! You'll slow me down."

"No, no...I can keep up."

"Do what you want, but stay out of my way."

He nudged Vernon into greater speed. Nothing seemed to matter anymore except for the voice in his head, guiding him onward.

But in the grayness of the day, Vernon suddenly reared. Behind Matt, Lavinia screamed, trying to maintain her seat. Matt controlled his panicked horse, then saw the dark bundle in the road ahead of him. He dismounted quickly, hunkering down, his heart in his throat.

It wasn't Darcy.

"Clint!" He set his fingers against his cousin's throat. There was a pulse. Clint groaned, turning. There was a massive lump on his temple. He stared up at Matt with dazed eyes. "Matt."

"What happened?"

"I don't know...I was lost. Then someone hit me. I saw the butt of an Enfield rifle come out of the smoke...and that was it."

"Where's Darcy?"

"She was with me. I was going to bring her to meet you at the far field...I was disoriented, tried to figure out which way I was going...I'm seeing black spots, Matt. I thought my whole skull was crushed."

Matt turned back to Lavinia, drawing his phone from

the historically incorrect pocket in his captain's coat. He threw the phone to her.

"Get help. And stay with Clint!" he told her.

"Matt, you don't understand, I need to come with you—" she said.

"Get off the horse and stay with Clint!" he commanded.

Lavinia went white. Matt leapt back on Vernon, and kneed the horse, the feeling of urgency now tearing into him. And the voice...

This way, hurry, this way, ride hard, hurry....

Carter held Darcy's ankle and was crawling forward with a deadly urgency, using her legs as a line to come closer.

Darcy kicked out furiously, trying to loosen his grasp.

"Killing me isn't going to help you!" she cried out. "Don't you see, they'll know, they'll all know!"

"You're going over the bridge, Darcy. You'll have fallen. Everyone knows you're accident prone."

"No, Carter! They'll find the bones. They'll identify the body, don't you see, it's over! Carter, I don't know what she knew, or what she saw, or what she wrote that so incensed you...but it didn't matter, did it? You'd already decided you were going to kill her. Who was she? The woman you supposedly loved so much?"

His eye was already beginning to swell. He looked horrible. Blood matted his beard; she had managed a few good strikes.

But his hands still had a strength like steel in them.

"Carter! I've scratched you. Your flesh is beneath my nails."

His hand moved; he got a solid grip on her calf, his face taut, muscles clenched, jaw in a grim and lethal line.

"The skeleton in the smokehouse, Darcy? She was Susan Howell. And what was she writing? She was going to tell Matt that I'd been having an affair with his wife—and more, of course. She was going to suggest that he look into my past. There were a few before her, you see. Catherine Angsley. Catherine didn't have to die, but she had loaned me some money, and then the little bitch got all furious and wanted it back when I didn't have it. But they'll never find her. She's deep in the Blue Ridge. They'll never find the others, either. I never should have brought any of them to Melody House, but you see, the old man had died, Matt was busy with his work and the fact that his marriage was falling apart...and that night, there was no one at Melody House. No one. Susan had gone there because I'd taken her there before, and because she wanted to feel that she had a right to be in the house. She was really not a nice person, Darcy. And you know, she was buried in that smokehouse for years...years! No one would have found her. But now, you have."

He got a fierce hold on her thigh. She struggled to sit, nails clawing at his flesh. He roared like a wounded animal, but didn't let go. Holding on to her despite the violence of her fight, he dragged himself to his feet, still clutching her. Dragging her.

"Carter, you're ill! You need help."

"Bull!" He went still for a minute, ready to laugh despite the circumstances. "I knew what I was doing every step of the way. There's nothing wrong with me. Hell, I have a mind and a will of steel. No one has ever so much as suspected me."

He had her against the rail. He tried to lift her but she fought too hard. Still, he had stamina. Little by little, he was pressing her back. Darcy could hear the water rushing over the boulders and stones below. Far below.

"Josh! Help me!" she cried out.

It gave him a start. He paused, if only for a second, looking around.

"Who the hell is Josh?"

"A ghost."

"A ghost! You're calling on a ghost? Shit, Darcy!" He laughed again, maintaining his hold. She struggled, getting a grip on his beard, pulling hard. He reached down to his calf, pressing his body against hers so that he didn't lose his hold. A second later, he'd drawn a Bowie knife from the sheath at his ankle and pressed it against her throat.

"You're going over, Darcy," he said flatly.

A blade in her throat…or boulders crushing her bones. Not much of a choice. But she could no longer fight him, not with the knife pressing into her flesh.

"Carter!"

The harsh cry, coming from the trail before the bridge, startled them both.

Matt burst out of the mist, drawing Vernon to a halt right at the foot of the bridge, just feet away.

"Carter, let her go. Now."

Carter was dead still for several seconds. Then a feral smile twisted his lips.

"Come make me, Matt. Be careful, though. You know how good these Bowie knives are. I can slit her jugular in less than a second."

His eyes never leaving Carter's, Matt dismounted from Vernon and strode firmly toward the bridge.

"Stop there, or she's a gusher, I promise," Carter said.

Matt stood motionless, aware of the knife at Darcy's throat. He didn't look at her, though. He kept his eye contact on Carter.

"It's over, Carter. The FBI is looking for you."

"They may be looking for me, Matt. But they won't find me. Hey, we both know this place. Get into the mountains…and we can disappear for good."

"Carter, if you let Darcy go now, we can work something out."

"I don't think so, Matt. Actually, this is rather amusing. There you are, the great Sheriff Stone. The Stone of Stoneyville. Negotiation, yep, that's one talent you really pride yourself with having. Talk, stall, talk, stall. And imagine, all this going on beneath your nose, and you didn't know! You know, once you kill, you figure out that's it's really pretty easy. Especially when you get involved with the right people. Women looking for something they can't have. Like the right guy, true love, support and warmth and all that crap. Pretty ones, of course. Only problem is, sometimes, when you think it just might be a go, they turn out to be bitches, all judgmental, not really what they pretend to be at all. I'm no maniac, Matt.''

Matt put his hands on his hips. "So what, then? Carter? You're going to kill Darcy in front of me? You make another move, and you're a dead man as well.''

"How you going to manage that, Matt? You've got a rifle there, but hell, no shot. You're a reenactor today. No real bullets—on anyone. Too much of a danger to the crowd.''

"I'll kill you with my bare hands, Carter," Matt said with low but vehement sincerity. "I swear it.''

"So…we all die. Here and now," Carter said.

"Carter!''

The cry came from a woman. Darcy could barely move her head; she could almost taste the steel at her throat, but she strained to see past Matt and was amazed to see Lavinia come running down the trail. Her beautiful violet eyes were huge; her usually perfect hair had escaped its Civil War coils and was a tangle around her face.

"Carter!" she tried again, gasping too hard to speak more.

"Did you know that we had a hot and heavy affair, Matt?" Carter said casually. "For once, I bested the great sheriff! It was actually hard not to let you know, but then again, I loved the ease of hanging around Melody House.''

"I don't give a damn if you slept with Lavinia, Carter.''

Carter smiled, looking past Matt at Lavinia. "Did you come to help me, sweetheart? Have you got a gun on you? If so, just go ahead and shoot the sucker.''

That, at last, drew Matt's eyes from Carter. He stared at Lavinia in amazement and horror. *Had she been in on it? Had she become so involved with Carter that she had actually been his accomplice in murder?*

And did she have a gun, secreted away in her voluminous skirts?

Lavinia found her voice at last. "Carter, for the love of God, let her go!" she said.

"Lavinia, you've turned pansy on me. Didn't you want a wild life of reckless adventure, far more than the sheriff intended to give you, no matter what his pedigree?"

Darcy could feel the blade, chafing into her flesh. She felt a thin trickle of blood drip down her neck.

"Carter, let her go," Matt said. "I swear, if you do, you'll get a trial with the best lawyers. If you hurt her in any way, I'll rip your throat out with my bare hands, I swear it."

Darcy felt his hand jerk. The blade cut more deeply. She was certain that she was dead. Matt would avenge her, of that she was certain, too.

But she would be dead already. A new ghost to haunt the realm of Melody House.

It was then that the white mist reappeared. It seemed to form at the base of the bridge, between Matt's position and the place where Carter had her back arched over the bridge.

"It's Susan!" she cried, "Carter, she's here! It's Susan."

"Bull—!" he began. But his eyes widened suddenly. Darcy didn't know what anyone else saw; she wasn't certain what she saw herself. But the mist moved, and Carter froze, as if paralyzed with disbelief and horror.

"It's Susan, and she's come to avenge her own death!" Darcy breathed.

Carter jerked, his grip barely slackening.

Matt chose that moment to lunge across the few feet separating them, and tackle Carter.

The impetus of his force, knocking Carter flat, and sending the knife flying, also sent Darcy flying. Her body twisted. Face forward, she went more than halfway over the railing. Grasping madly, she got a handhold on a support beam, just before the bulk of her body slipped. She held on desperately, aware of the rushing sound of water beneath her.

She heard the brutality of the fight going on above her, but she could only pray that Matt was winning. She was losing her grip.

"Josh!" she whispered softly.

She felt warmth, and knew he was there. Felt as if some of the weight was eased from her hands. And still...

"Darcy!"

Lavinia was looking over the railing at her, then lay flat on the ground, seizing hold of her hands through the rails. "I can't...I can't...get you up!" Lavinia cried with dismay. "I'm going to lose you."

Darcy felt her hands slipping. She saw Lavinia's fingers, losing their grip.

She smiled at the woman so feverishly trying to save her. "It's all right," she said softly. "It's all right...."

It wasn't all right. She didn't want to die. Even if she did know that there was an afterlife, that Josh would be there.

"Lavinia, hold on, hold on a moment longer."

Matt. He straddled the railing, balancing precariously himself. He reached down, catching hold of her arms above the wrists, and he squared his shoulders, and pulled. She cried out, the pain in her arms threatening dislocation.

But she was hiked over the railing. They fell to the bridge together. Gasping, she opened her eyes to see his. They both stared blankly at one another, hearing the sounds of Lavinia, as she sobbed with relief. She saw Carter's body, prone, just feet away.

"Is he...dead?" Darcy managed to whisper.

"I didn't kill him," Matt said. "Come on, Darcy, let me get you up." He came to his feet, muddied, his uniform torn and battered, his face bruised. He reached a hand down to her, drawing her up close to him.

A sudden roar proved the truth of the fact that he hadn't killed Carter. The man was up; he had apparently been gathering his strength for one last surge of fury.

"Move!"

Matt shoved Darcy, and she went ricocheting along the

bridge. He ducked himself as Carter raced forward, his knife in his hand once again.

But Darcy was gone, and Matt's sudden movement tripped up Carter, sending him flying against the bridge railing. He teetered precariously.

The white mist appeared again.

Carter let out a cry of horror. Surrounded by the mist, he went over.

They heard of the sound of his last terrified, strangled scream. And then the sound of his body, hitting the rocks below.

The reenactment that late June day would be remembered for the events that followed as much as for the battle itself.

Darcy's first concern, after they had looked over the bridge and ascertained that Carter was, indeed, dead, had been Oola. The dog had tried to defend her, and Darcy was afraid that Carter had given her a blow that had killed her. But when they found the dog against one of the ornamental pillars on the other side of the bridge, she was still breathing. Adam, following behind Matt and Lavinia, had arrived them, with a host of officers behind him, and so, Oola had been quickly rushed to the vet. Thayer had called to say that the dog had suffered a concussion, but would be all right.

Agents from the FBI, as well as local and state police, scoured the area. Darcy found herself questioned for hours, since her honest answers seemed to dumbfound many people.

Luckily, Randy Newton was in charge of the investigation from the government's side, and he, at last, said that they had enough information from her, there was nothing more she could explain to them on how she had first discovered the skeleton in the smokehouse.

It was an interesting investigation, Randy told her, somewhat amused. They had a confessed killer, but he was dead, so the only people who had heard his confession were her, Matt, and Lavinia.

Darcy deeply pitied Lavinia that day, because she had to explain that years ago, she had thought little of it when he had told her that Susan Howell would no longer be in his life. When her marriage to Matt had been fraying, she admitted, she'd thought an affair with Carter would be revenge against Matt, a foolish thing, and she thought that she and Carter had both tacitly agreed that they would never speak about it.

But when she had talked to Matt, and read about Darcy discovering the bones in the smokehouse, she had felt a terrible urge to come down, a feeling of dread that something just might have happened years before, something she hadn't even begun to fathom until she had returned to Melody House. When Carter had pretended that he wanted Lavinia to be with Darcy at the reenactment, something inside Lavinia had triggered suspicion, and she had realized that it was time to talk to Matt about Carter. She had stayed with Clint until one of the officers had arrived and an ambulance had been called, and then left, still anxious that she might still somehow prevent tragedy. Clint would be in the hospital for several days. He had suffered a concussion.

It was late when Adam, Penny, Lavinia, Matt, and Darcy returned to Melody House. Later still when they had all showered and changed, and come down to the kitchen to scrounge through the refrigerator for something to eat.

"Matt, your friend thinks I'm guilty of something," Lavinia said wearily.

"Lavinia, you're not guilty of anything when you assume that someone just broke something off with another person," he assured her.

"It's so scary. I can't even imagine. We all...we were all his friends. And more," she said sheepishly. "And all these years...he killed when it was convenient. Hid the bodies—and got away with it." Lavinia shivered. "To think...never mind, I don't want to go there. But I didn't know—I really didn't even suspect, way back then, that Carter could be…crazy. And yet, when you called me, I had to come here.''

Matt grinned at her. "Lavinia, it's all right. You're a good friend. You came here, and you followed your instincts.''

"Everyone has a certain amount of instinct, Lavinia. A touch of something deeper in the mind. It doesn't suggest that you might have known anything all those years ago. It just means that you have greater mental powers than you imagined,'' Adam told her.

"Yeah?'' she said, and shivered. "Did I do any good? No! And I saw the way you looked at me, Matt Stone. You actually thought that I might have been his accomplice in murder, when he made that ridiculous statement to me!''

"Only for a second of sheer panic,'' Matt admitted.

"You did a lot of good, Lavinia,'' Darcy told her. "I don't think I would have made it until Matt came if you didn't help me,'' she said.

"See there, Lavinia?'' Penny added.

Lavinia shivered again. "Greater powers….'' She stared at Matt, then at Darcy. "What did happen at the end?'' she asked. "Carter rose…and looked like a raging bull. Then he was teetering on the bridge, and I could have sworn…I can't say it.''

"You could have sworn that a ghost knocked him over?'' Darcy asked.

Lavinia's huge violet eyes fell on hers. "Yes,'' she said quietly.

"Carter lost his balance, and went over,'' Matt said.

"But, Matt…'' Lavinia began.

"When I told my story to the FBI, that's exactly what I told them,'' Matt said firmly. The house phone began to ring. "Excuse me,'' he said, walking out of the kitchen. "Hey, Penny, we've got all kinds of stuff to go in eggs. How about omelettes?''

Darcy smiled at Lavinia. "I think that Susan Howell did

make a return, Lavinia. She was the lady in white people kept seeing in Melody House. Because she was in a long flowing gown, everyone—including me—assumed that she had to be a victim of traumatic death from centuries ago. I think she faded away on me, too, every time Carter was around. He stalked me from the time I first came here. And she was still afraid of him. Even in death, she was afraid of him. But, today, when she had her chance, she helped us.''

"You think Matt really believes that?" Lavinia said.

"No," Darcy said. She smiled at Adam. "But I think it's what really happened.''

Matt came back into the kitchen. "They've recovered some of Susan Howell's bones. Carter had scattered them in the water. They were in the stream, near the bridge. They're still missing a few, but they'll find them. And hopefully, they'll find the other bodies.''

"So, Matt,'' Penny murmured, "you were right, in a way, being convinced that the things going on here were being committed by someone alive and well." She stared at him. "But there are ghosts, you know." She gave her attention back to the omelettes. As the rest of them moved around the kitchen, getting plates, drinks, silverware and napkins, they continued to talk about Carter. Shock, Darcy assumed. Every time she thought about it herself, the fact that so many people had seen him as such an entirely normal human being for so long, she felt goose bumps rise on her flesh.

"With Susan Howell, it must have been easy," Matt said as they ate. "My grandfather had just died. Lavinia and I were falling apart. Penny wasn't living in the house yet. It was frequently empty. And he probably brought Susan there often. She probably really thought that he was going to marry her, and she'd be part of the group that stayed on the property whenever they chose. And yet, that night, Carter would have known that he was alone. Maybe he thought that the smokehouse would cover the fumes when the body started to decay. Or perhaps he thought that he'd buried her so deeply, she'd never be found anyway. It's impossible to know now."

They talked late, over coffee, brandy, and dessert. Darcy felt Adam's eyes on her, and looked at him, and knew that though the situation was sad, he was proud of her for her abilities to touch what others could not.

She frowned suddenly.

"Adam, why were you so anxious that we come here?" Darcy asked him. "It was as if you knew that there was something going on here...but you hadn't been here in years, either."

Adam hesitated, then looked at Matt. "My actual gift isn't like Darcy's," he said quietly. "But I knew that such gifts existed, I'd seen them far too many times to ignore them. I have the ability to discover and channel such gifts. In fact," he admitted, smiling ruefully at Darcy, "one of my greatest heartbreaks has been the fact that although I know there is something beyond, and that so many of those powers are locked in our minds, I cannot touch my own son, while he and Darcy...sometimes it seems that they can converse as if Josh were still alive. But right before I sent you that letter, Matt, I had a dream about your grandfather. We were playing chess on the porch, just as we had done so many times, and he was talking about the house, telling me that it had been wronged. And as we were talking...a woman drifted by me. In mist. And I asked your grandfather if he had seen her, and he told me that so much that was so wrong had occurred there, and that she needed help. The house needed help, and so did you, Matt. Anyway, when I awoke, I felt as if I had really talked to him again, and I knew that something was going on here. I didn't, of course, know that it was a recent tragedy that had occurred, I just knew that I had been summoned." He looked back at Darcy. "The business I had in London could have been put off, actually, has been put off. But I wanted you to come here first. I wanted your impressions. Then, it seemed as if Matt just might be right, too, what with the things going on, and so, I was worried about bringing you here. That's why I decided you needed a dog, because the dog would always know when a living being was causing the trouble.''

"Oola did run after Carter, growling and snarling. And that's why he hurt her. She gave me warning, Adam. She's wonderful, and I love her," Darcy said. She smiled then. "And you had a dream, huh? And you talked to your old friend in it."

Adam flushed. "I don't think that I have what you have, Darcy. Not at all. But it's good to know that my instincts kick in as well."

"This is terrible," Penny said. "I don't think I can sleep a wink, but I'm exhausted."

"I am not going back out to that caretaker's cottage by myself, not tonight," Lavinia said firmly.

"Don't worry—we've plenty of room in the house."

Matt smiled, looking at Darcy. "The Lee Room is available."

"I will not be sleeping in the Lee Room!" Lavinia said indignantly, and they all smiled.

"If you're really uneasy tonight, you can bunk in with me," Penny told her.

"I may just be doing that," Lavinia said.

"Maybe we should all try to get some sleep," Matt said. "Let's pack up, and call it a night."

Darcy had insisted earlier that she was fine, but now every bone in her body seemed to hurt. Matt looked a little rough around the edges as well, but he jumped into a brief shower himself, and when he came out, Darcy discovered that he'd filled the tub for her with hot water and an aloe and oil bath that was guaranteed to ease sore muscles and be kind to tender, scraped, and bruised flesh. Darcy sank into the tub, troubling over one thought that had nagged at her during the day.

Josh.

He had been with her....

And he had disappeared. She couldn't understand why he would have left her under such circumstances.

"Have I lost you?" she whispered out loud.

She didn't get a reply. Then she smiled. Josh had always been so polite. He didn't make an appearance when she was in a shower or bath, or changing clothing.

She rose and slipped into one of the massive Melody House robes. Exiting the bathroom, she found that Matt wasn't in his bedroom, or his office.

He had walked outside, and was standing on the balcony.

She thought that this must all be very hard on him. Carter had been a friend for years. Matt had allowed Carter free access to his holdings. Carter had used his house to commit murder.

She walked out on the balcony, slipping her arms around him.

"It's all solved now, isn't it?" he said, "or at least on its way to being all solved." He caught her chin and tilted it upward. "You were planning on leaving, weren't you?"

She gazed into his eyes and flushed. "Being with you is incredible, but…I can't change what I am, Matt. If I wanted to, I couldn't. I tried at first."

"The psychic and the small-town sheriff," he murmured. "Hm. It could work."

"Matt, I'm here now. We weathered a lot together. But…I can't change what I am. And being what I am, I love working for Adam."

"We can make it," he said softly.

"You say that now, but—"

"I'm not the only one who says it," he told her.

"Oh?" She arched a brow to him. "Did…Lavinia suggest that I was right for you? Or Adam?"

He laughed. "Lavinia did prove that she is, at heart, decent. Quite decent. But, no, I'd never trust her suggestions as to my relationships. And Adam, well, of course, I have tremendous respect for him, but no, Adam hasn't said a word to me. He probably figures this is something we have to work out ourselves.''

"Can it be worked out?''

"Darcy, you were the last thing I wanted when you walked into the Wayside Inn that day. But you're the only thing I know I want for the rest of my life. I love you. Everything about you. And I think that you love me, too.''

"Yes,'' she whispered. "But, Matt, you don't believe in the possibility, even, that there can be something outside of logic and reason and scientific explanation. How could we survive, with our thoughts being so entirely different?''

"Maybe I've changed. And I know we can make it.''

"All right—who exactly told you that we can make it, and how have you changed?''

He smiled. "Josh.''

"Josh!''

"I've been lying, Darcy. To myself, as well as you. Today, I knew it. The first time I suspected it was the day you fell through the boards at the library. I was on my way to lunch—then somehow I was on my way to the library. Today...I was having a good time. A really good time. It's fun for us to play soldier—we don't really have to lose, and soldiers don't really die. Then Randy Newton called me with the information about missing persons last seen in this area. When he gave me names and I knew them as girls Carter had dated, I had to find you. Right away. I had no idea where you might have gone. But there was a voice in my head guiding me. And I followed it.''

He smoothed her hair back, cupping her head, bending down to kiss her lips very lightly.

"Whatever it takes, I know we can make it. Trust me. Josh told me so.''

"How do you know it's Josh?''

"Because we just had a great little talk out here, man to man, on the balcony.''

She cocked her head, looking at him doubtfully. "Where is he now?''

"Gone.''

"Gone?"

"Well, for the evening. He said that he never hangs around to intrude on your private life."

Darcy inhaled sharply. She eyed him, still skeptical.

"However," Matt continued, "he's promised that he will attend the wedding. In fact, he said that he'd best be the first one invited."

"Our wedding, huh?"

"If you'll have me, of course."

She was silent for a minute, her blood racing through her veins, pounding to her mind. *Could it really work? Could she really have this man, forever? And could it be that he really accepted her for all that she was, and had he really learned that the world went beyond all that could be seen by the naked eye?*

"I love you, Darcy. And I'll be there for you. Always. I'll never doubt you, ever again."

"Yes."

"Yes?"

"Yes, absolutely. I'll marry you. Anytime, anywhere. As long as Josh is invited of course."

He swept her up, and carried her back inside. And despite bruises and scratches and what should have been sore muscles, they indulged in the most sensual and passionate hours Darcy had ever experienced.

It was later, much, much later, when Matt slept himself and Darcy tiptoed out on the balcony.

She smiled, hugging her robe to her.

"Thanks, Josh," she said softly.

And there, on the balcony, she felt his warmth surround her.

And life, she knew, was very, very good.

* * * * *

Turn the page for an exciting preview of

THE AWAKENING
by
Heather Graham
writing as Shannon Drake

Available October 2003

September

There had been rain the entire time Finn Douglas skirted New York City. The Jersey Turnpike, never the easiest driving on the East Coast, was slowed to a torturous crawl, and with drivers becoming more impatient, fender benders lined the way. After crossing the Hudson, he nearly missed the sign that led to all of New England. Maine was still a hell of a long way away, and by this point, he was already exhausted.

He'd figured he might have at least made the state line that night, but it wasn't going to happen. By the time he crossed through Connecticut and followed the Mass Pike eastward, he realized he was becoming a hazard to himself, and everyone else on the road. At twenty, he could have stayed awake a solid forty-eight hours and not felt a desperate need for sleep. That hadn't been all that long ago, and he taunted himself that at the ripe old age of twenty-eight, he should still be in decent enough shape. Strange. Once he crossed the line into Massachusetts, he didn't feel just tired—he felt as if he were being drawn to leave the road. By the time he neared the signs that told him he was coming up on the city of Boston, the urge had become a compulsion. He had to stop, and he had to stop there.

It was stupid to stop in Boston. The city lived in a constant state of "under construction." The roads all went one way. The congestion was terrible, and the motels, hotels, and restaurants would be higher here than anywhere north. But still...

Off. Get off now. It's imperative.

It was almost as if there were a voice inside his head. *That of a state trooper,* he thought wearily. One warning him that he would kill himself, and someone else, if he didn't rest a while.

He should have gotten off the highway in Connecticut, before hitting the Mass Pike and the highway in the city.

There was an exit ahead. He was somewhere in the north of the city, near the old turnoff for the airport.

He didn't know exactly where he was when he followed a ramp and naturally, found himself on a one-way street.

Boston. He'd never even find a parking space.

Ah, but Boston. A great city. Food.

A drink.

Those were of the essence. He had left Louisiana during the wee hours of the morning, and driven straight, allowing himself pit stops only when the car was nearly on empty. How the hell many hours had he been driving? He was simply a fool. An idiot for taking so long to come. After he had sat home so many nights, telling himself that she would come back, that he hadn't done anything wrong. Megan would know it, and come back to him.

But she hadn't done so.

And there had been a moment of startling clarity and panic when he had realized it didn't matter that he was right. He had allowed certain perceptions to grow because of his pride, and since he had furiously refused to deny any of those perceptions, he'd given her little choice. He lay in their bedroom, feeling the breeze from the balcony, hearing a muffled version of the cacophony that never really left the streets of New Orleans, and noting every little thing that was a piece of Megan. The beige drapes that fluttered in the night, the headboard and canopy of the large bed, the antique dressers, not yet refinished. One of her drawers remained open, and a trail of something made of silk and lace streamed from a corner of it. He could swear he smelled her perfume.

And if he were to rise, it would be to turn on the CD player, and listen to the sound of her voice.

He had almost called, but then, he hadn't. They had exchanged too many harsh words. He could see the fall of her long blond hair in the clear picture in his mind, the passion, and the tears, in the endless blue of her eyes. Calling wouldn't do it, not after the way he had shrugged when she had warned that she needed to leave, go home...

He was parked, he realized. He squinted. He thought he was somewhere near Little Italy, and thanked God that he somewhat knew Boston, since he had played it, though he knew almost nothing of the surrounding area—he had flown in and out before. There was a neon light blinking almost in front of him. It was like a flipping miracle—he had gotten a parking space in the city of Boston right in front of a restaurant. Or a bar. Or something.

He couldn't make out the name. It wasn't just his exhaustion. There was a fog sitting over the city.

He stumbled out of the car and straightened, blinking. Wherever he was, it didn't matter. He needed something to eat, and something to drink. And no matter how desperate he had become to reach Megan in person, he was going to get some sleep, somewhere very near. Even if he paid too much for a hotel room. He'd die on the road, for sure, and take someone else with him if he didn't get some sleep.

But first...food.

And a cold beer.

Theresa Kavanaugh left the bar late, and, admittedly, a few sheets to the wind. However, she was deeply unhappy to realize that she would be walking home; George Roscoe was supposed to have given her a ride home, but that was before George hooked up with the pretty blond bartender. It hadn't mattered at the time, because Theresa had found the guy at the pool table to be totally fascinating, and she had been certain that he intended to give her a ride home. She had been rather careful *not* to introduce him to either Sandra Jennings or Penny Sanders, because though they were all coworkers at the office, they weren't really best friends, and even best friends, she had discovered, might hone in on a cute guy a girl met at a bar. She had seen him standing by the table first, chalking a cue stick. But he had no partner.

"I'm pretty good," she had told him. "Want to take me on?"

"What are the stakes?"

"We'll gamble a twenty."

"I had been hoping for something a little...more worth gambling on," he'd said, laughter in his eyes.

"Let's see how we play first," she had challenged, and he had agreed.

She'd taken the first game. He'd paid up immediately. They had laughed, they had talked—maybe she had talked more than she should have. Because after she returned from the ladies' room, he was gone.

And so was George.

And at closing time, she had realized she was alone.

So, feeling somewhat irritated, she left alone. Naturally, she looked for a cab, usually available in abundance. But there was so much construction in the downtown area the cabbies were avoiding the place, or they had already been taken, or, perhaps, because of the hour, they had given up and gone home. She could have tried calling, but when she returned to the bar to do so, the doors were locked and no one responded to her banging. She couldn't resort to her cell phone because she hadn't charged the battery. The whole thing had just gone bad.

Still...it was all right. There were plenty of lights in the downtown area. Her apartment wasn't that far.

And when she started out, it was fine.

But then...came the fog.

She thought she was imagining it at first. Even in Boston, it was rare for a fog to just begin on the ground and swirl to something as thick as pea soup in a matter of minutes. But that was what it did. She could see clearly when she left the bar, but she hadn't gone two blocks before it began to churn in puffy, blue-gray swirls around her feet.

She began to whistle, wondering why fog should make her so nervous. But it did.

She could hear the click of her three-inch heels on the pavement, and that made her wish she were wearing tennis shoes. But she was still dressed as she had been at work: smart business suit, with a great A-line skirt, and the tank that she liked so very much. Naturally, she had known they were going to dinner, and onward to party that night. Friday night. The workforce lived for Friday nights, or so it seemed in

Boston. At least, it did at her company. They were a broker-age firm, still a Monday through Friday, nine-to-five kind of company. She was young, ambitious, and good at her job, and still...

Well, young. And she liked to party. And since she and Beau had broken up several months ago, now, she was be-ginning to feel a little lonely, and in need of the Friday night companionship. She wasn't ready to crash into anything with a man discovered at a bar, but by this Friday, when she had met the man playing pool...all right, so she would have in-vited him back to her apartment.

"Don't know what you missed, buddy!" she muttered aloud.

The fog had risen to her calves. It was the most bizarre color!

She kept whistling. She passed old buildings, many of which had been around for the birth of the country, along with new skyscrapers. As she passed one of the city's oldest cemeteries, she felt a little twitch in her spine. Now, there, the fog was downright creepy.

She decided not to look, but rather, concentrate on her memory of the man at the bar. She realized she couldn't re-member his eye color, or his hair, or even what he had been wearing. Only that he'd had...

A magnetism.

Maybe he'd be there again. She might have been too talk-ative. But still...well, surely, he must have had some incli-nation that he'd get lucky. And she knew she was attractive, that the tailored suit accentuated her curves, and that she had a really nice head of long, natural blond hair, and a good face. One would think she'd meet someone at work, but in her department it seemed that the men came in married, gay, or bald and potbellied.

She had plenty of time to meet the right guy.

Her eyes strayed to the cemetery. Ghostly stones rose just above the blue mist.

Something touched her foot, and she screamed out loud.

"Hey, lady...got a buck?"

She recoiled in horror from the bum that had touched her. He was just there—lying on the sidewalk.

"No!"

"Okay...got a twenty?"

"Get a job!" she shouted.

And she started to run.

A block...

Then her heel broke. She nearly fell to the pavement. Swearing, she steadied herself. Home wasn't that far! It seemed to be taking her forever to get there. She wasn't walking—or running—or so it seemed. Rather, it was like wading through the fog. It was up to her waist now. Soon, it would obliterate everything.

She passed the cemetery...the buildings. Soon...just two... three blocks to go.

The fog kept rising.

She stopped dead suddenly, seeing a form before her in the fog. She held her breath, praying it wasn't going to be another bum.

"Hey! There you are."

It was him. The guy from the bar. Charming, magnetic, seductive. He was standing at the end of the block, right in front of one of the few trees in the area. There was something strange about him, but she didn't quite know what...

"Hey!" she called back. Limping on her one heel, she started for him. A frown knit her brow as she studied him, and tried to figure out what was different about him. "I thought you left."

"I thought you had left!" he replied softly. His voice...it was like silk. He stood so still, and yet it seemed he emitted so much energy and power. "I had hoped to see you again," he told her.

She smiled, thinking that the cemetery, with its stones, eerie in the blue fog, was behind her now. Just as the bum was who had reached out and touched her. And the night...it lay ahead with a sudden awesome and new mystery.

"Theresa...come on. Come to me, Theresa!"

Well, of course, I'm coming to you, gorgeous! she thought, smiling inwardly.

And she was.

Her one heel clicked on the pavement. A pathetic sound.

The fog was to her chest, swirling madly. She was so close to him. Together, they could brave it.

She could see his smile. The flash of his teeth, she was so close.

She saw what was different about him. It was what he was wearing, on such a night…it was weird.

But on such a man, what did it matter?

She came closer, feeling more intoxicated than she ever had due to the influence of liquor. Maybe there were a few remnants of the cosmopolitans she had been drinking that stayed to warm her bloodstream, to make her feel as if her heart jumped with excitement with every movement that brought her closer.

It seemed that even the strange blue fog was a part of his magic…

She came to a halt, standing directly in front of him. "I can't believe I've found you again," she murmured.

"Fate," he said softly. "Destiny. Great things are to come."

The sound was still so seductive. As were his eyes.

She couldn't have moved if she wanted to. And yet…

There was something…off. Something not quite right.

Fate. Destiny. Oh, yes. And yet…

She didn't even know exactly why she knew, or what she knew, or what exactly it was that she saw…or felt…except that it was…

She struggled to understand.

"Come with me."

"Yes!"

"Serve me!"

"Oh, yes!"

He moved…

Ah, the seduction of it all. The danger. Something forbidden, and thus, ever so tempting, and still…

It seemed she was simply swallowed into the depth of the night.

And the blanket of the swirling blue fog.

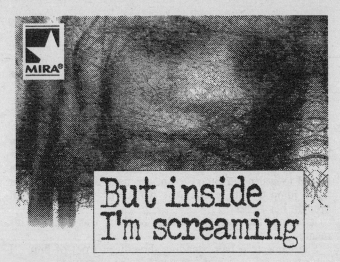

But inside
I'm screaming

A remarkable debut novel from

ELIZABETH FLOCK

While breaking the hottest news story of the year, broadcast journalist Isabel Murphy unravels on live television in front of an audience of millions. She lands at Three Breezes, a four-star psychiatric hospital nicknamed the "nut hut," where she begins the painful process of recovering the life everyone thought she had.

But accepting her place among her fellow patients proves more difficult as Isabel struggles to reconcile the fact that she is, indeed, one of them. In order to mend her painfully fractured life, Isabel must rely solely on herself to figure out what went so very wrong, and to begin to accept an imperfect life in a world that demands perfection.

"…an insightful, touching and, yes, even funny account of what it's like to lose control as the world watches…"
—*New York Times* bestselling author Mary Jane Clark

Available the first week of September 2003, wherever books are sold!

HEATHER GRAHAM

66665	HURRICANE BAY	___ $6.99 U.S.	___ $8.50 CAN.
66892	A SEASON OF MIRACLES	___ $6.99 U.S.	___ $8.50 CAN.
66812	NIGHT OF THE BLACKBIRD	___ $6.99 U.S.	___ $8.50 CAN.
66864	SLOW BURN	___ $5.99 U.S.	___ $6.99 CAN.
66787	NIGHT HEAT	___ $12.95 U.S.	___ $15.95 CAN.

(limited quantities available)

TOTAL AMOUNT	$_____
POSTAGE & HANDLING	$_____
($1.00 for 1 book, 50¢ for each additional)	
APPLICABLE TAXES*	$_____
TOTAL PAYABLE	$_____
(check or money order—please do not send cash)	

To order, complete this form and send it, along with a check or money order for the total above, payable to MIRA Books®, to: **In the U.S.:** 3010 Walden Avenue, P.O. Box 9077, Buffalo, NY 14269-9077; **In Canada:** P.O. Box 636, Fort Erie, Ontario L2A 5X3.

Name:_____

Address:_____ City:_____

State/Prov.:_____ Zip/Postal Code:_____

Account Number (if applicable):_____

075 CSAS

*New York residents remit applicable sales taxes.
 Canadian residents remit
 applicable GST and provincial taxes.

MIRA®

MHG0903BL